A DEATH
ON
LOCATION

A DEATH ON LOCATION

A Canon Clement Mystery

The Reverend
RICHARD COLES

WEIDENFELD & NICOLSON

First published in Great Britain in 2025 by Weidenfeld & Nicolson,
an imprint of The Orion Publishing Group Ltd
Carmelite House, 50 Victoria Embankment
London EC4Y 0DZ

An Hachette UK Company

The authorised representative in the EEA is Hachette Ireland,
8 Castlecourt Centre, Dublin 15, D15 XTP3, Ireland (email: info@hbgi.ie)

1 3 5 7 9 10 8 6 4 2

A CIP catalogue record for this book is
available from the British Library.

ISBN (Hardback) 978 1 3996 2141 0
ISBN (Export Trade Paperback) 978 1 3996 2142 7
ISBN (Ebook) 978 1 3996 2144 1
ISBN (Audio) 978 1 3996 2145 8

Typeset by Input Data Services Ltd, Bridgwater, Somerset

Printed in Great Britain by Clays Ltd, Elcograf, S.p.A.

www.weidenfeldandnicolson.co.uk
www.orionbooks.co.uk

For RC,
with thanks for the economies in
monogrammed luggage

When all the Ages of the Earth
Were crown'd but in this famous Birth;
And that, when they would boast their store
Of worthy Queens, they knew no more:
How happier is that Age, can give
A Queen, in whom all they do live!

The Masque of Queens, Ben Jonson

I

As she left the picture gallery, the queen staggered slightly. She had to lean against the wall for a moment to get her balance and her breath back. She hoped no one saw, for poise was everything – hard enough in such unforgiving dress, laced-in, huge-skirted, wigged and headdressed – but the masque was magnificent, and she on display, and in service to her glory. To encourage the other ladies to join in with it, she had danced and danced and danced, so much so that she had developed a horrible stitch and was forced to stop. The other dancers were still going strong. How the hell did people manage, so brutally corseted, if you got a stitch or a cramp or an itch?

She recovered, gathered herself, and swished along the corridor, past more portraits of different queens, of duchesses and marchionesses, done up in magnificent displays. Hers was not only magnificent but fantastical, for she was costumed as Candace, Queen of the Ethiopians – fantastical and improbable, for she thought it unlikely, in antiquity, to have glided along the banks of the Gihon in a gorgeously embroidered bodice and billowing silks.

Behind her the lights from chandeliers and stanchions flickered, and the sound of flutes and voices and the stamp of feet faded. She had managed the courante, recovered in the sarabande, but halfway through the jig the stitch had suddenly afflicted her. No wonder, she thought, when your viscera were crammed into an unnatural hourglass by laces and whalebone – and it wasn't just the ladies. One of the lords, the earl of somewhere – she wasn't sure where – had complained that he had only just managed to button his doublet.

She leant once again on the wood-panelled wall. The stitch was agony, her feet hurt, pinched in a sort of dancing slipper the costumier had thought suggestive of the topaz palaces of Ethiopia, and she had a headache coming on that felt like it might soon oblige her to take to her bed. But first, she needed to get out of her dress. She ran, half staggered, down a plainer corridor towards the great house's kitchens and sculleries. She was gasping when she pushed open the door.

The occupant of that humble room turned to face her, startled, and two spots of pink flushed on her cheeks.

'Miss March,' said the queen, 'could you be a pal and pop me a Nurofen?'

In 1603, after the accession of King James I, the then Lord de Floures welcomed his queen, Anne of Denmark, to

Champton House, as she and her retinue made a slow progress from Edinburgh to London. To delight and flatter Her Majesty, Lord de Floures put on an entertainment, which became famous as one of the great masques of the new era. His father and grandfather had become rich through wool, and of those riches he spent extravagantly on costumes, scene painters, musicians and singers, endured the rudeness of a poet and the insolence of a decorator, and cajoled his betters to join them there – not that he needed to cajole any more, for the presence of the queen ensured it. It was a coup for the ambitious peer and his lady, a demonstration of the renewal of the de Floures' prestige and power, its third flourishing since William the Conqueror settled his ancestor with a grant of land.

On that grant of land, or the part that remained, Bernard, the present Lord de Floures, was also ambitious, not for power and prestige, but simply for money; enough to reroof, rewire and replumb the house that had grown and shrunk and grown and shrunk with successive generations. Tudor, Baroque, Georgian and Victorian additions surrounded its medieval core, a fine but heavy inheritance. Next year Bernard's heir was to be married, a great day in every generation, and he knew it was his duty to welcome the bride in as generous a spirit as his ancestor welcomed the new queen nearly four centuries earlier. There would be no masque, but there would be a wedding breakfast and hot water, and working plugs, and fresh paint, and the fountains would play . . . the thought of the bills for these necessary improvements had not weakened his resolve, but they had darkened his moods, and as the estimates had arrived from the estate office he had become so relentlessly bad-tempered that only his daughter, Honoria, who loved him like a Cordelia, and the housekeeper, Mrs Shorely, who did not care if he shouted or not, could endure it.

And then came a turn in the wheel of fortune. The Rector of Champton St Mary, Canon Clement, who lived in the lovely Queen Anne rectory at the edge of the park, with his dauntless mother, Audrey, and two dachshunds, had a brother, Theo, who was an actor. Theo had come to stay one weekend and brought with him a film-producer friend. They lunched at the big house, and as they chewed their way through roast potatoes that tasted like Mrs Shorely had dug them shrivelled from desert earth, Bernard enquired of Theo's friend what sort of films she produced.

'All sorts,' she replied, 'but right now a costume drama, a film about the life of Anne of Denmark, wife of James I, who was famous for her glittering—'

Bernard held up his fork. He knew all about Anne of Denmark's glittering reign, for one of the most famous of her masques had been held here, at Champton, at the start of it.

The film producer put down her fork and the terrible potatoes were, in an instant, forgotten, for with almost an audible gasp, her need of a location and Bernard's of funds conjoined as expediently as the crowns of Scotland and England.

Six months went by, and location scouts – whatever they were – arrived, people expert in lighting and photography; art directors – whatever they were – arrived, and, one weekend, the producer and director, who were entertained almost as extravagantly as the royal couple. Estate manager and film producer did the deal, in which each party's desires were satisfactorily met – a splendid makeover for the grandest parts of the house and the park in return for a location where the real queen had been entertained, had bestowed her favours, and had danced and danced and danced.

Margaret Porteous had not enjoyed herself so much in years. The little village of Champton St Mary, where she and her late husband had made their home, was unusually stimulating for a place of only three hundred souls. The power politics of the Flower Guild, the Women's Institute and the Parish Church Council, the manoeuvrings at Harvest Supper, the Summer Fête and the Open Day at Champton House, were no less fascinating and complex than the doings of the harem of the sultan of Turkey. And then murder had come to Champton, and come again and again, and turned the village upside down, only to be turned the right way up again by the rector, who was rapidly becoming the C of E's answer to Father Brown.

Who would have thought three hundred souls, give

or take, could have provided so much diversion? You could not tell by looking at them, living quietly in the little cottages at the edge of Champton park, but this was a changing Britain, as the 1980s turned into the 1990s. The illusion of timelessness, which clung like ivy to the cottages in stone and thatch clustered along the brook, was ragged. There were cars parked along the main street, which occasionally lost their wing mirrors to the herd of cows that swayed through the village from pasture to milking, and there was – Margaret did not approve of this at all – a satellite dish fixed to the front of the Old School House by Councillor Norman Staveley. Only one so far, but they must be stopped before they spread like mushrooms.

At the centre of their life, and holding it all together like the sun, was Champton House. Margaret gave a sigh of pleasure when she thought of that great and stately home, where she not only coordinated volunteers on the occasions Lord de Floures opened it grudgingly to the public, but where today she was reviving in her own person its glorious history, its *royal* history. The de Floures' prestige may have dulled in the long centuries since Domesday, but at its most lustrous it had brought the great of their age through its gates: politicians, warriors, poets and painters, kings and queens. Queens plural, and Margaret was now one of them, not because of some utterly unforeseeable end to her widowhood, but because when the producers put out a call for locals to appear as extras in *A Woman of*

Boundless Intrigue, she was at the front of the stampede that followed. It had seemed especially fitting to her that she should have been chosen to play one of the queens in the masque, not only because she felt almost as attached to the house and its history as a member of the family, but because her experience in amateur dramatics, as she had advised the casting director for 'supporting artists', meant she would be able to bring a convincing queenliness to the role. And so she had, until the jig in the great dance scene at the masque asserted the priority of the body natural over the body politic, and, suffering the worst stitch she had ever known, she had stepped out – she hoped unnoticed – and made her way to the Old Dairy, where wardrobe had an outpost and she an ally.

Miss March, proprietor of Champton's dress shop Elite Fashions, had surprised everyone when Hollywood arrived by shutting up shop – unheard of from a woman who had sold Derby boots by candlelight in her old shoe shop during the three-day week – to volunteer as a wardrobe assistant and historical expert. She was decent with a needle and thread, and her inventory – at the request of Bernard's daughter, the Honourable Honoria de Floures – of the attic chests and wardrobes and presses at Champton meant she knew the difference between a leg-of-mutton and a virago sleeve, but she was neither professionally a seamstress nor a historian and felt, as a consequence, a stab of impostor syndrome, which added to her natural shyness. There was an accent of this in her appearance, for although she wore her unvarying grey suit and plain blouse, a garland of brightly coloured threads hung round her neck like a Hawaiian lei – threads of every colour for emergency repairs – and on her trestle table beside her were scissors and pinking shears and measuring tapes and an iron, and an extra-large pin cushion studded with so many items, from fine needles to giant farthingale pins, it looked like a punkish fairy toadstool.

'We're not allowed to give tablets, Margaret,' said Miss March, 'in case you have an allergic reaction. Don't you have anything in your bag? Or I can get a medic?' The latter suggestion was made unenthusiastically. It was a bore to have to fetch a medic, and it was only for Margaret, an extra, whom she thought was enjoying being a queen a little too much.

'It's a stitch,' said Margaret, 'worst I've ever had.'

'You don't want ibuprofen, you want unlacing,' said Miss March, putting away her sewing. 'Come into the light.'

Margaret tried to straighten up but gasped with the pain.

'Lean forward, hold on to the back of that chair, and keep still,' said Miss March, and she parted the long, gauzy veil that fell from Margaret's headdress down her back and over her skirt to the floor. She deftly undid and loosened the laces that fastened the bodice around Margaret's middle, and then the more robust laces that had been pulled to within tiny fractions of their tolerance to contain her middle within the corset beneath. Margaret gave a cry of what Miss March took for relief. But it was not relief, it was surprise; surprise at feeling a hot wetness spreading across her belly.

Miss March's first thought was that Margaret's costume had been fitted with a blood bag and it had burst.

Margaret's last thought was to wonder why the blood royal was supposed to be blue.

2

Early September was Daniel's favourite time of year. The heat of summer had cooled, a great benefit for a man who had to wear black all the time — how did those Greek widows manage? — but the trees were still in leaf and the winter jumpers and coats still stowed wherever his mother chose for that purpose, a location she kept secret from a habit of keeping all knowledge of her assets to herself. Most of all, he liked the beginning of the slow acceleration into autumn and the sense of promise it brought to a man who had always liked as a boy the beginning of the school year and stocking a new pencil case, and as a chorister rehearsing the music for Advent, the loveliest of all church music.

It was change he loved, not an obvious predilection in someone who seemed never to change, at least on the surface. But, as one of his heroes, Cardinal Newman, had observed, to live is to change. Without change, how do we become what we are called to be?

Bernard de Floures took a different view. He loathed

change, for to him it was always for the worse, even when it was for the better. How could it not be, for a man born into a decline that his own individual successes, if he had any, could not slow, let alone stop or reverse? He was at the end of things, he knew, his family's glory behind him rather than in front, no longer a force in politics and civilisation and empire and England, for history had other ideas. This gave him an affinity with Daniel, also at the end of things as the Church of England vanished into its own past, becoming quainter every day, little more than an opportunity for situation comedy as Champton House became a mere location for a period drama.

The parson and the peer were walking the rectory dachshunds, Cosmo and Hilda, in the park. Hilda had weaned her first litter of puppies at Champton House, and Cosmo, like so many males when females have young, had sought diversion elsewhere, in Bernard's study, where he had displaced Jove, the white Persian cat, and won the affection of a man in whom affection tended to run shallow. Was Bernard getting sentimental with age? Was Cosmo going against his dachshund nature and showing fickleness of feeling? Perhaps, for when the Clements had moved back into the rectory both dog and peer pined for the other and Bernard, exercising the faintest memory of *droit du seigneur*, had let it be known that if Cosmo ever needed a walk, he would be happy to oblige.

It was the dogs' second walk of the day. After elevenses

Bernard had knocked on the rectory door to complain about being banished from his own house by 'those awful minstrels'. Daniel, who was deep in the *Church Times* looking at advertisements for clerical posts in tempting places and wondering, in a vague way, what life as a parson in one of the gentler Hebridean islands might be like, suggested they walk down to the lake.

Hilda, who had started to waddle since giving birth to her first litter, waddled with Daniel, but Cosmo, spry as ever, stuck to Bernard. They made a peculiar pair. Bernard, in his late fifties and his father's tweeds, looked like a man with whom a Labrador came as part of the ensemble, so to encounter him on his estate with a little sausage dog trotting at his ankles seemed as unlikely as bumping into Johnny Rotten with a peacock. Daniel, who sought amity between all wherever he went, did not mind this. His mother took a different view. 'You need to watch that,' she cautioned. 'Before you know it, you'll lose Cosmo to the de Floures lot.' There speaks experience, thought Daniel, though he did not say so, for his mother was to the lustre of that family as a moth to a flame. She had seemed almost reluctant to move back from their temporary billet at the big house to the freshly done-up rectory, thanks to the generous insurance award she had grimly fought for following the fire. After a month in Queen Charlotte's Bedroom, even if dressed today in tattered silks and peeling wallpaper, she had found it difficult sometimes to conceal a certain feeling for the life of a grande dame.

Not today, Daniel corrected himself, for it was one of the rooms the production was using to shoot in and had been sumptuously restored for lights and cameras. A specialist in seventeenth-century decor had been hired for this, but his advice had not always been honoured, or not when it conflicted with the designer's vision of what the seventeenth century needed to look like for the purposes of the drama, and there had been rows on set. Bernard did not particularly care, being concerned with the needs of the present rather than faithfulness to the aesthetics of the past.

'All spick and span now,' he said, 'and they've done up all the state rooms.' He cackled. 'Must have cost them a fortune! And wait till you see the fountains playing. They haven't worked since the Second World War.'

They walked towards the lake as the late-morning sun flashed in the library windows in the Georgian wing of the house facing it. Or was it sunlight? Perhaps it was lights, the enormous lights they used for filming, standing on tripods, like creatures from *The War of the Worlds*, to create the effect of natural light even when natural light in abundance was available in the normal way. He had wondered about this to his brother, Theo, who had been cast as a Pembroke in this film as a reward for effecting the introduction to Bernard, but he had said it took all the ingenuity and artifice of Hollywood to create the illusion of reality, which Daniel immediately resolved to use in a sermon.

'A mixed blessing, I suppose, Bernard, to have your house taken over by a film crew?'

'An inconvenience, but they pay for it. Handsomely. Such *profound* joy in calculating how much I'm saving thanks to their spending. And not only doing things up. I especially like it when they break something – and they always do; it's like having the All Blacks rampage through the Louvre. We keep adding things to the bill. And they never question anything, they just cough up.'

'There's no business like showbusiness.'

'I do forget they're here sometimes and walk into a scene without thinking. I'm supposed to be confined to the family wing, but . . . Cosmo, I'm afraid, disgraced himself yesterday.'

'Oh dear.'

'Since he's been banned from the mess tent . . .'

'Oh, yes. The sausages.'

'Not his fault if the film people keep feeding him breakfast – that he should feel breakfast is for him also . . .'

'But all the same . . .' said Daniel.

'Snatching the sausage literally from what's-his-name's hand . . .'

'Mr Alleyne. The director.'

'Who feeds his own damn dog from his plate.'

'Like the Queen Mother and her corgis.'

'Quite so. One rule for his dog and another for mine. For ours, I mean.'

Daniel said nothing.

'So poor old Cosmo is confined to my quarters. And yesterday I let him out of my study, and he must have heard the commotion from the dancing in the picture gallery and off he went. I tried to call him back . . . he is barely trained *at all*, Daniel . . . but he ran onto the set in the middle of the scene. They were trying to dance a quadrille, or whatever it was, and a blasted dog was suddenly scampering under their feet. All the extras went "aah". Director not so pleased. And as for Her Majesty . . .'

'Ah.'

'Not amused. Stormed off the set and went to her caravan and wouldn't come out. Her agent phoned up the director and he had to go to her and grovel like a peasant to a real queen.'

'I hear she is rarely out of character.'

'I don't think the original would have been half as grand. She had a fit the other day because her caravan thing was facing the wrong way for the morning sun.'

'That *is* grand . . .'

'Have you seen the caravan? It's called a . . . sounds like lumbago . . . but it comes with a lavatory and a bath and a television set, like a suite at the Dorchester.'

'Theo says she refuses to speak to anyone on set other than the director and whoever's in her scene, and then only if they're playing a noble. She completely ignores the low-born characters.'

'What's it called when actors stay in their character even when they're not filming?'

'Method acting?'

'Yes, that. But she's not seventeenth century at meal-times. She's a vegetarian. Well, a pescatarian.'

'Is that fish?'

'Yes. And why that shouldn't count as flesh I don't know, but it doesn't. Mrs Shorely told me she had a tantrum about people eating meat when she was present. The crew all have to have their bacon butties hiding on the north terrace. If she gets so much as a whiff of a rasher she starts to rant and rave. And there's an awful drink she has for lunch.'

'What is it?'

'A sludgy brown mixture like a savoury milkshake, full of spinach and such things. Won't touch anything else. It's to keep her slim.'

'Oh, look,' said Daniel.

At the centre of the lake a jet of water leapt into the air. Four smaller jets arced away from it as the fountain, mute for a generation, gurgled into watery song.

'Splendid, isn't it?' said Bernard. 'But – this is a little awkward as I am officially an adviser, paid to help them get it right – it is completely wrong.'

'Not seventeenth century?'

'No, nineteenth. Installed by my great-grandfather to delight Queen Victoria when she visited. But if Anne of Denmark wants a fountain to play over two hundred years too early, she shall have it.'

Bernard and Miss March were not the only locals to have advisory roles. Daniel, too, had that task, appointed to ensure correctness of clerical dress and liturgy in early Jacobean England, trickier than almost any other reign because James, king of Scotland as well as England, had his own Protestant priorities, which were not the same as his predecessor Elizabeth's, which differed from her Catholic predecessor Mary's, so quite who was wearing what and where and when was not always clear. And his advice could be overruled, and frequently was, especially by the fearsome Angela, who was head of wardrobe. 'It may be wrong, vicar,' was her refrain, 'but it's what we've got.'

How quiet the village was, thought Daniel, now everyone, save Mrs Braines at the Post Office and General Store and a few of the less obliging and able villagers, was making movies up at the big house.

Then not so quiet. A tinny electronic voice came at them from across the lake. Someone was waving frantically and shouting something indistinct through a bullhorn.

'Oh dear,' said Daniel, 'do you think we've walked into the back of shot again?'

'Can't a man take a stroll beside his own fountains?' growled Bernard, but he started to move away.

Gillian Smith, as the world knew her, was walking crossly to her Winnebago again, attended like the queen she was playing by a gaggle of fussing women. Not ladies-in-waiting, but hair and make-up, costume, her PA and the second assistant director.

'Miss Smith, Miss Smith!' he said, in a voice simultaneously urgent and unguent. 'That was fantastic, *fantastic*, but there were one or two tiny issues with the supporting artists, and we will have to go again.'

'Walking off like that? *So* unprofessional. If they can't be professional, why should I? Carrie, bananas?'

'Yes, Gillian,' said the PA, who was experienced at dealing with her boss and managed to be both 'on it' and unruffled always.

'And properly ripe? The one I had this morning was like chewing a candle.'

'On the turn, I'd say.'

'And you?' She looked crossly at the AD. 'Who are you?'

'Martin, Miss Smith.'

'Tell Dick to come to me in twenty minutes.'

He looked nonplussed.

'Tell him!'

'Miss Smith, we're heading dangerously close to the lunch break . . .'

'Then the sooner you bugger off the better.'

There was another, what the French call *un excès de stress*, thought Carrie, at the Winnebago.

'These *steps*,' said Gillian, 'awful *plarstic* . . . and to have to climb them in these . . .' She pointed at her shoes, square-toed straights with a shaped heel, in pink silk braid and kid fastened with a ribbon.

Angela the wardrobe lady said, 'I can have you out of them in a minute, Miss Smith, and we can loosen your corset?'

'Hardly worth it,' she snapped as they manoeuvred her sideways in her huge skirt through the narrow door. 'If I have to be back on set before I've barely sat down. Really, really . . . you know!'

They manoeuvred her again onto a stool, and as Angela loosened her corset – 'More, more. MORE!' – Carrie gently unlaced the shoes, thinking, as she had thought more than once before, that no one has Hollywood feet, especially not when they had been doing service for . . . She even checked herself when the matter of Gillian's age came up. It was not difficult to shave off a year or two, but there comes a time when a year or two begins to shade into a decade and the discrepancy between the highly managed and expensively maintained appearance of relative youth and the actual tally of years is too obvious to sustain. Even the queen – the real, current queen – she thought, altered her likeness on the currency, appearing on the new fiver looking her age – sixty-four, like the Beatles song. She wondered if that were in part to avoid any suggestion of counterfeiting, unthinkable for coin of the realm; but then the real queen was allowed to age without any loss of status. This queen was not, and the careful management of presentation, and choice of roles, was critical to make the transition from ingenue to leading lady to legend. She was in the middle of these three, no longer ingenue not yet legend, and there the transitions were especially tricky. When to maintain the illusion of freshness, when to anticipate what is to come? The real Anne of Denmark was thirty when the events of the film took place. Gillian was fifteen years further on, and although she had, with extraordinary singleness of purpose, as well as the make-up artist's and photographer's art, stayed in her twenties until she was forty, she was not going to be able to do so for much longer. Carrie had started to think a suggestion of UHT was beginning to appear in her creamy complexion.

Gillian waved Angela away. 'Tah-tah-tah-tah-TAH!'

She said this when she was irritated but could not be bothered to explain why. Those around her had learnt to interpret her wordless vocabulary and departed, almost crouching and walking backwards, which Carrie thought especially fitting, for would Anne of Denmark's courtiers not have done the same?

Carrie was the one person who was not dismissible in that way, the Duchess of Marlborough to Gillian's Queen Anne – the other one, of England, not Denmark; her confidante, and the nearest thing she had to a friend outside the circle whose names appeared above the title of the films they were in, the only people she considered her peers. Carrie was not her peer and never could be; the demarcation of roles was essential for the relationship to function. Her selection, twenty years ago now, had happened when Gillian needed minding on promotional tours, when she was what was then known as a starlet and had to open supermarkets and pretend to like children at fêtes. Carrie worked for her agent and, after two or three of these tours, proved reliable, patient, self-effacing when the spotlight was on, resolute in ensuring Gillian's wishes were fulfilled, and plain. Plain in manner, in style and in appearance. Not being interested in style particularly – she was by nature more interested in how things worked than how they appeared – she had acquired a sort of anti-style, a look that in no way risked approaching, let alone eclipsing, Gillian's. Her diligence in maintaining this had meant she had survived in an orbit that showier satellites had not sustained. Agents, PRs, co-stars and lovers had come and gone, but Carrie had endured, and in the tenth or eleventh year of constant service she had started calling her Gilly when they were alone together – that neither could remember the first time it had happened was remarkable, for Carrie never forgot herself and Gilly never forgave overfamiliarity.

Carrie put Gillian's shoes out on the step to air and closed the Winnebago door. 'Do you want something? A tea?'

'Banana,' she snapped, 'I already SAID.'

Carrie took a banana from the fruit bowl on the coffee table, which was laden with magazines she had carefully chosen to offer such diversions and amusements as Gillian desired. There was *Tatler* and *Harpers & Queen*, there was British *Vogue* and American *Vogue*, there was *The Face* and *i-D*, and underneath them the magazines she actually liked: *Elle* for the lifestyle and the frocks, and her favourite, *Country Life*, for she liked to look at the houses and estates for sale, always finishing by saying unkind things about the portrait photograph of a girl ripe for the marriage market, usually in an Alice band and pearls, and with the gormless expression of someone not knowing what they were letting themselves in for.

'Do you want this sliced?'

'No, just peeled.'

Carrie half peeled it and handed it to her. Gillian held it as daintily as anyone could, and bit off the end. How rare it is, Carrie thought, for anyone to look menacing holding a banana.

'I think I'll keep Dick waiting a bit. Tell him I have a *migraine*.' She pronounced this as if it were a French delicacy.

'Are you sure? He'll want to get his scene in the can before the break.'

'He can shoot the extras then.'

'You are in just about every shot.'

'But in the long shots we're all in costume, and all queens. I've forgotten who I am . . .'

'In the masque? Bel-Anna.'

'Had you heard of Bel-Anna?'

'No, but she's the principal queen. That's why you're her.'

'One of the others can dress up as me and do a turn around the floor, no one will know. One queen looks very much like another in all this' – she fluffed her skirt – 'well, from a distance.'

'He won't like it.'

Gillian waggled her fingers at her, a gesture that meant 'just deal with it'.

Carrie said, 'Do you want a tea? I got in some Red Zinger.'

'Yes. No. Do you know, I think it might actually be a *migraine*?'

'Why don't you lie down? I can go and talk to Dick. Can you lie down in that?'

Gillian moved with a slightly deliberate stagger to the day bed. 'Cushions . . .' she said.

Carrie rearranged them and plumped them up and helped lower Gillian onto them in such a way as to cause the least disruption to her hair and make-up and costume.

'Thank you, darling,' said Gillian. 'I may just close my eyes.'

'Do you want a couple of codeine? And your Phenergan?'

'Angel!'

3

Elite Fashions on Champton's Main Street was, unusually on a day of trade, temporarily closed to customers. Miss March had bought it not for stampeding footfall but for its proximity to Champton House and the prestige that conferred. The previous owner, Mrs Harper, had offered High Class Ladies' Fashions — the sign was still in the shed out the back — but Miss March thought that unnecessary, a gilding of the lily, for the address alone conferred sufficient dignity for the clientele she sought to serve. This was the ladies of the smarter villages around the cathedral city of Stow, where Miss March and, until his death, her father had kept the shoe shop that shod that same clientele. 'Don't sell winklepickers to yobs for ten bob a pair when you can sell Oxfords to the quality for a hundred and fifty,' was her father's summary of what we would now call a business plan, and she adhered to the same principle now.

But today Elite Fashions was closed even to that select clientele, since showbusiness had taken her customers

away, the siren song of Anne of Denmark luring them
to Champton House like tars to the shallows. She, too,
had been lured not to show and display but to diligent
work behind the scenes, which she thought somehow
more respectable than cavorting around in historically
questionable costumes.

This was a view shared by Audrey Clement, the
rector's mother and her retail consultant, or 'shop girl'
as she was unkindly called at the Post Office. Audrey
could understand why the young people, or the coarser
sort of adult, might be interested in the flicks, but ladies
preferred the more genteel amusements of the National
Association of Decorative and Fine Arts Societies and
the WI and Braunstonbury's Music Appreciation Society, so when news broke that *A Woman of Boundless
Intrigue* was going to be filmed at Champton, starring
Gillian Smith, the ladies, chief among them Audrey
Clement, rather pursed their lips. Audrey said, 'It'll be
motley, not Tricoville, for our gels now the circus is
coming to town.' But then they heard that extras – or
'background artists' as Mrs Porteous pompously called
them – were being sought for the crowd scenes and
everyone wanted to take part. The genteel ladies, hoist
by their own petard, wavered and then Mrs Porteous,
again, assured them that the film was 'a historical drama
recreating one of the great events in Champton's long
and splendid history'.

Nearly everybody signed up. Margaret Porteous,
'local historian, chief guide to Champton House and

senior churchwarden', three titles she had mostly made up, was to be in the actual masque itself, dressed as one of the mythical queens who accompanied the real queen. When Audrey heard of this she found that her distaste for the whole enterprise changed to fascination. If the history of their Champton in all its greatness was to be shared with the wider world, its treasures displayed, its 'champains rich'd' with 'wide-skirted meads' rendered on Panavision, then it would be no less than her duty to join the pageant. And if Peggy Porteous was going to be raised to the dignity of queen in the process, she would not be the only one, so after negotiating a 'sabbatical' from Miss March, Audrey practically ran to the casting.

Success followed, but success so tempered it was almost more like a failure, for Audrey had been cast not as a queen, but as a servant. 'Do I look like a wench?' she had said to the casting lady.

'No, you're too old for a wench, more . . . I don't know . . . spit cook? But if you don't want to . . .'

Audrey was made of tougher stuff than that and would not let a mere miscasting ruin her chance to appear in a film with Gillian Smith. 'Nonsense! A wonderful opportunity for me to recreate history in the round. Like *Upstairs, Downstairs*! Who wouldn't rather be Rose than Lady B?'

News of this leaked immediately. When filming was mysteriously halted, Audrey took the opportunity to nip down to the Post Office to buy a packet of squashed fly biscuits and a pint of milk, and when the little bell over the door tinkled Mrs Braines behind the counter said, 'You rang, m'lady?' Miss Sharman and Mrs Achurch, who had gathered for that day's Post Office Parliament, both snorted.

Audrey pretended not to notice and dallied over her order, partly to inconvenience Mrs Braines, but mostly to see if there was intelligence to be gathered. 'Oh, and five first-class stamps, please,' she said, which obliged Mrs Braines to move from the shop counter to the Post Office counter, and then Audrey made her go back again when she remembered she also needed one of those cubes of blue chalk for snooker cues, an item so unlikely it would leave Mrs Braines in no doubt that it was a revenge purchase.

As she waited for it to be fetched from the back of the shop and brought to the till, she smiled at Dora Sharman and Cynthia Achurch. 'Will you be joining our band of merry mummers too?'

'Merry what?' said Dora.

'Signing up to appear in the film? Hollywood comes to Champton?'

'No. I couldn't bring Scamper and I'm not leaving him at home.' At the sound of his name, Dora's scruffy Jack Russell looked up. When he saw Audrey he growled, for his bitterest enemies in Champton were the rectory dachshunds, and enough of their scent adhered to Audrey's inaptly named Hush Puppies to raise the alarm.

'So I see. Not really lap-dog material, not really fit for a queen.'

This rather stung Dora. 'It's not my Scamper who made the queen lose her temper. Unlike your Cosmo.'

'I beg your pardon?'

Cynthia Achurch would have given another little snort but restrained herself, for her husband, Bob, was the rector's sexton and she felt a certain deference was prudent.

'Didn't you know?' said Dora. 'Cosmo was down at the big house yesterday and his lordship let him out of his study and he ran into a scene they were filming and ruined it. Margaret Porteous, all dressed up, had to chase him and pick him up and fetch him out. Everyone's talking about it.'

Audrey gave one of the rigid smiles she used when wrong-footed. 'Oh, how funny! I'm sure it caused great amusement.'

'Not for Gillian Smith. She had a fit.'

'Actresses!' said Audrey. 'I'm sure it happens all the time.'

'I expect you'll find out,' said Mrs Braines, 'co-starring as . . . what's your part?'

'I am a member of the household.'

'In the kitchen? Scullery? I wonder if you'll see much of Gillian Smith there,' said Dora.

'We all play our part, high born or low. *Toujours c'est la même chose!* How much is that, dear?'

★

Bernard did his best to shoo Cosmo and Hilda towards Daniel so he could put them on their leads, but
dachshunds are not sheep, and they were disinclined to
be rounded up, not with their walk barely begun and
their routine inspection of the lake's edge interrupted.
Hilda sat and refused to move, and Cosmo went his
own way until Bernard cornered him, scooped him up
and tucked him under his arm. Cosmo, so errant and
disobedient, typical of his breed's perverse nature, was
immediately docile, and when Bernard presented him
to Daniel, he showed no resistance when his lead was
clipped on. With Cosmo tethered, Hilda was easy to
tether too, but – always the alpha – she still refused
to move. Daniel had to pull on her lead until she began to
slide through the long grass.

As Hilda broke into a walk, Daniel's chain of thought
was interrupted by Bernard, who bellowed, 'We're
MOVING. We have DOGS!' He was shouting at the
distant figure with the bullhorn, who had reappeared
in a sort of golf buggy and was driving towards them
across the park. 'I SAID, WE'RE MOVING!'

The buggy stopped and the driver shouted again
through the bullhorn.

'We have an EMERGENCY! We need the vicar!'

'RECTOR!' shouted Bernard.

Emergency? thought Daniel. I wonder what that
could be? A solecism in clerical dress so urgent they
send a Mini Moke?

The figure – Daniel could see it was one of the

runners, a girl recruited from the College of Further Education at Braunstonbury whom he recognised from Guides – shouted again.

'You must come NOW! There's been an accident!'

Bernard said, 'Then you had better go. I'll take the dogs back to the rectory. Telephone me there.'

Daniel did not quite run to meet the buggy – the driver's name was Gayle, he remembered – not because it was beneath his dignity, but because it was above his competence. Never athletic, he was approaching fifty and instead of doing more to preserve his fitness, he was doing less, especially since Bernard had started to take Cosmo for walks. Cosmo would happily walk all day; Hilda would waddle for precisely as long as it suited her and then sit down. Such an interruption to his hardly punishing regime had already had a noticeable effect and he was puffing by the time Gayle reached him.

'Get in, vicar.'

He got into the seat beside her, and she set off with rather a lurch, which reminded Daniel of the dodgems.

'Gayle, isn't it?'

She nodded. 'You remember me? From Guides?'

'Yes. What's happened?'

'I remember you. You showed us round the church, and there was a separate bit like a little church with all the old graves in and statues of the people who were in them, and they had blank eyes, and it reminded me of the Cybermen . . .'

'What's happened, Gayle?'

She calmed down. 'One of the extras has been taken ill. She's one of your ladies.'

'Do you know who?'

'The Queen of somewhere, not England. Ethiopia? Chantelle?'

'Candace,' said Daniel. 'I think that is being played by Mrs Porteous. Is it Mrs Porteous?'

'I don't know,' said Gayle, 'but she goes to church here. That's why the wardrobe lady asked me to get you.'

They set off towards the house. 'Do you know exactly what's wrong with . . . this person, Gayle?'

'I don't know, but I think it must be serious. They looked worried.'

'Who spoke to you?'

'It was the wardrobe lady, the local. I don't know her name.'

'Miss March.' It must be serious if Miss March looked worried.

They drove on in silence for a while. Then Gayle said, 'I'm doing media studies at college. They came and talked to our lecturers. We get work experience and something to put on our CVs and they get us to do whatever they need doing.'

'What sort of things?'

'Teas and coffees. Making sure people are where they need to be. You know.'

'Do you get to meet the stars?'

'Not really. We see them, but they have their own

people. I did have to go and get Miss Smith some of her special tea, but I didn't give it to her myself. She has a person who looks after her – Carrie, it all goes through her.'

'Special tea?'

'Yes, not like proper tea. It helps you to sleep, or if you're bad with your nerves. Sounds like calamine lotion.'

'Chamomile?'

'That's it.'

'Where did you find chamomile tea in Champton? I don't think Mrs Braines would keep it at the shop.'

'In town. One of the drivers took me. Do you know the health-food shop?'

'Oh, yes, my mother gets her evening primrose oil there.'

'You wouldn't believe how expensive it is.'

'The simpler things in life so often are.'

Gayle drove round the side of the house to the old stable block, built in the same century as the film they were making but not considered useful for their purposes, so it had been conscripted to contemporary needs. There the production team had made camps: sprouting around the palatial accommodation intended for horses and grooms were the shiny white tents and bolted-together Portakabins for the various departments necessary for the making of motion pictures. Hair and make-up were here, and catering, and wardrobe, and a series of workshops where the technicians

and scenic artists and electricians and sound engineers
erected their temporary sheds. And then, slightly apart,
and facing the lake, were the Winnebagos for the stars,
parked like watering cattle in a circle. Then, yet more
distant, like the foreman's house separated from the
workers, was the most splendid Winnebago of all, reserved for Miss Smith. She was in it at that moment, attended by Carrie, nourished by half a banana, soothed
by Phenergan and codeine, lying on a sofa with a video
of the Horse of the Year Show playing quietly on her
television.

'Here we are,' said Gayle. 'I'll just tell them you're
here.'

The encampment, from afar, always made Daniel
think of the Field of the Cloth of Gold, when Henry
VIII, in tented splendour, met the King of France at
the Pale of Calais for a parley in 1520. This was more
Cloth of Polyurethane, but it was as costly a shanty as
Henry's in its way. It was quiet now, the usual bustle
of its various departments still, until from round the
corner nearest the house there came a stream of revellers dressed gorgeously for a Jacobean masque, the
women in long silk dresses with overskirts laid over
more overskirts and slashed capes in rich velvets, wearing flowers entwined as headdresses. The men looked
not so different, with what looked like tasselled skirts
and delicate armour, and billowing sleeves and headdresses more feathery and precarious than the women's.
It was like a Gobelins tapestry come to life, he thought

(though he couldn't remember if Gobelins was active in 1603), until he noticed some of the masqueraders were wearing glasses and smoking cigarettes.

Then he noticed, with a start, that many of them were his parishioners, temporarily costumed for a seventeenth-century masque. He started, not just in recognition, but because he was already on terms with their seventeenth-century selves. His job required him to be a custodian of the family histories of Champton and many of his parishioners today had names recorded, iteration after iteration, in the registers, some going back to the 1550s. There had been Braines and Staveleys and Stanilands and Achurches in Champton long before anyone wrote down their names, in different spellings, and the de Floures family had been here, in the same house, since the Norman Conquest. The last of the de Floures family to quit this life, Bernard's cousin Anthony, he had buried in the de Floures chapel in the north transept of his church, the place of blank-eyed statuary and grandiloquent memorials that had scared Gayle. To her, he supposed they looked like marmoreal ghosts; to him, they seemed not so long ago and not so far away, the proximity of the living and the dead being a daily experience for the parish priest.

As their pageant passed in front of him, one of the figures broke away and approached. At first Daniel thought it was a baroque Hiawatha, with a headdress of what looked like dyed eagle feathers and carrying a spear, or was it a torch? Then he saw it was his brother, Theo.

He smiled. 'Who are you supposed to be?'

'This? In the masque, Wingina, Indian chief – I think he was killed by Raleigh, or someone like Raleigh, I can't remember, but . . .' – he held up a hand – 'I can't really say much, Dan, and please don't divulge your source, but Margaret Porteous has had a heart attack or something. It's serious. No one's saying much, but I thought you should know.'

'Where is she?'

'Old Dairy. Wardrobe has an outpost there. Miss March's spot, where she awaits with needle and thread. But everyone's being mysterious. I hope she's all right. You didn't hear this from me.'

Daniel was about to ask why it was such a mystery, but Theo just turned and went and rejoined the revellers, who were more excited by the catering than the casualty.

Then Gayle, looking more scared than before if anything, arrived with a man who looked like an off-duty commando, wearing a belt with a walkie-talkie and headphones over a baseball cap. He had the distracted and irritating air of someone thinking about more important things.

He was wearing dark glasses so Daniel could not see his expression, but he sounded slightly impatient.

'You're the vicar?'

'I am Canon Clement, Rector of Champton.' He paused, waiting for the man to introduce himself. He did not.

'And you want . . .?'

Daniel paused a beat and said, 'I understand one of the extras—'

The man interrupted him. 'Supporting artists.'

Daniel said, 'Yes, supporting artists. I understand one of them has been taken ill. I believe it's Mrs Porteous. She's a parishioner. I understand she's asked to see me.'

'A parishioner?'

'Yes. Mr . . .?'

The man did not reply to that but said, 'That won't be possible.'

'I beg your pardon?'

'I can't let you see her. She's with a medic.'

Daniel said, 'She will want to see me.'

The man looked steadily at Daniel. 'As I said, one of our medics is with her, assessing her. I can't let anyone in at the moment, for reasons of privacy. And safety.'

Daniel said, 'I would like to see her straight away, please. Could you take me at once? As I said, I know she would want to see me.'

The man held up a finger, then turned away as a hissing sound came from his headphones. He started having a conversation for which only his half was audible, and it made Daniel think of people with psychosis who have conversations with the voices in their head. Daniel, mild by nature, was not easily irritated, but this man was unusually irritating, in part for his lack of basic courtesy, but mostly because he was standing in the way of a priest and a parishioner in need. By nature and experience he had learnt to compromise himself almost into invisibility when required, but there were some matters in which he would not compromise, and this was one.

'I need to go to her, Gayle.'

Gayle looked awkward. 'I'm not allowed to take you.'

'The Old Dairy?'

Gayle looked nervously at the man with the headset continuing his half-audible conversation while pacing up and down. It was as if he was creating a personal vortex of stress, Daniel thought, like a tiny dust devil. So Daniel smiled at her and started to make his way through the stables courtyard towards the house.

After a second, he heard someone shout, 'Hey!' and turned to see the man with the headset running over.

'What are you doing?' he said.

'I'm minding my business, Mr . . . I don't know your name, so forgive the discourtesy.'

'You can't be here.'

'And yet I am.'

'You can't just wander around our location.'

'Your location is in my parish. You have your priorities, I understand, but you must understand that I have mine, and my priority at this moment is the welfare of my parishioner. If you won't take me to see her, I will take myself.'

'I'm going to have to call this one in,' said the man.

Daniel said, 'I don't care what you do, but I'm going

to go and see my parishioner. If you would excuse me?'
The man hesitated for a second, so Daniel walked away.
He heard him behind him again on his walkie-talkie,
only this time sounding a bit more urgent.

Daniel had the advantage of knowing the house well,
so he slipped round to the service wing, where there
was a separate entrance that led to the family quarters
and to the kitchen. He let himself in and said a tentative
'Hello?' outside Mrs Shorely's door, but there was no
reply. This part of the house, usually occupied, was not
used for filming, so it was unusually empty, but Daniel
could hear the peculiar din of filmmaking on the other
side, where the state rooms lay in their magnificent
sequence. He did not walk towards the din but along
the kitchen corridor, until he turned the corner to the
Old Dairy. There was another man with headphones
and a clipboard standing as if on sentry duty outside the
door. Next to him was a forbidding-looking man in a
bomber jacket and dark glasses. He moved to intercept
Daniel and held up a restraining hand.

'I have to stop you, padre,' he said.

The other man motioned towards him with his clipboard, a gesture of welcoming that also ushered him
away from the door, like a sheepdog funnelling a flock
into its pen. On the clipboard, Daniel noticed, a document was precariously fastened, a spreadsheet, covered
with different-coloured highlighter stripes that made
him think of Bridget Riley.

'You're the vicar?'

Daniel resisted the temptation both to compliment him on his powers of observation and to correct the wrong use of vicar.

'I am. And you are?'

'I'm Martin. Second AD.'

For a moment Daniel thought he was referring to the second century after the birth of Christ.

'Assistant director. Martin Clancy.'

'I would like to see Mrs Porteous, Mr Clancy. I understand she is here?'

'Can you hang on? A medic is with her.' He looked to the side as he said this.

'What's the matter with her?'

'I can't say, sorry. We'll know in a minute.' He looked to the side again. Then he said, 'I can look round the door?'

'Thank you.'

He hesitated again in a cleft of indecision. Then he knocked and opened the door. Someone on the other side growled. He went in and closed the door behind him.

Daniel, suddenly alone, tried to shift his mood from combative, or as near to combative as he got, to pastoral, for whatever was behind the door would require him to be at his most pastoral.

'What was your unit?' he said to the security guard.

'The Skins.'

'An Ulsterman.'

The guard nodded and relaxed a little. 'Sorry about this.'

Daniel nodded and leant back against the wall. He could hear a quiet conference happening beyond the closed door, and from its cadence he could tell it would be a while before anything happened. He noticed on the wall opposite a set of prints of pastoral scenes, of sheep grazing in a meadow, and of cattle chewing the cud, and on either side of the door itself, milkmaids a-milking. They were the Marie Antoinette kind of milkmaid, ornamental rather than agricultural, the nicer kind of cows led on ribbons to their dainty labours. He wondered what the real dairymaids who had once worked there made of them as they churned butter and scalded pans.

A man came out, but it was not Martin. He was older, too old, Daniel thought, for a baseball cap, but he wore one, and he had no headphones, which gave him an air of authority, like the tycoon at a desk without a telephone, because other people do the telephoning.

'Canon Clement?'

They also do the briefing, thought Daniel, and he said, 'Yes.'

'I'm Dick Alleyne. I'm directing this film. We've met.'

'Yes, I remember,' said Daniel.

'I think you're our religious adviser.'

'It was mentioned.'

'We have a situation. Not an advice matter.'

'Mr Alleyne, would you let me in, please?'

He shrugged. 'You had better come in.' He nodded at the security guard, who followed them in.

The Old Dairy was a long, cool room built when a

new service range was added to the house in the reign of
Queen Victoria. The gently sloping floor was laid with
Minton tiles; a gutter ran through them and around an
indoor fountain, no longer working, which once kept
milk and butter and cheese cool. The walls, too, were
tiled, behind the marble counters and shelves; running
over the top of them was a narrow porcelain frieze, made,
Daniel noticed, from repeating reliefs of the de Floures
circlet of flowers. In spite of this flourish, it felt more like
a cottage hospital than a dairy, clean and white – but not
only white; a dribble of blood had congealed in the gutter.

It had come from Margaret Porteous, who was sitting
back in an old armchair, still in costume but without the
wig, her own hair still flat and hair-gripped beneath it.
Around her, like ladies-in-waiting, stood mannequins
wearing clothes as extravagant and lovely as hers, only
they were headless. Wigs on blocks stood on the shelves
and it looked for a moment like an early Terror had come
to Champton and they were its decapitated victims.

Margaret had suffered a different wound. A deep-red
stain, almost black, spread across her bodice and down
the inner and outer skirt of her costume. The long, en-
veloping veil, so recently diaphanous and rippling, was
now clogged and stiff where the blood had congealed.
This was no heart attack, but it was obvious that her
mortal life was done. Her mouth gaped open – how
she would have hated to be seen like that – and she
had the unmistakable stillness of flesh and blood from
which life has just departed.

No medic, he noticed; not that a medic could do anything for her. He could, and said a prayer for her immortal soul.

'Depart, O Christian soul, out of this world;
In the Name of God the Father Almighty who
   created you;
In the Name of Jesus Christ who redeemed you;
In the Name of the Holy Spirit who sanctifies you.
May your rest be this day in peace,
and your dwelling place in the Paradise of God.'

'Amen,' said the security guard by reflex.

There was silence and Daniel felt a moment of intense pathos. There was nothing in Margaret's life that gave any presentiment of the death that had ended it. He felt then the desolation he had felt before when a person innocent of any conceivable offence suffered an act of blank cruelty. And then he felt resolve.

'What happened?'

'As far as we know, she came in complaining of a stitch. She'd been in the masque scene we're filming today, and when the wardrobe assistant loosened her corset, she started bleeding.'

'Miss March.'

'Yes.'

'Where is she?'

'I had her taken home. She was very upset.'

'The police will need a statement,' said Daniel.

'Yes, I suppose they will.'

'You have called the police?'

No one said anything at first, but they looked at Dick. 'It's in hand,' he said.

'In hand?'

'There's a protocol.'

'Yes, there is,' said Daniel. 'It's called the law, and if you do not report a suspicious death, you will be in trouble with the police and the coroner.'

Dick said, 'It's just, we need to assess the state of the casualty . . .'

'No medic, I see. Unless you are also a medic, Dick?'

'And our security officers are first-aid trained,' he said feebly, 'and we need to secure the . . . you know, the scene. And we don't want the story to break until we're on top of it. Better for all concerned, you see?'

Daniel had had enough and made to leave. The security guard held up a hand, but Daniel gave him one of his Old Testament looks and he yielded.

Daniel stalked rather than walked down the corridor, angry at the self-importance of a film crew that thought it had jurisdiction above and beyond the law of the land, and – a special provocation, which he was canny enough not to express – their lack of regard for his rights and responsibilities as incumbent of the parish.

The corridor to the service range led to a door, green baize on the corridor side, mahogany and gilt on the more splendid side, which opened onto the hall. There the house telephone stood – Badsaddle 264

– and Daniel was going to telephone DS Neil Vanloo at Braunstonbury Police Station. This was a call he did not want to make, not only because no one would want to be in a situation when this sort of call had to be made, but also because he had not spoken to Neil for a while – honouring an agreement they had made, or rather one he had forced on Neil, in the turbulence of a disrupted relationship. The hall, which was one of the rooms used for filming, was not part of any scene that day, so it was littered with the debris filmmakers strew around their sets. There were sections of track, there was equipment, there were tables and chairs set up with monitors, there were enormous lights on tripods, and smaller lights – the great light and the lesser light he called them, though Theo had called them something else – but there was no telephone. The set dressers had removed anything out of period that could be moved and had hidden what could not.

'Allow me.' Dick was standing behind him with the security guard who was holding a small black device like a walkie-talkie, only smaller.

Daniel recognised it at once. A Motorola MicroTAC 9800X. It was the first one he had seen.

'Calling 999?' said the security guard.

'I'll call the station direct,' said Daniel.

'You know how to use it, padre?' He flipped it open and passed it to him. 'Don't forget to use the STD code.'

4

Miss March thought she might be in shock. After Margaret had died in front of her – she knew she was dead, she did not need to be told – she had done everything she needed to do: notified Angela, waited for security and Dick to come, and then she had really, really wanted to go home. She had seen her father die a violent death, a death caused by a lout in the street, and to see another had revived the horror of that night. Mr Alleyne arranged for a driver to take her. Most considerate, she thought. She said she was aware she would need to speak to the police, and that they would find her in the flat.

She was taken in a silver Mercedes to Elite Fashions, the driver opening the door for her as if she were a star, which she disliked, and which drew a small crowd of three to the Post Office and General Store window on the other side of the road. She went up the narrow flight of stairs to the flat and felt suddenly very alone and very sad. She remembered her last flat, and looking out of the window into the street at midnight, and her father challenging a group of youths, and one of them threatening him, and suddenly he was on the ground and she was kneeling by him in her winceyette pyjamas, screaming . . .

She made a cup of tea, to which she added two spoonfuls of sugar, for she believed that was the right thing to do when someone was in shock. At least she knew she was in shock; she had experienced it before, so she decided to do what she always did: let routine get her through this terrible moment.

She went down to the shuttered shop, switched on the lights and set herself the task of arranging silk scarves so they cascaded down a cone she had made out of chicken wire. When the chicken wire was invisible after all the scarves were in place, she hoisted it onto a stick fixed into a stand. It looked like a little Christmas tree by Hermès, and was free to spin, or rather wobble, in a manner she hoped would show off their – what was the word Robert Herrick used? – their liquefaction. She thought about opening the blinds to see it in proper light, but that would perhaps invite attention from Mrs Braines, and she didn't want that.

When news that the film was going to be shot at Champton had spread, Miss March had responded not by scouring the pages of *Hello!* to see what Gillian Smith had been up to lately, but by familiarising herself with the history and literature of the period. She loved the seventeenth century – she had moved to Champton

partly to be next to where quite a lot of it happened
– she had catalogued what was left of it in the attics
at Champton, or hanging from beds in the grander
rooms. Daniel thought she would be uninterested in
such shallow diversions as filmmaking, like his mother
had pretended to be, but he had noticed an *Anthology
of Jacobean and Caroline Verse* she had ordered from the
library at Stow on the counter at the shop one day, and
had directed her to Herrick, a poet he especially loved.
As the proprietrix of a dress shop – as Audrey had
mockingly called her predecessor behind the counter,
Stella Harper – Miss March turned immediately to
'Upon Julia's Clothes', and found it wonderfully brief
and wonderfully observant of the effect a dress could
have, simultaneously to flow and to fix.

She had seen, too, her customers, temporary extras,
talk about the costumes they had been given to wear,
particularly those fortunate to be chosen to dance in the
masque. Seen, and endured, in the case of some, like
Margaret Porteous (who was not usually a customer),
who, Miss March thought, had no feel for clothes at all.
And yet Margaret had been in to buy a pair of gloves, or a
knocked-down scarf in the sale, or to browse, but mostly,
she suspected, to talk to anyone who would listen about
her wondrous vesture as Candace, Queen of the Ethiopians in the forthcoming scene. When she described her
costume – the gorgeous slit overskirt, the tight bodice,
the headdress – Miss March, who was usually good at
imagining a customer in an outfit, could think only of

the slacks and moccasins Mrs Porteous typically dressed in, and there was nothing liquid about those. Audrey Clement, forgetting for a moment the high standard of customer service one might expect of that establishment, observed to Margaret that it must be difficult in an era of marine conservation to obtain whalebone in sufficient quantities to corset the ladies of this temporary court, even if they were only in the background.

As if summoned merely by the thought, the back door half crashed open and Audrey Clement came bustling through the slash curtain dividing the shop from the kitchenette. She was wearing a sort of housecoat, the kind of garment Miss March would have thought suitable for a cleaner rather than a 'retail consultant'.

'Mrs Clement . . .' she said.

'Saw the light on. Margaret Porteous,' interrupted Audrey. 'What's happened?'

'What do you mean?'

'Filming has stopped for the day and that never happens because everything is so far behind schedule thanks to Her Majesty Gillian Smith, who seems to have forgotten that punctuality is the politeness of kings . . . I mean Mrs Porteous?'

'She was taken ill on set and came to wardrobe, and then a medic came, and Mr Alleyne came and sent me home. I asked one of the runners to find the rector and take him to her. I wanted to be here, to be alone . . .' – a slight emphasis on 'alone', ignored by Audrey – '. . . so I told them I was going and where they could find me if they needed to speak to me, and . . . here I am. Do you like what I've done with the scarves?'

'And here I am,' said Audrey. 'They wanted to keep us all in the . . . enclosure . . . but I managed to nip off round the back of the stables and cut through the park.' She gave the cone of silks a twirl. 'Oh, yes, I see they move if it moves. How clever. But Margaret, what happened? How is she?'

Miss March did not reply, for she was watching an ambulance followed by a police car drive along Main Street towards the gates of Champton House.

One of the security guards had pressed the button to open the gates before the ambulance and the police car got there and waved them through. On either side of the gates stood the lodges where once gatekeepers lived and whose duty it was to admit visitors. They had long gone, and the lodges were now occupied by Alex de Floures, Bernard's younger son, who had rather found his own way in the world as an artist of some notoriety, if not renown, associated with the London art collective Long Pig. He could not quite manage the collective part of that, so maintained his own house-hold in London, in a house in Islington, and at home – it was always home – at the lodges. Their situation, literally at the edge of the park, suited him, he said, 'for its liminality', and it also allowed him, while on the estate, to maintain the degree of privacy he required to share them with his scandalous boyfriend, Nathan

Liversedge, grandson of Bernard's last gamekeeper, who everybody knew about but few wished to have to deal with socially. This was a mistake, for Nathan was not only handy, but handsome and obliging, and, after a couple of years under instruction from Alex, had acquired a feel for wine, film, furniture and sun-dried tomatoes. 'Has Alex found his forbidden love,' said Audrey once, 'or a knock-off Jeeves?'

Nathan had also acquired Alex's lively taste in dress. After the punk phase and New Romantic phase, he had gone a bit rockabilly and now – a new depart-ure – they were both wearing clothes that looked like they had been stolen partly from a quartermaster in the Norwegian army and partly from the Battle of Waterloo. Combat trousers with pockets on the thighs; big black boots and khaki T-shirts; dark serge capes with scarlet piping; nylon bomber jackets; tunics with elaborate frogging; parkas with a hood fringed with a sort of synthetic candy floss.

For Nathan, Army Surplus was already his look – his only look long before the Pygmalion promotion – and he had the build and physicality for it. Alex looked less persuasive in fatigues, like the posh one who played the piano in *It Ain't Half Hot Mum*, said his sister Honoria, ungenerously. The addition of the dressier items, which Alex had found in the attics at home, worked less well on Nathan and he had started to lay them aside, but Alex, with his magpie inclinations, looked more and more the gay hussar.

The face that appeared in the window as the little emergency cavalcade passed through the gates was Alex's. He immediately went to the telephone and called the house switchboard. After six rings the answerphone clicked in. 'This is Champton House. No one is available to take your call . . .' He tried his father's extension but got the same message. He tried the stables too, but no answer. He was in the north lodge, where he lived by day – the south was where he slept and bathed – so he went to the door and said to the security guards, 'What's going on?'

'Accident,' said one.

'Who?'

'Don't know.'

'Must be bad if the cops are there too.'

'Couldn't say.'

'Oh, come on.'

But the guard shrugged and pretended to scrutinise his clipboard. Alex, while interested, was not sure he was interested enough to make the trip up the three-quarters-of-a-mile-long drive to find out for himself, and was calculating how long it would take him to acquire the intelligence without going to unnecessary lengths. This was interrupted by the sound of a commotion from that drive. He went again to the door and saw what looked like a stand-off. The drive was not particularly wide, and the ambulance and the police car going towards the house had encountered a silver Mercedes coming from the house. The Mercedes had stopped; the ambulance and the police car had stopped. Nothing was happening, but both parties seemed to think they had priority over the other. The Mercedes sounded its horn. After a moment the ambulance switched on its blue flashing light. The Mercedes flashed its lights too and sounded the horn again. The ambulance gave a surprisingly loud blast of its siren. Then the passenger-side door of the police car opened. A uniformed officer got out and went to one side, where the Mercedes driver could see him, and used one of those imperative gestures police use to firmly direct traffic that might have other ideas. Nothing happened, so the policeman went to have a word with the driver. On the way he stopped, looked down at his feet and then performed a little suite of giant strides, and Alex saw what the problem was. It had rained very heavily for the past few days and the grass on either side of the drive was waterlogged. Even so, he would have thought the driver of the Mercedes would have appreciated that an ambulance with blue lights, a siren and the escort of insistent police officers really should not be argued with. There was an exchange at the Mercedes driver's window and eventually the car reversed a few yards, then drove very slowly onto the grass. The ambulance and police car, no longer with lights and sirens, went past with a rather noticeable acceleration, which seemed to Alex to add a note of reproach.

He thought it prudent to retreat to the kitchen, from

where he could observe without being observed. The Mercedes, as he thought, was going nowhere. As the driver must have feared, it sank into the waterlogged grass and even the most expert and gentle effort to move was thwarted. After three goes it stopped trying, the horn sounded again, and it flashed its lights. One of the security guards went up from the gates. Another driver's-side-window conversation happened and then the guard gestured to the other and there was a short interlude, almost slapstick, when they tried, without success, to help the driver get out.

Another conference, and then the two security guards went round to the rear passenger doors and slowly and inelegantly began to extract the passengers. First out, and more concerned for the other passenger than herself, was a middle-aged woman in dark slacks and a coat in a houndstooth check, which seemed to Alex too masculine. She was also wearing suede moccasins, which she surrendered without any hesitation to the puddled mud as she went as nimbly as possible under the circumstances to assist the removal of the other.

At first Alex could not tell who it was, or even what it was, so swathed and bundled was the figure that emerged, but then he saw a lady in a state of half dress, her head turbaned, wearing a cashmere tracksuit under a cashmere blanket and clutching a soft leather shoulder bag. Even in dark glasses the size of paired soup bowls she was unmistakable.

Ooh, thought Alex, it's Gillian Smith.

The two security guards, assisted by the driver and the other woman, manoeuvred her into a fireman's lift, and very gently and slowly and smoothly they began to carry her towards the drive, like porters at Christie's moving the Badminton Cabinet. Even from that distance, Alex could see there was an exquisite quality to the discomfort this caused their passenger, as if each flinch and wince had been planned to create an effect. Once she was safely on dry land, the other woman squelched back to the car and fetched from the back seat a large shoulder bag and a briefcase. Another conference followed on the tarmac, and Alex's first impulse was to go and offer temporary accommodation in the lodge – for a second he imagined himself a Walter Raleigh, laying his MA-1 bomber jacket across a puddle so Miss Smith could step with unmoistened foot across it – but a more calculating impulse stayed the gesture to see if they would come to him rather than he to them.

He was right. After speaking into their walkie-talkies, and then with the woman in houndstooth check, and then again into their walkie-talkies, one of the security guards stayed with Miss Smith in an attitude of professional vigilance while the other approached the lodges, accompanied by the woman with the bag and the briefcase slung over her shoulder – which wouldn't do her back any good, Alex thought. He slipped into the corridor where he could not be seen through a window and awaited the knock on the door.

It came, and he waited some more – he did not want to look like he had nothing better to do – and then, after twenty seconds or so, he answered it.

The security guard said, 'Alex, sorry to bother you, but we have a situation.'

'Yes?'

'This is Miss . . .?' He looked at Carrie.

'Carrie,' she said. 'Just Carrie. I look after Gillian Smith, who as you may be aware is starring in the film they're making at your house.'

'Oh, yes.'

'Transport has let us down – we're stuck in the mud over there – and we're waiting for another driver to come and pick us up, but I was wondering if we might prevail on your hospitality until they do?'

'Of course. Shall I put the kettle on?'

'Oh, no need, it will only be for a couple of minutes. But could you take these?'

Before he could say yes, she was unburdening herself of the bag and briefcase and, in one fluid movement, had burdened him with them instead and turned to convey the good news to her boss. Before the security guard could say how many sugars he and his partner wanted, Alex turned away too and went into the drawing room.

It was a grander name than the dimensions of the room merited, though not the contents. He had furnished it from the attic swag the de Floures had acquired over the centuries. There was a table too large for the room, portraits too big for the walls, forks too heavy and too grandly crested for beans on toast. He quite liked this, especially when it allowed him to give rein to his subversive nature. Nothing quite matched; paintings were hung next to each other for the jarring effect they produced, stuffed endangered species were ghoulishly displayed, and over the fireplace he had made a display of swords and bayonets brought to Champton by his military ancestors, arranged in a sort of giant cutlery fan, a mixture of ancestral relics and punk aggression, which he particularly liked.

He plumped the cushions on the sofa and armchairs, then removed the ashtrays, which had been filling all morning, and a fruit bowl, which bore a bunch of bananas so black and ripe they had almost started to purée. There was another knock at the door.

On the step was Gillian Smith. 'Angel,' she said, 'I could kiss you.'

Daniel and Dick were waiting to meet the ambulance and police car at the courtyard at the back of the house. Security had moved everyone away, off set and out of the house, so the camp pitched at the stables was unusually busy, and the house itself suddenly quiet and still, as if it had been abandoned in the middle of a great party.

Daniel knew the ambulance drivers, who nodded professionally, and went to get what they needed from the back of the ambulance. He also knew the police officers, two uniformed PCs, one of them PC Scott, who moonlighted as a pall bearer for the funeral directors at Braunstonbury, had served with Bernard in the army years ago, and was always the police officer despatched when events at Champton House required one.

'Hello, Daniel,' said PC Scott, 'what have you got for us?'

'Casualty. It's Margaret Porteous.'

'Oh. Anything I need to know?'

'It's one for DS Vanloo.'

'He's on his way.'

'This is Mr Alleyne, he's in charge of the production . . .'

'Dick Alleyne, and I'm the director, not in charge.' He offered his hand, and PC Scott shook it without saying his own name.

The drivers appeared with a trolley. 'Lead on,' said PC Scott.

The trolleys rattled over the cobbles to the kitchen door, which Mrs Shorely had opened. She was waiting for them there and said, 'You don't need me?'

'We can manage, thank you, Mrs Shorely.'

Daniel led them along the corridor to the Old Dairy. The security guard outside nodded to the two policemen and the ambulance drivers, and opened the door for them. They went inside.

After a minute PC Scott appeared and said, 'No one in or out, please.'

The security guard said, 'No one's been in or out apart from the wardrobe lady and the boss and us. And the vicar.'

'No one in or out from the house and the park, I meant.'

'I don't understand,' said Dick. 'We've cleared everyone for the day.'

'Unclear them.'

'But there are hundreds of people. It's a film shoot.'

'It's a crime scene.'

Audrey was a little out of puff by the time she got to the rectory. After catching Miss March displaying merchandise – a shock reaction, she thought; she had seen it in the Blitz, people behaving as if nothing had happened, scrubbing the step of a house that was no longer there – she had made unusually good time, heading back along Main Street and up Church Lane. Normally she took advantage of stops along the way to pick up and transmit intelligence, but apart from the ladies in the Post Office, who were in the habit of being so *unnecessarily* satirical, she thought, there was no one else about. They were still corralled at the stables, where she should be had she not had the wit and gumption to make her escape.

She hurried up the drive and round the lovely balanced front of the rectory to the jumbled back, where the kitchen and the outbuildings formed an uneven cobbled courtyard open on one side. As the door opened, Cosmo and Hilda ran to greet her, their tails wagging so fast they looked like propellers. 'Good girl! Good boy!' she said in a way that seemed dispropor- tionately perfunctory compared with their welcome, but she had news to impart and that took precedence.

'Dan!' she shouted. 'Margaret Porteous! She col- lapsed, though there's more to it than that . . . Miss March was being her annoyingly discreet self . . . Anyway, they're *saying* Margaret had a stitch prancing around in that ridiculous costume, poor thing, in the masque. She's Queen of Camelot or something, but you'd think she was Empress of All the Russias from the airs and graces – I imagine she'd expect Bernard to give her a low bow. Anyway, one minute she was stately as a galleon, the next she's staggering off the set and only just managed to get to Miss March, who was in the Old Dairy, I think. Shouldn't you go?' Cosmo, who had an extraordinary instinct for an expedition, started barking in anticipation. 'Be quiet, you ridicu- lous beast,' she said and drew breath. 'Gillian Smith went storming off set again and then we were told to go to the stables and await instructions, only I'm very surprised they've done that because the schedule is very tight indeed and they wanted to get it all done today. And it's the lunch break, and God forbid anything should interrupt that. And it's lasagne, or it is for us, and no one wants to miss that, though I expect Mar- garet will, and you know what she's like when a free lunch is involved. Dan?'

Bernard said, 'Not Daniel, me. He's up at the house. I brought the dogs home.'

'Bernard! Have you been here all this time?' Her mind whirred like a Rolodex for anything unfortunate she might just have said.

'He said to wait. What's this about Mrs Porteous?'

'I'm not sure. What did I say?'

'Quite a lot. How serious is it?'

'I don't know. I suppose we will have to wait for Daniel. Cup of tea? Drink? Lunch?'

'Drink,' said Bernard, 'but what of poor Mrs Porteous?'

Audrey always felt unusually restrained talking to Bernard. To her, even though they had come to know each other well and were now on first-name terms, he was more like the Archbishop of Canterbury than a confidant. She still felt he was owed a deference because of his rank. To a woman of Audrey's generation and background, the meanest landed gent deserved deference, whereas a celebrity, even the internationally celebrated Gillian Smith, deserved nothing more than curiosity and judgement. She would never admit this to anyone, but as a girl she had kept a scrapbook of cuttings from newspapers about her favourite tennis players and rising clergy, and one reporting the marriage of Bernard's parents at St Margaret's, Westminster, which the Duke and Duchess of Gloucester had attended. Although she loved the gloss that came from their association, she simultaneously resented the awkwardness it caused, for Audrey was not given to introspection and she took such factors as the status quo and her place in it as granted. She did not like having her world shaken.

'Sherry?' she said.

'If you will.'

'I will.'

'Drawing room?'

She felt a faint sense of relief leaving the kitchen with her distinguished guest for the more formal setting of the drawing room, but Cosmo, realising there was to be no expedition after all, gave a whimper.

'Cosmo!' Bernard called him and patted his twilled thigh – and the little dog ran to him.

5

DS Neil Vanloo was doubly apprehensive as he slowed at the gates of Champton House. Not only because his professional attendance was required for what sounded like a murder, but because it would require the professional attendance of the rector. Their overlapping interest in the suspicious deaths of members of this parish – and other parishes too – had led to a personal as well as professional relationship. To the surprise of both of them, that had got very tricky when each misunderstood the attraction of the other, and then there was an excruciating comedy of errors, which led to Daniel fleeing to a monastery, Neil's secret affair with the Honourable Honoria de Floures ending awkwardly, and a lot of bruised feelings and difficult realisations.

Things like this happen, and when they do a decent period of purdah is wise, in which poise may be recovered, embarrassments cooled and normal service restored. And then suddenly there had been another murder, so delicate feelings and tactical handling had to be put to one side. The murder had been solved, Daniel and Neil working together as well as they ever had, but there had been a surprising coda to that episode which made things awkward again; and without a fresh murder investigation to distract them, their relationship stuttered. They became nervous and polite around each other, which in a way was worse than a failure of composure and just as unbearable. Nothing explicit was said, but suggestions to meet were half-heartedly offered and easily declined, and eventually they ceased. Two security guards – ex-military, Neil could tell – were on the gates, one on his side, one on the other. The one on his side approached his window.

'Sorry, sir, house and park are closed.'

Neil showed him his warrant card.

'Just a minute.' Neil thought the guard had gone to open the gates, but instead he talked to his colleague and then started speaking into his walkie-talkie.

Neil sounded the horn. The security guard glanced at him and held up a finger. Neil got out of the car. 'Open the gate,' he said. 'This is not a suggestion.'

The guard came over again. 'Hold your horses, sergeant, we have a situation,' he said.

'You will have if you don't open the gate.' Neil had the physicality of a boxer and the unruffled air of someone without fear in conflict, and the security guard could see that, but then a car appeared coming down the drive on the other side of the gate. It stopped next to another car – both Mercedes, both luxurious and slightly sinister

– which was parked (or was it stuck?) on the grass.

Then the door to the north lodge opened and an un-likely procession emerged, a woman in a houndstooth jacket leading another woman in a turban and dark glasses and the sort of tracksuit that had never seen a track, followed by Alex, who was wearing the sort of outfit an irregular Croatian militiaman might wear in an escalation of ethnic conflict.

'I can't open the gate right now,' said the security guard. 'No one's allowed to leave – your orders.'

'So don't let them leave.'

'You don't understand,' he said, 'it's Gillian Smith. You try telling her.'

'Happy to do that,' said Neil.

'It's not you who gets fired.'

The woman in the houndstooth jacket had gone ahead and was having what looked like a particularly tense discussion with the security guard on the other side of the gate and the two drivers. When Gillian Smith arrived at the side of the car, they all fell silent, apart from the other woman, who Neil assumed was her agent, or manager, or whatever people like that had. Gillian Smith ignored her and looked expectantly at Alex, who opened the back door of the car and helped her get in.

'I have to deal with this,' said the security guard and left Neil in the car. What he did not know was that Neil, thanks to his secret affair with Honoria, knew the code to open the gates. He entered it on a keypad on a post to his right – 1603 – and the great ironwork gates creaked and slowly swung open.

When the security guard on his side noticed, he started. 'Don't open the gates!' he half shouted, half hissed to his colleague, who shouted back that he hadn't.

Neil drove through, enjoying for a moment the privilege of access for his humble Ford Escort that was denied the Mercedes, but this was dashed when the sleeker car did not move as he approached. There was another tense discussion happening, and even when he flashed his lights there was no sign of a response, so he got out of the car.

Alex saw him walking over and intercepted. 'Hello, Neil. This is not, I take it, a social call?'

'No, it's very much a business call and it's soon going to be very much concerned with a police officer being obstructed in the course of his duty.'

'Maybe you could have a word? We have an incident of – what's it called? – cognitive dissonance?'

'You'll have to explain that to me.'

'You know when Admiral Beatty ordered his ships to turn onto a collision course at Jutland because he got mixed up, and his officers obeyed the order even though they knew it would cause a disaster? Something similar is happening right now.'

'What?'

'Orders from HQ' – he pointed in the direction of the house – 'not to let anyone in or out. But orders, too, to oblige Miss Smith in all things. Somewhere between her being released for the day and your arrival, the former overtook the latter.'

'OK,' said Neil, 'leave it with me.'

'She's notoriously difficult,' said Alex.

Neil spoke first to the driver of the second car. He showed him his warrant card. 'Move, please.'

'I can't, mate, we've already got one stuck and I have to get Miss Smith home.'

'Please get out of the car, sir.'

He sighed. 'Do I have to?'

'Yes, sir,' said Neil.

As he got out Neil moved away a few feet, so the driver had to go to him. 'Miss Smith isn't going home, not until I say so,' he said.

The man sighed again. 'My job is to pick up Miss Smith and take her home. She's already been delayed and . . . that just doesn't happen.'

'This is a crime scene,' said Neil, 'and I don't care if you have the Queen of Sheba in the back, no one's going home.'

'Queen of Sheba? Pushover. You don't know Miss Smith.'

'Hello?' said a voice behind him.

It was the woman in the houndstooth check. 'Are you a police officer?'

'DS Vanloo, ma'am,' he said. 'And you are?'

'Carrie Palethorpe, personal assistant to Miss Smith. We seem to be having some difficulty persuading these gentlemen to let us through.'

'They can't let you through.'

'They can't? Why not?'

'Because I said so.'

Carrie smiled. 'I'm sure we can work together to resolve this.'

'We can. Turn around and go back to where you came from.'

'I don't think you understand, Detective Sergeant. Miss Smith—'

'I don't think *you* understand, ma'am, this is a crime scene, an investigation is underway, and we need to talk to everyone.'

'Of course, I completely understand, but surely you can talk to Miss Smith at her place? It's not as if she had anything to do with whatever's happened.'

'We don't know. We need to establish . . . no, enough, turn around, go back to the house and we'll let you know when you can go.'

Carrie put on her sympathetic face. 'This is delicate, Detective Sergeant, but Miss Smith has a medical condition that makes it imperative for her to get back to where we are staying.'

'If Miss Smith requires urgent medical attention, I will arrange for her to get it. Now go before I arrest you for obstructing a police investigation.'

Carrie sighed. 'You couldn't cut me some slack? You don't know what she's like.'

Neil said nothing. Carrie went back to the car and leant in through the window. Although he could not hear the exchange that followed, something obliged them to get Miss Smith out of the car again. She made her own way back to the lodge, not quite at a run but more nimbly than seemed possible after the fuss she had made a moment ago.

Neil approached Carrie. 'What's the delay now?'

'Medical condition,' said Carrie. 'She needs to go sometimes. I did tell you.'

Alex followed Neil. 'Can I assist in any way?'

'I think she can probably manage on her own,' said Carrie.

'Only she seems so . . . dependent,' Alex added.

'She's not an invalid. I'm not her carer,' said Carrie irritably, and then went back to the car and started to rearrange the nest of blankets and cushions in the back seat in anticipation of the reinstallation of her employer.

'Another drama,' said Alex.

'Drama?'

'Whatever has happened to make you drive out from Braunstonbury when you could be having your sandwiches. And a catch-up with the rector. If you two are talking?'

'Not now, Alex. I'm at work.'

'I see. What a peculiar job it is too.'

'It has its moments.'

They stood in silence for a while as Neil tried not to let his irritation show. Then Miss Smith emerged from the lodge again and, at a statelier pace, made her way back to the car.

'Imagine working for her,' said Alex. 'I only had five minutes of her in the drawing room. It was like having Turandot drop in for elevenses.'

Neil walked away. He had to reverse back to the turning area in front of the gates to allow Miss Smith's car to turn around. He waited for it to set off slowly down the drive again, back towards the house, and then followed.

The lunch break was by now so extended that quite a few of the cast and crew had made a second pass at the catering. There was a danger of the more popular items on the menu running out, so the caterers were told to press the vegetarian option as a way of slowing demand. But the cast and crew had been working hard and looking forward to lunch, and even though it was a double satisfaction they sought, to find the lasagne they wanted substituted by a spinach and chickpea curry was still disappointing. The tight little communities that filmmaking creates, though short-lived, are involving and intense, and minor disappointments that don't matter much in the wider world matter disproportionately more there. This required a degree of sensitive management, and Martin, the assistant director responsible for keeping everyone happy, knew that if the catering was disappointing, morale was threatened.

Opposite the catering wagon was a marquee where two long lines of picnic tables – the kind with the bench seat attached – were available for the use of the cast and crew. You could tell who the cast members were because they were wearing black bin liners as improvised ponchos – an efficient and expedient way of protecting their costumes from food fragments, but it made them look like Jacobean punks. Actually, he thought, a blindfolded person could tell them apart because they always sat separately, partly because people tend to sit with the people they know, but also because there is a kind of unspoken hierarchy, or ordering principle, when it comes to location catering. Crew sit with crew, and seniors take precedence. Supporting artists sit with supporting artists, and cast sits with cast, again with precedence going to those with seniority – a distinction in a late-twentieth-century film location that mirrored that of the period and place they were filming.

There were distinctions within distinctions too. Martin had noticed – and this was true of both supporting artists and cast – that those who were playing high-status characters started to sit with others of equal status, and those playing servants started sitting with others playing servants. Martin, who could not afford to discriminate when it came to a character's social class, went from table to table to keep everyone 'updated with information'. But there wasn't any new information, so he had started repeating himself, and the questions about when they were going back on set, or when they would be released, grew more insistent.

Martin had bigger problems to deal with than frustrated supporting artists. Different standards applied

for the important actors, for whom distinction was observed in all respects. A little distance from the catering
marquees, down a path made scruffy by the passage
of golf-buggy wheels, was the corral of trailers and
Winnebagos for their use. At the end of that path was
Gillian Smith's, the most splendid and most isolated.
Martin overheard Alex describe it to Theo as Sanssouci
crossed with an HGV.

Gillian was quite easy to deal with in the sense that
she was the apex star, and so there was no arguing with
her precedence in everything, but it was more difficult
with lesser creatures, for whom hierarchy was sometimes quite hard to establish. What about an actor who
had been in a soap opera, like Theo; once PC Heseltine
in *Appletree End*, recognised wherever he went, and
an opener of supermarkets and fêtes? His soap-opera
days were behind him, but his celebrity endured, in
part thanks to a heavily rotated advertisement for a
chocolate bar, and his expectations of treatment were
consequently quite high. The problem was, he had not
yet reached equivalent status in film, so it was someone's job – Martin's, day to day – to ensure that he was
treated nicely enough but within his proper bracket.
Most of the time that worked reasonably well, but there
were moments when the fact of his junior status was
made plain. More than once, Gillian Smith had commandeered the car that was meant to be driving him,
leaving him suddenly at the back of a queue he had forgotten existed. Her wishes came before his, however,

and an insult to him was worth the tribute paid to her.

It had happened just now. Theo had been waiting for a knock on the door and for someone to tell him they were released for the day. He was expecting wardrobe to come to divest him of his costume, and a car to drive him the half-mile through the park to the rectory, where he had elected to stay with his mother and brother, rather than at the nearest thing to a deluxe hotel the county could offer. No knock came, and he had been obliged to descend his trailer, look for Martin, and ask what was happening but had found his car being dispatched as a relief vehicle for Gillian Smith, who had somehow got stranded at the gates. Perhaps, he thought, unkindly, her ego was wedged between them? No point in making a fuss, no point in showing the slight, but there it was for all to see.

Theo went back to his trailer and the rattling convection heater at his feet. He tried to get the television to work but it wouldn't, so he put on Radio Four instead and half listened to the news. Trouble in whatever they called Burma now. Why did they keep changing the names of things? There was a knock at the door. 'Hello, wardrobe, here to sort you out, petal.' It was Sandy: tiny, bald, of indeterminate age. Alex, on one of his frequent visits to Theo's trailer, once described him as the most intense concentration of camp in a defined space since Charles Hawtrey moved to Deal. Sandy was the first wardrobe assistant, and the first point of contact for actors when they needed urgent sewing up, or lint-rolling, or loosening. He stood just off set with bobbins and needles and bull clips and wire brushes to roughen the soles of your boots lest you slip on the polished wooden floors.

'Am I released?' said Theo.

'As far as I am concerned you are. Do you want me to help you out of your drawers?'

Theo presented himself to Sandy's expert way with buttons and bows and hooks and eyes.

'We're done for the day because of the . . . accident.'

'I know her,' said Theo. 'She's a friend of my mum's. Margaret Porteous. Is it bad?'

'Och, I don't think I can say,' said Sandy, 'and far be it from me to spread rumour, but let's just say she won't be reprising the role.'

'Dead?'

'And worse.'

'Worse?'

He unpeeled Theo from his doublet and held it up to the light. 'Couple of stitches needed, I think.' He sniffed it. 'And I can freshen it up for you.'

'Sandy, what's happened?'

'Sweat. You know, standing around all day under the lights, giein' it laldy with the dancin'. Of course you're gonnae sweat, hen.'

Sandy's swoop between high camp and unsoftened Glaswegian had become his trademark, and even if he wanted to, he couldn't switch it off.

'What's happened with Margaret Porteous?' said Theo.

Sandy put the doublet on a hanger. 'All I know is that she came off set in a hurry and went to wardrobe and somethin' happened and she's deid. And Angela's away talking to the polis.'

'A heart attack? She wasn't young.'

'Heart attacks, to the best of my knowledge, do not cause fountains of blood.'

Theo blinked a couple of times. 'Angela murdered Margaret Porteous?'

'It wasnae Angela, she wasnae there. Tell you who was, that woman from the dress shop doon the road who's suddenly the seventeenth-century costume expert, all grey, grey, grey. I'm just telling you what I'm hearing. No one's saying your dress-shop leddy did anything. But I'm hearing that no one's going any-where until the polis have done what the polis need to do, so I'd settle in if I were youse. Can I do your shirt? In fact, gimme the lot.'

Theo undressed to his boxer shorts in the unselfcon-scious way of an actor with a dresser. 'Margaret Porte-ous. No one would want to kill Margaret Porteous. I can't imagine Miss March . . . You might want to shut her up, but . . . And how? Stabbed?'

'I dinnae know. It's all a big mystery. Where's your poignard, by the way?'

'Poignard?'

'Your dagger.'

Theo blinked again. He wore a sword belt with his costume, from which hung a sword in a scabbard on his left hip, which apparently denoted his status, though why you would wear a sword to a ball he did not know. On his right hip, held in a smaller scabbard, was a dagger with an ornate carved handle made of bone, or ivory – he wasn't sure – and a narrow blade, more a spike. The whole thing was about a foot long.

The sword was in its scabbard, but the dagger was not.

'I dunno. I had it with me. I haven't touched it. I didn't even know it came out of its thing.'

'Well, it has.'

Both were silent.

Sandy said, 'I'll need to let someone know about this.'

'Of course.'

'Don't go anywhere.'

Theo nodded.

Sandy took the costume away. 'Shall I close the door?'

'No,' said Theo, 'leave it open, I could use some air.'

Margaret Porteous dead. Margaret Porteous murdered? Stabbed? Surely not by Miss March! But with his dagger? The dagger he had been wearing when he went on set and danced the masque – more a melee than a dance by the end, because Dick wanted it to be an expression of passions normally restrained by the discipline of the court and the status of the dancers. He supposed that was why masques existed, to temporarily subvert the status quo and give a thrill of unbridled liberty to a world where everything was bridled. He had talked about this with Daniel over dinner one night, who said he thought it highly unlikely that a court masque would have ever been unruly, especially because the queen, who loved them, was one of the masked and costumed dancers. That would be thought daring enough by the standards of the time. But the director and the writer and the producers were keener on passions than historical accuracy, and you have to accept the jarring infelicities of trying to portray a distant world in a way that is easily digestible for contemporary film audiences with equanimity. 'The past is a foreign country,' said Daniel, 'they do things differently there,' which Theo knew was a quotation, but he couldn't remember where from.

There was another tap on the door. 'Hi, Theo.'

It was Brandon Redding, Braunstonbury tearaway but temporarily employed as an extra on *A Woman of Boundless Intrigue*. He was also a menial – like Audrey Clement, a kitchen servant – dressed in plain hose and tunic in what Theo thought rather fashionable Armani colours, but the black bin-liner poncho thrown over it restored a punkishness that was much more him.

'I've got your order.'

'Come in. Close the door.'

Brandon reached into a leather pouch hanging from his belt and produced a little white paper envelope. 'A gram of Charlie for you. I've got more if you're interested?'

'What have you got?'

'Whizz, Es, acid.'

'I'm too old for amphetamines,' said Theo, 'and there's quite enough make-believe going on for me to float around set hallucinating. I could definitely do with some more Charlie, though, and have you got any puff?'

'Weed or hash?'

'I don't know. What would you recommend?'

'Do you want a little puff now?'

Theo thought about it. 'I don't suppose a small one will do any harm.'

Brandon knelt in front of the coffee table on which a runner had left a fruit bowl containing a trio of unripe bananas and a choice of salt and vinegar or smoky bacon crisps. He reached into his pouch again and produced one of those small, grey-lidded black plastic pots for camera films. He tipped out what looked like an irregular OXO cube. 'Moroccan. Very mellow. It's the business.' He produced a large packet of cigarette papers, took a Marlboro Light cigarette from Theo's packet, split it and shook the tobacco into one of the folded papers. Then he took his lighter, gently singed a corner of the OXO cube, pinched it off and crumbled it along the tobacco. He tore off a piece of card from the cigarette packet, formed it into a little tube and then positioned it at one end of the cigarette paper. Then he rolled it expertly, and licked the gummed strip. It reminded Theo of his mother making brandy snaps, each one done so skilfully they looked like they had been produced by a machine. Brandon lit it, took a couple of drags, then passed it to Theo. 'This is my favourite for chilling out.'

Theo took a drag, held it in his lungs for a second and exhaled. A smell of smoky spice, somewhere between cookery and aftershave, filled the trailer. 'Oh, I say. That's nice. Have you got any more?'

'Only this. But I have got something very special – sinsemilla. The best weed in the world. Do you want some? I can get as much as you like.'

'Maybe a bag of that too. Put it on my account.'

Brandon frowned. 'Since when did you have an account?'

'I haven't got readies. And you know I'm good for the money.'

'I only give accounts to my steadiest customers.'

'I must be one of them, Brandon. When I'm here. And I'm going to be here for weeks.'

'What do you want?'

'Just Charlie and puff, while I'm working. And weed.' He took another drag and handed the joint back to Brandon. 'This *is* mellow!'

Brandon indicated for Theo to budge up and sat heavily next to him on the narrow sofa. It was too close, even for Theo, who usually liked a frisson.

'Do you know what's going on?' said Brandon.

'Someone taken ill. One of the dancers.'

'Taken very seriously ill. Dead.'

'You know?' said Theo.

'Everyone knows. Or knows something. You know who it is?'

'Margaret Porteous. One of the queens in the masque.

She was one of my brother's churchwardens. Looked like an older Judith Chalmers.'

'I knew Mrs Porteous. Mrs Porthole we called her. She was a governor at the school when I was there. Did me no favours. Got me thrown out.'

'What did you do?'

'Fucked up the boys' toilets. I did some cock-and-balls graffiti. Wrote something about the headmistress.'

'How careless of you to get caught.'

'Nicked red-handed. And I was the only eleven-year-old who knew what the cock-and-balls thing was, so . . . Didn't go down well at all with Mrs Porthole. So I was expelled, and that was the end of a promising academic career.' Brandon handed Theo the joint. 'Do you know how she carked it?'

Theo took a drag. 'I heard something, which is why the cops are here.'

Brandon jumped up. 'Already? Why the fuck didn't you tell me? I've got my gear on me!'

'I don't think they'll be interested in that, Brandon.'

6

Daniel and Neil were standing in the Old Dairy.

'Poor Margaret,' said Neil.

'Yes. Poor Margaret.'

They were both silent for a moment, paying the necessary respect, in their different roles – to a departed soul, to a victim.

Neil was first to speak. 'What does it look like to you?'

'What we're *looking* at,' said Daniel, 'is a stabbing. A murder. But it's complicated. Was she stabbed here? In which case, is Miss March a murderer? Or – and this is to my mind more likely – was there a lapse of time between the action and the consequence? She wasn't stabbed here, where she died, so we need to find out where it happened. Why would she come to wardrobe rather than first aid?'

'She might not have known she'd been stabbed,' said Neil. 'I remember a guy telling me he just thought he'd been punched and he only realised he'd been stabbed when he saw the blood.'

'That would rule out Miss March as the murderer. But I think she may have played an unwitting part in poor Margaret's death. Do you remember how the unfortunate Empress of Austria died? Sisi? She came up when we were at the monastery. A favourite subject of that poor novice who was murdered.'

'Remind me.'

'It was the 1890s. She was on holiday in Switzerland and went for a walk by Lake Geneva – I think it was Lake Geneva – with just a lady-in-waiting. And in an extraordinary stroke of bad luck, she was recognised by an anarchist who was there to assassinate the Duke of Orléans, but he'd left town. If he couldn't get the French pretender, an empress would do, so he stabbed her with a stiletto. She was so tightly corseted – I think she had the record for the narrowest waist of her day, sixteen inches – that it acted as a kind of compression bandage, and nobody realised she had been stabbed. It was only when they got her to a hotel and the lady-in-waiting loosened her corset that she started to bleed and was dead in a couple of minutes.'

'You think the same thing happened here?' said Neil.

'Margaret is stabbed, she doesn't know she has been, she comes to wardrobe, Miss March unlaces her corset, and she bleeds out. A striking resemblance, no?'

'But Margaret was not the Empress of Austria.'

'No. For the purposes of the scene they were shooting today she was Candace, I'm guessing.'

'Who is she?'

'The Queen of Ethiopia,' said Daniel. 'One of the dancers in the masque. The ladies of the court all dressed up as characters from myths and legends. You know there was a masque for Anne of Denmark at Champton in 1603? It's why they're filming here. I was reading about it. Ben Jonson wrote it, and Inigo Jones put it together – sets, costumes.'

'So they were recreating something that actually happened?'

'Yes and no. This is based on *The Masque of Queens*, actually performed some years later in London, but they preferred it for dramatic reasons. And for dramatic reasons they took some liberties with it too.'

'Like what?'

'From what Theo has told me about it, I think it un-likely that the Jacobean court was quite as uproarious as the film version.'

'But explain who Margaret is,' said Neil.

'Candace. The Queen of Ethiopia. More properly, Kandake, a Meroitic name, and the sister of the King of Kush, which we would now call Sudan, and by matri-lineal descent a queen mother, we would say—'

Neil interrupted, 'And the point?'

'Candace had one of the key roles in *The Masque of Queens*. The queens all appear in the second part, after the witches in the first part – these were all played by actors – but the queens, all queens of virtue, were played by the ladies of the court. It was quite a daring thing to do, for high-born ladies to appear on stage, as it were. Off the top of my head, the Countess of Derby played Zenobia, Queen of Palmyra, and the Countess of Bedford played Artemisia . . . no, not Artemisia, that was someone else . . . Bedford played Penthesilea, the Amazonian queen – that must have been quite a sight – and for the queen herself to appear in a masque? That must have caused a *sensation.*'

'Is there a point, Daniel?'

'It was a masque of *queens*. Queens plural. All the ladies played queens and the queen, the real queen, Anne of Denmark, played Queen Bel-Anna – a play on her name, I suppose. Bel-Anna was Queen of the Sea – there's a drawing of her, more a costume design, by Jones, at Chatsworth, I think—'

'Daniel!'

'They were all queens. So how could you tell the real queen from the other ladies?'

'What are you getting at?'

'Why would someone kill Margaret Porteous?'

'I have no idea.'

'Neither do I. So perhaps the intention was to kill someone else. And they got the wrong queen.'

'Mistaken identity?' asked Neil.

'Yes. Think about it. A dozen queens dancing, in costume, masked, in simulated candlelight. It would be very easy to make a mistake.'

Neil thought for a moment. 'So who, then, is the right queen?'

'Miss Smith.'

'Oh, I see. The murderer thought it was Miss Smith. But who would want to kill her?'

'From what I gather, she is not without her enemies.'

'What do you mean?'

'Not the most popular colleague in her profession, according to Theo. I don't suppose anyone climbed so tall a tree without, I don't know, knocking some competitors off on the way up,' Daniel said.

'Unpopular enough for someone to murder her?'

'Boundless ambition, nameless acts?'

'What's that from?'

'I just made it up.'

'So we need to check who in the cast might have a grudge against her?'

'Or in the crew,' said Daniel.

'But if the blow was struck in the confusion, it would have to be another actor, surely?'

'We don't know precisely when it was struck.'

Neil was quiet for a moment. Then he said, 'Does that sound plausible to you? That another actor, or stagehand, whatever they're called, took the opportunity to kill Miss Smith on set with the cameras running?'

'No, but Margaret Porteous being stabbed to death in the costume of Candace, Queen of the Ethiopians does not sound plausible either.'

There was a knock at the door. Forensics had arrived, and with them the pathologist, Doctor Cheseman. Charlie Cheseman. His real name was Nigel, but no one called him that apart from his sister. He had remade himself, in name and character, bow-tied, scented with pipe smoke, in a waistcoat and with a pocket square. It was a look, thought Daniel, common among medics and lawyers: 'I am a professional but not typical of my profession,' it said, as if they were embarrassed by their callings.

'You two', said Dr Cheseman, 'are becoming quite the pair of psychopomps. Whom do you have for me today?'

'Margaret Porteous,' said Daniel. 'You know her, I think, but you won't recognise her.'

Dr Cheseman took a look at the body. 'What on earth was she doing?'

'Candace, Queen of Ethiopia,' said Daniel, 'dancing in *The Masque of Queens*, or a version of it.'

'Poor Mrs Porteous,' said Dr Cheseman. 'And how did she come by that wound?'

'Not sure,' said Neil. 'What does it look like to you?'

'Stabbing,' he said, looking more closely. 'Narrow-bladed instrument – very narrow – but there's something peculiar about it.'

'What?'

'The blood. Did someone try to staunch the bleeding?'

'Don't know,' said Daniel, 'but she was wearing a tightly laced corset. Could she have been stabbed through it but only started bleeding when the corset was unlaced?'

'Like that unfortunate Austrian queen?'

85

'Empress. Elisabeth of Austria.'

'Queen of Hungary too, wasn't she?'

'Yes, but you said Austria.'

'So you're saying she was a queen. Good. The corset? It's possible. Hard to imagine how you could be stabbed without knowing it. But I stopped being surprised by what can happen where the human body is concerned long ago. I need to take a proper look. Remind me who she is?'

'Margaret Porteous. Actually, one of my church-wardens.'

'I remember. Bit of a snob. Fond of mu-u-sic.' He inclined his head fondly like Queen Mary acknowledging someone. 'Who on earth would want to kill her?'

'We have no idea,' said Neil,

Dr Cheseman stepped back to look at the position of the body. He then said, 'Have you ever seen the Westminster effigies?'

Daniel at once saw what he was thinking of. 'Oh, yes.'

'What are they?' said Neil.

'Effigies of grand people who had funerals at Westminster Abbey,' said Daniel. 'Life-size, made of wood and wax, and dressed in all their finery and regalia. They were left at the Abbey after the funerals, and nobody really knew what to do with them. They're known as the ragged regiment. But they're in the museum now.'

'I remember going to see them,' said Dr Cheseman, 'and wondering what it was like for the makers, to clothe and unclothe their kings and queens, and paint their faces and fit their wigs. How do they hold to-gether the poetry of majesty and the prose of corsets?'

'A perennial question,' said Daniel, 'at least since someone first embalmed a pharaoh.'

'Not for me, or not any more. They're just bodies, like any other. But *you* have to make something of it. You preach the resurrection and the life,' said Dr Cheseman, 'against the fact of death, if I may say so, padre' – he added this, noted Daniel, in the tone of Robin Day saying something brutal to a politician – 'but we establish the fact of death.'

'Oh, I don't deny death,' said Daniel. 'I preach the resurrection, and death is required for that to happen.'

Cheseman shrugged. 'No one gets up again, Daniel.'

'She wants ice.'

'There's ice in the freezer section of her fridge,' said Martin.

'She needs more,' said Carrie.

'OK,' said Martin. 'Can you tell me what for?'

'For her feet. Her feet are hot.'

Martin looked puzzled. 'Wouldn't applying ice be uncomfortable? Or harmful? We don't want her to get – I know this sounds ridiculous – frostbite.'

Carrie shook her head. 'She wants lots of ice in a bucket, or something, and a fan set up to blow air over it to cool her feet. She gets hot feet sometimes. I can sort out the fan but not the ice.'

Martin thought about it. 'I can send someone to check with catering.'

'Thank you,' said Carrie. 'As an urgent priority, please.'

Martin went to find a runner and Carrie went back to Gillian's luxurious caravan.

She was lying on the sofa, four times the size of Theo's, propped up with cushions and in her cashmere tracksuit. Her feet, naked, were propped up by an open window.

'Carrie, darling, where's the ice? This damn air is . . . all *wrong*.'

'It's coming,' said Carrie. 'They're talking to catering.'

'Christ, it's not the United sodding Nations, I just want my . . . you know . . . *feet*!' She waved her hand at her feet and then, as if exhausted by the effort, fell back into the pillows.

'Can I get you anything else?'

'I'm not sure. What is there?'

'Let me have a look.' The kitchen for Miss Smith's Winnebago was as luxurious as such a thing could be but limited, for a Winnebago was essentially a mobile home, not so different from Carrie's static caravan at Newhaven. It was the same with yachts, she thought, or private jets: no matter how much you zhuzhed them up, trying to satisfy an employer's demands was like trying to cook Sunday lunch in a bus shelter.

'There's hummus in the fridge,' she said. She'd had

it fetched from the Waitrose at Stow. The runner said
that when she asked for it the lady didn't know what
she meant and said, 'Humus, like for the garden?'

'Sushi!'

'There isn't any, Gilly. Nearest is seventy miles away.
Can you believe it?'

'Can't catering get on top of that?'

'I think you need a special diploma.'

Gillian sighed. 'If this was LA . . .'

'What about a piece of fruit?'

Gillian licked her lips. 'I think I want savoury.'

Carrie looked through the cupboard next to the
fridge. 'Ooh, they've given us a tin of pâté de foie gras.'

'Wouldn't touch it with a barge pole! Imagine if that
got out? Cruella de Gill. A Woman of Boundless Cal-
ories. I don't know which is worse.'

'Smoked salmon?'

'Perfect.'

Carrie took a packet of Ry-Krisp – Gillian's favourite, sent over from LA – and cut thin slices from a side
of smoked salmon, which she had brought herself from
Fortnum & Mason, because Gillian wanted her to make
sure the fishmonger pin-boned it properly. She made a
delicious little mound of them on the crispbreads, with
a squirt of lemon, a twist from the black pepper grinder
and some tart little capers, and placed them on a bone-
china plate. She arranged everything on a tray with a
can of Diet Coke from the fridge. 'Voilà!' she said as
she put it down on the coffee table.

Gillian had rather lost interest in the minute or two that had elapsed between request and satisfaction, and had other things on her mind now. 'How long is this going to go on for, do you think?'

'I don't know. Dick will. He's coming.'

'He was coming an hour ago . . .'

Twenty minutes ago, thought Carrie.

'. . . and you know how I hate to be late.'

To be delayed, thought Carrie, or inconvenienced in any way, and it's partly my fault because I have taken most of the resistance and friction out of your life by being so good at my job, and thereby made a rod for my own back. You got used to that within about three days, and now, if there were a giant meteorite heading towards Earth, you would expect me to divert it so you could go shopping in Sloane Street. 'I suppose if the police are involved . . .'

'I didn't think much of that plod who caused the contretemps at the gate. If we'd been a minute earlier, we could be *home* by now . . .' She made her cross face. 'We need to pick it up, *pick it up* . . .' She snapped her fingers twice with this statement, which Carrie thought not so much a way of emphasising urgency but more a sly reminder of her servility. 'Mind you, handsome. Didn't you think?'

'I didn't really notice,' said Carrie.

'In a rugby-club sort of way. Not that beach–bum blond beefcake schtick, you know?'

'I don't think I get the difference, really.'

'Throw a frisbee on Santa Monica beach and you'd hit a dozen. No, an English country copper is much sexier.'

'If you say so, Gilly.'

'Taking down your particulars . . .' She glanced at the tray. 'Glass, I think, if Dick's expected.'

Carrie went to the cupboard and took out a tumbler of Waterford crystal, as heavy as a dumbbell, and then thought better of it and chose a highball glass of more manageable weight. 'Do you want ice and lemon?'

'Please . . . So there *is* ice?'

'Just a tray of ice cubes from the little freezer.' She popped a couple of cubes straight out of the tray into the glass, cut a slice of lemon so thinly it looked like a dragonfly's wing, and laid it over the ice. A pointless adornment, she thought, giving neither flavour nor substance. She took it to Gillian. 'Shall I pour?'

She nodded.

There was a tap at the door. It was Martin.

'Carrie? Mr Alleyne for Miss Smith?'

Carrie looked at Gillian, who nodded briskly and said 'my blanket' without vocalising, and it took a second for Carrie to understand what she wanted. 'Just a minute!' She pulled the blanket up over those parts of Gillian allowed a respite from the confinements of her costume, tucked it under her feet, then looked at her with a raised eyebrow. Gillian nodded. Carrie opened the door and, observing due form, spoke to Martin, not to Dick, who was standing about three feet away. 'Miss Smith can see Mr Alleyne now.'

Martin turned to Dick and said, 'Miss Smith will see you—'

'Yes,' interrupted Dick, a bit irritably. 'Gilly!' he shouted. 'Are you decent?'

'For you, *always*, darling,' she said.

Dick Alleyne was tall, in his sixties, thicker round the middle than he used to be, his hair thinner and greyer, and his movements slower than when Gillian first worked with him, but he had been in charge of things for so long that his presence had not diminished with age. If anything, it had grown stronger – something, she thought, that happens to men (alpha males, she had heard them called) rather than women, who depreciate faster than Austin Allegros. His physical presence and charisma were both too big for the Winnebago and Carrie looked almost pushed to one side as he installed himself on the small sofa opposite Gillian's, with the naturalness of someone who never wondered whether or not he was entitled to his place.

Dick was not only the director; he was Gillian's favourite director. If he were not, she probably would not be here, on this production. Although it was likely to do her no harm (if everything that should work worked), *A Woman of Boundless Intrigue* was more like something for television rather than the studio movies she had made in Hollywood, and would like to continue making. It was tiring to pretend – at least when no one important was around – that she was cheerfully mucking in without a sushi chef and her reflexologist to hand . . . but, as the reflexologist kept saying, 'Don't wait for favourable change to come to you, go to it, make it happen. Become the change you want to be,' or something like that.

'Can I get you something, Dick?' said Carrie.

'I'll have a Coke too. No need for a glass.'

She went to fetch one.

'Don't need you now, thanks,' he said to Martin, who slid away like a Tudor secretary.

Carrie handed him his Coke. 'Anything else?'

'No, thanks.'

Carrie looked at Gillian.

'You stay right here,' she said to Carrie.

Dick nodded. 'So sorry to mess you about, Gilly, but something awful has happened.'

'I assumed something of the kind.'

'One of the extras has died and . . . not to put too fine a point on it' – he immediately regretted the phrase – 'it looks like she was murdered.'

'Murdered? Oh, my goodness! How?'

'I'll let the police tell you that.'

'And by whom?'

Carrie noticed the 'whom', a queenly formality of speech, but she wasn't sure if it came with the part or if it was a way of asserting status over Dick.

'Don't know. Don't know very much about it at all, but the police want to speak to you.'

'Me? Whatever for?'

You would be irritated if they didn't want to speak to you, thought Carrie.

'I don't want to say too much, but I think she may have met her murderer on set.'

'Her?'

'Yes. I don't remember the name of the lady, but she was playing the Queen of the Ethiopians.'

'A murderer? On location?'

At the rectory, Audrey and Bernard had lapsed into silence as they waited for Daniel to return with news. Cosmo was sitting curled up on Bernard's lap and he, in a most unusual display of tenderness, was stroking the dog's head like a lover. Audrey was doing the *Telegraph* crossword, the most rigorous intellectual activity she ever undertook – the only one, in fact, unless you counted social strategy, a particularly complex matter at Champton, in which case she was a Carl von Clausewitz.

Now that everyone was home from the holidays, the autumn social calendar was coming into play – Harvest Festival was a month away – and there were urgent matters to attend to. The most pressing was assigning places in church for the parishioners to display the fruits of God's creation with the customary flair and innovation – but not too much flair or innovation. Determining what was enough and what was too much was potentially awkward. There could be no repeat of

the unfortunate time when the primary-school seniors'
ingenious effort with a marrow and two onions left
a windowsill in the chancel looking frankly indecent,
but no one wanted to say anything for fear of being
thought smutty-minded. Who made the decisions was
a difficult question too. Because Harvest Festival involved things that were grown, it was thought to come
under the Flower Guild's jurisdiction – thought by the
Flower Guild, that is. Audrey considered this quite
wrong, and symptomatic of an overreaching attitude
that was typical of Stella Harper, its late 'chairman',
whom she had once described as Papa Doc du Dah-
lias. Because the harvest loaf was the principal tribute
brought by those who had ploughed and scattered (or,
more accurately, found a tin of chickpeas at the back
of the cupboard), the catering committee – for which
Audrey was chairman – thought the decision about
displays should come under her remit, a remit she ex-
ercised also with dictatorial tendencies.

There had been a clash with Anne Dollinger, who
took over from Stella, when Audrey removed from the
windowsills Anne's display of autumn fruits without
telling her. When Anne remonstrated with her, with
a mildness that made Audrey (who liked a fight) more
rather than less combative, Audrey said she thought
someone had forgotten to clear up a few mouldy leftover
apples, and in her judgement they constituted not only
an affront to the theme of bounty but a health hazard.
This had made Anne cry and Audrey, who thought a

lack of backbone a moral failure, cross. Daniel, rather than back up his mother, had tried to make peace between them — one of his more irritating habits — and Audrey had suddenly had enough. She had majestically informed him that if the harvest congregation were to be infected with malaria by fruit flies (Daniel thought better than to suggest the epidemiological unlikeliness of this) on his head be it, and swept out. Anne, Daniel had noticed, had stopped crying almost immediately.

Audrey squinted again at the crossword — she really must get her bifocals adjusted — and said out loud, 'Crack sailor.'

'What?' said Bernard, and Cosmo stirred on his lap.

'Two across, seven letters, something, B, something, something, something, something, E.'

Cosmo stretched and Bernard took the opportunity to free the arm the dog had been lying on and look at his watch. 'Past lunchtime,' he said.

'How rude of me. Would you like something?'

'I wouldn't dream of troubling you.'

'Not any trouble! I have pints of soup and mountains of cheese . . . and leftover apple pie that needs eating.'

'I should really go home.'

'Nonsense. I could heat up the pudding.' She checked herself. Was pudding U or non-U? '*Un peu de dessert*,' she said in an exaggerated French accent.

Cosmo yawned and stretched out again on Bernard's lap, delicately lowering his head onto his arm.

'Matelot,' said Bernard.

'Matelot?'

'Crack sailor. Seven letters.'

'Doesn't fit,' said Audrey. 'Something, B, something, something, something, something, E.'

'I'm afraid I have no idea.'

Audrey tossed the paper onto the pile at her feet. Daniel always gathered them up when they were no longer required, folded them neatly and kept them in a box in the scullery for use as firelighters. Audrey's appetite for the news, however, was greater than the rectory fires' for accelerants, and boxes of old *Daily Telegraph*s and *Braunstonbury Evening Telegraph*s and *Church Times* had to be taken to the tip when Daniel thought them more than a manageable fire risk.

'I'll put the pie in the Aga.'

There was nothing much Bernard could do as he waited for lunch but sit in the armchair with the little dog asleep on his lap. Hilda waddled in through the door Audrey had left open, came over to him and sniffed his ankles, and then turned and waddled straight out again, back to her bed by the Aga. She spent hours there now, aged, he supposed, by her motherly efforts and the consequences of her first litter. It had been a bit like that with his first two wives, both of whom had taken to their boudoirs after discharging their motherly duties of providing heirs and spares and an extra, Honoria, his daughter, whom he loved more than his sons. Both asked for and got divorces, and his third, whom he had met and married in Italy, was not interested

97

in motherhood and consequently had returned to Italy almost as soon as the coronet had settled on her head. 'Why did you marry me?' he had asked. '*Such* a lovely house,' she'd replied.

There was the sound of crockery and cutlery from the dining room. 'Audrey?' he said. 'Hello?'

She appeared in the door. 'Did you just call me?'

'I didn't want to disturb the dog,' he said, 'but are you laying the table?'

'I was.'

'In the dining room? But there's no need. We could sit in the kitchen.'

'You can if you like.'

'I mean, I think we are on a footing where we need not stand on ceremony.'

Audrey would once have thought there nothing finer than a peer of the realm assuring her of his equal esteem, but now it had happened she found it did not suit her so well. It was a bit like being found suddenly attractive by someone you had once pined for fruitlessly. The fulfilment of a desire was its end, and she preferred to decide when things began and when things ended. And it spoilt her fun, for she was looking forward to letting the ladies at the Post Office know she had given lunch *à deux* to his lordship. She wondered if she should just say she had given lunch to 'Bernard'. But more crushing, surely, to say 'Bernard . . . his lordship'? And then it occurred to her that it would be even more crushing if they were to discover that it had been a kitchen lunch. Two old friends sitting down to a bowl of soup, a crust of bread, a wedge of Wensleydale and a slice of apple pie, rather than the rector's mother and the rector's patron. No, not a bowl of soup, a *mug* of soup.

'Absolve,' she said.

'I don't understand.'

'The crossword. Crack sailor. Sailor AB, abbreviation for able seaman. Crack as in crack a puzzle. Absolve. Anyway, *à table*.'

Bernard lifted the sleeping dog onto the floor, who stood a little unsteadily before he woke up properly and trotted behind them to the dining room.

7

Daniel and Neil were standing in the now-deserted hall – deserted by actors and extras and crew, but with the jumble of filmmaking still in position: the lights and cameras and those little train lines they used to push the camera along on a special trolley so it could glide around. Are there special people, Daniel had asked Theo, to do the pushing? There seemed to be hordes of special people to do all sorts of things. Yes, Theo said, dolly grips, which sounded like something from hair and make-up but actually referred to senior technicians who were highly paid for the skilled job of ensuring the camera was where it needed to be at precisely the right moment, so the focus puller could keep everything sharp and clear no matter where the camera went. They could use a focus puller, thought Daniel, to bring some sharpness and clarity to working out what had happened. There was so much that was out of focus, or blurred, or in shade. And so many people involved.

'What's a psychopomp?' asked Neil.

'A spirit who guides us after death into the next world. Charon, ferryman on the Styx, is a psychopomp.'

'Cheseman. He's a psychopomp.'

'He doesn't actually accompany you into the afterworld.'

'He accompanies you into the investigation, and that's the only afterlife I'm really concerned with at the moment.'

'Oh, yes.'

Neil said, 'Maybe psychopompous is better.'

'Well, yes . . .'

'*If I may say so, padre* . . . Did you notice that?'

'I certainly did.'

'*If I may say so, padre* . . . pompous twat.'

'They so often are.'

'Pathologists?'

'Medical people. And clerical people. Pomposity comes with the black cassock and the white coat.'

'Why?'

'Because we think we know better.'

Neil said, 'We'll have to wait for Dr Cheseman's report to find out more, but what are you thinking?'

'I'm trying to think of reasons to murder Margaret now. What don't we know? What have we missed? You?'

'I want some facts, I want some evidence. A murder weapon would be good. Who was where and when?'

'That's going to be complicated. But you have

something to your great advantage. Witnesses. To the murder, and the murderer. Dozens of them, whether they know it or not.'

'A lot of people to talk to,' said Neil.

'And don't forget, we have one unblinking eye who sees everything.'

'God?'

'The camera.'

'The camera never lies,' said Neil. 'Unlike us.'

Daniel nodded. 'Shall we go and see Mr Alleyne? He'll want to know what's going to happen. I don't suppose shutting down a film is a straightforward business.'

They walked out of the hall into the courtyard that stood beyond the Tudor facade. It had once been the front of the house, but two wings now protruded on the west and east sides, and across the fourth side they had built a magnificent baroque range, in another period when the de Floures were flourishing. It looked so splendid you would think it belonged to a palace, with a portico and a balustrade and pedimented windows. 'Inigo Jones?' said Daniel when he first saw it. 'I'd love to say yes,' said Bernard, 'but it was probably his pupil, John Webb.'

'Us,' said Neil.

Daniel walked on.

'We are going to have to talk about it sometime.'

'I know,' said Daniel, 'but not now.'

'More pressing matters . . .' said Neil. They walked

on. Then he said, 'You know, I'm enjoying this.'

'What?' said Daniel.

'Being together again. I've missed you. I'm quite glad of a murder if it means we can get on good terms again. Do you think we could?'

'I don't know.'

Neil stopped. 'You know why I did what I did?'

'Yes, I think so.'

'I wasn't toying with you, though I can see how it could have looked like that. I needed to do something to stop you doing some—'

'Can we concentrate on the task ahead of us?'

Neil said, 'OK. A rain check?'

'I don't think I know what that means.'

'From baseball. If bad weather stops play, you get a free entry to the next game.'

And Daniel said, 'A rain check. But what do you want to do first?'

'We need to talk to everyone, find out where they were. Find out if anyone saw something. Or saw something without knowing what they were seeing. If someone actually saw her get stabbed, we would have heard by now. So I think we need to choose who can be interviewed by uniform – we've got some extra lads coming – and who *we* should be talking to.'

'Theo can help with that.'

'We'll have to talk to him too. Not you alone, though. Us. Formally.'

The way from the courtyard to the stable block

passed through a gatehouse surmounted by a pediment. Under the point of the triangle was a relief sculpture, in the lovely golden stone of that place, of the de Floures circlet of flowers. There was another over the door to the hall in the Tudor range behind them – an exercise in branding we would call it now, thought Daniel, leaving an arriving visitor in no doubt as to who had the power in this place. But it was also showbusiness; on the reverse side there was no circlet, no lavish decoration, just blank stone, for the departing guest did not need to have the de Floures power and wealth blazoned again.

Neil said, 'I want to see what they filmed today, and as soon as possible. How long does it take to get the film – not developed – what do they call it?'

'Processed,' said Daniel. 'I know they have what they call the rushes, a preview of what they shot the day before, so the director can see what it looks like. I think they can do that more or less overnight.'

'So we could be looking at Margaret's murder in the morning?'

'You'll have to ask Mr Alleyne.'

'We need to talk to him first,' said Neil, 'and he will want to know how long he's going to be out of business.'

They turned towards the stable block; it was at an angle to the house and disproportionately large, Daniel thought, but when it had been built the house was bigger than it was now, and intended to be even bigger, before the de Floures' palatial ambitions were scaled down again. It, too, had columns and a portico and a pediment and the de Floures circlet, but it was mostly open space within, cobbled, and with stables down either side and little rooms above with dormers where once dozens of grooms and coachmen and stable boys lived. The cobbled centre had now been laid over with temporary flooring that slotted together and reduced the chances, Daniel supposed, of people turning their ankles or rattling expensive bits of equipment to pieces. There was an area at the centre under a giant gazebo where Dick liked to work at a large table and where people came and went as supplicants or penitents or messengers.

The stables on each side had been converted for the use of different departments, and outside, on the terrace and lawn on the opposite side to the house, was the corral of tents and marquees. Beyond them, with views of the lake uninterrupted by production shanties, were the leading artists' Winnebagos.

There was a cluster of people around the central table looking intently at something, and Daniel supposed that from there Dick was directing operations, as far he could direct anything when his location was suddenly transformed into a crime scene.

That changed reality meant that as Daniel and Neil approached there was a faint but coordinated parting of the security guards, and they passed between them, no longer impeded by the unarguable priority of the shoot. Dick was sitting at the middle of the table's short edge with a large sheet of paper unfolded in front of him. It was like graph paper, divided into rows and columns, some highlighted in yellow, others in pink, blue and green, so they formed strips and blocks of colours configured in different ways. Daniel's heart always beat a little faster at a colour-coded schedule, for he loved nothing more than organisation. But what was this organising?

Dick said, 'Detective Sergeant, just who I wanted to see.'

'You have something for us?' said Neil.

'I was hoping you would have something for me. We need to rewrite our production schedule, and we can't do that until we know what we can do and where we can do it. And when we can do it.'

'I would put a temporary stop to everything if I were you,' said Neil. 'This is a very complex crime scene, and anyway, I was hoping you would be able to help me.'

Dick looked a bit disappointed but said, 'Of course, anything we can do to help, it goes without saying.'

'Is there somewhere private we could talk?'

'My office,' said Dick, folding and picking up the schedule. There were others lying on the table, and he nodded to a woman with a scatter of highlighter pens in all colours in front of her who had a fresh copy, as yet unmarked in pink or yellow or blue or orange or green. 'Hold off, Fee, I'll have more for you in a minute.' Then he turned to them. 'Is it both of you? Or just the Detective Sergeant?'

'Both,' said Neil.

'No Miss Marple?' said Dick.

'Not today, sir.'

Dick led the way across the cobbles to a doorway into the stables themselves. At the end of a range of stalls was his temporary office, which had a closing door and a chance of relative privacy. 'Head groom's office,' he said, 'back when people had such things.'

Inside, a black Labrador was asleep on a blanket in front of a plain pine desk. When Dick took his seat behind it the dog got up stiffly and came to him, his tail wagging in a creaky way.

'Hello, Jasper,' said Dick and scratched his head. 'You don't mind dogs?'

'No, not at all,' said Daniel.

'Jasper comes with me everywhere,' said Dick, in a way that made Daniel think he, like his star, had a persona to sustain. Dick indicated for them to sit down in two canvas-backed folding chairs, the kind that might bear the name of the star on the back, although these had none. It was not a star's sort of room, but plain, with deal tongue-and-groove panelling halfway up the plainly painted wall. On it there was a cork-board, bits and brasses, and pictures of prized horses, probably treated better than the people who looked after them, thought Daniel. And it gave the suggestion of a certain equestrianism to Mr Alleyne. The dog, who seemed well suited to that scenario, went back to his bed and lay down. 'Drink? Cup of something?' said Dick.

They both declined.

'What's going to happen next?' he said.

'Next,' said Neil, 'is drawing up a list of everyone involved in today's shoot. Who they are, where they were . . .'

Dick held up a hand. 'What are we dealing with here? No one has actually said.'

'It's a murder investigation at this stage, Mr Alleyne.'

'Hmm,' he said, 'what else could it be? But how terrible. Who was this Mrs . . . Porter?'

'Porteous,' said Daniel, 'Margaret Porteous. Widow, churchwarden, very highly regarded in this community.'

'Why would anyone want to kill her?'

'We don't know,' said Neil. 'There's nothing in her life we know of that would make anyone wish her any serious harm.'

'Person or persons unknown,' said Daniel.

'How was it done?'

'She was stabbed,' said Neil. 'You saw the wound. We don't know where or when exactly – the pathologist is looking at her now – but it was most likely on the set during the dance.'

'Why do you think that?'

'I don't think she knew she had been stabbed.'

'The wardrobe assistant thought the same.'

'It's not unusual, sir. What people feel – or feel at first – is a blow, like a punch. Then they bleed. She didn't bleed until they got her corset off. Miss March, the wardrobe assistant, will be able to tell us more.'

'I can arrange that if you like.'

'We'll take care of it, sir.'

Daniel said, 'But you spoke to Miss March?'

'Yes, of course. Security called me and I came at once. Miss March – she's one of your people, I think? – was a bit unnerved, so I sent her home.'

'And you sent for an ambulance and the police?' asked Neil.

'Yes, Daniel came with me.'

'How long after the incident was that, sir?'

'Just a few minutes.'

'How many minutes?'

'I don't know, fifteen?'

'Nearer half an hour,' said Daniel.

'Half an hour?' said Neil. 'Why did you not summon help at once, sir?'

'I did. We have our medics and our own security people. They were there before I was.'

'But no one called an ambulance? Or the police?'

'Of course, but in the first instance . . . look, it was obvious the lady had died – our guy checked for signs of life – and then we made sure everything was secure.'

'You should inform the emergency services in the first instance.'

'It's not that clear cut on a film set, Detective Sergeant. It was a very complicated scene, there were people everywhere, no one knew what was going on. It takes a while to establish the facts.'

'I would have thought', said Neil, 'that dialling 999 was a clear priority.'

'And we did. As soon as we could.'

'Not as soon as you could, Mr Alleyne,' said Daniel. 'I had to offer you some encouragement.'

Dick nodded and took a cigarette from a pack of Silk Cut on the table. He offered the packet to them. 'They're not full strength. Like jumping from the tenth floor instead of the twentieth.' Neither acknowledged a tired joke. Neither accepted. He lit the cigarette with one of those American army lighters that smell like a paraffin fire and are said to work in a hurricane, then took a drag and exhaled. 'You have to imagine what it is like making a film. It is a parallel world. You become so absorbed by it, and you are under so much pressure from producers, and . . . others' – he grimaced – 'that you get out of step with the world outside and you cannot just re-enter it without adjustment. Does that make sense?'

'It does,' said Daniel. 'Monasteries are like that too.'

'Oh, that's interesting,' said Dick. 'I'd love to talk to you about that sometime. But my point is, don't be surprised, or suspicious, if our reaction was not as quick as you would expect it to be.'

'The trouble with that is,' said Neil, 'we need to preserve a crime scene as quickly and efficiently as possible, and while you are getting in step with the world outside, we might be losing evidence.'

'And leaving a dying soul without succour, if I may say so,' said Daniel.

'We all have our interests in this,' said Dick. 'But point taken.' He said this with finality, as if he was directing the exchange. 'What do we need to do now?'

'Like I said, we need to know where everyone was and when.'

'I can definitely help you with that,' said Dick, pushing the folded piece of paper he had taken from the table towards them. 'This is the schedule for today. It has exactly that information on it. Cast and crew. Fee, our production coordinator, does them every day.'

'Can you show me how it works?' said Neil.

'Sure,' said Dick, 'gather round.' He unfolded the sheet of paper and laid it on the desk. 'So, the yellow ones are cast and the blue ones are crew and the others are hair and make-up, wardrobe and so on. The grid shows who needs to be where and when, not just those on set shooting a scene, but who needs to be in make-up and when, who needs to be in wardrobe and when. That can be hours before we start shooting for someone like Gilly – Gillian Smith. She has her own hair and make-up team. Also, the sparks and the grips and the set dressers and drivers and the weapons master—'

'Weapons master?' said Daniel.

'Yes, whenever there are weapons on set there are weapons masters. Sounds like something from warfare, but they're an extension of props. They take care of all the cutlery for a shoot like this, swords and daggers, and make sure they're safe and accounted for. They're also armourers if you have any firearms, like muskets or cannons.'

'We'll need to talk to him urgently. And we urgently need to see what you filmed. Daniel says you can see footage you shot pretty quickly?'

'Yes, the dailies. Though I don't know how much we've got that's going to be of use to you. We were only doing general shots this morning, so it's all from a distance, nothing close up.'

'But would the choreographer know who was where?'

'We haven't got to the dancing yet.'

'I thought you were shooting the masque this morning?'

'It was more melee than masque this morning. It's the masquers, but at the end of the dance when it sort of degenerates into a bit of a scrum.'

'I don't think early Jacobean masques did that,' said Daniel.

'Yes, so you said, though we don't really know. We're not going for historical recreation here, we're going for drama, and we need it to get . . . physical.'

'What do you mean by physical?' asked Neil.

Dick took another drag of his cigarette. 'We need to show the constraints of court life giving way to . . . er . . . earthier impulses.'

'What does that entail?'

'It's meant to get a bit wild. The dance gets into a fast orbit and then it falls apart and they . . . sort of knock into each other. You know the dance in the gym in *West Side Story*? Like that. The queen gets closer to the Venetian ambassador than diplomacy normally encourages, if you see what I mean.'

'Anne of Denmark?' said Daniel.

'What's boundless intrigue all about if not the passions?'

'Statecraft. I don't think the masque was quite a rave.'

'I know, I know,' said Dick, 'but we're at the movies.'

'If we put this all together,' said Neil, 'any film you've got, the production schedule, interviews with cast and crew, we would end up with a pretty comprehensive picture of this morning's events.'

'I hope so,' said Dick. 'Who do you want to start with?'

'We'll work something out and let you know.'

'Do you want the office . . . the stable . . . next to mine to work in?'

'Thank you, that would be helpful.'

'It would help me if I could get some idea of how long this will take. I don't mean to sound unfeeling, or unhelpful, but this is a very expensive operation, and I need to talk to the office.'

'I appreciate that, sir,' said Neil, 'and as soon as I can, I will let you know. But at the moment this is a crime scene, and as I'm sure you will appreciate, the investigation must take priority.'

'Of course, of course. But as I'm sure you will appreciate . . . I also am a man under authority. There are people shouting at me down the phone. The show must go on, you know? But let me sort you out with somewhere to work.'

'One more thing, Mr Alleyne,' said Daniel.

'Yes?'

'Can you think of a reason why someone might want to murder Miss Smith?'

'Gilly? Yes, easily.'

'Can you explain why you say that, sir?' said Neil.

'I could give you a dozen reasons why I would want to murder Miss Smith, and I'm sure I'm not the only one.'

'A difficult person?'

'And then some. Not only difficult but irrational and difficult. And powerful. She can make or break a film. She can make or break a career. Her caprice could make Henry VIII look like Abraham Lincoln.'

'But, seriously . . .'

'I am being serious.'

8

Miss March had tidied the shop twice now, hung and rehung the autumn scarves, and was at a loss for what to do next. She still wanted to do something, to occupy herself with a repetitive and undemanding task, but one with enough momentum to keep her from recalling the death, too awful to contemplate for long. The shop was shut, so no customers came in to divert her. Her retail consultant was at that moment lunching with her landlord, and all her regular customers were up at the big house anyway, which was closed for the duration of filming, which meant also there were no tourists coming through Champton. She would never use fading footfall as an excuse to close the shop, but the offer of employment as a wardrobe assistant and adviser was irresistible. She had written a sign in her surprisingly simple hand – 'Due to Unforeseen Circumstances Elite Fashions Is Temporarily Closed' – and stuck it in the window, which was a struggle, for it went against everything she had learnt in more than a quarter of a century in retail. She put on a pair of dark-grey leather gloves, locked the back door behind her and walked a few yards to use the zebra crossing to cross the road, which was empty of any traffic at all as far as anyone could see to left or right, and thence to the Post Office.

The Post Office's door and windows were painted in the de Floures livery of putty grey and white – very nearly her own preferred palette, which perhaps was one of the reasons she was drawn to move there. All the de Floures properties were painted in those colours; you could see what was estate and what wasn't from half a mile away, for those who lived in properties bought from the estate repainted them in different colours, partly to be more fashionable, but mostly to indicate that they were owner-occupiers. The shop was very much still part of the estate, with a white-painted sign announcing Post Office and General Store surmounted by the de Floures circlet of flowers, and next to it, sticking out from the wall of creamy limestone, was the Post Office sign, in scarlet and gold, striking rather a jarring note.

Miss March pushed open the door and the little bell over it dinged, which caused Scamper, Dora Sharman's very old, almost sightless and thoroughly bad-tempered Jack Russell, to growl. Miss March gave the dog a tight little smile and an incline of her head, an irrational gesture of politeness for a dumb beast, but Miss March did not like dogs, yet did not wish to seem especially standoffish to Dora. She was at the shop counter, in one of her coats that looked like it was made from Axminster carpet, which she wore in every season regardless of the weather, with one of her countless crocheted bonnets – this in rather garish acrylic colours.

'Good morning, ladies,' said Miss March.

'Morning,' said Dora, doing the work of welcome for Mrs Braines too.

'What can I do for you, Miss March?' said Mrs Braines, shifting her weight from one elbow to the other on the counter.

'Pint of milk, please, Mrs Braines, just ordinary. And a KitKat, please. A single.'

'Very good.' Mrs Braines slowly and painfully stooped to open the fridge door and get the milk.

'I understand there has been an incident at the big house,' said Miss March. 'Mrs Clement called in on her way home . . .'

'Well, you probably think we won't know any more about that than you then,' said Dora, 'seeing as the Champton bugle has blown.'

Miss March ignored the sentiment behind this. 'Margaret Porteous was taken ill.'

'Taken ill all right,' said Dora, 'poor old gal.'

How Margaret would have hated the 'old gal', thought Miss March, but said, 'How unfortunate, whatever the cause, and perhaps it would be better if we did not—'

Mrs Braines interrupted. 'There's your pint, Miss March,' she said. 'Was it a big or little KitKat you wanted?'

'Little.'

'No one's supposed to know,' said Dora, 'and it's not my place to go chopsing out of turn. There are enough contenders for parish pump in Champton St Mary. Well, you would know.'

'Fifty-five pence, Miss March,' said Mrs Braines.

Miss March took sixty pence from her purse and put the change in the NSPCC collecting tin that poor Mrs Porteous had organised when she got in a panic about Satanic sexual abuse spreading to Champton from Nottinghamshire. She went to open her bag but, fired with curiosity, she had forgotten to bring one.

'Do you want a bag, Miss March?' said Mrs Braines.

'No, thank you, I'm only going over the road.' She took the pint of milk and the KitKat in her gloved hand.

'She was murdered, wasn't she?' said Mrs Braines bluntly.

'I couldn't possibly say.'

'They're saying a heart attack, but I heard different from Jean Shorely, who heard from one of the extras – that tearaway, bad lad who lived here for a while but got chucked out of the school. Anyway, he's one of the extras and he got it from one of the actors, that Margaret – Brandon summat, that's his name – was . . . stabbed. And that you was there.'

There was a sound like a small explosion. Miss March had dropped her pint of milk on the floor. Scamper yelped and tried to hide behind Dora's legs.

White milk splashed on red quarry tiles, like a negative image of the scene at the Old Dairy . . . red blood splashed on white glazed tiles.

Daniel and Neil had taken over one of the stalls next to the head groom's office and were going over the production schedule that Dick had surrendered, like the captain of a ship handing over his charts to a boarding party. Neil was making a list of whom to prioritise for interview, assigning each name, each position, as A, B or C. 'Daniel, I don't know who these people are and what they do. What's a best boy? What's a boom operator?'

'I could make a guess, but it would be a guess. Shall I find Dick?'

Neil thought for a moment. 'Not Dick. He has his own agenda, *as I'm sure you will appreciate*. Is there someone . . . what about Theo? He knows how a film set works, doesn't he?'

'Do you want me to get him?'

'Please. And make sure people see you bringing him in.'

The commotion around the big table in the gazebo had died down. Those who had been leaning in were now sitting back in chairs, drinking coffee, smoking – waiting, he supposed, for instructions. There was so much momentum in filmmaking, so much to get in the right place at the right time, and quickly, and so much pressure that an unexpected hiatus would, he supposed, fill everyone with frustration and impatience, like a tea clipper becalmed in the doldrums.

He stood outside Theo's Winnebago. The door, unusually, was closed, for he liked it open to watch the comings and goings. Daniel tapped on the door. There was a sound of movement within and then nothing.

He tapped again. 'Theo? Are you there?'

'Just a second!' Theo opened the door a crack. 'What is it? I'm not decent.'

'I need to talk to you.'

'Can it wait?'

'Not really.' Daniel slightly pushed on the door and it yielded.

Theo was wearing only a T-shirt and boxers. 'I've only just got undressed; I was going to take a shower.'

'I need your help. And I wanted to speak to you before you're interviewed, which will be happening soon. But I have some bad news.'

'I know.'

'What do you know?'

'Margaret Porteous is dead.'

'How did you find out?'

'It's a film location, Dan. It's more gossipy than the Long Bar at the Troc.'

'Apropos, dear brother, your caravan smells like an opium den.'

'Oh, never mind that now. What happened?'

'She was murdered.'

Theo blinked. 'So it's true! Are you sure?'

'We're sure, but I need your help.'

'Of course, what can I do?'

'May I sit down?'

They sat down.

'I need someone to explain who the people are on set. And the cast. What's a best boy? What are sparks? What's a camera assistant? Who was standing where when it happened?'

'When what happened?'

'When Margaret was stabbed.'

Theo blinked again. 'So, she *was* stabbed.'

'You had heard?'

'Heard something. Poor Margaret. But where? When? And who could possibly want to kill her?'

'We think she was stabbed on set. During the filming.'

'Christ,' said Theo, reaching for a cigarette. 'But that's mad. I think we would have noticed if someone was stabbed during a scene.'

'Not necessarily. We think she didn't know she had been stabbed, or not at first. She might have thought she'd just knocked into someone or got a stitch.'

'So that's why she left the set. Most unprofessional. A real actor would have carried on till they said cut, even if they knew they had been stabbed.'

Daniel thought this in rather bad taste but said nothing. Then Theo said, 'Dan, there's something I need to tell you. My dagger has gone missing.'

'When?'

'I only noticed it when wardrobe came to get my costume just now. It was in a scabbard on my belt when I went on set this morning – it must have been because wardrobe checked me first. When I got back here it had gone.'

'You don't remember anyone getting too close, bumping into you?'

'Yes, everyone. It was supposed to be a sort of Bacchanalian scrum – everyone was bumping into everyone.'

'Could someone have taken it from you without you knowing?'

'I think so.'

Daniel thought for a moment. 'Can you describe it?'

'Yes, I can, it was a poignard. Do you know what they are?'

'A stiletto?'

'It's a narrow dagger, like a stiletto. Very smart in Renaissance Europe, though mine was extra-smart because I'm an earl.'

'Was it usable?'

'I really don't know.'

'Was it sharp?'

'I didn't try it.'

Daniel noticed Theo glance nervously at the bathroom door.

'Wouldn't a prop be made to be harmless?'

'If it were a prop, yes, but a lot of this stuff isn't props, they're the real thing.'

'Did the weapons master . . .'

'You know what *that* is . . .?'

'. . . show you how to use it, how to wear it?'

'No, I mean yes, but I wasn't really listening. It's just costume, Dan, I wasn't going to gut a deer with it. But how do you know about the weapons master?'

'I spoke to Dick about it.'

'Oh, God, about me? Please don't!'

'No, not you specifically, but about what was on set, what could be used to stab someone.'

Theo glanced again at the bathroom door. 'We all had daggers and swords. Everybody did back then.'

'Is something bothering you, Theo?'

'Of course something's bothering me – someone's been stabbed, and my dagger has gone missing.'

'Does anyone know about this?'

'Wardrobe.'

'Not the police?'

'Not as far as I know.'

Daniel got up. 'No one thinks you stabbed Margaret, Theo.'

'You don't, but the cops might. Dick might.'

'It would help, or at least show willing, if you would tell me what's in the bathroom?'

Theo started.

'You keep looking at the bathroom door.'

The sound of a listless flush came from behind it.

Theo sighed. 'It's like having Sherlock Holmes for a brother. He had a brother, I think.'

'Yes, Mycroft.'

'What *names* he gave them!'

The bathroom door opened. 'Hello, rector,' said Brandon.

'Hello again, Brandon.'

'I was just visiting. Had to go to the toilet.'

'I hope you've washed your hands.'

Theo got up. 'I forgot you two knew each other. Brandon's one of the extras.'

'Supporting artists,' said Brandon.

Daniel nodded. 'Well, he knows how to make himself useful.'

'I'd better be off. Thanks, Theo.' He was through the door before Theo could reply.

Daniel looked at his brother and raised an eyebrow.

'He's a friend,' said Theo. 'I met him through Alex.'

'A bringer of good things, then, for Alex and for you?'

'If you like.'

'How apt for the harvest season.'

Theo looked puzzled.

'Brandon Redding doth provide for our wants to be supplied.'

'Spare me the sarcasm, Daniel. Most unbecoming in a parson.' He sat down again. 'Don't tell people.'

'I'll have to tell Neil.'

'It's just a little . . . herbal cigarette. I find it relaxes one. And for God's sake, don't tell Dick. I don't want a reputation.'

'I don't think Neil will be interested in what you or

Alex or Nathan like to smoke. He will be interested in Brandon.'

Theo stubbed out his cigarette. 'You really don't like him, do you?'

'No.'

'He's not Pablo Escobar.'

'I suppose he connects eventually to people like Pablo Escobar. And connects with you.'

'Don't be so pompous, Dan. He just provides a service. For consenting adults.'

'Do you remember who brought the first fruits of the harvest as an offering in Genesis?'

'Not off the top of my head, no.'

'Cain.'

Neil was in the Old Dairy. The scenes of crime officers were setting up and before they got seriously to work, and before the undertakers arrived to take the body away, he wanted to get a feel for the place, not in the rigorous technical sweep of evidence gathering, but something more subtle than that. He had always done this instinctively, without thinking about it much, but Daniel did it too, and better, and since they had started working together he had begun to explore more purposely the grey, the ambiguous, the flicker at the edge of vision, the mood that hangs to a crime scene like mist to a lawn. This was not approved of in police orthodoxy, which was founded on systematic investigation and was suspicious of that kind of priestcraft. How

interesting, Neil thought, that priestcraft was used by
his profession as a pejorative – but they all did it, they
all had hunches and instincts and practised their arcane
arts, or the good ones, even if they did not talk about it.

He was standing next to the counter. He looked
at the pinking shears – you could do some damage
with those – the measuring tape, the bobbins spread
across the surface, and wondered if there might be a
pattern to their distribution, something that would
tell him who was standing where, about the angle of
their stance, about what they could have picked up
or put down. His eye was drawn to the pin cushion,
and he bent to look at it closely. It was large and drab,
covered with something like canvas, and looked like
an old man's chin after three days without a shave. Pins
and needles stuck out of it like stubble; occasionally
there were ornamental interruptions from pins with
coloured beads on the end. Some were as big as hat
pins, others like tacks, but there were some made from
brass, with fleurs-de-lys, or coils, or barley-sugar twists
on the end. He took one and pulled it out to examine
it. It was much longer than he expected, as long as a hat
pin but much stronger. What were they for? He made
a note in his pad.

Daniel was at the catering van getting a cup of tea he
did not want and a sausage roll he would not eat, but he
needed a reason to sit at one of the trestle tables. There
is a cordon sanitaire around a dog-collared person;

on a train you can usually guarantee the seat next to you will be unoccupied for the entire journey, but this was not a normal day, and there was an unusual press around the catering van, for no one was at work but no one could go home. And there had been a death, and when there is a death, people – even against their better nature – turn towards the dog-collared person rather than turn away. A man came and sat opposite him. Daniel could tell he was crew, for he wore what they all seemed to wear: trousers with pockets sewn on the side, a baseball cap, and what Daniel still thought of as plimsoles but were known to everyone else as trainers, although what one trained for in them was not clear. He was Daniel's age and had a greying beard and moustache, as standard in that profession as a full set in the Royal Navy.

He nodded. Daniel nodded back. The man looked at the polystyrene cup of coffee in front of him and looked up at Daniel.

'You're Theo's brother, aren't you?' he said.

'I am. Daniel Clement.'

The man nodded again but did not reply.

'I didn't catch your name,' Daniel said with the in-direct reproach for a lapse of manners typical of his calling.

'I didn't say. It's Roger.'

'And you work with my brother?'

'I do. I'm the weapons master. I've just had a tricky conversation about his dagger.'

'With the police?'

'An interview. His missing dagger. It's my respon-
sibility to ensure everything is accounted for when
weapons are being used. But I can't weld them onto
the actors, can I?'

'No, I don't suppose you can. And anyway, Theo
could lose his DNA in a careless moment.'

'It is not unusual for actors', said Roger, 'to be careless with their DNA.'

'No,' said Daniel. 'Forgive me, but the dagger . . .'

'I don't know where it is.'

'Not that. Could it have been used to hurt someone?'

'Yes. That's why there's a weapons master. To reduce
that risk. It's quite a new thing. Guns and swords used
to come under the props master, but there have been
accidents, so it's a specialism now.'

'Do you acquire the weapons? Are they made for you
or adapted or, I don't know, bought in antique shops?'

'All of those. Especially on a show like this when
everyone's carrying one.'

'And Theo's? A poignard, yes?'

'Yes. Or a replica of a poignard.'

'So not a real one?'

'No, a prop.'

'So made to look like the real thing but not dangerous, not sharp?'

Roger said, 'In theory. But a poignard is basically
a stiletto. It's long and thin and pointed and made of
steel. Get enough force behind it and it will do as much

damage as you like. That's why they're ornamental. I would never use one in a fight scene. There was a movie last year, *Cyborg*, sci-fi epic with Jean-Claude Van Damme. The muscles from Brussels. Mate of mine worked on it.'

'I must have missed it,' said Daniel.

'Literally took someone's eye out with a dagger. Jean-Claude Van Damme. Accidentally stabbed another actor with a prop dagger in a scene. I think he's suing him. That's the nightmare scenario. Someone does someone a mischief and I end up getting sued.'

Miss March was still trembling when she got home. She went steadily upstairs, one step at a time, holding onto her banister like an old lady. She was not an old lady, she was in her thirties, but the kind of thirties her parents' generation had, already into middle age. Now, they would still be skateboarding.

In the flat she calmed a little and decided to make a pot of tea. As it brewed, she fetched a mug from the cupboard over the sink. It was her father's, brown Bakelite, once white inside but now darkened by tannin, one of the set they had growing up. She did not like to recall her mother, who had walked out on them when she was nothing more than a girl, but her mother came to her obliquely sometimes and did now. Why did she choose these mugs? she wondered. Was it wartime, and the world was sombre? Was it demob, when everything was plain? Why these?

No milk. The bottle she had just bought from Mrs Braines had smashed on the floor and she had been too flustered to get another and had left. She wondered if Coffee-mate worked in tea. There was a tin of it downstairs in the shop's kitchenette, which Audrey kept for emergencies. Then the doorbell rang. She thought it would be the police, and it was.

'Miss March.'

'Detective Sergeant, won't you come in?'

Neil followed her up the narrow stairs, carpeted with an exuberant Axminster that cannot have been her choice. It was the same as his parents' in Oldham, a fussy pattern of petal shapes and foliage crammed into a red background, which always made him think of bacteria in a Petri dish.

'I can offer you tea or coffee,' she said, 'but I've only got Coffee-mate to go in it.'

'No, thanks, Miss March.'

She indicated the sofa and sat in the chair opposite, knees together and to the side. She was trembling.

'Are you all right, Miss March?'

'Just the after-effects of shock,' she said. 'It will fade. I've experienced it before.'

'Then it must have been very upsetting for you.'

'Yes, it was.'

'And I'm sorry to put you through it, but I have to ask you some questions.'

'I understand. I made a few notes,' she said, and took a little notepad that was on the coffee table and opened it as he opened his police notebook in a moment of symmetry.

'Can you tell me what happened? In your own words?'

She wondered how she would tell it in another's words, but said, 'I was in the Old Dairy from early in the morning. It's a sort of staging post between the set and wardrobe proper, and I'm there usually with Sandy. He's on the set doing running repairs and I'm there to help and look after the kit. Really to advise. I know something about the dress of the period, you see, and the historic textiles at Champton House. I had checked how the principals looked, and cast an eye over the supporting artists, and it was . . . well, not perfect. There were a couple of solecisms in dress, and how they wore it, but it is never perfect, and I suppose if it looks credible to the average viewer, then that's good enough.'

Neil nodded and pretended to write something down. She had not yet said anything he did not already know, and she was digressing in the way of people in shock, but he did not want her to know that.

'Then Mrs Porteous . . . appeared in the doorway looking awful.'

'How did she look?'

'Flushed. Breathless. Wincing. In pain. She asked me for an ibuprofen, but I'm not allowed to give one – we have to get a medic for that – but then she said she thought it was a stitch, so I said I'd loosen her corset.

It would have been more stays than a corset, like our great-grandmothers would have worn, at that time of course, but no one can see that, so it was just a stage corset underneath her bodice, but still tight. So, I unlaced the bodice, and then the corset, and then . . . the blood came, and it kept coming. I couldn't see where from at first, it just gushed. I got her into a chair, and—'

'Where was she to begin with?'

'She was standing, holding on to the back of the chair so I could unlace her, and then I moved her in front of it, or she staggered in front of it, and then fell back and I think – I thought – she must have fainted, and then I called and called for help, but no one heard me, and I didn't know what to do, whether to look after Margaret . . . Mrs Porteous . . . as best I could, or find someone who could. Oh, I took off her wig, I remember that; she had said it was very uncomfortable. And then she spoke – I don't know if she was conscious, or fully conscious, but she said something about being young and believing in fantastic things, and then she said that was wrong, quite wrong.'

Neil wrote it down and read it back to her. 'Are you sure that's what she said?'

'Yes, more or less. I didn't catch it all. She spoke clearly, but I don't know how aware she was of what she was saying. It was the first thing I wrote down when I got home.' She showed Neil her notepad.

'Any idea what it means?'

'No, none at all.'

'And then?'

'And then she gave a couple of little gasps. And that was that.'

'She was dead?'

'Yes.'

'How did you know?'

'I've seen someone die before, Detective Sergeant.'

'Your father?'

'Yes. Murdered too.'

'I seem to remember he was involved in an altercation?'

'He tried to stop some youths from . . . making a mess in our shop doorway. This was when we had the shoe shop at Stow. When the pubs chucked out it would happen. You know what lads are like. Some lads.'

'A heart attack?'

'Yes, but they might as well have stabbed him.'

Neil made another note. 'Then what happened?'

'I went to look for someone and found Angela, and she alerted the medics while I went back to sit with Margaret.'

'Anyone else with you?'

'No.'

'Could anyone else have got in?'

'Yes, but I don't think so. The next thing I knew a security guard was there with Angela and Mr Alleyne. He saw I was in a state and had them fetch a driver to take me home.'

'He didn't say anything about the police coming? Or ask you to wait until we arrived?'

Miss March thought for a moment. 'No. Now you ask, I suppose that was unusual.'

'But you did not think so at the time.'

'No. I suppose I was in shock. I wasn't thinking straight. And Mr Alleyne . . . he is the director. One tends to do what he asks.'

Neil wrote in his notebook. Then he said, 'I think that's everything I need to know for now.'

'Let me show you out,' said Miss March, with a faint note of urgency.

Neil put his notebook and pen away and stood up to go. 'Oh, one thing . . .'

'Yes?'

'I noticed in the Old Dairy, in the pin cushion, there were these sort of long needles, made of brass. Hat pins?'

'Farthingale pins,' said Miss March, 'used to fasten . . . well, farthingales, if you know what they are.'

'I don't.'

'The hooped underskirt. Anne of Denmark rather liked them. They were made of stout stuff and the dresses that went over them were heavy and quite stiff, so it needed a hefty pin to hold everything in place.'

'Where do you get them?'

'Angela gets them. I assume they're replicas.'

'How many do you have?'

'I couldn't say. Couple of dozen? We would only use

them for the principals. Everyone else gets safety pins.'

'You haven't noticed any missing?'

'No,' said Miss March. 'But I'm not sure I would notice.'

Neil smiled. 'Thank you, Miss March. Don't bother seeing me downstairs.'

'Very good, Detective Sergeant.'

Neil smiled again and left.

When Miss March heard the gate close she returned to the pot of tea she'd made. As she poured the dark liquid into the mug she noticed her hand was shaking.

Carrie was sitting in one of the huge armchairs in Gillian Smith's Winnebago. It was so luxurious, so packed with cushions and throws and upholstery, that it had become almost impossible to sit on. So often the way, she thought, that creating ever more comfortable environments for the blessed of the Earth has the paradoxical effect of making a space less rather than more inhabitable. Gillian's house in Los Angeles, a mini gated estate as it was preposterously known, was high in the Hollywood Hills with a view across the diamond-bright grid of downtown by night, and had been designed by an architect so fashionable in the Seventies that it was now a stop on a tour of modernist Los Angeles. Twice a day buses full of architecture fans stopped outside for them to take photographs and ooh and aah. Gillian had at first thought they were on a tour of the homes of the stars, and smiled graciously when she ran into them coming or going, even stopping at the gates in what could almost be mistaken for a pose, until she noticed they weren't taking photographs of her but of her chimney, and there were no gracious smiles after that.

Carrie was waiting for Gillian to wake from her nap. The ice in the bucket intended to cool her feet had long ago melted, and she, bundled in cashmere, ear plugs in, eye mask on, had fallen asleep and almost immediately started to snore. How impossible it is, thought Carrie, to maintain an air of glamour when you are making a sound like a warthog drowning in a swamp. But she quite liked it when Gillian took a nap because it meant she did not have to do anything and could just sit quietly, not reading, or listening to music, or thinking about anything in particular, just savouring the deep, brief joy of not having to be attentive to anyone.

The warthog sound was interrupted by something between a cough and a splutter, and then another, and then another, and a rustling, and then Gillian's reedy voice calling for her. 'Carrie? Carriee?'

'I'm right here, Gilly,' she said. 'Do you want anything?'

'Yes. To get out of here. What time is it?'

'Quarter past three. Do you want a cup of tea?'

'Quarter past three? For God's sake! Why aren't I home?'

'The police say we can't go.'

'Why?'

'Because they need to interview everyone.'

'Oh, for . . . why didn't you *tell* me?'

'Dick said. Don't you remember?'

There was a soft rustling and a creak and Gillian, still wrapped up in cashmere, came stumbling by. 'Loo,' she said, 'and then tea.'

'What tea do you want?'

'Just normal.'

She closed the bathroom door behind her and there was the sound of a voiding so powerful it reminded Carrie of the sound of milk yanked from an udder hitting her father's tin bucket when she was a girl.

'Carrie,' called Gillian from the bathroom, 'will you tell Dick I'll see the police now? Might as well get it over with – I can't tell them anything – and then we can bloody well go!'

'You want to talk to them now?'

'Give me five – make it fifteen – to freshen up.'

Carrie paused for a second and then said, 'I'm not sure they're quite ready yet . . .'

'Yes, but I will be, in fifteen minutes. Make it twenty?'

'I'll go and see. What about your tea?'

'Leave it, I'll do it myself. I just want to get out of here.'

There was a peculiar stillness over the production village, as Dick called it. The stars were in their Winnebagos, the actors in their tented seclusion, and there was no to-and-fro of technicians and drivers and runners as Carrie made her way to the head groom's office. She knocked on the door. 'Come!' was the reply, which she found grand and irritating. Inside, Dick and Neil were standing at his desk with the production schedule unfolded in front of them. They reminded her of air vice-marshals looking at a map of the Kent and Sussex coast in the late summer of 1940.

'Carrie,' said Dick, 'come in, come in . . . Do you know the Detective Sergeant?'

'We met at the gate.'

'Oh, yes. Gate-gate,' said Neil. 'Miss . . . something beginning with P?'

'Carrie Palethorpe.'

'Executive assistant to Miss Smith,' said Dick.

'I'm her PA,' she said.

'You are so much more,' said Dick, and with that Carrie knew the conversation would be awkward. 'Would you like a drink?'

'No, thanks. Is this a good time?'

'For what?'

'Miss Smith is ready to talk to you now, Detective Sergeant.'

Neil paused, then said, 'Much obliged, I'm sure.'

'Shall we head over to her Winnebago?'

Neil paused again, then said, 'Perhaps I need to explain to you how this works, Miss Palethorpe?'

Carrie was expecting this. 'OK,' she said with a faint sigh of boredom.

Neil noticed that and said, 'Sorry to disappoint you . . . and your employer . . . but we're dealing with a murder here, and that takes precedence over any inconvenience it might or might not cause Miss Smith. Or you.'

'I understand that, but perhaps I need to explain to you how it works with her?'

Ooh, thought Neil, I like her. 'Please do.'

'If you want to get any sense out of her, I'd do it soon.'

'And why's that?'

'First, unless she's on set and working, she's generally not great after lunch, if you get my meaning. Second, it will put her back up, and when that happens reason rarely prevails. Third, I can understand why you might not mind putting her back up – believe me, I understand that temptation better than most – but if you want to get anything of value out of her, I would do it now while the going is good.'

'I see,' said Neil, 'thanks for the advice.'

'You're welcome.'

'Carrie's right,' said Dick, 'she can be awfully stubborn if she wants to be.'

'OK,' said Neil. 'Would you kindly inform Miss Smith that I accept her gracious invitation and will be over in twenty minutes?'

'Thank you, Detective Sergeant.'

As Carrie left, Daniel arrived. 'Who was that?'

'Miss Smith's executive assistant,' said Neil. 'We

have been summoned by her mistress for the gracious grant of an interview.'

'Best to accommodate, I would have thought.'

'We've just been discussing that. And, Dan, I need you to track down Bernard.'

'At the rectory with Mum, I think.'

'We're going to need his help – and his permission – to set up some spaces to interview people. I don't want to piss him off any more than I have to.'

'I'll call him.'

'But why's Audrey at the rectory? Shouldn't she be here?'

'She comes home for her lunch. Not even Hollywood could make her eat a lasagne.'

Bernard and Audrey were sitting back in their chairs at the table in the rectory dining room. The remains of Audrey's apple pie – 'Bramleys from the garden!' – lay in crumbs in front of them; crumbs and a smear of Elmlea for thrift, which Audrey had made extravagant by decanting it into a silver creamer. Bernard was silently checking his tooth with his tongue to see if a clove he had accidentally bitten had done any damage.

'Do push that awful beast away, Bernard, if he's bothering you,' said Audrey, who was pained to see Cosmo curled up in Bernard's lap at the table, though he had the manners at least not to feed him titbits from his plate.

'He isn't bothering me at all. But I wonder where Daniel has got to? I should perhaps make my way home, if they allow me in. They keep trying to stop me going where I want to go.'

'But can't you just stay in the family apartments?'

'I do, but I can't even pick my own apples or fish my own lake' – when was the last time you did either of those? thought Audrey – 'without someone shouting at me through a megaphone to get out of the way. How am I supposed to know if I'm in the background? And I can't put the wireless on or have people to lunch.'

'It really is too much.'

'I should have gone away for the duration. Italy is lovely in September, but I've rather gone off it since my wife bolted. She's Italian . . .'

'So I gathered.'

'. . . and she went back to Siena and now I feel I can't.'

'But look on the bright side,' said Audrey, 'the house done up for nothing.'

'Yes. Well, you would know, after . . .' He looked round the room.

'After the fire? Yes, the insurers were very obliging. I thought we might have a tremendous fight on our hands, but no – they agreed to everything. In the end.'

Bernard said, with a cooler tone, 'And I hope we did everything that we could at the estate to assist you and make sure everything was . . . ship shape?'

The telephone rang. Cosmo was suddenly alert and

sat up to contribute an unnecessarily noisy and point-less tattoo of barks.

'Oh, it's incessant!' said Audrey, although this was the first time the telephone had rung that day. 'Please excuse me, Bernard.'

Bernard, who did not care if she answered it or not, put Cosmo on the floor, who skittered off after Audrey to the hall, where she insisted on keeping the telephone on a table set aside for that purpose. Bernard went back to the auto-examination of his dentition.

'Champton St Mary Rectory,' she said. 'Oh, there you are! . . . We've been . . . we've been . . . Bernard . . . Yes, he is . . . but what ha— . . . Why? . . . What? . . . Oh dear . . . Oh dear, that's awful . . . I see . . . What about the dogs? And you have Deanery Synod, or is that next Wednesday? I'll ask him. If he's not there in fifteen minutes he's not coming . . . Of *course*, don't be so dense.'

Bernard had been listening on the other side of the door, which Audrey had left open to facilitate precisely this. She started talking before he could.

'You have been summoned, summoned by the con-stabulary, to your house, which seems very impertinent to me, though under the circumstances . . .'

'Why?'

'I'm sorry to say, Bernard, your fears were not mis-placed. Your house is no longer a film location but a crime scene, and you are required to assist in the in-vestigation into the murder of Margaret Porteous.'

'Murder? Dear God! How? Why?'

'That is the business of the investigation to find out.'

'Poor Margaret.'

'Yes, poor Margaret.'

They were both silent.

Then Bernard said, 'I wonder how long this is going to take?'

In the north lodge, Nathan Liversedge was making Alex de Floures a cup of tea. Nathan, the grandson of Bernard's shadowy former gamekeeper Edgy, had crossed the barrier between servant and master since he and Alex had become lovers. In the old days, Alex's father had said, that sort of thing would have been tolerated but never discussed – brute appetites and all that – but he was damned if he were going to sit down to dine with the gypsy nancy boy rogering his son. Alex, despite his protestations at his father's bigoted attitude, actually preferred it that way, partly because he, too, winced at Nathan's social faux pas, but mostly because he liked feasting with panthers and did not want to turn his panther into a pussy cat.

But both he and Nathan adapted to the other, inevitably, and while Alex was unlikely to take up wart-charming, one of Edgy's specialisms, he had begun to learn how to take care of himself, a skill he had never had to acquire in a life that had provided, without fail, someone to pick up the things he dropped, like clothes, or cutlery, or newspapers, or anything. In the two years since he and Nathan had started to form a life together, he had learnt how to stack a woodpile. His way of doing it tempered pragmatism with aesthetics, and his woodpile took four times as long to build as Nathan's, but he had experienced for the first time the peculiar satisfaction that comes with a physical job well done. Nathan had also changed, acquiring a polish that came about not because Alex wished to remake him, like Henry Higgins, but because convenience demanded it. If he wanted his dinner cooked it had to be cooked to Alex's specifications, and Nathan had become quite the chef – 'If you can bake a hedgehog you can bake an Alaska,' Alex once said, laughing at his own joke. Nathan had also discovered a palate for wine, and not the oaky Chardonnays, the best that Braunstonbury Sainsbury's could offer, but the far more magnificent wines that lay in the cellars at the big house. Nathan had a degree of access to the house, because in spite of the notoriety of his relationship with Alex, he was the only person on the estate who could raise a boiler from the dead, or deal with rats, or fix a rattling window, so in a quiet arrangement with Mrs Shorely, the housekeeper, he would come when required, his presence under-stood but not acknowledged by Bernard. In return, Alex thought it quite fair to take payment in the form of wine, but this was not an argument Bernard would even begin to understand, so it was transacted in an even quieter arrangement with Mrs Shorely, the only person who knew what was in the cellar since the last

butler had gone. Nathan now knew the difference between a Sancerre and a Puligny-Montrachet, a Pauillac
and a Graves.

He also knew the difference between PG Tips and
Earl Grey. In the afternoon, Alex liked the latter, in a
proper cup and saucer, with a slice of lemon to cut the
smoky perfume of the tea.

Nathan set it down on the old coffin stool Alex had
repurposed into a side table and then sat next to him
on the sofa. Alex grunted an acknowledgement but did
not look up from his copy of *i-D*. There was an article
about a Manchester band, the Happy Mondays, who
looked like kids in a playground rather than refugees
from the Twenties Weimar Republic, which was what
everyone else in the magazine looked like, and he felt
that mixture of alarm and anticipation that his look
was going to need radical revision.

It was a moot point if changing the look would
really make much difference to his appearance. His
aristocratic English genes had made him tall and slen-
der, red-blond and frog-faced. Nathan was stocky and
dark and contained, more of a blank canvas, Alex liked
to think, but his effort to make them look more like
equals, as Champton's twin icons of post-punk mili-
taria, did not really touch the points of difference.

The blank canvas had not given up PG Tips for Earl
Grey, and preferred it in a mug rather than a cup and
saucer. He also slurped it in a way that Alex found
difficult.

'Must you, Nathan? You sound like a horse at a trough.'

Nathan ignored the slap. 'How long is this going to go on for?'

'I don't know. As long as it takes.'

'I don't like explaining who I am every time I come and go.'

'You don't.'

'Only because I know other ways to get in and out. I *do* like pissing off security, though.'

Alex put down his magazine. 'Your place here is always a bit . . . questionable?'

'I'm a gypsy boy. My place is always a bit questionable.'

'Oh, yes,' said Alex, still feeling a frisson that he had made such an excitingly unsuitable match.

'Jean Shorely wasn't best pleased to be messed around again. Having to find rooms for the coppers to do the interviews.'

'I don't suppose Daddy was overjoyed.'

'I didn't see him up there, but I did spot the rector. Looked flustered.'

'Daniel? I wonder how calm he is, now he's reunited with his beloved bobby. They seem . . . fated, don't you think?'

'What do you mean?

'To be together. Only not as Daniel wanted it to be, but because they are the only ones who seem able to figure out who's murdered whom.'

'Maybe it was a madness.'

'A *folie d'amour*.'

Nathan grunted.

'Something happened. But I don't know what. One minute Daniel's practically announcing he's off to the cloister again, but then it's business as usual, only his passion for the policeman has suddenly died. What do you think happened?'

'I don't know. Maybe he likes it here?'

'Hard to imagine Champton without him. But something happened. Do you think they had a thing?'

'I don't think Neil was interested in that at all.'

'I don't know. A one-off, a moment of madness? And then they wake up in the morning and . . . aaargh!'

Nathan thought about it for a moment. 'No, I can't see it. More likely the rector got a grip.'

'I liked him losing his grip. So unflappable. It gets boring. And I don't believe it.'

'What don't you believe?'

'That someone can be so in control all the time.'

'It's his job. It's the person he is.'

'No one's completely in command of themselves. Their passions, their desires, their subconscious.'

Nathan nodded. He was not what Alex would think of as an introspective person, but was not so much ignorant of the tension between another's inner and outer life as indifferent to it. His life had been tough growing up, and he had acquired the useful habit of not maintaining unrealistic expectations of people. Indifferent, and therefore not surprised or disappointed.

He understood the drives to eat, to find somewhere to live, to have sex, to acquire sufficient power to achieve a liveable life, but he was not interested in why people were so often at war with themselves, inconvenienced by their desires or unable to face the truth of their natures.

'Did you see Brandon?'

'I did,' said Alex. 'He's supposed to come round to-night to drop off some gear, but he's not going to want to do that with coppers everywhere. And he'll have to make a statement like everyone else.'

'Are they interviewing everyone?'

'Everyone. Somebody must have seen something. You know how this works.'

'Yeah. And I know how it's always me they come after.'

'Not this time, darling. You weren't there.'

'They'll think of something. And Brandon *was* there, and if they go after him and discover his sideline, they could connect him with us.'

'I don't think Neil will be interested in a bit of puff in the middle of a murder inquiry.'

Nathan slurped his tea again. 'No, but there's some-thing about Brandon . . . you know?'

'Bad boy?'

'Yes.'

'I quite like bad boys.'

'You like a fantasy bad boy. The real thing I don't think you would like so much.'

'And that's Brandon?'

'I reckon so.'

'Why?'

'I dunno. Something about him. Makes me wary.'

Alex put on a witchy voice and said, 'By the pricking of my thumbs, something wicked this way comes.'

Theo was sitting in his trailer. He was still in his T-shirt and boxers and had opened a bottle of wine because he was bored and reluctant to skin up as there were so many police about, not all of them friendly. There was another knock at the door.

'Who is it?'

'Police, Mr Clement,' said a familiar voice, 'we need to speak to you.'

'Come in.'

It was Neil. 'What's with the Mr Clement all of a sudden?' said Theo. 'I usually only get called that at the clap clinic.'

'Professional standards for a professional job,' said Neil. 'But it's nothing to worry about.'

'Nothing to worry about? In a murder inquiry? When I supplied the murder weapon?'

Neil, suddenly serious, said, 'We don't know that.'

'What else could it be?'

'There was a lot of cutlery on the set, Theo.'

'Yes, but it's all accounted for except mine.'

'Could have been any one of a dozen daggers. We haven't heard from forensics, nor seen the pathologist's report, so they're all potential murder weapons. But that's not what I want to talk to you about.'

Theo gestured towards the sofa. 'It's not quite up to Miss Smith's standard. Very much Dressing Room 3. Or 4. Have a seat on my uncomfortable sofa.'

'How do they work out who gets what?'

'Pecking order. Sometimes it's obvious – Miss Smith is prima ballerina assoluta; no one needs telling – but it's harder when you get lower down. I get my own trailer because I've been in a soap and am semi-famous.'

'Quite a step down, though. No Jacuzzi.'

'It's not about the Jacuzzi, it's about location: who gets closest to Gilly. And if you are close, it doesn't mean you get upgraded facilities. The opposite, in fact. If we want to be near her Jacuzzi then we must put up with a dribbling, lukewarm shower. It's like Versailles. The aristocrats lived in broom cupboards because there were far more of them than rooms to accommodate them, but they simply had to be there; it was all about being close to the king. The Oscars are just the same. Would you like a drink? No cocktails, but I can give you a glass of wine.'

'No, thanks.'

Theo poured himself another glass from the bottle of red wine on the counter of the kitchenette. 'What did you want to talk to me about?'

'Two things: first, Brandon Redding.'

'Brandon Redding?' said Theo, looking up and to the right as if consulting his memory.

'The lad you buy coke from.'

Theo started. Then shrugged. 'Oh, that Brandon. I didn't actually know his name was Redding.'

'He called on you here today.'

'Daniel tell you?'

'Doesn't matter.'

Theo took a gulp of wine. 'Would it make a difference if I told you I was helping him with his acting?'

'How's he getting on with that? By all accounts his principal interest is commerce.'

Theo took another gulp. He was slightly drunk – squiffy, he would say – and it made him bolder, or franker. 'Yes, I suppose it would be fair to say that. He is helpful to have on set, which, as you have probably noticed, can be a demanding environment. Sometimes we like a little something to calm us down or pep us up. Are you going to arrest me?'

'No plans to, but I would like to arrest him. And that might be awkward for you.'

'A friendly warning . . .'

'I'm saying you might keep your distance from him,' said Neil. 'It's not just his concierge services, you see, Theo. He's involved in some nasty business with some nasty people and . . . I would keep away.'

Theo was so cheered by the realisation that he was not about to be marched off location in handcuffs that he did not really notice the warning in what Neil had said. Theo was geared to gratification, and had made his way cheerfully through life without looking for reasons not to seek it whenever and wherever he could. So what he heard was not 'stay away', but 'I am not going to take this further', which meant all he had to do was make different arrangements, and that could be easily done through Alex de Floures, who had been a customer of Brandon's for some time, and had introduced him to Theo.

'And there's another thing,' said Neil. 'Not business, personal.'

'Is it my brother?'

'It is.' Neil paused for a moment. 'Things between your brother and me have been quite difficult.'

Theo wondered if a 'Just Say No' lecture would be preferable, but there was nothing he could do.

'As you are aware, or I think you are, a while ago I discovered that Daniel has . . . feelings for me . . .'

What an odd and untranslatable expression, thought Theo, to *have feelings* for someone – sounds like the collywobbles rather than desire.

'. . . which came as a complete surprise to me. I thought it was just, you know, a friendship. But it was important to me, and I didn't want to be unsympathetic, but it was . . . I had never thought of myself in that way . . .'

What's he trying to say here? wondered Theo.

'. . . and I think I handled it badly.'

'How do you mean?'

'When we came back from the monastery after the murder, I . . . I snogged him.'

'You snogged Daniel?'

'Yes.'

There was silence, and then Theo burst out laughing. 'Oh, my God, how I would love to have seen that. Why on earth did you snog him?'

'If he wanted a snog, I thought why not give him one? See what happens.'

'And what happened?'

'He jumped like a kitten.'

'And then?'

'We've barely spoken since.'

'Hmm.' Theo nodded. 'That's Daniel. But that's not you. Or is it, you dark horse?'

'I thought he was going to rejoin the monastery. Not a good idea that, so I decided to give him something else to think about. It was spur of the moment.'

'Would you have followed through?'

'No! Not my thing at all. Very prickly, snogging another bloke.'

'I know,' said Theo, 'but weren't you throwing fuel on the fire?'

'The opposite. Instantly extinguished it. Daniel – I think the phrase is "made his excuses and left".'

'Of course,' said Theo.

'Why of course?'

'It's one thing to like the idea of something, another to actually like it.'

'I thought I was giving him a taste of what he wanted.'

Theo sighed. 'A middle-aged man who's never had sex, who's never been physically intimate with someone – well, not since he was a baby, and that doesn't count – and who lives in a tradition that has long believed that a horror of sexual contact is not weird but holy. If you were him, how would you feel if a policeman suddenly snogged you?'

'Flattered? Vindicated?'

'Come on! You were the object of his newly awakened desire because you were *never* going to snog him. He yearns for you, but he cannot have you. It's his cross to bear, Neil. Catnip to Dan.'

Neil looked helpless. 'I'm a regular bloke, Theo. I do my best, but I'm no good at this.'

'I dunno, a snog was rather brilliant, and *very* sporting. And he didn't go back into the monastery, which would have been a *disaster.*'

'Imagine him walled up somewhere like that forever.'

Theo took another slurp of wine. 'Imagine me having to take in our mother? Are you sure I can't get you a drink?'

'Quite sure.'

'What can I do for you?'

'I don't want to have to rely on murders coming along to get back on terms with him.'

'You want your friend back.'

'I do.'

'Maybe he doesn't want you back? Maybe it's too difficult for him. Like you and Honoria.'

'It's not like me and Honoria. We were having a love affair . . .'

'*You* were.'

Neil faltered at that. 'Ooff. OK, we were having an intimate relationship, with everything that goes with an intimate relationship. Well, it was to me, if not to her. That wasn't me and Dan.'

'You always looked like you were in love with him.'

Neil was silent for a while. 'You know when you're in love with someone you think they can give you something you need but lack. That they can complete you?'

'Not really.'

'I felt that with Dan, but not romantically.'

'What does he have that would complete you?'

'Faith.'

'Get your own.'

'I had my own and it went, and I want it back and Dan makes me think I could get it.'

Theo sighed. 'That's catnip to him too – a sheep looking for a flock.'

'Can you help me?'

Theo said, 'Why don't you just ring him up and go round?'

'I don't know if he would be up for that.'

Theo finished his wine. 'OK. We're having dinner this evening, just me and Mum and Dan. Why don't you come round?'

'I haven't been invited.'

'I just invited you.'

9

On the Field of the Cloth of Gold Neil and one of his uniformed constables and Dick Alleyne (accompanied by Jasper) and Carrie formed up to go in procession to Gillian Smith's trailer. They looked like ambassadors on a diplomatic mission, and ceremony attended them, formalising the testing of strength, the compatibility or incompatibility of their objectives. Power, Daniel thought as he watched them, in Tudor England, Hollywood, Church House, the City, flowed around people and places in much the same way wherever, whenever, they contended. And then he wondered if it was really more like a European embassy to a Chinese court, where the visitors did not really understand who or what they were parleying with, and did not know if their diplomatic skills would work, or if their conventions would be observed or respected, or if they might just be particularly unfortunate and end up beheaded.

Daniel made his way back to the house through the courtyard and then through the grand space of the hall to the corridor that connected them to the Tudor wing and Bernard's study, a lovely room with linenfold panelling, a pointed, arched fireplace and diamond-paned windows, which looked over the deer park. Bernard spent more and more of his time here alone, reading *The Times*, watching Formula One, until recently with just the company of his cat Jove. A vicious and beautiful beast in long white fur, he had belonged to his last wife, but she had declined to take the cat home to Siena, and the cat liked the fire, which was steadily tended in Bernard's study from September to May. He had taken up residence there, and after a while Bernard had got used to him. It made him look like Blofeld in a Bond film, Daniel thought; all the cat needed was a diamond collar. But misfortune had come to Jove not in a final showdown with 007 but with the arrival of Cosmo who had come to stay in the big house temporarily after the fire at the rectory, had bonded with Bernard while Hilda was weaning her puppies, and saw no reason why Jove's domain of Bernard's study should not be surrendered to him.

There had been tremendous fights, Jove's agility and viciousness on one side, which saw him slashing at him with his claws, racing up curtains and along bookshelves Cosmo could only bark at, Cosmo's tireless territorial vigilance on the other. On the rugs and floorboards there had been some more spectacular dog-and-cat fights – two very low-flying missiles, one white, the other reddish-brown, twisting and turning after the other's heat trail.

Cosmo had more or less prevailed, for Jove had not his unsleeping instinct to see off an intruder, and rather than confine himself to his usual place on the third bookshelf up where classic literature was kept and he therefore would be undisturbed, had ranged through the house in search of new places – the library steps, Mrs Shorely's fireplace, the top of the great stairs from where he could see who was coming and who was going, and the kitchen range where the cat flap gave him access by night to the smorgasbord of the Tenter Yard and the kitchen garden.

Bernard, who was disinclined to make an effort to attract or keep the company of anyone or anything – they came to him, he had found – rather liked Jove for his cold indifference to matters of affection and loyalty, so when the arrival of Cosmo inconvenienced him, and he went off to find fresh fields and pastures new within the house and park, Bernard barely noticed. What surprised those around him was not only that Cosmo had taken Jove's place as the creature with the closest proximity to his lordship, but also that Bernard should suddenly find such an affinity with that creature. Feelings of affection and even devotion began to rise within him. He had Labradors, in the days when he hunted and shot – lumbering outriders of his presence around the house and estate – but they were not lap dogs, cute dogs, little sausages, companions of his heart. They did not receive titbits, as Cosmo received titbits, or sleep on the sofa with their head on his lap, or curl up at his feet when he settled to work or watch television or read the paper.

Audrey's warning about this, when she and Daniel reoccupied the rectory, was borne out. Cosmo had pined for Bernard, continually sniffing at the door, or leaping up when he heard the sound of his Land Rover. Again, to everyone's surprise, Bernard had pined for him too, and sometimes telephoned or called round on a pretext to see if he could 'borrow the little brute' for an afternoon, or 'spare your legs, Audrey, and take him for a walk'.

For this reason – to stimulate Bernard's better nature – Daniel had brought Cosmo with him when he tapped on the study door. Not a 'come in' or even a 'come!' came from Bernard, more a rising grunt, somewhere between a 'bah' and a 'yeah'. Daniel opened the door and Cosmo, who had his snout stuck in the gap at the bottom, was pushed back by it across the polished parquet, so determined to get a scent of Bernard that he did not notice the way ahead was clear.

Not entirely clear; there was a hiss and a streak of white fur as Jove, who returned when it suited him to his place on shelf three, realised his nemesis was back, and tore off down the corridor. Once, this would have been a temptation that Cosmo could no more ignore than a greyhound a rabbit, but it was Bernard he wanted, even more than a fight with a cat, and as soon as he saw him he ran to his lordship, his hind quarters so misaligned due to the furious wagging of his tail and the lack of traction on the polished floor that he looked like a fishtailing car.

Bernard sank to his knees, a tribute he would offer no other person or thing, and Cosmo skidded into them, flipped onto his back and squealed with such pleasure it sounded like pain as Bernard rubbed his tummy.

'Who's a STERLING FELLAH? Who's a STER-LING FELLAH?' he gurgled, which made Daniel think of Rudyard Kipling.

Cosmo was so excited he let himself go and an arc of urine rose and fell like the play of the restored fountain outside, only it fell across Bernard's knees.

'Oh, Bernard, I'm so sorry!' said Daniel, but Bernard was unconcerned and just kept on rubbing Cosmo's tummy. Was he like that with his wives, wondered Daniel, generous with his physical attention, solicitous of their feelings? Another person's sex life was not an area where Daniel felt he had expertise to offer – indeed, he had only discovered he had his own sex life in his late forties. On occasions when someone came to see him and confessed bedroom matters, Daniel adopted a smile that he hoped was warm and sympathetic, but it concealed a sense of mild panic. Although he was aware that in his time Bernard had enjoyed quite a busy one, he had never once broached the subject with Daniel. Daniel was grateful for this, and he liked to imagine that the two of them looked on the passions and emotions of others with what Daniel thought was Stoic detachment, though in Bernard it was more likely to be boredom. And to see Bernard, whom he thought incapable of understanding what an emotional exchange might be, let alone engage in one, billing and cooing over a little dog was disconcerting, for Daniel had assumed Bernard's emotions had been smothered at birth. But then he thought of Bernard's wives urinating with unchecked delight at his touch, and this was too difficult to entertain for longer than a fraction of a second.

'What happened with the police?' asked Daniel. 'Is there a plan for the investigation?'

'I was not so much consulted, Daniel, as informed. My house, or that part of it that has not been occupied by minstrels, is now commandeered by plod.'

'How long?'

'As long as it takes. There are hundreds – and I mean hundreds – of people they have to talk to. They've set up in the kitchen wing, in the Rudnam Room, in the stables, in the library. It's like Scotland bloody Yard. And if you think I'm put out, you should hear that awful fellah in charge.'

'Mr Alleyne?'

'The one in charge. It's messed up his schedule, which seems to be far more important than catching whoever stabbed Mrs Porteous.'

'I imagine making films is a complicated business.'

'You'd think it was the D-Day landings.'

'Not unlike it, in a way . . .' said Daniel, 'moving hundreds of people around to the right place at the right time. There is something of Monty about him.'

'Daniel, it's *H.M.S. Pinafore,* not the D–Day landings. Who's a STERLING FELLAH?' Bernard scratched Cosmo's tummy one more time, then got up jerkily and went to sit in an armchair in front of the fire. The little dog followed him, and he picked him up with the ease that comes with frequent handling. Maybe his mother was right, thought Daniel, Cosmo is becoming another's dog. 'Sit down, Dan. Help yourself to a drink if you want one. Sherry? Whisky?'

'Not now, Bernard.'

They settled and looked into the fire, which was burning so low it was more ash than ember.

'What do you think?' said Bernard.

'I really don't know. The whole episode seems unreal somehow.'

'Yes, it feels like it's in the film rather than in life.'

'That won't last. It's why Dick – Mr Alleyne – is feeling so fraught; his business is the enchantment of storytelling, not establishing the facts in a murder inquiry. He's lost control.'

Bernard said, 'I suppose I should be annoyed with you.'

'Me? Why?'

'One expects gentleness and benevolence to attend one's parsons.'

'Oh, I see.'

'And yet with you we get murder and mystery. It's like having Hercule Poirot as the rector.'

'That is rather my job.'

'To attract murderers?'

'To face, not flinch from, the worst of us.'

'Hmm. I sometimes think you encourage it.'

'Encourage murder?'

'Well, not encourage it, but . . . I don't know, draw it out.'

Daniel said, 'I really don't go looking for it.'

'I dare say you don't think you do, but I don't recall any other parson here followed so closely by flashing blue lights and forensic pathologists.'

Daniel wondered what to say to this. 'Perhaps I have an unusual calling.'

'Did you ever think it would suit an average man better if you had a plain one? Wouldn't a parson who said his prayers and gave us Holy Communion and told the children bible stories at assembly and judged the dog show be more suited to Champton?'

'I do all those things, Bernard.'

'It's hard to imagine you doing Harvest Festival without someone ending up with a scythe stuck in their back.'

'And I would point out to that average man, if he'll allow me, that I don't instigate such things, I just clear up after them.'

'And yet so many just happen while you're around. Not just here, I mean. There was that business at the monastery when you ran away. And now here we are again, with a highly respected member of the community stabbed to death in my picture gallery. You're a lightning conductor for evil.'

'I promised at my ordination, Bernard, to seek Christ's sheep that are dispersed abroad, and for his children who are in the midst of this naughty world, that they may be saved through Christ forever.'

'What the hell does that mean?'

'I don't do anything to stir up hatreds, or open old wounds. I do what I can to remedy what has gone wrong.'

'And to shake sleeping dogs,' said Bernard, aptly, for Cosmo was now snoring softly on his lap. 'I think perhaps you like that.'

'Not in the way you mean.'

Bernard said, 'Pour me a whisky, would you? I don't want to move the old chap. Whisky and soda?'

Daniel went to the sideboard where Bernard kept on a tray the everyday whisky he preferred, the Famous Grouse, which Daniel thought was to Scotch what Lucozade was to Veuve Clicquot. Why such parsimony from a grandee? By the time he put the drink in his patron's hand, Bernard was thinking about something different, drawn to his theme by self-pity, partner to accidie. 'I don't know how I'm supposed to live here with the place overrun by rozzers and minstrels.'

'I'm sure you can find somewhere to hide away from them.'

'It's *my* house, it's my *home*. I feel like I am trespassing in it.'

'You invited the minstrels in, Bernard, and there is nothing you can really do about the police.'

'Yes,' he said testily, 'but knowing that does not find me somewhere to close my eyes for a few moments, to play with the dog, to eat a morsel of food.'

Daniel understood. 'Would you like to dine with us tonight?'

'I couldn't possibly. I've lunched with you, or your mama, already. And anyway, I'm not permitted to leave. No one in, no one out.'

'You wouldn't be leaving. The rectory technically is in the park.'

'Is it?'

'That's why your incumbents have so often trespassed on your kindness and generosity. So the least we can do is offer you a dinner in return.'

'But this is late notice for Audrey!'

Daniel said, 'She would be delighted to have you, and it will be the most kitchen of kitchen suppers.'

Daniel's image of an embassy going forth to an inscrutable potentate when he saw Neil's deputation leave the stables to interview Miss Smith was prescient. Carrie went into her trailer first to ensure Miss Smith was ready to see them. She emerged a minute or two later to inform the waiting party that Miss Smith was not quite ready, for she had a raging migraine, but she understood the urgency of the inquiry and, mindful of her duty, had taken a powerful combination of paracetamol with codeine and expected its palliative effect would be sufficient to make her testimony intelligible. If they could perhaps wait a few minutes for the flashing lights and disabling pain of the condition to subside, she would then feel able to do her best to answer their questions.

Neil said he was sorry to hear of it and they would return in fifteen minutes, and the deputation went back to the stables, where Dick lost his temper. He had been struggling to contain it since Neil had arrived and imposed his rule on Dick's, a situation he found difficult to deal with in the smallest degree, but this was not the smallest degree. When he lost his temper, it was volcanic and everyone around him quailed, because that was what was expected of them. It did not apply to Neil, who was unaffected by loss of temper. People lost their tempers around policemen all the time and he simply waited for the energy of the explosion to dissipate, then continued where he had left off with no alteration of tone or pitch. This took him efficiently where he wanted to go in an interview, not only because the energy of his interlocutor was spent, but because the stratagem of having a tantrum had not succeeded, and therefore they were disarmed too.

So he waited for Dick to run out of steam. There was a beat, and then Neil said, 'Once we've talked to Miss Smith, sir, that's another name off our list, and you'll be one step closer to resuming your schedule.'

Dick's tantrums did not work on Carrie either, who

had quite enough to deal with in Gillian Smith and was impervious to bad temper, due to a mixture of personality and the frequency with which it arose in the everyday course of her employment. Tantrums were easy, actually; it was caprices that were difficult, perverse and unpredictable, and if Gillian set her mind on one, it was very difficult to change it.

Carrie said, 'If I may?'

'Go on,' said Neil.

'I would suggest that a certain degree of management on our side would help you on your side. Miss Smith is not always ready to . . . align with the wishes of others, if I can put it that way, and it would not matter to her who those others were. I can help you with that, prepare the way – not to interfere with your investigation, but to get you together in a way that expedites it.'

'I see,' said Neil. He liked Carrie. She was a northerner for starters, and he felt an automatic solidarity even if she was from the other side of the Pennines, and in this highly strung world she seemed level and even. 'Well,' he said, 'shall we go and see if she's in a fit state to share her recollection of the events of this morning? And, Mr Alleyne, perhaps you could chase up the . . . do you call them dailies? So we can see for ourselves what happened on the set earlier?'

'I've got the first AD on it. You'll probably need me to – what was the word you used, Carrie? Expedite? – Miss Smith's recollections.'

She said, 'It might be helpful.'

They set off again on their mission to the circled Winnebagos, only this time they were distracted by the sight of a black van making slow progress down the drive towards the house. It was what is called a private ambulance, but the kind no patient wants summoned, for it is driven by undertakers and collects bodies for removal to their premises, or the coroner's jurisdiction. It had come to take away Margaret Porteous, what was left of her, and its solemn glide was a reminder to everyone of what had happened that morning. People stopped and were silent, and while no one doffed a cap or bowed a head, there was that wordless acknowledgement of the subtraction of one from our number, and the recognition of a common destiny, that we, too, will be subtracted eventually.

Mrs Shorely telephoned Bernard in his study. He turned to Daniel. 'The undertakers are here for Mrs Porteous.'

'Thank you,' said Daniel, and he made his way to the Old Dairy where the pathologist had finished his job, to leave Daniel to his.

Audrey was in the rectory drawing room, her feet up on what she called the 'pouffay'. Strewn around it were several editions of the *Telegraph*, as yet uncollected by Daniel. Hilda, who had bonded with Audrey in maternal solidarity after she had her puppies, and more so when they went to their new owners, had created a temporary billet out of the *Sunday Telegraph*, which had more to offer for that purpose than the daily version, and she was at that moment sleeping on what you might think a comfortless prediction of recession. Hilda suddenly looked up and there followed a ring on the doorbell, which sent her scuttling out into the hall and across its slippery black-and-white tiles. Audrey was of the generation that never ignored the doorbell, no matter how inconveniently it sounded, but she did not rush to answer.

It was Miss March. 'Mrs Clement, forgive me for calling on you without notice, but I was just passing and thought . . .'

Just passing? thought Audrey. You never *just pass* anything.

'. . . I would take advantage of this break in the schedule to—'

Hilda started sniffing around her shoes, and while Miss March tried not to show her distaste for this, she really did not want dog slobber on her suedes.

'Such a sprightly dog! – to see if you . . . well, know anything more about what is happening?'

'Hilda! Away! Away!' said Audrey, with a firm note of command, and the dog at once waddled back to her nest of newspaper. 'Let us have tea, Miss March, and I shall fill you in.'

In the kitchen the lunch things were by the sink but not yet washed up. Miss March detected not only a hint of bohemianism in that, but also marks of grandeur about the crockery and crystal. Whom – it was always 'whom' with Miss March – had been for lunch?

'India or China?' said Audrey, lifting a lid on the Aga hot plate and sliding the kettle onto it.

'I don't mind,' said Miss March, 'but isn't it a China sort of day?'

'Is it?'

'You seem to have had lunch guests?'

'Oh, only Bernard. Lord de Floures,' she added unnecessarily. 'He called in. Much as you have. But no ceremony, just a quiet lunch, the two of us.'

'How very plain the dress shop will seem to you now!'

Audrey said, 'The shop? Not at all! But empty for now. And even if you were open, everyone's up at the house.'

'Shouldn't you be there? Helping the police?'

'Shouldn't you?'

'I have spoken to them already – I was at the scene, as they say – and they know where I am if they need me.'

'Just as they know where I am. It will be our old friend Detective Sergeant Vanloo, though we don't see so much of him as we used to. India, I think.' She fetched down a Brown Betty teapot from its place on the shelf over the Aga. Oh, thought Miss March, no Spode for me.

'What is the news?'

'You know better than I,' said Audrey, 'and it's almost too awful to talk about.'

Almost, thought Miss March.

'It is as you feared but could not say. Margaret was murdered,' said Audrey. 'Stabbed to death on the set while they were shooting the masque scene. And she was *so* looking forward to it. She was playing one of the queens in the masque, as you know . . .'

Miss March nodded.

'And so did everyone else — she wouldn't stop talking about it.' The kettle came to the boil. 'But I think she must have seen it as the crowning moment of her career.'

'Her career?'

'As chief guide to Champton — self-appointed, I might add. She organised the rotas for the Open Days with all the confidence of a chatelaine. And she knew the house's history — who slept where, and when — better than anyone. So, to recreate a masque like the masque that was held here when Queen Anne stayed on her way from Edinburgh to Windsor was simply marvellous.' She took down a caddy from the same shelf as the teapot — loose leaf, thought Miss March, very good — shook tea from it into the teapot, like a baker who knows how much flour to use without measuring, and poured on the boiling water.

'I heard it was not the right masque,' said Miss March.

'No, it wasn't. They applied a certain poetic licence, I think — with a trowel sometimes, according to Daniel — but it was the nearest I suppose Margaret got to reliving one of the most glorious moments in the house's history.'

'Not knowing,' said Miss March, 'that she was about to become a very sad chapter in its history.'

Audrey nodded. Then said, 'Footnote, perhaps. But it is, as you say, very sad. And alarming. For if Margaret Porteous can get herself murdered, any one of us can.'

Miss March nodded too. 'Any ideas?'

'None at all. She could be annoying, but we can all be annoying.'

Yes, we can, thought Miss March.

'Cup or mug?'

Miss March paused, because she didn't do mugs, but she didn't want to be awkward either. 'Whatever's easiest.'

Audrey fetched two rather plain and solid cups down from the dresser. 'Please excuse the china, Miss March. Daniel bought a set for me from a pottery in a windy little place in Suffolk. I call it lentilware.'

'It's charming,' said Miss March, taking the cup and saucer, which looked like it had been made from a mixture of Ovaltine and cement. 'There is another possibility, Mrs Clement. Perhaps Margaret was not the intended victim? It occurred to me that in a crowd of queens it would be easy to mistake one for another. Is it not plausible that the murderer intended to strike someone else?'

'I suppose it must be *her*,' said Audrey.

'Whom?'

'Gillian Smith.'

'Why?'

'I don't really know. I suppose I think people don't get to be film stars without making someone or other want to kill them.'

Miss March nodded, said, 'I see,' and sipped her tea. 'Have you had much to do with Miss Smith?'

'We barely see her. She arrives on set when everything's ready for her, does her scene — we just stand around or carry things in the background — and then she's whisked away. They drive her around in one of those little carts you see on golf courses.'

'But it must be marvellous to see someone so gifted at work.'

Audrey paused the elevation of her cup to her mouth to say, 'Are you a fan, Miss March?'

'I wouldn't say that,' said Miss March, 'but an admirer, yes. My father and I saw her playing Eliza Doolittle in *My Fair Lady* at the Prince of Wales. I couldn't believe it was the same person, the before-Eliza and after-Eliza. Remarkable. How do they do it?'

'We don't get close enough to tell. And it's terribly bitty. Sometimes they just film a sentence or two and she's whizzed away again. Such an odd business.'

'Do you get to spend much time with the other extras?'

'SAs, dear. Supporting artists. Yes, hours and *hours*. We go to a sort of tent and have endless cups of tea and wait to be summoned.'

'What do you do while you wait?'

'Some read, some knit, some play cards, some talk nonsense. We stay in our groups, which is a bit inconvenient when most of your friends are playing courtiers and countesses but you're a humble servant in a plain dress and bonnet. Such an irony that today in make-believe I waited on the pleasure of my betters, but in life I lunched a peer.'

Miss March stirred her tea. 'Anyone you know at the kitchen end of things?'

'A couple of ladies from the WI, Cynthia Achurch, a woman who used to do for Mrs Hawkins at Upper Badsaddle Manor. But not really. You seem unusually curious, if I may say so, Miss March?'

Two spots of red appeared in Miss March's cheeks. 'I am afraid I formed too hasty a judgement when I heard they were coming to make a film at Champton. I thought it . . . vulgar.'

'Like the navvies coming through with the railways.'

'Not quite that, but not something of interest to me. Or others,' she nodded at Audrey.

'I thought the same thing, Miss March, and then half my friends signed up for it and I . . . reconsidered. If I'd been quicker, I might be Lady Bedford now.'

'Do you mind being a servant?'

'I rather enjoy it. And, with a bit of wit, standing around with a jug or a charger can sometimes offer more to the audience than bowing in a ruff.'

Miss March sighed. 'Oh, well. I shall be off and . . . stock-take again.'

Audrey looked at her over her cup. 'You sound a little forlorn.'

'There are times when it is difficult to be alone.'

'Miss March, why don't you join us for supper tonight? It will be Dan, and Theo, probably, if he can get away at a decent time. It won't be anything fancy, just a fish pie and mincemeat tart.'

'I don't mean to add to the stampede to your table today, Mrs Clement, but if you're sure, I would like that very much.'

'Then come at seven. Actually, a quarter past, or you'll barely have time to brush your hair.'

'Can I bring anything?'

'Don't think so. Unless you've got any cream? We had the last at lunch.'

On the way home from the rectory Miss March picked up a carton of Elmlea from the Post Office and General Store. As she put it in the fridge in her little kitchen in the flat over the shop, she wondered if there were some way of decanting it and passing it off as the real thing. A jug, she thought. Her nice little crystal jug with a bit of cling film over the top. And then she wondered if the chicken pizzaiola she had taken out of the freezer that morning for her supper tonight would freeze again. Probably not, which was an unforgivable waste, because she wasn't going to risk it tomorrow with all the salmonella about, which she was sure they were trying to hush up, but it would have to go. 'Needs must!' she said, and tipped it into the bin.

★

Gillian Smith had to be helped to sit up on the pile of cushions heaped on her sofa. She was wearing something between a pant suit and a tracksuit, but it, too, was cashmere, only brownish rather than the pinky-lilac she'd had on earlier. She was also wearing a pair of large dark glasses to protect her unnecessarily from the pale sunshine of the end of the day. She looked like a chinchilla, thought Neil. Not a chinchilla, a lemur. The big eyes, though, made her look vulnerable, innocent? She winced when she moved; she asked Neil to repeat his name when he introduced himself; she had a list of exacting requirements for Carrie to prepare a soothing refreshment. The curtains were drawn, which made her sunglasses even less necessary than they already were, and the crackle of the PC's walkie-talkie made her jump like a startled okapi. It was typical Gillian Smith behaviour, Neil could see that. She saw herself in a role, a leading role, and she created a character accordingly, but one that was useful also to serve her interests. How do you interview an invalid? If a question was too challenging, she would no doubt fade or crumble and someone would stop the interview, like a doctor with a patient in intensive care being badgered by a detective. But Gillian Smith was not in intensive care, was not an invalid, and even though the others formed themselves around the role she had cast herself in, handling her as gently as the Sophilos vase, Neil would not. There was a clash almost immediately.

'Thank you, all,' he said, when the introductions had been made. 'You can leave us to it now.'

They all froze. Then Dick said, 'You want us to . . . leave you on your own with her?'

'Yes,' said Neil. 'Thanks for your help.'

'But . . . I think it would be better if . . . I could help with the schedule and where Miss Smith would have been on set, and . . .'

'All in good time, sir. But for now, we just need to speak to Miss Smith.'

Carrie turned to Dick. 'If you want to get on with the schedule, I can manage things here.'

'No,' said Neil, 'everyone out except me and the constable. That includes you.'

Miss Smith feebly raised her hand. 'I'm afraid that's out of the question, Detective Sergeant. I'm going to need Carrie.'

'I'm afraid *that's* out of the question, Miss Smith,' said Neil. 'It's not how police interviews work.'

'But . . . I can't possibly talk to you without Carrie here!'

'Why? I don't think we need an interpreter.'

'I never speak to anyone without Carrie.'

'Never?'

'Not if it's a business matter.'

'It's a police interview, Miss Smith, and a murder inquiry.'

Gillian Smith's face froze as this unusual reality confronted her. In the daily round of making her way through the world, she rarely experienced much resistance from others. She was so used to getting her own way that she sometimes forgot it was necessary to negotiate your wishes with others who also have wishes. Of course, there were circumstances when she had to accept that wanting something was not the same as getting something – gravity, for example, or age, though she had worked very hard to mitigate the deleterious effects of the latter – but where people were involved, there were only a very few who could better her. She had had some difficulties of this kind with ex-husbands, and Dick, too, sometimes told her what she did not want to hear or to go where she did not want to go, and it was only because of their mutual success that she had not professionally divorced him in the same way she had her husbands. Even so, Dick understood that getting the best from her required his 90 per cent acquiescence. There was Carrie, uniquely placed to speak truth to power, but as an adviser and an employee, not a peer.

'A police interview?' Gillian said eventually.

'Yes, madam.'

'In that case I want my attorney.'

Neil said, in a patient tone, 'You are not answering a charge, Miss Smith. These are preliminary enquiries, and your attorney, or solicitor, would not usually attend. Unless you wish to admit to a crime? In which case a solicitor would be advisable.'

'Don't be ridiculous. But why can't I have Carrie here?'

Neil sighed. 'We need to build up a picture of what happened, and speaking to people individually allows us to do that.'

Carrie interrupted. 'But I know better than Miss Smith where she was and when, that's part of my job.'

'That's what I was trying to say,' said Dick.

'It is sometimes the difference in people's recollections that makes for a fuller picture. And we will appreciate speaking to you both in due course, but for now, just Miss Smith.'

There was another silence as the courtiers – for that's what they were – had to resign themselves to leaving their queen – for that's what she was – to face her questioners alone. It was Carrie who got there first. 'I see. We will wait outside, Detective Sergeant.'

'I wouldn't do that if I were you,' he said. 'I don't know how long this will take. Why don't you go back to the stables, and I'll send the constable to get you when we're finished?'

None of them moved. Neil got up and indicated the door.

Carrie picked up her bag and said, 'Gilly, do you have everything you need for now?'

'How can I possibly know? What am I supposed to do if I have an attack?'

'Everything's in your bag,' said Carrie. 'Spinhaler, Migraleve, Piriton, and everything.'

'If there's no choice.' Her face, or the part that was visible, crumpled a little and she turned away to look out of the window, despite it being covered with a drawn curtain.

Neil saw the others out, a small file of uncertain courtiers descending the plastic steps. He was just about to close the door when Carrie said, 'She never has to do these things on her own, you see. When we were filming once at MGM she had nervous exhaustion and collapsed in her trailer. I had to take her to the ER at Cedars-Sinai. She refused to speak to the nurse; it all had to go through me.'

'Why?'

'They get used to it. Having a buffer between them and the world they can't control. And when all your courage is in the front window – on screen, on stage – I don't think you have much out the back. They scare easily.'

'She doesn't look like she scares easily.'

'Out front. You might find her a tricky interview.'

10

When Mr Williams the undertaker and his men arrived in the private ambulance from their yard in Braunstonbury they were not quite sure how best to manage Mrs Porteous. She lay in the awesome stillness of death – they were used to that – but she was dressed as a mythical queen but in the style of the reign of King James I. Her hair was pinned to her head under a sort of cap, the loosened bodice of her extravagant costume was stained dark with dried blood, and her wig, removed by wardrobe, lay like a scraggy kitten sleeping on the make-up counter.

'Like picking up Mary, Queen of Scots from the scaffold at Fotheringhay Castle,' said Mr Williams to Daniel. 'Who's NoK? Have they been informed?'

'I don't know,' said Daniel. It had not occurred to him that there were next of kin.

'We need to put something on the form. Can we put you until we find them?'

'Yes. I'll try to find out.'

There were considerations, too, about preserving evidence, which added another dimension of delicacy to the business of removing her body, and Mr Williams and his man worked with a sort of respectful thoroughness, for which Daniel was especially grateful. Margaret was a sheep of Jesus' flock, as the prayer book put it, and in the benefice of Champton St Mary and Upper and Lower Badsaddle Jesus had entrusted his shepherdly duties to Daniel, and those duties did not end with her death. Respect was due from him in his profession and the undertakers in theirs, for the least we can do for those undone by death is respect their equal dignity.

They moved her as gently as they could onto the lowered wheeled trolley they brought with them on call-outs and made sure she was securely fastened and covered before they raised it. Daniel went with them, like a priest leading a cortège, down the corridor and out of the house by the kitchen entrance, not because Margaret Porteous did not rank highly enough for the front door, but to be unobserved. Jean Shorely was standing at the door to her office and bowed her head in a gesture of ceremony as they passed. The kitchen courtyard was cobbled and the trolley so rattled across it that the men had to slow down to ensure stateliness. Funeral processions so often look rickety, thought Daniel. We want them to be like Viking funerals, black-sailed ships slipping over the horizon as a burst of orange flames engulfs the single honoured passenger, but what you get is hand hearses pushed up a hill to the cemetery, a cortège stuck at roadworks on the bypass and once, when he was vicar of a smart parish in London, a limousine following the coffin having to jam on the brakes when an oblivious pedestrian stepped onto a zebra crossing and all the mourners fell forwards in a black crêpe crumple.

The men loaded Margaret into the windowless back of the private ambulance and drove even more slowly out of the courtyard and up onto the long drive leading to the east gates, which Nathan had quietly gone to open for this purpose at Daniel's suggestion.

Another murder at Champton was notoriety enough, but a murder that involved one of the most celebrated English actresses of her day was a story few editors would be able to resist when word got out, as he knew it soon would.

He walked back through the kitchen wing to the study, where Bernard had put the wireless on. Cosmo had gone to lie on the rug in front of the fire, which was burning more brightly now, and his pale tummy flushed with a flicker of rose. He looked up when Daniel came in but then lowered his head again.

'Nothing on the news,' said Bernard, 'not yet. I don't suppose it will be long.' He switched it off.

'No, and we should brace ourselves. This time will be worse than the last. There will be a feeding frenzy.'

'Because of Her Majesty?'

'Yes.'

'If this death rate continues, Daniel, your celebrity will soon rival hers.'

'I'm not exactly Hollywood.'

'No, you're not,' said Bernard with more emphasis than usual. It was becoming a refrain, and not one Daniel particularly liked.

He said, 'I had better phone the rectory, let Mum know you're coming to supper.'

Neil was sitting next to the uniformed policeman on a small sofa that was more than snug with the two of them side by side, but also offered more in comfort and luxury than police officers are used to. It was not an easy interview. Miss Smith was not only uncomfortable being alone with the two officers, but she struggled to give a plain statement of the facts. When Neil had asked her what her role was in the scene she had said 'ambiguous' and then talked about the way the masquerade both concealed and revealed Anne, in the paradoxical way of such things, which was quite a challenge for an actress, trying to convey simultaneously contradictory things.

'If you could just say where you were and when, that would help,' he said.

She gave him rather a cold look at that. Then she said, 'I think I see what you mean. I make my entrance at one end of the picture gallery as one of the queens, but not with any special ceremony. I'm just one of them – in fact, I'm not, I'm the real queen, but I play

Queen Bel-Anna in the masque, Queen of the Sea, like a female Neptune or whatnot. Of course, it's my name too, or a derivative of it, and so while I'm not the only queen I'm still *primus inter pares* – or is it *prima inter pares*? Mrs what's-her-name, poor woman, was also a queen, but I don't remember which one, and I don't remember her especially – there were so many of us. The scene we shot this morning is actually at the end of the masque, when the more formal parts are over and it becomes a bit of a scrum, if I can put it that way . . .'

'How do you mean?'

'The formality of the dance breaks down and something more basic emerges.'

'What do you mean by "more basic"?'

'Something closer to our baser human instincts – sex and violence, you know . . .'

Neil remembered one of the droller elders in the Moravian Brethren church remarking once that sex was frowned upon in the church lest it encourage dancing.

'. . . and the point of the scene was to show control breaking down, and suddenly the queen, who was pretending to be just another dancer, really was just another dancer, and people laid hands on her and shoved her around and it all got a bit revolutionary for a moment until order was restored.'

'Who restored order?'

'The queen's men.'

'Who are they?'

'Oh, earls and dukes and such like.'

'What was different about them to the men who got frisky in the scrum?'

'Lords-in-waiting? I don't know. I get rescued, though, and bundled out.'

'Take me back to the scrum. Where were you and who do you remember being around you?'

'It was a long shot, for cutaways really.'

'What does that mean?'

'It's shot from a distance, so it is not for detail, but to establish where we are and what's happening. It's like any crowd scene – you show the crowds, then you get in close to the characters.'

'And how precisely were the actors for that shot positioned?'

'Loosely. It's not really choreographed. That section, much more complicated, comes later, and then it's very precise.'

'So do you remember who was where?'

'Not really, no.'

'Could you describe to me exactly what you do remember?'

Miss Smith stiffened again. 'I just did.'

'Talk me through it step by step, please, Miss Smith. You may remember a detail that seems insignificant but isn't.'

'I see. I was called to the set and brought in a buggy by Martin, who's the second AD. That's assistant director – he's the one who looks after me. Us. The actors. Then hair and make-up and wardrobe had a final look. Then there was playback – they play the music we dance to on loudspeakers, and it's all synched up later. Then, when the camera is at speed, the clapper loader marks the shot—'

'Explain?'

'There's a clapperboard – I'm sure you've seen them in films, like a slate with a hinged top? At the beginning of a take they do a clap, which allows them to synch the picture and the sound, and it has the scene and the number of the take on it . . . it used to be chalked on a board but it's all electronic now . . . and the clapper loader says what scene and take it is too, so that's on the soundtrack. It's so they know which shot is which in playback, I suppose.'

'I always wondered what that was for,' said Neil.

'Now you know. Then the director calls action and off we go.'

'Describe exactly where you were and who you were with.'

Gillian Smith had never taken direction well, and as her star had risen and acquired more wattage, she had got worse, which is why she only liked to work with directors she knew and trusted, and why a growing number of them did not like to work with her. She frowned.

'I told you, I was on set, in the picture gallery, at the end nearest the big staircase. Oh, I remember, I was just in front of – well, under – a big portrait of a chap in doublet and hose, big white ruff. And there were extras

– sorry, supporting artists. I can't remember who was who; they all look pretty much alike to me . . . That sounds awful – I just mean, one sees them on set but one doesn't *know* them. I do remember there being a lot of queens. More queens than Hyde Park Corner after Trooping the Colour.' She laughed at her joke, but nobody else got it. 'And I suppose Mrs . . . what is her name?'

'Porteous,' said Neil.

'Mrs Porteous must have been one of them. Who was she supposed to be?'

'Candace, Queen of the Ethiopians.'

'In blackface?'

'I'm sorry?'

'Blacked up? Made up to look like an African?'

'No, ma'am. It was a very liberal interpretation of what a queen of Ethiopia would have looked like.'

'What was she wearing?'

'I don't really know. A tight bodice.'

'We all had tight bodices.'

'And . . . would there be a record of what she was wearing?'

'Yes, of course. Wardrobe would have the design and a Polaroid of her in it.'

Neil put his pen down. 'Go and find Mr Alleyne,' he said to the constable, 'and get him to send the wardrobe lady with the picture of Mrs Porteous in her costume.'

The young constable said, 'Do you want the design as well?'

'Anything she's got. Quick as you can.'

Gillian Smith seemed even more tense when she was left alone with Neil. When Neil caught her eye, she looked away and then pretended to check her diary.

'Somewhere you have to be, Miss Smith?'

'I was rather hoping to be home by now,' she said, 'but my hopes are fading.'

'Where are you staying?'

'At . . . somewhere hall. It's a lovely old house that's a hotel now, about half an hour away.'

'Glassthorpe Hall?'

'Yes, that sounds right.'

'It's the poshest hotel in the county.'

Miss Smith inclined her head to the side. 'That's gratifying to know. In one sense. But it's not the Sunset Marquis.'

Neil wondered why she would want to compare Glassthorpe Hall to a tent but did not pursue it because there was something about Miss Smith that sparked in him an impulse to unintentionally wander off the path of objective enquiry into the thickets of personal curiosity. 'Is this your normal way of life, ma'am? Posh hotels and film locations?'

'Actors are troubadours, Detective Sergeant, not so different from our forebears travelling the roads and lanes in their wagons . . .' – she gestured at her Winnebago with its considerable, gleaming comforts – '. . . looking for a village green on a feast day.'

'I'm not sure your forebears' wagons had Jacuzzis,' said Neil.

'They never work,' she said. 'You can never get anything on the telly either; we just play videos. They're there to make me feel special, and quite right too, but really, we've just made camp in our caravans like gypsies.'

'Where is home, Miss Smith?'

'Los Angeles, mostly. Have you been?'

'I have not.'

'It's like living all the time in the summer holidays.'

'That sounds like the good life.'

'People dream of it. But then you realise holidays, like parties – like life – are only fun because they finish.'

'Very true, madam. But to get back to my questions, where are you from originally?'

'Clapham.'

'A long way from LA.'

'Nobody ever dreamt of living in Clapham. You? I think I hear Lancashire?'

'Very good. Oldham.'

'Nobody ever dreamt of living in Oldham.'

'They did. My ancestors did.'

'Where on earth were they living to dream of Oldham?'

'Germany. It was a freedom-of-religion thing. Moravian Brethren, kicked out of Germany, needed somewhere to go.'

There was something about Detective Sergeant Vanloo that sparked curiosity in Miss Smith also. 'That explains the blond hair and blue eyes,' she said.

'I think we were from Belgium originally, but a long time ago.'

Miss Smith was thinking she rather liked the blond hair and blue eyes and wasn't really interested in where these genetic characteristics had been acquired. 'What a fascinating mixture you are, Detective Sergeant . . .?'

'Vanloo, madam.'

'Oh, yes, that's very Low Countries.' She tucked her legs up on the enormous sofa, a gesture that wordlessly invited Neil to respond by sitting back in his chair, with a consequent alteration in tone. But he did not want to do that.

'Where is Smith from?' he asked.

'Anywhere you like,' she said. 'That's one of the reasons I picked it.'

'Is it not your real name?'

'Not the one I was born with, but the one I go by and have done since I started in this business. And now it's the name everyone knows me by.'

'What is your real name?'

She gave him a steely look but one that was somehow sort of playful. 'Detective Sergeant Vanloo, what a question to ask!'

'I could look it up.'

That was not so playful, she thought. 'Butters,' she said. 'And it's not Gillian. It's Iris.'

'Perfectly good name,' said Neil.

'Starring Iris Butters?' she said.

Neil shrugged.

'So I changed it to Gillian Smith. Gillian because I had a friend I *adored* at school called Gillian, and Smith because it was nondescript, and my agent at the time thought that when you said the two together it sounded like a drum roll and people would remember it.'

'Is there anyone you're still Iris Butters to?'

'No, I changed it legally, by deed poll in the end. Easier.'

'I meant family, friends?'

She looked a bit put out. 'No. There isn't an Iris any more.' She picked up her diary again. 'When do you think we will be finished?'

Back at the house, Daniel knocked on the door to Jean Shorely's office.

'Yes?' she said, not looking up when he opened the door until she had finished writing on what looked like an invoice. 'It's you, rector.'

'Mrs Shorely . . .' She was Jean at the WI or at church, but at the house she was always Mrs Shorely to respect the formalities laid down between employer and employee. 'I wonder if you can help me?'

'I don't know until you ask me.'

'What do you know about Margaret Porteous?'

'She's dead.'

Daniel said, 'Yes, we know, what I meant is—'

'Not everyone knows, and not everyone knows she came by her death in this way, but that won't be for much longer.'

No, it won't, thought Daniel, especially since Jean Shorely's phone must be red hot from all the use it had been put to once the news started to spread.

'That's why I want to talk to you,' he said. 'Before long, as you say, this will get out and then we will no doubt have the newspapers turning up, and I need to make sure that Margaret's family know what's happened before they read about it or see it on the news, but – I'm embarrassed to tell you this – I realise I don't know anything about them.'

Jean thought for a moment. 'Do you know, neither do I. I don't think there were any family, just her and Dennis, and he wasn't the most sociable of men.'

'She, I suppose, did enough socialising for two,' said Daniel. 'It was only when he died that I really paid him any attention, I'm ashamed to say. And it wasn't a church funeral, even though Margaret was a church-warden. He wouldn't have wanted it, she said, so it was just Margaret and me and half a dozen mourners at the Braunstonbury Crem.'

'I was there,' said Mrs Shorely, 'out of respect for Margaret; I didn't know Dennis at all. He was the type of chap who didn't want attention, no matter how kindly meant. So I don't see why that would cause you shame, rector.'

'Once or twice, I have buried someone, a parishioner, and realised I knew nothing about them. I don't mean I wasn't nosey enough, but if you have the cure of souls, you should have at least noticed them. And I don't think I did notice Dennis Porteous.'

'There wasn't much to notice,' said Mrs Shorely.

'I doubt that, Mrs Shorely,' said Daniel. 'But do you remember any other Porteouses?'

'Not that I ever heard of. They would have been at the funeral, though, surely?'

'There were a few from here and a god-daughter, but I don't recall anything about her. Do you remember when they came to Champton?'

Jean said, 'Years ago. Twenty years ago?'

'What about family? No children or stepchildren, no nieces or nephews?'

'Not that I know of. But I do remember her talking about the god-daughter.'

'Did you meet her?'

'I shook her hand after the funeral, but that was all. Margaret mentioned her a few times, especially after Dennis died. Too many times.'

'How do you mean, "too many times"?'

'She said it too much and too often. As if she really wanted you to know she had people in her life.'

Daniel felt a smart of guilt at Margaret's unrelieved loneliness, and the funeral he had taken for her husband without knowing anything about him.

'But, rector,' said Mrs Shorely, 'you gave the tribute. Margaret must have told you something about Dennis for you to write it.'

'I don't remember anything about it at all, Mrs Shorely.'

'You'll have it still, though?'

'Yes.' Daniel kept all his funeral tributes, handwritten in his curacy and then typed, in specially marked folders in the ugly filing cabinet in his study.

'Why don't you fetch it out?'

'Thank you, Mrs Shorely.'

Miss Smith's trailer was now busier, with the constable, Dick Alleyne, Angela from wardrobe and Carrie all looking at a pile of documents and photographs spread out on the coffee table. They seemed to think this was pretext enough, thought Neil, to gatecrash the interview. 'Thank you for these,' he said, 'but there's no need for you to be here.' Jasper, Dick's dog, got up from the rug where he had curled up, came over to him and licked his hand. 'Not even you,' said Neil.

'I think,' said Dick, 'it would be helpful if I were here to stir Miss Smith's memory?'

This was the wrong thing to say, for Miss Smith said, 'Thank you, Dick, but I think even at my grand old age I should be better able than you to recall what I was doing this morning.'

'I merely meant,' he said, in a tone that few would get away with, 'that I was better placed to know who was where when you were on set.'

Miss Smith smiled her brightest smile. 'I merely meant,' she said, 'that we should comply with the detective sergeant's instructions. His investigation, Dick; not your shot.'

Angela from wardrobe wordlessly deposited her cache of designs and Polaroids, and the disappointed ambassadors retreated again. Jasper looked behind him at the top of the stairs. 'Bye, Jaz,' said Miss Smith, waggling her hand at him as she waggled it at her underlings.

Neil began to look through the designs.

'So this is what Mrs Porteous was wearing.' He handed Miss Smith an A5 costume design sketch.

'Oh, yes,' said Miss Smith, 'it's based on Inigo Jones's design for the original *Masque of Queens*. He worked here at Champton, did you know?'

'I did, madam,' said Neil, with firm confidence thanks to Daniel having enthused so relentlessly about the masques of the court of James and Anne.

'It's quite something,' said Miss Smith, 'the headdress, the veil – it would have moved beautifully – and the *crown*. Of course it was a crown, she was a queen.' There was a tiny hint of the proprietorial about this, as if Miss Smith were mindful of her character's sole authentic claim to the title. 'One wonders, for of course one always does, how the costume as imagined by the designer eventually looked when worn by the actress.'

'No need to wonder, Miss Smith.' Neil passed her the Polaroid of Mrs Porteous in it. Miss Smith gasped.

'Do you recall seeing Mrs Porteous in the costume?'

After a second Miss Smith blinked and said, 'Not really the ideal model for it.'

Even Neil, who was about as sensitive to the nuances of ladies' fashions as the Wurzels, had noticed the gasp. What was that about? 'Do you recall seeing her, Miss Smith?'

'I mean, rather a stretch getting that bodice round her. And I'm not sure a lady of her years is best served by so generous a décolletage . . .'

'But do you remember seeing her?'

Miss Smith frowned and looked to one side. Neil wondered if she was playacting to conceal from him an unspoken thought or if she was just always like that.

'I don't think so, no. I mean, there were lots of queens, lots of costumes just as extravagant as hers. And when you've seen one . . . and they were all whirling around in a crowd, so . . . I must have seen her, I suppose, but I couldn't swear to it.'

Neil said, 'Can you think of any reason why someone would want to kill Margaret Porteous?'

Miss Smith looked affronted. 'Me? Certainly not! Why would I?'

Neil wondered again where for Miss Smith the line between spontaneity and calculation fell.

'Can you think of any reason why someone would want to kill you?'

The stable clock began to chime. Daniel realised he did not know what hour it was; he thought it might be four, but then it struck five and he had evening prayer at six. It did not occur to him that under the circumstances evening prayer should be cancelled. He had no difficulty in seeing that the making of filmed entertainment must stop to suit a police investigation's demands, but the offering of prayer and worship to God was not subject to those demands, so he walked round the stables, rather than go in, and walked down the path that led through the park to the rectory. The trees were beginning to look tired of their burden of leaves, which were starting to curl at the edges and change colour. Why red and orange and yellow? he thought. Why go out in a blaze rather than fade? He wondered if a leaf was like Violetta in the last act of *La traviata*, giving a last extravagant burst of song before expiring. He had seen people in real life die like that too, a soar before a final dive, the body making one last effort with all its resources to keep inertia at bay.

There was a plume of smoke rising from the drawing-room chimney, a fire lit by his mother, who would normally think it immoral to heat one's house before the first hint of frost, and heaping on knitwear rather than fuel the proper remedy for hypothermia. But Bernard was coming to supper, and while Audrey was not likely to wear her jewels for a scratch supper on a weekday, she would not wish to impose discomforts on so grand a guest. Miss March – also invited, his mother had told him in the telegram English she used on the phone – would not get that consideration. This pained Daniel, who shared the presumption of Abraham that any guest should be afforded the honour due to God himself: the traveller on the threshold, or the simple shepherd, or possibly the proprietor of a high-class ladies' dress shop. It bothered his mother not at all, who had no less an instinctive sense of who was entitled to what, based on comforting prejudice, class bias and the status quo.

He let himself in through the kitchen door and Hilda waddled to greet him, her tail wagging but without the propeller blur of Cosmo . . . Cosmo! He had quite forgotten that he had left him with Bernard in his study. He felt like a new mother who gets home and realises she has left her baby outside Pricerite. 'Bugger!' he said.

Audrey looked up from the kitchen table, where she was peeling potatoes into a large aluminium pan. 'I beg your pardon?'

'I left Cosmo at the big house. With Bernard.'

'Then I'm sure he'll be fine.' She paused, then said, 'Actually, Dan, I'm not sure he'll be fine. I'm beginning to feel it's not only Bernard who would like that dog adopted.' Cosmo abandoning the rectory for Champton House was not something Audrey would mind overmuch. Her fondness for dogs in general did not equal Daniel's, nor her fondness for his dogs in particular, though she did feel a certain solidarity with Hilda in her matronly estate. 'But I'm sure Bernard will bring him with him.'

Daniel felt a stab of guilt again. 'I've never done that before.'

'One of your parishioners has just been murdered,'

said Audrey. 'I know that's hardly a unique occurrence, but you might be forgiven a momentary lapse of attention. I did it with you.' A potato divided perfectly in half by one stroke of the peeling knife against Audrey's thumb plopped into the saucepan. 'I left you at the station once when I was meeting your father from the London train. Didn't remember until we got home and he asked where you were. We raced back and discovered you fast asleep in your pram, your face covered in smuts.'

'Should I call?'

'I don't think even Bernard will fail to notice that he has a miniature dachshund trailing him around. Miss March on the other hand, I think, feels rather neglected since the circus came to town.'

Daniel stepped round Hilda, who had waddled back to her bed by the Aga, and put the kettle on the boiling plate. 'I can't think of anything Miss March would be less likely to do than appear in a film.'

'I'll need you to move that kettle in a minute. But I don't know about Miss March, she seems suddenly very interested in it. Asking lots of questions, not just about Margaret Porteous – though she does, of course – but about what it's like being an extra . . . supporting artist, I mean.'

'Really?'

'Yes, I wonder if there's a tiny part of her that wants to be a film star.'

'She wouldn't be the only parishioner of mine

queuing up to put on the slap who only a week or two ago was denouncing the whole thing as vanity.'

Audrey ignored this and said, 'But then she does look like a character from a film already, don't you think? Someone from the Fifties with a crush on the curate.'

Yes, thought Daniel, you're right, a woman of banked-down passions and high respectability.

'And always the same,' said Audrey. 'Same palette, same good taste, gloves, shoes, the lot.'

'Not always the same,' said Daniel. 'I called round to the flat once to see her about an ad in the parish magazine and she answered the door in pink fluffy slippers. She went as pink as them when she saw it was me.'

'Perhaps that's Kimberley struggling to get out.'

'For goodness' sake, don't call her that.' Miss March's Christian name, a moment of madness on the part of her late father, was a closely kept secret. 'Do you want a cup of tea?'

'No, I've got a fish pie and a mincemeat tart to make. Have you got time before church?'

'A quick one.' Daniel took a mug and a tea bag, which Audrey looked at with distaste, and stirred the infusion he made until it reached the teakish colour he liked. He went to his study, sat at his desk, and looked up the readings for the day in his lectionary. These were the dullest weeks in the Church of England's year, the long stretch after Trinity and before Michaelmas, when finally the vestments went from green to lustrous white and the readings got exciting.

There was nothing particularly exciting for evening prayer today, just that awkward passage in Mark when Jesus kills a fig tree and the congregation always looks puzzled. What he really wanted to look up was in the filing cabinet. He found the folder where he kept his funeral tributes and silently congratulated himself on the method of his filing when he found Dennis Porteous exactly where he was meant to be, between Kathleen Poole and Walter Powell – company he would keep only in death, for in life they were not sympatico nor sympatica.

He sat back in his chair with his mug of tea and read. After a minute he lay down the single leaf of paper, typed, double spaced, and felt shame. There was nothing to it – a few details of dates and places, a few comforting words, and this:

> Dennis was a quiet man, not one for the social whirl, nor for seeking attention, and I think I will remember him most readily sitting quietly with the crossword. Once not so quietly, for when I was round at the Laurels seeing Margaret about church business he discovered an answer to one of the questions, which must have been bothering him all day, and he gave, if not a whoop of delight, at least a small sigh of satisfaction. I don't know if Dennis was much of a believer, that's not my point, but I wonder if we might imagine him again giving a small sigh of satisfaction at an answer, finally, to a question until now unanswered?

Daniel cringed. Was this the best he could do? Was this all he had to say? A theology as shallow as his knowledge of the man he was conducting into the mystery of the eternity? When he had been a curate he was sometimes put on crem duty and had to take six funerals a day for people he did not know and with a next of kin, if they had a next of kin, who had nothing to say about them. How often he had wondered out loud if Doris, doing her knitting, ever reflected on the one thread that held the whole pattern together? Once, the organist, tired after the fourth reprise of 'All Things B&B', had sighed with a sort of desolate boredom at the mention of the one thing holding the pattern together. He could forgive himself more readily for funerals of that kind, but Dennis was his parishioner, and Margaret his churchwarden, and they merited his fuller and more careful attention. It was noise and trouble and fun that got the attention, and attention is not a limitless resource. 'Fair shares for all, the second rule of ministry,' his training incumbent had said. 'What's the first?' Daniel had asked. 'Don't fuck the flock.'

But there was a god-daughter, and there was a name – Heather – and she lived at Northeye.

11

It was highly unusual for an invitation to be issued from the number-one trailer to any other trailer when Gillian Smith was on location, so it was with surprise that Theo answered the knock on his door to find Carrie standing there.

'Hello,' she said, 'are you by any chance free for a cup of tea?'

'With you?'

'With Miss Smith.'

'Me? She's barcly said hello to me. In fact, she hasn't even said hello.'

Carrie pursed her lips, then said, 'I could say she's terribly shy, but what's the point?'

'What does she want?'

'To exchange notes.'

'I haven't had a scene with her yet.'

'Not those kinds of notes. Can you come?'

'Of course I can come,' he said, 'give me a second.'

He half closed the door and pulled on a pair of

tracksuit bottoms and a dark V-necked jumper over his T-shirt. He stepped into a pair of mules Audrey had bought him for Christmas from Clarks in Stow, and which he had never worn till now, then paused before deciding to drape a dark-blue flowery silk scarf round his neck, loosely in a loop, which he had bought in Florence.

Carrie was waiting at the bottom of the steps.

'I'm barely dressed,' he said. 'I look like a prisoner.'

'We're all prisoners,' said Carrie, 'at least until the police tell us we can go.' They set off, turning right down the path to the gloriously isolated trailer rather than left towards the stables. 'Have you had your interview yet?'

'Yes, sort of,' said Theo. 'A preliminary one. It's a bit difficult, because I . . . oh, I'm not supposed to say. It's a secret!'

'A secret is just something you tell people one at a time,' said Carrie, 'and I think I know anyway. I was talking to Sandy in wardrobe.'

'He told you about the dagger?'

'He told everyone about the dagger.'

'So now everyone thinks it was me?' said Theo.

'I don't think they do. But it sounds like the murder weapon.'

'It wasn't me.'

'Of course it wasn't you. But let's not have this conversation without Gilly.'

They had arrived at her door. Theo found he was

suddenly nervous and took a breath. Carrie went ahead and announced him like a butler at a ball. 'Theo Clement!'

'Come in, come in,' came the voice from behind the door. He came in, and there on the sofa, arranged in something more completely pant suit than tracksuit, was Gillian Smith.

'Miss Smith,' he said, and almost bowed as he would if they were in character.

'Theo, darling! It's Gilly, please. I'm about to have a gin and tonic. You?'

'Yes, please,' he said.

'Or a martini? Carrie makes a very special martini.'

'That sounds very nice.'

'Carrie?'

She was already in the kitchen.

'Now, Theo, come and sit next to me. It's been an *age* since Stratford!'

Twenty years, in fact, since she was Cleopatra, and he the Messenger, when he spoke his first professional line on that most famous stage, 'News, my good lord, from Rome.'

She spoke even less to him then – not a word, in fact – but from her attitude now you might think him the friend of her heart.

As they slurped their cocktails, Gillian went through a list of people they had both worked with, so comprehensive that Theo did not remember some of them, and although he realised that she was pretending to pluck the names from memory – Carrie had made the list – he was still flattered by the mood of intimacy. Then came the reason for the invitation.

'So unfortunate about poor Mrs . . .'

'Porteous,' said Theo.

'. . . Porteous. I'm sure you must be all the more devastated, seeing as you knew her. Your brother's churchwarden, I hear. Are you coping?'

'I hardly knew her,' said Theo, 'but it is very shocking. And especially for me, because the police think I may have provided the murderer with the weapon.'

'Goodness! What was it?'

'Yes, the dagger that came with the costume. It was missing from the scabbard after we stopped shooting and it still hasn't been found, as far as I know.'

'Are they sure?'

'I don't think so – I suppose the pathology report will tell us more – but if a dagger goes missing around the time someone gets stabbed, what are you supposed to think?'

Gillian nodded. 'Well, quite. And you don't remember anyone knocking into you?'

'Everyone did; it was meant to be a melee. But no one stands out. Apart from you.'

'Me? It wasn't me who pinched the dagger, darling . . .'

'No, of course not, I just remember you in the throng because . . . it was you.'

'You could tell it was me even in disguise?'

'Yes.'

'How?'

Theo was about to say 'because there was such a fuss made over you when you came on set', but he thought better of it and said instead, 'The bearing, Gilly, the bearing.'

Miss Smith shifted in her seat to lean into Theo confidentially. 'There's a question I want to ask, but it makes me feel uncomfortable.'

'Not on my account, I hope?'

She appeared to make up her mind. 'Darling, do you think it might not have been Margaret who was the intended victim?'

'The thought had crossed my mind. Like I said, I didn't know her well, but it's very difficult to think of her arousing murderous rage in someone. My brother said the same thing, and he has an unusually good nose for such things.'

'Your famous brother. The sleuth.'

'He hates being called that.'

'Then I shan't call him that.'

'You haven't met?'

'Not yet, but of course I'm *dying* to meet him. What did he say?'

'He thinks Margaret was maybe not the person the murderer wanted to kill.'

'Then who?'

'You.'

Miss Smith gave a gasp of shock, nicely delivered,

thought Theo, almost masking the pleasure in being promoted to leading lady in this story.

'The thought must have occurred to you,' he added.

'You'd think so,' she said, 'but something that awful? It's too much to contemplate.'

'Too awful,' said Theo. 'But, Gilly, why you?'

'There are . . . people . . .' she said, 'who form a jealous attachment to one. You know how it is?'

Theo had once had some correspondence from a fan of *Appletree End*, which revealed an intense devotion to his character, PC Henry Heseltine. The writer, a lady called Yvonne from Cwmbran, took to standing outside the studios to ask him for his autograph, sometimes for hours, and Theo, being an obliging person, obliged. The correspondence took an unsettling turn when she started mentioning that she had seen him in his local in Islington, a long way from Cwmbran, and then he found her outside his house. To deflect this unsolicited interest, he pretended he was gay, enlisting the help of Alex de Floures to masquerade as his boyfriend, so that she might finally abandon her conviction that destiny had chosen him for her and her for him, but it only made her conviction stronger. He found that he was thinking about her every day, which was a version, he supposed, of what she wanted, only it wasn't with affection. He started to feel very uneasy about it, and his agent and his brother suggested he notify the police, but he did not want to do that, or not at first. Then, one day, he realised it had stopped. No more

Yvonne outside the studios, no more Yvonne at his bus stop on Upper Street, and no more correspondence. Years later, he saw her picture in the newspaper and discovered that she had been bound over after pestering a different policeman in a different soap. His relief was slightly tempered by wondering what that policeman had that he did not, but it had not been a pleasant experience and he did not want to repeat it. If that was an unpleasant predicament for him, then how much more for Miss Smith, a film star for more than twenty years, and admired and adored by numberless fans? 'I do,' he said, 'but I expect you've had more than most.'

'You bet I have,' she said, 'but it's all dealt with by my agent and studios and people, and if someone should, sadly, feel poorly treated, they don't get anywhere near one. They do try to frighten one. I had one devotee send me a bullet through the post.'

'That would frighten me.'

'The police caught him. He was an inadequate, I'm afraid, not a real threat at all, but one doesn't *know* that. And of course, John Lennon . . .'

'*Nothing to kill or die for . . .*' said Theo, then he realised she wasn't thinking of 'Imagine' but of his murder. 'Awful, poor man.'

'And if they wanted to do me harm, that's how you would do it, no? Bang-bang, goodbye, Gilly, rather than going after me with a dagger on set?'

'I suppose so. But we don't know for certain if it was a dagger.'

'We must find out. You know, now I've met you, I really would love to meet your brother.'

Theo knew there would be a reason for his unexpected invitation, and here it was. 'I'm sure I can sort that out. But when?'

'I'd invite you both to dinner normally, but I can't now we're effectively locked down.'

'Why don't you come to ours for dinner? To his, I mean. The rectory's on the estate, so we wouldn't need to break out.'

'That would be lovely. What time?'

'You mean tonight?'

'Would it be too much of an imposition? We're stuck here, after all. And you wouldn't need to kill the fatted calf, I'm a cheap date.'

Theo thought that betrayed perhaps a lapse in self-awareness, but what a coup it would be for Audrey to have a film star to supper. 'I'm sure my mother would be delighted. I'll call to let her know.'

'You can call from production,' said Carrie. 'And I've booked a car for seven-fifteen.'

'Have another drink, Theo. Carrie?'

Daniel sat in his stall in the chancel at St Mary's. The south doors were open to admit worshippers, but worshippers there were none – an unsatisfactory situation in one sense, but in another he quite liked being left alone to say his prayers, and the community's prayers, without the inconvenience of people not knowing when to stand and sit, or their place in the prayer book. There was one congregant, Hilda, who had come with him, for she liked to sniff around the building, which was always lively with the scents of visitors, human and animal. After her circuit, she would come and lie down on a kneeler next to his and follow the long-hallowed Church of England tradition of responding to the call to worship by falling asleep.

That evening she was already snoring next to him twenty minutes before he rang the bell. Evening prayer, like morning prayer, was preceded by silence in which to calm the clamours of the day and raise up those things most necessary to hold before God. The day could not have been more clamorous, and his burden was heavy. He found his way through to the peculiar frequency of God by tuning out the competing frequencies. It was like listening to music through tinnitus, which a life-time of liturgical singing had brought to him relatively early. He called to mind Margaret and held her and the outrage of her death; and he held Dennis, remembering them as best and as generously as he could.

Just before he went to ring the bell, fruitlessly to summon the faithful, he heard the door creak. He got up from his stall, gave his knees a minute or two to adjust, then went down the aisle. Sitting at the back, almost camouflaged in her greys in a shadowy corner, was Miss March. She did not look up. He pulled on the bell rope that hung in the choir vestry and, with the delay that always made him think of a yo-yo on its counterintuitive travel, the bell sounded from the tower above. Nobody came but everyone heard it, even if they did not hear it consciously; and if he didn't ring it there would be complaints, another Church of England tradition of people getting indignant about what is done in the church they don't go to.

He went back to the chancel and into his vestry, where he put on a cotta, which his mother said looked like a starched negligee, and a stole round his neck in the worn green of the long season of nothing much happening. In his stall he took his prayer book, opened it, and said, 'Dearly beloved brethren . . .' which to contemporary ears would sound inaccurate aimed at a congregation of Miss March and Hilda, but that was how it was done. He and Miss March confessed their sins in the slightly perfunctory way the prayer book allowed, and he read the psalms and the Old Testament reading, and they said the Magnificat together, and then he read the portion from the New Testament, with its troubling image of Jesus turning a tree from fruitfulness to waste.

'And on the morrow, when they were come from Bethany, he was hungry. And seeing a fig tree afar off having leaves, he came, if haply he might find anything thereon: and when he came to it, he found nothing but leaves; for the time of figs was not yet . . .'

Daniel thought of the fig in his own garden, which grew against the wall and had put forth hard little figs for ornament rather than degustation.

'. . . And Jesus answered and said unto it, No man eat fruit of thee hereafter for ever . . .'

And then, in a way typical of Mark, his favourite gospel, the story of Jesus overturning the tables of the moneychangers in the Temple followed, another disruptive image, but people liked it because nobody likes moneylenders. That was the word most readers and congregations heard rather than moneychangers, which meant something different, and perhaps that revealed something about an anti-Semitic feeling people harboured without acknowledging it . . .

'. . . And when even was come, he went out of the city. And in the morning, as they passed by, they saw the fig tree dried up from the roots.'

And then he prayed, the prayers of the church for the queen and her ministers, and then the prayers of this community, for Margaret and the repose of her soul, for the memory of Dennis who had gone before her, for calm for troubled souls, for justice for the wronged, and for light in darkness and a quiet night.

After the blessing, for which Miss March bowed her head, making Daniel think of a heron, he processed out to the south doors to catch her, although 'processed' seemed too ceremonial a word, for it was only him and Hilda who followed.

He stood at the porch to say goodbye to his congregation of one.

'Miss March. I was sorry to hear of your experience this morning.'

'Thank you, rector. It was dreadful.'

'And I know not the first time you have witnessed a violent and untimely death.'

No. My father . . .'

'I remember you telling me. Often an event like this can evoke very difficult memories, and of course you know where I am if you need to talk, or just some company.'

'Your mother has been a stalwart friend, actually. Do we know any more about . . . I'm sorry, how rude of me to ask. And insensitive.'

'I don't think we know very much at all. But the investigation has begun. You must feel very distant from it in the flat.'

'I don't mind being on my own. But I dine with you tonight.'

'I know. I'm very pleased to hear it.'

She made to go, then turned. 'May I ask you a question?'

'Of course.'

'The New Testament reading. I don't think I have noticed it before.'

'The overturning of the tables in the Temple?'

'No, the fig tree.'

'What did you notice?'

'That Jesus kills something that could produce fruit. I'm no hippy, God forbid, but it seems so destructive.'

'It's one of the difficult sayings,' said Daniel.

'But what does it mean?'

'What do you think it means?'

Miss March blinked. 'I don't know. Can't you tell me?'

'Can't you tell me?'

Miss March thought for a moment. 'Is it Jesus showing his power to judge and punish?'

'Some have said so.'

'But I thought he came to save the world, not condemn it.'

'I suppose you could say he is not condemning it; it condemns itself. There are other interpretations.'

'Like what?'

'The fig tree is a symbol of Israel, God's people. And if God's people do not recognise that God is with us in Jesus Christ – like the moneychangers in the Temple – then their harvest will not be of fruitfulness but of waste.'

'I see,' said Miss March. 'Withered fruits.'

'And what do we do when a fig is fruitless?'

'Prune it, rector. Prune it hard.'

There was something in Miss March's voice that reminded him of his mother.

'I really don't want to sound disloyal,' said Miss Smith. 'I may have many flaws, but disloyalty is really not one of them. Having said that, Dick can be awfully stubborn. I love working with him, of course, and I adore him, but there are times when I have to put my foot down . . .' – Miss Smith was on her third gin and tonic

– '. . . and I'm not scared of putting my foot down. I haven't done thirty years in the business without learning how to squish when squishing is called for. No one has your best interests more at heart than you do. Isn't that right, Carrie?'

'It certainly is,' said Carrie.

'But I'm sure you know all this, Theo, you're not far behind me. Well, in age . . .' There was a knock at the door. 'Carrie . . .' She flapped her hands in the way she did when she couldn't be bothered to think of words.

It was Dick Alleyne. 'Sorry to bother you again, Gilly,' he said.

'Oh, what is it? Not more police? I told the Detective Sergeant everything I know. I was quite hoarse by the end of it.'

'No, I just wanted to check to see if you are OK. And that you have everything you need.'

'I wouldn't mind the restoration of my civil liberties, but that might be a big ask.'

'Quite so, can't do anything about that. But they're working through the interviews. Can't last forever. They have to go home too, some time.'

'I don't think we need anything else,' said Carrie.

'But I'm glad I caught you here, Theo.'

'Me?' said Theo.

'Yes, first to say I love what you're doing, thank you so much for your excellent work . . .' – always praise, always praise – '. . . second, can you talk me through what happened with the dagger?'

'I actually have a dinner to get to.'

'It won't take a minute.'

'You go on,' said Miss Smith, as if her assent were required. 'The driver's on standby. He'll wait until we send for him.'

'It's not for three-quarters of an hour anyway,' said Carrie. 'Do you want a drink, Dick?'

'I've got Jasper with me.'

'But do you want a drink?'

'Are you making martinis?'

'I am.'

'Then as dry as you dare.' He sat down on an armchair opposite Theo and Gilly, who were not exactly canoodling on the sofa; more like a queen indulging her favourite. How life imitates art! Jasper sauntered over to Miss Smith, she made a little fuss over him, and then he lay down again in the same place on her rug.

'So what happened?' said Dick.

Theo, with the flat tone of a man telling a story he's told enough times, and no matter how fascinating to his audience it has palled for him, said, 'I came off set after we were told to go and went straight to my trailer.'

'Not straight away, I think. You saw your brother?' said Dick.

'Oh, yes, only in passing.'

'And you told him what had happened?'

'I didn't know what had happened.'

'So what did you tell him?' This was said not with menace but with a firmness that made Theo feel uneasy.

'I told him Margaret had had an accident or a stroke or something. I can't really remember.'

'Why did you tell him?'

'Because it happened.'

'But why did you go out of your way to tell him?'

'He's the rector of the parish, Dick. Mrs Porteous is – was – one of his ladies.'

'It just looks a bit . . . I don't know, crafty?'

'Not crafty at all. Of course I was going to tell him if I saw him.'

'OK,' said Dick, holding up a hand, as if it were Theo who was coming on too strong. 'Now, tell me about the dagger.'

'Sandy came to my trailer and he got me out of my costume and that's when he noticed that the dagger was not in the scabbard.'

'And you didn't notice?'

'Not till then, no.'

'Why not?'

'Why would I?'

'I would have thought you would notice if someone took a deadly weapon from you.'

'Oh, Dick,' said Miss Smith, 'you don't notice these things after a day or two. I've gone home in a wig before, just forgot I had it on.'

'But this was a dagger. When were you last aware you had it?'

'I've told all this to the police.'

'Yes, but I need to know,' said Dick.

Need to know? thought Theo.

'I suppose when I put it on. Yes, I remember, Angela was coming to check me, and I remember making sure I had it. No, not just when I put it on. Later on set too, there was another check between takes. But I didn't notice it had gone until Sandy said.'

'Could you have dropped it?'

'I don't think so. Maybe? But it was snug as scabbards go.'

'So how did you lose it?'

'I can only think that someone took it towards the end of the dance when everyone was bumping into each other. It must have been then. I'm sure I would have noticed if someone just came up to me and helped himself.'

'Why do you need to know, darling?' said Miss Smith.

Dick looked rueful and said, 'West Coast.'

'What's West Coast?' said Theo.

'Doesn't matter,' said Dick tetchily. 'But, Theo, as I say to all my actors, my door is always open. If there's any problem, bring it to me. I like to know what's happening on my shoot. Is that unreasonable?'

'Not unreasonable,' said Theo, 'and I don't mean to be awkward, but the police rather jealously guard the information they turn up in an inquiry. It wouldn't do for a suspect to know what they know, you see.'

Dick looked at him darkly. 'I bow to the bobby off *Appletree End*, but apparently it doesn't work both ways.

The cops don't know about filmmaking. I've offered to help but they just go silent.'

'Procedure,' said Carrie. 'In court they need to show they followed procedure.'

'And it *is* a murder inquiry,' said Theo. 'That comes before anything else, surely?'

Dick and Gilly looked at him blankly.

Then Dick said, 'If you think of anything, let me know, Theo. Captain of the ship and all that? Anyway, I must go and see if we can save anything from the schedule. Goodnight.' He nodded to Theo. Jasper, who had only just got comfortable, grizzled at having to get up and go out again. 'Gilly, Carrie,' said Dick, and he left.

'What was that about?' wailed Theo.

'I wouldn't worry about it, darling,' said Miss Smith. 'He's just under pressure. Makes him grumpy.'

'And vindictive? I don't want to piss him off!'

'It's not you, it's the West Coast. The money. The people in LA who write the cheques. They'll be wanting to protect their investment.'

'I thought this was a British film.'

'It is,' said Carrie, 'but the money has more nationalities than the World Cup.'

'And what do you mean, "protect their investment"?'

'Film star, murder, police inquiry? That could add a chunk to the budget. They'll want a nice, quick, tidy resolution. And . . . well, you can understand their concern if one of the cast should mislay his dagger when another's been stabbed to death.'

Theo blustered, 'But that's the police's concern, not Dick's or the money men.'

'Nothing is more important than the movies, Theo.'

At the north lodge the curtains were drawn and a fire lit, but the bonfire smell that pervaded the drawing room came not from the fireplace, but from a massive joint rolled by Brandon Redding. Alex's joints were feeble things, clumsy affairs rolled in a bamboo mat and held together with spit-sodden strips of Rizlas, compared with Brandon's. This looked like a wind instrument, a smaller version of the kind of horn, Alex supposed, that Joshua fit de Battle of Jericho with. Its effects were almost as marked. He and Nathan and Brandon had been smoking a new kind of weed with a pretty name, like Cinderella, for an hour now and the mood had gone from giggly to mellow to not quite anaesthetised, but attempting the Cresta Run in this condition would be rash indeed.

'What's this weed called?' said Alex.

'Sinsemilla,' said Brandon. 'It means seedless.'

'Like grapes?'

'I don't know. They take the female cannabis plant and separate it from the males before they can fertilise them so they produce seeds, and that means it produces more of the good stuff that we like, putting the waccy in the baccy.'

'At school we used to smoke dried banana skins,' said Alex. 'Someone said it would get you high. I don't think it did. Not like this.'

Not like this, thought Brandon, because the sinse-milla he was trying to sell them was not sinsemilla at all. He had heard about it, and read about it, but could not find any in Stow, so he improvised by adulterating normal weed with a little heroin. It had become one of his most popular lines.

Alex felt a presentiment of anxiety, which usually came about now when he had been smoking weed.

'Coffee,' he said. 'Nathan, be a darling, make some coffee?'

Nathan giggled. 'I can't . . .'

'Please.'

'You'll have to make your own. I'm not going anywhere.'

Alex tried to get up but was immediately giddy and sat down, and then felt sick.

'Are you all right?' said Nathan. 'You don't look all right.'

'I feel sick.'

That's the heroin, thought Brandon, but said, 'It'll pass. It's like your first drink or your first fag.'

'I don't feel well at all.' He got up and just made it to the kitchen, where he threw up in the sink but had to hang on to it, too, because he was so wobbly.

'Alex, are you OK?' shouted Nathan, but then he started giggling again.

Brandon produced a little clear plastic bag, the sort they put notes in at the bank, but this contained what looked like a couple of pinches of mixed herbs. 'Do you want some of this? I've got some deals you can have.'

Nathan said, 'Not today, Brandon, I don't think it agrees with him.'

'What about you?'

'Not today.'

'Is it cool if I Ieave it with you? Theo wanted a bag. He could pick it up.'

'Nah,' said Nathan, who was not daft even when he was stoned. 'Why don't you go round to his trailer?'

'It's a crime scene,' said Brandon, 'there's police everywhere. How am I supposed to run a business?'

Alex called from the kitchen. 'He's staying at the rectory. They won't bother you there.'

'I can't go round and knock on the door. The vicar hates me.'

Alex reappeared looking a little better. 'It's the rectory. Anyone can come to the door.'

'Yeah, if you want the vicar. But I don't want the vicar.'

'Why don't you call first? You could meet him somewhere.'

Brandon thought about this for a minute. 'Yeah, OK. Can I use your phone?'

'Yes.' Alex flopped back in the chair. 'It's a bit early.'

'I could skin up?'

'Oh, go on then,' said Alex. 'I'm feeling much better now.'

Nathan murmured something, but Alex could not tell if it were protest or assent, for he looked half asleep. He decided to close his eyes for a minute.

12

As he and Carrie walked over to the production office there was a moment's awkwardness as Theo mentally composed how he was going to phrase the telephone conversation with his mother about the late, and self-invited, VIP supper guest. It occurred to him that Carrie might be expecting to come along too, and adding two late supper guests might stretch Audrey's tolerance more than he would like to.

'Um, Carrie . . .'

'Yes?'

'About supper.'

'I'll tell you what you need to know.'

'What do I need to know?'

'Normally I'd give you the information sheet, but we've left it a bit late.'

'The information sheet?'

'Yes, when she's invited out anywhere, I fax the information sheet first just so people know what's expected. I suppose I could get it faxed from the West Coast.'

'Fax? They don't have a remote for the telly. And if they did, I'd like to see Mum's face if a guest sent a list of requirements. What requirements?'

'It's a list of dos and don'ts — mostly don'ts — for hosts and hostesses when Miss Smith is attending a dinner, or lunch, or the opening of a suspension bridge, or anything.'

Theo laughed. 'You're pulling my leg.'

'No.'

'Like what?'

'Seating, other guests, menu, the finer points of pescatarianism . . . My favourite section is temperature.'

'Temperature?' said Theo.

'She likes to eat outside. If it starts getting chilly then sweaters will be worn, but if it gets below twenty degrees you will go inside. It's more for LA than Champton St Mary, but you get my drift.'

'I've never heard of anything like it!'

'Welcome to Hollywood. You're having Gillian Smith to supper, there are protocols.'

Theo began to feel a faint foretaste of panic, which intensified when Carrie knocked on the door of Dick Alleyne's office. Theo would never have done this — 'My door is always open,' said Dick, but whenever anyone said this, it meant you would not get past their secretary in Theo's experience. If Dick was in a bad mood, and more than usually disinclined to oblige, then Theo had good grounds for extra wariness — not just because of his careless custodianship of the dagger, but because his adoption as a favourite by Miss Smith caused a disruption of the hierarchy that was necessary for the director to do his job. Dick did not really want to be accessible in this way to actors 'below the line', whose names appear after the film title at the beginning rather than before it.

Theo – who was tricky anyway because he had been in a soap, and Dick did not approve of soaps, nor subscribe to the view that appearing in them conferred on actors a distinction he should respect – was about to ask to use his phone while he was taking calls from 'the West Coast', now that the time differences permitted. He wanted to give them good news about the production schedule, but that could not be settled because nothing could be settled until the police allowed them back on set with cameras rolling.

This was why Carrie was there. She brought with her the authority of Gillian Smith, which meant that what Theo asked for was what Gilly wanted. Dick understood, of course, and with a rigid smile and a steady look, he conceded the instrument.

'Champton St Mary Rectory?'

'Mum.'

'Champton St Mary Rectory?'

'Mum, it's me. Theo.'

'Hello, darling. Where are you?'

'I'm still up at the big house – major drama as you know . . .'

'Poor Margaret, I can't believe it!'

'No, me neither, but I'm calling to say I'll be with you for supper.'

'Oh, good. We've got Bernard too and Miss March. I've augmented a fish pie with prawns from the freezer – don't tell.'

'And I wonder if I might bring someone?'

'Two of you? Oh, Theo, we're already stretched . . .'

Theo knew two things. First, his mother liked nothing more than rising to meet a challenge. Second, a film star at the table trumped even a peer.

'You can do miracles with fish pies . . .' he said.

'I'm not bloody Jesus, darling.'

'And . . .' – this was tricky because he wanted a big reveal for dramatic reasons, but it would not do to look star-struck in front of Dick and Carrie – '. . . and . . .' He lowered his voice. 'It's Gillian Smith.'

'What about Gillian Smith?'

'She's my guest.'

There was silence at the end of the phone, and then Audrey said, 'You're bringing Gillian Smith to supper?'

'Yes. If we can squeeze her in?'

'Of course we can squeeze her in.'

'Mum, there are . . . rules.'

'Rules?'

'More, expectations. When she accepts an invitation to come to dinner she likes things to be a certain way – menu, heating, who goes where . . .'

There was a pause. 'There are indeed rules, Theo,' said Audrey. 'But they are my rules.'

'Just don't be . . . difficult?'

'Perhaps you would like to inform Miss Smith that we would be delighted to welcome her to supper, but to be aware that it's a plain affair, fish pie and a mince-meat tart. Oh, blast, is she a vegetarian?'

'She eats fish. Not meat.'

'Heavens, the mincemeat tart! Can she eat that? A sliver of mincemeat tart with, I don't know, ice cream or something?'

'That's fine. She probably won't eat anything anyway; she doesn't really eat food.'

'It's like having the queen to supper.'

'It *is* having the queen to supper.'

'When? What time?'

'About half past seven OK?'

'I suppose it will have to be. What does she drink?'

'Anything. Everything. Gin and tonic.'

'Oh, blast, it's nearly quarter past! Lemons! Have you got lemons?'

'I can get lemons.'

'Make sure you do.'

Theo heard, tinnily in the background, the doorbell ring and the sound of dachshunds barking and claws clattering across quarry tiles.

'That'll be Miss March. What shall I tell her?'

'Tell her Gillian's coming.'

'God almighty!'

Audrey put the phone down.

Carrie said, 'All sorted, Theo?'

'All sorted. But we need to take some lemons.'

'Got lemons,' she said. 'She's fussy about gin, though. And tonic. Got to be Plymouth. And slimline. Have you got any?'

'Slimline, yes, but I think we just have Gordon's. What is Plymouth gin?'

'Literally gin from Plymouth. I can't tell the difference, but she says she can. She acquired a taste for it when she was in rep there, or so she says. Maybe it's just to be difficult.'

'Have you got any?'

'Cases. I have a bottle for you to take.'

'Ah, that sort of answers a question.'

Carrie raised an eyebrow. 'Were you worried about inviting me?'

'Honestly? Yes. I don't want to seem rude.'

'We're way past rude when it comes to Miss Smith.'

'But what will you do?'

'Wait in the trailer and maybe eat a banana and half a tub of hummus.'

'Not exactly a feast.'

'It's a feast of my own uninterrupted company. Delicious.'

Daniel did some tidying up before locking the church after evening prayer, and when he got back to the rectory Miss March had preceded him and was now assisting his mother, a reversal of the normal polarity of their joint labours, which he thought his mother might enjoy. Miss March was in a pinny and Audrey was in her element, with a purpose and a velocity to her movement, from pantry to Aga to kitchen table, which made him think of a brilliant general on manoeuvres.

'Be useful, darling,' she ordered, 'lay the dining-room table.'

'How many are we?'

'Six.'

'What are we having?'

'Fish pie, mincemeat tart. Not fancy. Do you think you could lay the fire?'

'It's laid. Do you want it lit?'

'And the drawing room.'

'Not fancy, you say . . .'

She did not have time to counter this so said nothing and got on with her pastry and her capers and her parsley.

When Daniel was finished, he stepped back to look at the table, the glasses already beginning to shine as the fire rose in the grate. He liked it when people came to dine or to lunch; it felt entirely fitting for a priest, doling out not only spiritual nourishment, but the material kind too. And he was also quietly pleased that he had in his time at Champton St Mary lengthened the list of those invited. His mother would instinctively edit it, so shopkeepers and peers of the realm should not have to sit together elbow to elbow. Her motive for this was, as far as she was aware, to save both from embarrassment, but it was also because what to Daniel seemed like barefaced snobbery was to Audrey just a given. She had been born into a world of fixed order and saw it violently disrupted when the Second World War came. She had served as a nurse in the Blitz, when ambulances arriving from Belgravia and Bermondsey decanted their indiscriminately pulped passengers into her teenaged care. Daniel had preached a sermon once about the end of the First World War, when men returned from the Western Front having seen aristocrats and ploughboys alike turned inside out and could not thereafter sustain the necessary belief in the status quo for the old England to be quietly restored. Audrey thought differently. After the Blitz, when she had returned to Braunstonbury and embarked on married life, and children, she was all the more eager for the old order to be restored so she would not have to think about it, just know instinctively that shopkeepers and peers dined separately. In reality, her own life was evidence to the contrary; she now worked for the shopkeeper, and the peer had surrendered his house to the circus, but that need not affect how she actually felt.

'Mum' – he put his head round the door – 'table's laid, fires are lit. Can you manage? I just need a minute at my desk before everyone arrives.'

'Of course I can. Of course I can. I have the estimable Miss March.'

The estimable Miss March was no cook, however, and Audrey Clement was no teacher, but a pair of hands, now divested of their grey leather gloves, was a pair of hands. She now wore a novelty pinny sufficient to prevent the spoliation of a carefully chosen grey wool suit – not a day suit, but an evening suit; a distinction lost on most, but not on Miss March.

Audrey set to making another mincemeat tart to replace the insufficiently decent one she had already prepared.

'The key to pastry, Miss March, is speed, speed, speed,' she said, and so brisk had she been, it was as if the lightest layer of snow had fallen across the kitchen table. Rolling out had been tricky, for it had not had time to chill and rest, but Audrey was not going to be beaten by a reluctant paste, and the flouring of the rolling pin and the flouring of the board was deftly done to keep things moving.

The tin was lined, and Miss March was spooning mincemeat out of a large jar that Audrey had made well in anticipation of Christmas, but she had fetched it from the pantry, for an unexpected feast had arrived early.

'Palette knife, Miss March, smooth it with a palette knife!' said Audrey, gesturing towards the earthenware jar next to the Aga, in which she kept her spoons and spatulas and such like.

Miss March was not sure what a palette knife was, but she guessed correctly and was soon getting the filling as neat and level as Audrey required. What pleasant work, she thought, and how well we do it when the chief and subordinate roles are reversed.

Audrey, meanwhile, was wielding a lattice cutter and then, 'Quick, quick, quick!' she said, and rather hoofed Miss March out of the way to brush the edge of the pastry with milk and then lay what looked like a very pretty pastry string vest over the tart. 'Phew!' she said. 'That's the tricky part! But it's not a *complete* disgrace, is it?'

'It looks lovely,' said Miss March. 'What can I do now?'

'Entertain the guests when they arrive, which will be any minute.'

'Guests?' said Miss March nervously.

'No one you don't know, or nearly no one. Dan and Theo, and a friend of Theo's. Oh, and Bernard – sorry, Lord de Floures – dines with us tonight too, but you know him.'

Miss March's stomach gave a flutter. She did not like company much, and would not have sought it this evening had it not been for the trauma of the morning, so to have to deal with her grandee landlord took nothing from her anxiety. And the last time they had shared the rectory table, one of the other guests had expired during a game of charades, an episode she would sooner forget than have to revisit.

'Wouldn't it be better, more proper, if the rector looked after his lordship, Mrs Clement?'

'Nonsense, and he's working and cannot be disturbed, so you will have to make small-talk solo, but it's not for long. Everyone will be here soon. I need to egg-wash this pie and think seriously about peas, so . . .'

Miss March undid the pinny, only then noticing that it was hilariously printed with the image of a buxom girl in a bikini, only without head or arms or feet, so when she put it on it looked like her body. Miss March would no sooner be seen in a bikini, even if it were merely a trompe-l'oeil, than in a suit of armour, and again her pale face admitted in an instant the reddening shame that always afflicted her when dignity was imperilled.

'Ha-ha,' said Audrey, who had acquired a fondness for broad humour when she was a girl that had never left her. Also, she thought a little humiliation heaped on friend and foe alike never hurt either, a calculation based not so much on the discomfiture of the person it was inflicted on so much as the limits of Audrey's natural capacity for empathy.

There was a ring on the doorbell, which woke Hilda. She looked out from her bed by the Aga, but then seemed to change her mind; she tucked her head back into her blanket and closed her eyes again. Miss March, flustered, did not know what to do with her pinny, so Audrey took it and said, 'The door, Miss March, if you would be so kind.'

'Who is it?'

'How would I know?' Audrey knew that it wouldn't be one of the boys, for they would come to the back door, or, if it were Theo bringing Miss Smith, then he would let her in himself, so it would have to be Bernard.

'What shall I do with them?'

'Put them in the drawing room and I'll get there as soon as I have done this, and we'll give them a drink.'

Miss March felt a distant surge of panic. She was unused to entertaining peers in someone else's drawing room and felt ill-equipped for the demands this would make on her savoir faire.

She went to the door and checked herself in the tall mirror in the hall. Daniel poked his head round the study door. 'Can you answer that, Miss March? I'm on the telephone.'

She nodded and he shut his door with an air of firmness.

Neil Vanloo was standing on the step. 'Hello, Miss March.' He was wearing a burgundy V-necked jumper under a blue anorak and was holding a bottle of wine.

'Detective Sergeant Vanloo!'

'Yes.'

Miss March could not think of anything to say.

'Can I come in?'

'You may,' she said, recovering herself.

Neil's entrance woke Hilda again; she recognised his voice before Audrey had even heard it and came scooting out of her bed and into the hall. He would have knelt to greet her but was encumbered with the bottle, and also Miss March's awkwardness, which made him feel a little awkward too, so Hilda ran around his ankles, jumping up in her excitement, and he half bent towards her while trying to talk to Miss March at the same time.

'A difficult day, Miss March. How are you holding up?'

'I'm quite all right, thank you, Detective Sergeant.'

'I'm glad to see you have company.'

'Mrs Clement insisted I come to dine.'

'Me too!'

This wrong-footed Miss March, for she knew Daniel had laid the table for six and there was no place for Neil. 'Mrs Clement is busy in the kitchen. May I take your . . . coat?'

'Can I give you the wine?' He handed her the bottle and then took off his anorak. How easy it is for the handsome, thought Miss March; they can wear a horrible anorak and still look good, still turn heads. 'Thanks. Where do you want me?'

'Drawing room,' she said, 'make yourself at home. I'll just get this wine in the fridge.'

Neil went into the drawing room, followed by Hilda, still doing her best in her excitement to be a trip hazard.

In the kitchen Audrey was filling a large saucepan with water. 'Peas!' she said. 'It's all we've got, but nobody wants anything else with a fish pie, do they?'

'How far do you think that pie will stretch?'

'Far enough.'

'Are you sure? We're seven, and the table is laid for six.'

237

'We are six.'

'That was Detective Sergeant Vanloo arriving.'

'I don't think so.'

'It certainly was.'

'What's he doing here?'

'He seems to think he's invited. He brought this.'

It was a Sainsbury's Chardonnay.

'That'll go nicely with the fish pie. Would you put it in the fridge – the pantry fridge? But why does he think he's invited?'

'I suppose the rector invited him.'

'I would be surprised if he had. They seem to have not exactly fallen out, but I don't think he's been here since Christmas.'

'Oh, this could be awkward.'

'Neil's never awkward, or he's too thick-skinned to notice if he should be. Daniel will be Daniel. Years of experience of looking like he's enjoying what he doesn't enjoy. But let's find out.'

Audrey breezed into the drawing room. 'Neil, how lovely to see you! It's been ages!'

'Hello, Mrs Clement.'

'Mrs Clement! Have you come to arrest me? It's Audrey, please! Drink?'

'Thank you.'

'There's gin and tonic, there's wine, there's . . . I think we have beer. If we do it will be what you brought at Christmas.'

'A bottle of that then, thanks.'

'I can do that,' said Miss March, looking for a reason not to be in the room. 'I think I saw some in the pantry.'

'Won't be cold, I'm afraid. Does it matter?' said Audrey.

'As it comes is fine,' said Neil.

'Forgive my appearance, Neil' – she flapped her WI pinny – 'some late alterations to the menu tonight.'

'I hope I'm not causing any inconvenience.'

'Not at all, I'm delighted Daniel asked you. He's in his study, but he won't be a minute.'

'Not Daniel, Theo.'

Barely missing a beat, Audrey said, 'Ah, yes, Theo, of course!'

It was enough for Neil to notice. 'He did tell you he'd invited me?'

'Well,' said Audrey, 'I'm sure he did, but it's been a very difficult day and . . . it doesn't matter, Neil, we've plenty and I'm delighted you're here.'

Miss March appeared with an opened bottle of Stella. 'Where do you keep your glasses, Mrs Clement?'

'In the corner cupboard in the dining room,' she said.

Miss March disappeared again.

'You must be exhausted,' said Audrey. 'And hungry. I don't suppose you stop to eat in these circumstances.'

'It's the best-catered murder investigation I've ever conducted,' said Neil. 'My lads have chilli con carne coming out of their ears.'

'From the van? I've not tried a lunch there yet. I'm

not sure I'm quite ready to discover what a chickpea is. But how is the investigation going? Perhaps you cannot say.'

'Nothing to tell you, Audrey,' said Neil, 'but we're continuing to make enquiries.'

'You and Daniel on the scent of a killer? Reunited again?'

'I'm always glad of his help.'

'And he of yours. In so many ways.'

They both retreated from this remark like lambs who have brushed innocently against an electric fence.

Miss March appeared with Neil's beer. She had poured it into a half-pint glass, the same shape as the dimpled kind you get in pubs, only this was not cheap but crystal, and cut not with dimples but with the pattern you see on a whisky tumbler. How very Audrey, thought Neil, to gentrify a beer glass.

'Is this all right, Detective Sergeant?'

'Just right, thanks. And, please, it's Neil.'

Miss March smiled politely but was no more likely to call him by his Christian name than he would hers. Then it occurred to her that he did know her name, because he had to ask for it when he took down her statement, and that he might start using it, and the second most carefully kept secret of her life would be known.

'Miss March, what will you have?' said Audrey, with a slight but unmistakable emphasis on the 'Miss March'.

'A tonic water? Anything soft.'

'Actually, would you mind helping yourself?' said Audrey. 'They're on the tray in the dining room. I really should get back to the kitchen.'

Daniel was listening at the study door. It was Neil. He recognised the timbre of his voice even if he could not hear it distinctly – that slightly nasal Mancunian sound. And there was still a flutter, still a leap in his pulse. He went back to his desk and felt the contrary force of attraction and resistance contending. Attraction he could do nothing about except let it fade, and he knew that it would if he allowed it to. But he knew it was not dead, and he feared it could flicker into life when they were obliged by circumstances to come together again, as colleagues in mystery.

Daniel had managed to find Mrs Porteous's god-daughter with one enquiry. All he had was the name Heather, and Northeye, a little town on the south coast, which he knew nothing about save its vicar, Father Derek Driver, who was at the camp end of the Church of England spectrum, and known as Deirdre by his fellow students – among them Daniel – at theological college, and to them still known by that name. Daniel had looked him up in Crockford's Clerical Directory – still vicar of Northeye – and telephoned.

A solemn voice answered, 'Northeye Vicarage.'

'Hello . . .' In that moment Daniel forgot Derek's real name and said, 'Deirdre, it's Daniel Clement.'

'Trude!'

Daniel's nickname at college was Trude the Obscure, due to his impenetrable thesis on a tiny textual variant in the Epistle to the Ephesians.

'I don't really answer to Trude, Deird— Derek, these days, but it's lovely to hear your voice.'

'And yours, my dear, but to what do I owe this pleasure?'

'I think you may be able to help me track someone down.'

'Not *another* murder?'

'I cannot say.'

'You're quite the Mountie, Trude, aren't you? Always getting your man!'

Daniel winced at that. 'It's not really like that.'

'I dare say. But whom do you seek?'

'I don't have much to go on, a parishioner's god-daughter, who I think lives in your parish, but I only have a Christian name.'

'Which is?'

'Heather.'

'Eight-five-five-seven-three.'

'Sorry?'

'Her number, eight-five-five-seven-three. Same code. It's Heather Merriman. She does the parish magazine. She's been boasting about meeting you since you caught your first murderer.'

'Thank you. Anything I need to know?'

'Don't think so. Nothing out of the normal range. She has an extraordinary number of knitted owls.'

'Ah. And how are you?'

'Holding on by my fingernails.'

'Will you stay, or will you go?'

'Would like to go but don't think I can. You?'

'Not a resigning issue for me.'

'I heard of your apostasy.'

It was said lightly, but it was said. Daniel had not only declared himself in favour of the ordination of women to the priesthood, but had received communion from a woman priest of one of the other Anglican churches at a much-publicised service. It had divided his circle of clerical friends and colleagues, half in favour, half opposed, and of them a number were so bitterly opposed that it required a parting of the ways.

'Just another variation in the evolution of distinctive forms in the Church of England, father.'

'That *does* sound splendid! Perhaps we could evolve the distinctive form of ordaining tea cosies?'

'Let's not fall out, Deirdre.'

'That ship has sailed, my dear, but I wish you well.'

'And I you.'

He was rattled by that conversation. Daniel, a true Anglican, was habitually predisposed to seek a *via media* when people were at odds. The bias towards a middle way was one of the characteristics he most liked about the Church of England and why he could not imagine leaving it. At theological college – no hothouse hotter for the nurturing of resentments – everything from the correct amount of swing for a thurible in a procession at a patronal festival to union with the Methodists was the cause of schism. Sometimes a *via media* could be found, sometimes only a barely credible compromise, designed to keep both parties just happy enough until something else came along that they wanted to fall out about more.

He was trying to think eirenic thoughts about this when he heard Neil arrive, and that obliged him to return to the urgent matter that was the subject of his call.

'Northeye, eight-five-five-seven-three,' he said out loud, and then telephoned the number Deirdre had given him.

'Hello?'

'Is that Heather . . .' – Daniel had to think for a second – '. . . Merriman?'

'Speaking.'

'Hello, this is Daniel Clement, rector of Champton St Mary and the Badsaddles. You may remember, we met at Dennis Porteous's funeral?'

'Oh, father, of course I remember! How nice to hear from you . . . but is everything all right?'

'Is this a good time?'

'Yes. But what's happened?'

'I'm afraid I have bad news.'

'Auntie Margaret?'

'Yes. I'm sorry to have to tell you that she died today.'

Heather gasped and said, 'I knew something awful had happened!'

Daniel said, 'I'm afraid it has.'

'I had the most terrible feeling of foreboding. After lunch. When did it happen?'

'Before lunch. But that's not important.'

'How did it happen?'

'We're not entirely sure,' said Daniel, which was not wholly untrue. 'It was sudden. We'll know more in due course.'

'Poor Auntie Margaret!'

'Please be assured of my prayers, Heather, for Margaret and for you.'

'Thank you, father. I must call the vicar. But what about funeral arrangements?'

'That is one of my reasons for telephoning. You are down as next of kin.'

'Am I? I suppose I am, although strictly speaking we're not kin.'

'Auntie Margaret?'

'An honorary auntie; she was my mother's friend. Her best friend. They grew up together.'

'I'm embarrassed to say this, Heather – may I call you Heather?'

'Of course.'

'I know next to nothing about Margaret, in spite of her being my parishioner and a churchwarden, and having buried her husband . . .'

'She was a very private person.'

'I would very much like to know a little more about her.'

'What sort of thing?'

'Where she was from, her family, how she met Dennis, why they came to Champton?'

'Why?' asked Heather.

'I need to serve her better in the address at her funeral than I did Dennis.'

'Yes, I see. I don't know where to start.'

Daniel used the technique he used whenever he was taking notes from a grieving family about the person they were mourning.

'I'd like to do it in the form of questions, then I can write down what you say and keep it in order.'

'I would quite like to say something at the funeral. Perhaps I should write something down and post it to you? For your approval.'

'I was just going to ask you if you would, so yes, please, but would you mind if I just sketched the details now?'

There was silence for a moment, then Heather said, 'All right, fire away.'

'Where was Margaret from?'

'Devon, she was a country girl – well, not country, maritime. Her father was something in the shipyard at Devonport. Clerical rather than manual. Her mother was a teacher. No brothers and sisters. She met my mother at school, the Secondary School for Girls, they were in the same house, St Ursula. Auntie Margaret did her teacher training at Bristol, I think, but then the war broke out and she had to go to . . . I can't remember where . . . but she came back to Devonport and taught at the Secondary School for Girls herself. She met Dennis through the Operatic.'

'The Operatic?'

'Am dram.'

'Dennis was a performer?'

'Good lord, no, he was a technician. Lighting. He wasn't very good. My mother called him the Prince of Darkness.'

'Was she in the Operatic too?'

'Yes, all the young ones in their day were.'

'And Margaret married Dennis.'

'Yes, my mother was her matron of honour. Margaret had been her chief bridesmaid.'

'And then?'

'Nothing much. I came along and my mother asked Margaret to be my godmum.'

'No children of their own?'

'No, don't know why. Their life was very quiet. Dennis became more and more withdrawn. He didn't like company much.'

'What did he do for a living?'

'He was something in the Town Hall. In charge of something – payroll, accounts, something.'

'What was Margaret like as a godmother?'

'Very nice. Remembered birthdays. Gave me my first prayer book. Postal order at Christmas.'

'Did you see much of her?'

'Not really. After they each got married, she and my

mum saw less of each other, like you do. And then Margaret left the Operatic. I think there was a falling-out – can't remember why.'

'And then?'

'She was big at church, like my mother, so they had that. And she was very dedicated to teaching. She became head of history at school. And then Dennis retired early – he inherited some money, I think – and she retired and they moved to Champton.'

'Why?'

'I think that was Auntie Margaret. History was her passion. She came to see Champton House with the Arts Society. She said it was love at first sight.'

'So it was the house?'

'And its history, and the de Floures.'

'And she ended up becoming the head guide?'

'Yes, that meant a lot to her. And she was so excited about the film. I suppose it's a comfort to know that she got to do that before she went.'

Daniel said nothing.

'When do you think the funeral will be? I'll need to book some time off.'

'I'm not sure yet. The funeral directors will be in touch in due course. Best if we arrange everything through them.'

'I see.'

'Thank you, Heather, you've been very helpful. And again, please be assured of my prayers.'

'Thank you.'

After the call, Daniel sat for a moment reproaching himself again for knowing so little about Margaret and Dennis Porteous. It was not that he felt entitled to that knowledge – it was theirs to share or not – but that he had not realised he had known so little, not noticed the absence of the normal transmission of details. Dennis did not trouble anyone much, nor wish to be troubled, and Margaret was just a steady presence. He tried to think of other parishioners who had been as steady a presence in parish life about whom he knew so little.

There was a knock on the door.

'Yes?'

It was Neil. 'I've been abandoned in the drawing room. Thought I would come and say hello. Hope I'm not bothering you.'

'I was just coming. I had to telephone someone. I didn't know you were coming to supper.'

'Theo invited me.'

'Did he?'

'He did.'

Daniel got up. 'Shall we join the others?'

'There aren't any others. Not yet. And I wanted to talk to you alone.'

How much he would have liked that, Daniel thought, not so long ago. 'Ominous words,' he said.

'Not ominous. Business, not personal.'

'Oh, I see. Shall we sit?'

They sat.

'Won't take a minute,' said Neil.

There was something uniquely wretched, thought Daniel, about having to go through the formalities of conversation when you can't say what you want to say.

Neil took his notebook out of his back pocket. 'I need some help with something. I interviewed Miss March earlier – very useful witness, by the way: clear and thorough, and she had written everything down. Margaret said something just before she died. Miss March wasn't sure if she was aware of what she was saying, but it is this . . .' He turned up a page in his notebook. 'She said something about being young, believing in fantastic things, and that was wrong, quite wrong. Does that mean anything to you?'

'Say it again?'

'Being young, believing in fantastic things, and that was wrong, quite wrong.'

Something pinged in Daniel's memory. 'I think it may.'

'Is it something she had spoken about to you?'

'No, not that kind of a thing.'

'Then what sort of a thing?'

'I think it's a quotation.'

'From what?'

'I'm not sure. I'll have to think about it.'

'And there's another thing. I was going through her stuff in the Old Dairy and I found these long brass pins . . .' – he looked at his notebook – '. . . farthingale pins. Do you know what they are?'

'A farthingale was a sort of hooped skirt, I think.'

'Yes, and it was all held together with these pins, but they're not really pins, they're the size of tent pegs. And they're not flimsy either.'

Daniel said, 'I see. Do you think you could inflict a serious injury with one?'

'I do.'

'Like you might with a long, narrow, bladed weapon?'

'I do.'

In Miss Smith's trailer Carrie was making up a bag for Theo to take to supper at the rectory. It contained a cashmere shawl in case Gilly got cold, a bottle of the gin and the tonics she liked, a banana, and a small pharmacy of remedies for everything from hay fever to anxiety. It was like sending a kid off to school, she thought, and wondered if she should get Gilly a pair of mittens connected by the thread that goes down the arms and across the shoulders, so they never get lost.

Miss Smith was still on her sofa, wrapped up for the journey of half a mile across the park from the stables to the rectory. She had changed her mind about a car and asked for a buggy instead, not wishing, in her words, to inconvenience a driver, and because she thought it might be fun to arrive that way. Carrie had to make the necessary arrangements, which meant standing down a driver and a car and then organising a buggy with another driver at the last minute, thereby causing more inconvenience, not less. She remembered reading about a member of Gandhi's staff, who said people had no idea how much it cost them to keep him in poverty.

Why did Gilly want to go to supper at the rectory with an actor she did not know, who was only really known to the public for soap operas and advertisements, and was a co-star – co-star! – she had not even acknowledged until just now? It couldn't be for the pleasure of his company, nor was she especially charmed by Queen Anne rectories, no matter how handsome, and Carrie had seen Champton's and it was indeed very handsome. Lord de Floures would be there, and that might conceivably be a temptation had Miss Smith not made the acquaintance of Princess Margaret, whose royalty just about made up for her rudeness (and a trip to Mustique). It must be the rector. She had shown an unexpected fondness for clergy before. Why? Perhaps it was because they were on terms with God and Miss Smith would quite like to make His acquaintance too? While going to supper at the rectory would be typically impulsive, it was unnecessarily daring too. A murder had happened, the murderer was at large, and the rector was a lightning rod for murderous passions. Carrie's instinct was that they should keep their heads down, have something from catering on a tray, but Gilly's impulses overruled Carrie's instincts.

Theo and 'Gilly' were doing that thing actors always do, discussing other actors, and how they knew them, and the shows and the films they'd worked on. Miss Smith was inevitably at an advantage in this, having worked longer and more luminously, but there is only so much pleasure to be had by telling a story in such a way that your interlocutor eventually has to ask who else was in the cast and you reply 'Larry' or 'Burt' or 'Glenda'. So she had gone into the more distant past, to her years in rep, and was trawling through the casts of shows by Terence Rattigan and Noël Coward and Sir Arthur Wing Pinero with which she had enchanted Wednesday-matinee theatregoers from Aberdeen to Exeter. Occasionally Theo would almost yelp 'Yes!' when they found they had someone in common, though he had to remind himself not to make too much of it, as she had appeared with them when they were in their salad days, and he when they were in their after-dinner-mint days. Parts too; they had both done seasons at Stratford – she as Juliet and Viola and Desdemona, he as Oswald and Autolycus, and the Messenger in the same production in which she had been Cleopatra, but only once in the same season – and occasionally they had appeared in the same play but in different productions. He had recently been Charles in *Blithe Spirit*, and she, when she was starting out, had played Elvira.

'Seven-thirty,' said Carrie when there was a tiny but serviceable pause in the barrage of anecdotes.

'Thanks, Carrie. Ooh, my goodness, we mustn't be late, not for your mama!'

'It's just across the park,' said Theo. 'It's only five min-utes. And it's just an ordinary supper, no formalities.'

'But I would hate to be the cause of an incinerated

dinner. And it would be very rude to be late. We must go. Carrie, is our buggy here yet?'

'Here and ready,' said Carrie. It had been here and ready for twenty minutes.

'Do you have everything, Theo?'

'Yes, I think so.'

'Here's the gin,' said Carrie and handed him Miss Smith's supplies. 'Call me in production when she's ready to go. I'll come and pick her up in a car and take her back to her hotel. They don't need her to stay now she's given her statement. She won't be late. She probably won't eat anything; I wish I had the information leaflet to show you.'

Outside, Gayle was waiting behind the wheel of the buggy she had been driving all day, or rather not driving, with everyone confined to their quarters. She hadn't taken it out since she'd delivered Daniel to the stables when news of what had befallen Margaret Porteous had first arrived. She was quite glad of a chance to finally do something, and to drive Miss Smith was quite the honour, even though she could be a difficult passenger. All the runners and riders had been instructed not to address her, not even to look at her, as if she were a divinity whose radiance would blind and burn them. If they were to chance upon her on set or in production, they were expected to stand against the wall with their eyes down. Carrie was so used to laying down the law for the convenience of Miss Smith that she no longer noticed how strange it was. At first, when

Carrie's predecessor – sacked for 'narcissism' – told her of these requirements, during a rushed handover, she had thought it was a joke and then, when she realised it wasn't, a foible that shaded into madness. But what is madness, she had come to believe, if not living in a minority of one? And stars of Miss Smith's magnitude were all minorities of one, or very nearly one. There were a handful of other stars whom she would consider peers and meet on level terms, like sovereigns attending the funeral of Queen Victoria but still jostling in their feathers and frogging for precedence. Everyone else was, if not an untouchable, beneath her degree, and while they entered and left her world in the normal course of business, they were not of her world, and that distinction was unarguable and non-negotiable. Her life was crowded, but she was alone and always had been for as long as Carrie had known her. There were lovers (although that word was misleading) who came and went like members of a cast, necessary and useful for the job, but not people to whom she offered any intimacy apart from physical. Carrie, in a rare moment of thoughtlessness, and after three martinis, had once asked Gilly if she had ever loved anyone. There was a cold pause and then Gilly – for she was Gilly by then – said, 'Have you ever had a dog, Carrie?'

Carrie said, 'Yes. A cocker spaniel when I was a girl. Monty. He was a house dog, not a working dog. I loved him.'

'That's love, you see. The wagging tail, always pleased

to see you, the relentless adoration. That's what love is, but it only comes on four legs, not two.'

That's why people like you love dogs, thought Carrie, because unlike people, they don't choose. 'Why don't you get a dog, Gilly?' she'd said, and immediately regretted it, for it was another clumsy trespass.

There was a longer pause and then Gilly said, 'Because they die when they're teenagers. If you're lucky. And I'm away all the time. It's the work, Carrie, with me. The work.'

Carrie's work at that moment required her to get Gilly into the buggy, an operation that had almost an element of ceremony about it, as if she were a camerlengo assisting a pope into the sedia gestatoria. She wondered again if it was a problem she had at least part-created, her efficiency engendering helplessness in her employer. Why should Miss Smith get in the buggy like anyone else when the person who minimised the friction of encountering the wishes of others or the inexorable facts of time, gravity and entropy was there to do all the work for her? And – a more difficult thought – her efficiency not only compounded Gilly's helplessness, but also bound Carrie to her and made her no less helpless. Had she passed the point of no return, she and Gilly each to the other indispensable?

'Carrie!'

She lent her arm and gently guided Gilly into the seat. When she was comfortable she tucked the rug Gilly had specially requested over her knees.

'Carrie!' Gilly gestured to her to lean in. 'Have a car and driver on standby. I don't know how long I'll manage.'

'Already sorted,' she said. 'You might enjoy it. Nice vicar and Lord de Doodah.'

'For an hour. I'm already longing for a bath and a bed.'

Theo had thought he might travel on the back seat next to Gilly, but she had taken the whole of it, so he squeezed into the front seat next to Gayle, Carrie's bag on his knee. 'Do you know where you're going?'

'I think so,' said Gayle. 'Down to the church.'

'Let's *go*, people!' came an already impatient-sounding voice from the back.

The buggy lumbered over the interlocking plastic sections that had been laid over the grass and cobbles.

'Slow down, please! It's not Le Mans!'

This was easier said than done, for like a dodgem the buggy rather lurched into motion, and that lack of smoothness was exacerbated by nerves, for Gayle was scared of her passenger. She slowed down, but then had to speed up to get up a low slope.

'Slow down!'

She could not slow down on the slope, but at the top she did and the buggy lurched to a halt.

'No, don't stop!'

They sped up again going down the other side.

'Slow down!'

They stopped and started and lurched and slowed

down as they made their way towards the path that led through the park to the rectory. Bernard was watching from the library, he and Cosmo having made the daily inspection of the parts of his house that had been taken over by 'the minstrels' to note damages. It made him think of the account of Marie Antoinette in a tumbril on the way to her execution, her head nodding up and down as it went over the cobbles.

Also watching the buggy stop–start on its way to the edge of the park was Brandon Redding. He was crouching in a copse of trees in the park, cover for two hundred years for those availing themselves of his lordship's game for their own pots. It stood between the house and the lodges, where he had left Alex and Nathan more or less passed out on the sofa. He had taken the opportunity to hide some of his products where they would not find them by removing the fancy ends of the curtain poles, inserting his stash inside and then replacing them, so if he were by some mischance nicked, he would not have a surfeit of Class A drugs on him. But he had in his pocket a couple of bags of his home-made 'sinsemilla' and some wraps of coke that he had reserved for Theo. He wouldn't normally stalk a customer like this, especially not when the place was full of police, but he had lost a substantial amount of his stash into the blue chemical flush of Theo's Winnebago lavatory, and he needed to make a sale.

He wasn't going to intercept the buggy like a high-wayman – delivering rather than demanding they deliver; he did not need to, for he could see where it was going. He would make his way to the rectory and wait for Theo to step outside for a cigarette, as he certainly would.

He broke cover as close to the park wall as he could and loped along it towards the rectory, a poacher's route he had learnt as a boy from Nathan's granddad Edgy, before Mrs Porthole had got him thrown out of school and his foster family gave up on him. Thanks to her he had ended up in Stow, where there were no woods and lanes and rabbits, but shops to nick from, smaller kids to intimidate and, as he got older, more to worry about than being nicked for poaching and fighting and being expelled for scrawling cocks and balls on toilet doors. There was another copse that filled the corner between the park wall and the rectory garden's wall. He would find a place there from where he could see Theo step into the garden for a fag.

13

In the drawing room, Daniel and Neil and Miss March were standing in an uncomfortable trio holding cheerless drinks: a sherry for Daniel, a warm lager for Neil and a slimline tonic for Miss March. It was the first day of the year when a fire needed to be lit, but it was smokier than usual, as if it took a while to remember its purpose after the summer. The half-perfume, half-chemical smell of woodsmoke began to pervade the room, and every now and then a little shower of soot fell from the chimney into the grate.

This was more than usually noticeable, for the conversation was not flowing. Daniel felt wrong-footed by the appearance of Neil, and Miss March felt inadequately prepared for the additions to the dinner guests. Neil was always bluff in social circumstances, but he was not insensitive to the awkwardness between him and Daniel, and there was something unusually forced about his bantering, which compounded it. Even Hilda, whose repertoire of moods was really only delight or aggression, had sensed something was wrong and had retreated from the drawing room, with its temptations of society and a lit fire, and gone to her bed by the Aga, where she had fallen asleep.

Miss March had asked Neil how the investigation was proceeding, realising as she said it that it was clumsy of her to ask and that he could not answer the question. He had replied as he always did when people asked this, 'We're continuing with the investigation,' but there was something about the formula that made recovery by swerving to a more fruitful topic even more difficult, and they stood in an almost unbearable silence until Miss March found herself observing that the nights were drawing in.

Rescue came in the form of Audrey, who burst through the door as host rather than cook, with only a faint dusting of flour on her right sleeve to indicate that she had been in the kitchen.

Miss March, who was always startled by Audrey's way of bursting into a room as if she were clearing an obstacle in the 400-metre hurdles rather than making a carefully judged entrance, was even more startled because Audrey had dressed up beyond what Miss March had been led to believe was the standard expected for the evening. She was wearing a dove-coloured Jaeger twinset she had bought at a generous discount from the shop, over a smart dark skirt with two strings of seed pearls that had belonged to her mother round her neck. She wondered if it was, consciously or unconsciously, a way of Audrey asserting social superiority, to restore her diminished status since she had gone to work for Miss March, even if it were as a retail consultant.

'Here we are!' said Audrey. 'And so lovely to have a fire. I adore this season of mists and mellow fruitfulness, don't you, Miss March?'

'Yes,' she said, 'but I would rather have spring and the sense of something coming rather than the sense of something going away.'

'And such lovely things in the shop.'

'If only there were customers to buy them.'

'I heard you were closed, Miss March,' said Neil. 'I thought you were like the Windmill Girls.'

Anyone less like a Windmill Girl would be hard to imagine, and Miss March's blush bloomed again. 'Elite Fashions is closed for the duration of the filming, Detective Sergeant,' she said.

'Practically the whole parish is involved in some way,' said Daniel, 'even my mother and Miss March.'

'Oh, Daniel, so are you!' said his mother.

'As an adviser. Like Miss March.'

'That's not fair, Dan,' said Audrey. 'You make me feel like a chorus girl. In actual fact, Neil, we are making history come alive. I think that's terribly important.'

'And we will be done before the Christmas rush begins,' said Miss March, 'and besides, it's always slow after the summer holidays.'

'I wonder if anyone would like to get me a drink?' said Audrey.

'Your usual?'

'Thank you, Dan.'

Daniel took one of Audrey's favourite 1950s cocktail glasses, etched with stars in the spirit of the atomic age, from the corner cupboard and the bottle of Noilly Prat, or 'noily' as his mother called it, and took both to the kitchen for ice and lemon, leaving his mother with Neil and Miss March.

'What a pleasure to have everyone round for a scratch supper! And on a Wednesday!' declared Audrey.

Neil said, 'She didn't know I was coming, Miss March. It was Theo who invited me, and he must have forgotten to mention it.'

'Typical Theo,' said Audrey, 'he was always the absent-minded one of the two. You would think it would be the parson.'

'Nothing absent-minded about the rector,' said Miss March.

'No. But I think they like to be thought of as absent-minded,' said Audrey.

'Why's that?' asked Neil.

'To get out of things.'

'How do you mean?'

'Too unworldly to do what the rest of us have to do. Earn our keep. Make small talk. Polish our shoes.'

Miss March didn't like the sound of that.

'And most of them are not good, not good at all,' said Audrey with some feeling, 'at fighting their corner. They think they have to be nice.'

'That doesn't sound like Daniel either,' said Neil, and nobody said anything for a moment.

Audrey eventually went to the window. She appeared to be looking for something.

'Expecting anyone?' said Neil.

'Theo,' said Audrey, 'and Bernard. Is it half past?'

'It's gone half past,' said Miss March. 'I hope it won't spoil the fish pie.'

'It's a famously robust version,' said Daniel, returning with Audrey's 'noily'.

'Essential for anyone who cooks for a parson – thank you, darling,' said Audrey, taking her drink, 'because they're always late, and they always bring the waif and the stray. See also Lancashire hotpot and apple crumble . . . Holy moly, the mincemeat tart . . .' She rushed out.

'Am I waif or stray?' asked Neil. Miss March wondered if she too was waif or stray, but did not say anything.

'She didn't mean you,' muttered Daniel.

'Did she mean Bernard?'

'When I was in London,' said Daniel, 'we would feed the homeless on a Wednesday night.'

'But your mum wasn't with you in London.'

'No, but . . . it's what we're called to do, isn't it? Whatever you do to the least of these, you do to me.'

'Very proper,' said Miss March, silently glad that there were other people doing this charitable work, so she didn't have to.

'It was not quite as picturesque as that sounds. This was Belgravia and we used to get leftovers from the splendid afternoon teas at the Motcombe Hotel. That's how I met Honoria, by the way. She was working there . . .'

'*Working*,' said Neil sarcastically.

'. . . and she said yes, they would only be thrown away if they weren't eaten. Think of that, throwing away smoked salmon finger sandwiches, glorious cakes, little slices of quiche . . . And, of course, word got out and people used to call in who weren't homeless at all. In fact, some of the regulars turned out to work for a very respectable bank, and the real homeless got rather elbowed out.'

'The first shall be first and the last shall be last,' said Neil.

'Yes, that's often how it goes, I'm afraid. But this is a long-winded way of saying that there are many places at a rectory table.'

'In my father's house there are many mansions,' said Neil, surprising himself again with a line of Scripture that had been drilled into him in his youth and was still there, dormant but ready to rise when bidden. 'We had the same philosophy in the Moravian Brethren. The love feast. Anyone could come for a cup of tea and a bun. It was meant to be a sort of holy communion, although we had proper Holy Communion – not what you'd think proper, Dan. It was one of the first trad-itions the mother church at Herrnhut started. And we still do it today. Mug of tea and a bun, come one, come all.'

'That sounds lovely,' said Miss March, 'and I suppose Harvest Festival, or Thanksgiving in the United States, is the same sort of thing?'

'Thanks for the fruits of the earth and the offer of a share in them for all,' said Dan.

'Sounds so Communist when you say that,' said Audrey, returning from the kitchen. 'Free grub for everyone, but someone has to sow the seed and reap the crops and make the tea and buns, no?'

Neil said, 'From each according to their ability, to each according to their needs.'

'Is that from the Sermon on the Mount?' said Miss March.

'It's Marx,' said Daniel. 'But you can trace it back to the Acts of the Apostles, I think.'

'I don't think Christianity has ever really been improved since the C of E got the hang of it,' said Audrey, and she went again to the window, peering through the gap in the curtains. 'Evensong. Maundy Money. Lighten our darkness, we beseech thee, O Lord. So much nicer than Che Guevara . . . Oh, here they come!'

'The starving refugees from Champton House,' murmured Neil, but Audrey wasn't listening.

'Look, but don't make it obvious,' she said as she smoothed her skirt and then went out to the hall to check herself in the mirror.

Daniel looked through the window and saw something he could not at first make out. It looked like a very slow, very small motorcade, led by a motorcycle or something, with a single headlight shining in the darkness making a lurching progress towards the drive. Behind it was another vehicle with twin headlights – a car, he supposed, but stuck behind the motorbike.

Both stopped at the gateposts and then lurched into movement again and came up the drive. What was the one in front? A tiny milk float? Funny time for the milkman to be delivering, and he always went to the back door. Then, as it got nearer, he recognised it as one of the cast and crew buggies. It was being followed by the glossy Mercedes reserved for the important people. Had Theo asked Dick to dinner? And how typical of Theo to make someone drive him the half a mile from the house. And how typical of him to keep the car waiting.

'Here they are!' called Audrey from the hall.

'Who is it?' said Miss March, a little anxiously.

'Theo and his friend,' said Audrey.

'Dick, the director? I wouldn't call them friends exactly.'

'No,' said Audrey, 'his film-star friend.'

'Who?'

'Gillian Smith,' said Audrey. 'Didn't I mention she was dining with us tonight?'

14

Bernard had fallen asleep in front of the fire in the library. He had allowed himself a pink gin, which he made himself from the tray on the sideboard after the minstrels had retreated to their camp, and the policemen to theirs. Then he made another, and his thoughts turned morose as he sat alone under portraits of his ancestors – and their judgement – wondering how many of them would have let their house to a troupe of acrobats? The last time there was a masque for the queen here his ancestor had hired the minstrels, not the other way round, and the minstrels were Ben Jonson and Inigo Jones, and the masque as splendid as anything seen at court. And now they paid him to allow them to recreate his ancestor's glory as entertainment and he was banished to diminished quarters with nothing but a tray of drinks and the rector's dog. Cosmo, who seemed to sense this thought, stirred on his lap and gave a little contented sigh.

Cheered by this, Bernard had then started to think of the money he had not only made from this woman of boundless intrigue, but also saved by getting them to do up the shabby state rooms and faded silk hangings and restart the stilled fountains. His son and heir was to marry next year and he would marry if not quite in the style of his ancestors then not disgraced by mouldy hangings and chipped paint.

He had closed his eyes for a minute, and when he opened them, something caught his eye moving across the park. At first, he thought he was half dreaming, for it looked like a carriage of some unusual type, but then he saw it was one of the buggy things they ferried the minstrels around in. One of those Jerry motors they used for the important people drove up behind it from the stables and then slowed to creeping pace to follow.

He puzzled over this, but the second pink gin had an additional soporific effect, and he closed his eyes again for a moment.

Then Mrs Shorely was standing over him.

'Is it dinnertime?'

'Excuse me, m'lord, but have you forgotten you're dining at the rectory tonight?'

'Damn!' said Bernard, and he pushed Cosmo from his lap, who was not quite ready for this sudden ejection and landed on his back. 'What's the time?'

'It's gone half past.'

'Thank you, Mrs Shorely. Do you know, it's the second time today I've eaten there?'

'Quite so, m'lord,' she said, using one of her phrases of studied neutrality.

'Then I should . . . get ready.' He hesitated before saying this for he never really went out. He felt seedy in the way of a man in middle age who has fallen more soundly asleep after a cocktail than he anticipated, so he went to his study, Cosmo following, and up the back stairs to his bedroom and bathroom and dressing room. He cleaned his teeth and washed his face, because there would not be time to take a bath. He considered shaving, but then thought it not worth it, so he gave himself a squirt of Blenheim Bouquet, brushed his jacket with the narrow, ivory-handled clothes' brushes that bore his father's initials and the de Floures circlet of flowers, and then brushed his hair with the oval, ivory-handled hairbrushes of the same set, also crested and initialled. Cosmo made the low, keening noise he always did when he knew an excursion was to be made but did not know if he would be included. So, when Bernard summoned him to follow, he leapt after him like an athlete out of the blocks.

He let himself out of the kitchen door without bothering to take Cosmo's lead, which Mrs Shorely had hung there in anticipation. Why would he? Must a man leash his dog to walk his own park? He liked the way Cosmo faithfully followed him around without having to be tethered, but this was what he expected of dogs, or the retrievers and gun dogs he had known all his life. Dachshunds, he was discovering, were a different kind of beast. The first lesson he had to learn was the propensity of the breed to present a trip hazard.

Bernard had never been balletic, but he was almost nimble in his efforts not to step on Cosmo, who grew ever more inventive in keeping close to him. There are other reasons why dachshunds would not make good retrievers, as Bernard discovered when he was a good way down the path that led to the rectory.

Cosmo suddenly stilled, trembled, then shot like a very low-flying missile towards the copse of trees to their left, disappeared into it, and then released a round of unfeasibly loud barks, like a submachine gun firing, and in an instant every feathered and four-legged creature burst out of the cover.

'Cosmo!' shouted Bernard. 'Cosmo, come here! Come HERE!'

Cosmo's neurology, never a sophisticated system, was firing one message and one message only now, and it was to confront the intruder, the one two-legged creature who did not break cover as Cosmo attacked.

A miniature dachshund attacking a human is not an unusual scenario – ask any postman – but they are not German shepherds, and while their bark and their courage might be large, in size they are similar to a draught excluder, so Brandon Redding was not as scared as he might have been of a gamekeeper's hound, and he knew the dog was one of the rector's so not likely to be red in tooth and claw. But Cosmo was loud and persistent and stood his ground when Brandon tried to shoo him away. Then he heard someone calling for him, but it wasn't the rector; it sounded like Lord de Floures. There was a part of Brandon, deep down and unacknowledged, that was scared of authority, a reflex that he had perhaps acquired from Edgy, who sometimes used to talk with a peculiar sort of nostalgia about the days when tough off-the-books punishment followed if you were caught poaching by a landowner and his men. He felt that twitch, and his response normally would be to override it with bravado, a habit that had caused him considerable trouble in his short but confrontational life. So much trouble that you would think it would amount to a lesson he would eventually learn, but he had his neural circuits too, which fired up as dynamically as any other creature's. He wanted to walk out of the copse with a sneer and a 'fuck you' and a 'what are you going to do about it?' but if regard for law and custom could not temper his reaction, self-interest could. He did not want Lord de Floures to know he was there, not while there was business he was trying to transact, and particularly not in the middle of a police investigation. So he scaled the wall, almost in one movement, and dropped down on the other side. Cosmo, losing his prey, gave another barrage of barks.

'Cosmo! Come here! Come here!' shouted Bernard, but Cosmo didn't come, and Bernard realised he was going to have to go to him. He was late, and the rectory was tantalisingly close, so to be delayed was especially annoying. Also, he had not brought a torch because the night was not dark and he did not want to have to poke around in the rough looking for a dog too stupid to realise that whatever creature he had scented or heard or seen in the trees was long gone. This was why he didn't like dogs, he thought, giving a little grunt of irritation and stepping out across the grass towards the trees.

Miss March was even paler than her normal shade of pale. It was bad enough to discover that on the suddenly lengthened list of supper guests was not only a peer of the realm, but also a film star — a film star that, very secretly, very quietly, Miss March had admired and even adored since she was a girl. She silently cursed Audrey for having 'neglected to mention' this newest and most terrifying recruit to the table. She looked at Audrey, who at that very moment chose to look at her, and Miss March saw her eyes widen with the triumph of knowing that she had not only scored the greatest social coup in Champton since the original Anne of Denmark came in 1603, but in so doing had also reminded Miss March that while she may be on her payroll, the status quo was still the status quo. Audrey only glanced at her, for her gaze was really on her new guest, who was at that moment being extracted from the buggy that had drawn up in front of the rectory in a manner more like a bride on her wedding day than a Wednesday supper guest.

'Mrs Clement!' Miss Smith's salutation emerged indistinctly from the bundle of soft, sound-suppressing textiles in which she had been wrapped by Carrie for her short journey across the park. Theo and Gayle did not quite perform a fireman's lift to get her safely onto the gravel, but it was not perhaps quite as dignified as Miss Smith would have liked and she made a fluttering, chiding gesture at them and said, 'Oh, don't make such a fuss. I'm not an invalid!' Then she just stood and smiled and didn't move.

Audrey realised that it was she who was expected to move. She put her head to one side, said 'Miss Smith!' in an ingratiating way, and came down the steps holding onto the rail firmly. Why is she doing that? thought Daniel, and then realised that if Miss Smith was going to make Audrey descend the steps to her level, then Audrey would pretend to struggle to have to do so.

'Oh, please, it's Gilly,' said Miss Smith, 'and allow me to take in for a moment your simply glorious house.'

'Queen Anne,' she said, 'like you . . .' She paused a moment for the brilliant joke she had thought of earlier to be appreciated.

'Queen Anne?' said Miss Smith with a hint of steel.

'Anne of Denmark. *A Woman of Boundless Intrigue.* And I'm Audrey.'

'Oh, I see! A different Queen Anne, of course.'

Audrey thought it best to retire her brilliant joke and advanced on her distinguished guest. 'Yes, much loved by parsons and their mothers, for she bestowed on us not only lovely rectories, but lovely money to do them up with as well. So, God save the queen!'

'Thank you,' said Miss Smith, thinking Audrey meant her.

'Won't you come in? Theo, darling, will you help Miss Smith?'

'Gilly,' she said, 'while I'm here! Theo, send the buggy away. Audrey, this looks very extravagant, but I have my car and driver here too to take me to my hotel later. Would you mind if he waited in your drive?'

'It's Daniel's drive, really, but of course he can wait here. Does he . . . need anything?'

'I don't think so,' said Gilly, without bothering to ask him.

Theo offered her his arm, she leant on it unnecessarily, and they followed Audrey up the steps, Gayle bringing up the rear with Miss Smith's precious bag.

Daniel, with unconscious formality, was standing in the hall under the brass lantern light to greet her.

'Miss Smith,' he said, 'welcome to the rectory.'

'Rector,' she said, '. . . if that is what I am supposed to call you?'

'I prefer Daniel, if you don't mind?'

'I don't at all. I've been dying to meet you.'

'But what am I supposed to call you?'

'I prefer Gilly, if *you* don't mind. And who is this splendid fellow?' She pointed at the portrait of Daniel's favourite predecessor, wigged, suave and looking at them with a worldly glance from a heavy gilt frame.

'That is the Reverend Sir Gilbert Mackworth,

Baronet,' said Daniel. 'Rector of this parish in the time of Queen Anne, and builder of this house.'

'He looks awfully naughty,' said Miss Smith, 'if it's not too naughty of me to say so.'

'He was a man who loved the world,' said Daniel.

'And the world loved him back,' said Audrey, 'over and over again. May I take your wrap, Gilly?'

Miss Smith lightly heaved the burden of cashmere from her shoulders.

'The portrait is by Kneller,' said Daniel, '1717, after the queen had died, when he had married a rich heiress. He was a cousin of the de Floures. He ended up with the Golden Prebend.'

'What is that, and what do you get it for?'

'It was one of the richest appointments in the Church of England, the eleventh prebend of Durham, in the gift of the bishop, whose favour you must have won somehow – Gilbert was related to the then Archbishop of York – and it came with an estate, which brought in about £1,400 per year. Must be about fifty thousand in today's values.'

'What did prebends do?'

'Nothing much.'

'I don't suppose anyone had a cushier life', said Theo, 'than Sir Gilbert.'

'It was a life of comfort and ease,' said Daniel, 'until the poor man got the stone.'

'Kidney stones?' said Miss Smith.

'Yes. He left his body to a friend who was a surgeon

in the hope that it would reveal the cause of the terrible agues he had lately suffered and spare his children and grandchildren from suffering the same.'

'Into every life a little rain . . .'

'Come and meet everyone,' said Audrey. 'And what would you like to drink?'

'One of my G&Ts, please.'

'We have gin, we have tonic, we have everything.'

Theo said, 'Mum, Miss Smi— Gilly has a special kind of gin.'

'Oh dear, I'm afraid we have only ordinary gin.'

'She's brought her own,' said Theo, holding up the special bag.

'House present,' said Gilly, 'not just for me!'

'I'll fix it, Mum,' said Theo, and he retreated into the kitchen.

Audrey's smile failed for a tiny moment, but flickered back on only with a hint of Tipu's Tiger about it. 'Come into the drawing room, the fire's lit. Special logs. From the estate.'

While this was happening, Miss March, whose dread had only increased as she heard Miss Smith's voice in the hall, had inched her way towards the corner furthest from the door. She had not meant to, but the thought of meeting Miss Smith socially made her feel like a rescue puppy evicted from its cage to meet a potential owner. At that moment a dog barked distantly, which made her more nervous and even more anxious to wedge herself into a corner. As she had retreated,

Neil had perforce retreated with her. He could see she was uncomfortable, more than uncomfortable, and he did his best to make her feel easier, which in his clumsy way had the opposite effect and compounded Miss March's anxiety. So when Audrey led Miss Smith in to make the introductions her distinguished guest could not see at first where her other, less distinguished guests were.

This was not an unknown predicament for Miss Smith, whose presence among strangers tended either to draw them towards her or propel them away. In this situation it rather suited her, for it gave her control of Audrey's drawing room, and she could see already that Audrey did not surrender territory easily; it also gave her the opportunity to appear amiable.

'Hello, who's that hiding over there?' she said.

Neil stepped forward. 'Miss Smith.'

That did surprise her. 'Is it our Detective Sergeant?'

'It is. Neil, Neil Vanloo.'

'Crikey, I didn't expect to see you here. Or are you working?'

'Off-duty now.'

'Thank goodness, I'm hoarse from explaining where I was and what I was doing, I don't think I could go through it again. And I think I see another familiar face.'

Miss March half shuffled out of the corner.

'I know I know you,' said Miss Smith, 'but I'm not quite sure . . .'

Then Miss March crumpled at the knees and fell to the floor.

Brandon dropped into a scrubby bank of nettles and briars on the other side of the wall. It was where the rectory glasshouse once stood, but that was long gone. Broken bits of brick and glass still lay under the scrub and Audrey had declared it out of bounds, very firmly when Daniel, with a characteristic lack of pragmatism, suggested rebuilding it. It had become neglected, the wild end of the rectory garden, and a sign of the decline of the country parson who not that long ago would have had people to keep it.

It meant that Brandon landed with a crash, all the louder in the coolness of the night, and the dog on the other side of the wall released another barrage of furious barking. Brandon stayed absolutely still, in a crouch, knowing with a poacher's instinct that the less he did, the sooner this moment of danger would pass. He was not dressed for poaching, in baggy jeans with a hooded top over a T-shirt, and a pair of British Knights trainers that looked too big, with the tongues flopping out in front of the laces. His bumbag, in which he had stashed Theo's order, was highly practical for raves, or what passed for raves in shire counties in Middle England, but he was well ahead of Braunstonbury's curve in the fashions of the rave scene after the Second Summer of Love when somebody had shouted 'Weebles wobble but they don't fall down' at him in the bus station, and he had had to teach them a lesson.

He just hoped he had not landed on something that had cut him, or could cut him. He could not feel the beginning of a sting or the warm spread of blood as his body issued a short and welcome damage report. He was more concerned with Lord de Floures calling for the dog. Maybe that would be enough for it to give up, but it sounded determined. Stubborn and aggressive, sausage dogs, someone had told him. He quite liked it when things people thought were cute turned out not to be. He had given a masterclass in that to the kid who'd mocked him for looking like a Weeble.

The dog's barking began to subside a little, but Brandon did not move. He did not want to start it off again if someone came looking for him. He could hear his lordship's voice – the HMV logo popped into his head – still some distance away, but if a dog won't come to you, you have to go to the dog.

He looked to see if there was a safe route out of his confinement, and he saw in one of the lit windows of the rectory the to-and-fro of the Clements. There was the rector's mother – he recognised her from her walk, for she was, like him, an extra for the kitchen and pantry scenes, and he thought no one who worked in so humble a position walked like her. It was like having Margaret Thatcher come to mop your floors. He saw Theo and Daniel, too, going one way and then the other at the speed not quite of panic, but certainly of urgency. All hands on deck at the rectory tonight, and Lord de Floures among the guests. It was one of the things he hated most about Champton and its parson, fussing over the posh ladies and the peer. Weren't parsons supposed to help the poor? He'd hated those assemblies when he was at the school here, being told to be meek and mild by someone who lived in a house like this for free and only worked one day a week.

A peak of resentment made him stir in his place. It was getting very uncomfortable and he was going to have to move. There was an alcove a little further along down in the wall with a bench in it, somewhere once to sit, but the way to it was full of briars and thistles. If he could get to it, he could sit there quietly, keeping an eye on the back door for his client to emerge, as he knew he soon would, for Theo wouldn't get halfway through his first cocktail without wanting a fag and Audrey had a strict no-smoking rule in the rectory. Unless, he supposed, Bernard wanted to puff on a hookah or a bong, in which case she would have lit up a cheroot herself.

He gently moved his weight from one knee to the other, which caused the brick and broken glass to shift and that started another barrage of barks from the dog on the other side of the wall. Better to make the move now; it couldn't get any worse, and the quicker the better. Still in a crouch, and feeling like he was in the SAS on an operation, he picked a way through the tangles and jagged edges and fallen bricks towards the alcove. How could a dog that was only a bit bigger than a ferret make so much noise?

This was most peculiar, thought Miss March as her senses returned, to be flat on your back on the floor with absolutely no idea how you had got there. She then realised her legs were hoisted up in the air, as if she were about to give birth, and that leaning over her and looking down was not a midwife, but Gillian Smith.

'It's the wardrobe lady!' said Miss Smith. 'Normally it's you taking care of me!'

It would be difficult to imagine a scenario more embarrassing for Miss March. It was so awful, so off the scale of insufferable indignity, that it was almost impossible to believe. 'What happened?' said Miss March as she tried to regain her composure, her dignity, her legs.

'I'm afraid you fainted,' said Miss Smith. 'Thank goodness Mrs Clement has medical experience.'

It was Audrey who had taken control when Miss March fell palely to the floor, putting a cushion under her head, hoisting her legs in the air and sending Theo to get a glass of water and Daniel to get a brandy – 'Kitchen brandy is fine.' It was Audrey who then appeared next to Miss Smith, faintly blurred in the wedge-like shape between Miss March's legs.

'You fainted,' said Audrey, as if she were speaking to an invalid.

'I suppose I must have,' said Miss March.

'Shock of the day,' said Audrey, 'and I don't suppose you had any lunch.'

Miss March sat up and tried to smooth her skirt. 'I think I should go,' she said and tried to stand, but her knees gave way again.

'Come and lie on the sofa,' said Audrey. Neil helped her up and led her gently to the sofa. She did not want to lie down, nor did she feel the need for it, but it was easier to submit to the fuss than try to leave.

Daniel appeared with a little glass of brandy.

'Drink this,' said Audrey, but Miss March did not drink, and the smell of the brandy held up to her face made her feel nauseous.

'Oh, lord,' said Miss Smith, 'are you going to vomit?' She not so subtly backed away.

Miss March shook her head. 'Perhaps a breath of air?'

'You're not going anywhere, Miss March, until you're a bit steadier,' said Audrey.

'No brandy,' said Miss March when Audrey tried to get her to take a sip.

Miss Smith would not normally dine with a wardrobe assistant, even if it were a wardrobe assistant who was at the expert end of that role rather than the seamstress end, and therefore a notch nearer to her, so there was a tone of reproach in her next solicitous remarks. 'Jolly good job you didn't have one of these fainting fits when you were pinning my costume,' she said. 'You could do someone a mischief!'

'I'll be all right in a moment,' said Miss March. 'I was just a bit overwhelmed. I really think I must go home.' She was actually quite desperate to leave. She stood up slowly, but it was fine, no more whooshing in her ears or feeling hot. 'I'll be fine, really.'

Audrey wasn't having it. 'Nonsense, you need to eat, and supper is ready. It may be a plate of cinders – where the hell is Bernard? – but you must have *something*. I really think you should step outside for a moment, Miss March, in the back garden. I'm sure a breath of evening air will make you feel better and then I think we should eat, Bernard or no Bernard.'

'Yes,' said Miss Smith, 'I think I can go with that,' as if it were a matter that required her consent. It was not a pleasant experience for Audrey to find herself displaced from the apex of the rectory hierarchy by an upstart guest, and the instinct to reassert it that rose within her contended with her desire for the social cachet Miss Smith's visit conferred. It was a complicated matter, for her earlier luncheon with Bernard had also not fitted comfortably with her sense of the status quo. Bernard, the sun around which all Champton's planets orbited, shed his light evenly, and Audrey had managed to bring her orbit closer and closer to him, which made her shine and glow, but at luncheon today she had sensed that he did not always want to be the sun, or did not think he did. And if he were to dim his light, or cease to turn, then where would she be? And now a greater sun had appeared in their galaxy and all orbits were off.

'Do the gallant thing, Theo,' said Miss Smith, 'I'll be fine!'

She did not feel fine, for she was suddenly without her point man in a new social environment, and one in which the elements were difficult to assess. Normally she only went to places where her peers presented no potential threat to her pre-eminence, but here there were policemen and wardrobe assistants, and while they were perfectly fine – the policeman was also rather comely – they were not her people. Lord de Floures passed inspection; Theo, her temporary lieutenant, was acceptable; the fascinating parson did not really fit into any social metric – and it was him she was really there to see – and in Audrey she recognised someone who, while not quite Dorothy Parker, would at least give her some sport. She nodded at Theo.

'Allow me,' he said, and offered Miss March his arm. She was glad of a reason to get out of the hot and uncomfortable drawing room and away from the solicitous but unflinching inspection of the others.

'Thank you,' she said, 'and I wonder if I could have my bag?'

Theo hooked her glossy black handbag over his free arm, and with as much dignity as Miss March could muster, they left.

Audrey said, 'I'll call the house and see where Bernard's got to. It's Badsaddle 264, I think, Daniel?'

She knew perfectly well what it was, but she wanted Miss Smith to know that she did not need to look it up.

'Would you excuse me, Miss Smith, but I must leave you for a moment to telephone Lord de Floures.'

'Of course,' said Miss Smith. 'I can monopolise the copper and the vicar.'

'Rector,' said Audrey as she left.

'Rector. Now,' she said confidingly to Daniel, 'you must tell me what the difference is between a vicar and a rector.'

'Nothing much now. Originally it meant a rector got the greater income – the rectorial tithe – but we all get the same now, so it's historic. In America it's different.'

'How long have you lived there, Miss Smith?' said Neil.

'Since my twenties, on and off.'

'Do you like it?'

'I love it. The weather, the . . . I don't know . . . people are easy, and it's where we make the movies.'

'Don't you miss England?'

'When people ask me that in interviews I usually say something about red buses and Ovaltine, but actually no, I don't. Partly because I'm from Clapham, so . . . you know? But really, it's because I like the lightness there. You breeze along, no one looks backwards, it's all forwards.'

'I can't think of anywhere less like Oldham,' said Neil.

'No,' said Miss Smith, 'very distant from LA.'

'Yes, do you know it?'

'I certainly do, from rep. Alexandra in *The Little Foxes*, Vicky in *Hobson's Choice*. Lyceum, or was it the Coliseum? Can't remember. Which is the one with the ghost?

'Coliseum.'

'Not that one. But you're too young to have seen me in either.'

'I could have, but we weren't allowed to go to the theatre when I was a boy.'

'Whyever not?'

'Not a suitable entertainment for the Brethren.'

Miss Smith looked suddenly alert. 'You're Plymouth Brethren?'

'Moravian Brethren.'

'Oh, yes, you said. From Belgium or somewhere?'

'Then Germany, then here.'

'Do you know the Plymouth Brethren, Miss Smith?' said Daniel.

'I do. My family was Brethren. Very strict. No musical instruments, I wasn't allowed the wireless, heads covered, and no boys. Can you imagine?'

Audrey appeared in the door. 'Very odd,' she said. 'I called the house and Mrs Shorely said Bernard left about twenty minutes ago.'

'Walking or Land Rover?' said Daniel.

'Walking, and he's got Cosmo. I wonder where he can have got to?'

Neil said, 'I can go and look for him if you like?'

'Would you mind? I imagine you have a torch.'

'I do,' said Neil. 'Excuse me, folks, I shouldn't be long.'

'They come, they go, they don't come at all,' said Miss Smith.

'I'm afraid I have to go and do some remedial work in the kitchen,' said Audrey.

Daniel and Miss Smith were alone.

'Could Anne of Denmark have come here, do you think, and talked to the then rector as I am talking to you now?'

'Not quite here,' said Dan, 'this house wasn't built then. But there was another house here before this. The cellar here is thirteenth century, so she could have been on the spot.'

'Anne of Denmark and the Rector of Champton, revived.'

'I'm the Rector of Champton St Mary and the Bad-saddles actually.'

'I'm Denmark, Scotland and England.'

'What a burden that must be.'

'Quite. But I'm playacting. You're not.'

'Not always.'

'What's the heaviest thing you have to carry?'

What a question, thought Daniel, for a pre-dinner drink. 'It can be lonely.'

'Check.'

'There's a boundlessness to it sometimes. The task. The demands.'

'Check.'

Daniel didn't actually know what she meant by 'check'.

'And I'm more and more aware of how often I can't do anything useful, or anything at all, to help.'

'How about now?'

'A death like Margaret's is always difficult to face. A death like that, while we're all in the middle of play-acting – theatre, film, is so like play, don't you think? Play for grown-ups? The unreality is compounded and everyone and everything goes out of focus. My job is to help get it back in focus.'

'You're a focus puller.'

'Oh, I thought the same thing, or something like it, if I understand what you mean.'

'Someone to make sure everything is always crisp and unblurred and steady, no matter what's going on.'

'Yes, a bit like that. In an extreme way.'

'And that's how you catch killers? Getting everything back into focus?'

'Yes, I suppose so. It is when everything is in focus that our deeds are uncovered. Or rather they uncover themselves.'

Miss Smith gave a shudder. 'It reminds me of a print my grandparents had of God's all-seeing eye. It was on the wall of the spare room. It used to stare down at me when I went to stay.'

'I remember those. I think they were intended more for boys' bedrooms, if that is not too indelicate a way of putting it.'

'Oh, vicar! I mean, rector! Why does that stick in my mind, do you think?'

'I don't know. Perhaps it frightened you?'

'It did a bit, but I think now it was more than that. You see, I liked the idea of being looked at. I still do.'

'I suppose you must be one of the most looked-at people . . . anywhere?'

'I suppose I am. Actually, there's no suppose about it. I wanted it, I got it. Be careful what you pray for.'

'I would find that very difficult,' said Daniel.

Miss Smith's eyes narrowed. 'But you are looked at all the time! In church and going round the place in your dog collar and your . . . costumes.'

'Yes, but it's hardly on the same scale, and no one's interested in my star sign.'

'So you regret taking this role? You would rather not be looked at?'

'I don't regret being Rector of Champton, not at all, I love it. I love being a priest. But I don't much like being looked at. Be careful what you pray for.'

'Right,' Gilly said.

'It's a common predicament for clergy. There was some analysis done, which found that we are by nature introverts, but most of us are forced to live an extrovert's life. Some of my colleagues are made miserable by having to go on parade, perform, go to things.'

'And you?'

'Most of the time I don't mind it, but sometimes it gets a bit much. Managing people's expectations, realistic and unrealistic. Trying to have a private life can be difficult. The hardest thing, I find, is when trouble comes your way, when you're turned upside down and you don't know what you're doing. I've been through something like this lately. I found I couldn't bear looking at faces looking at me in the expectation that I will unfailingly provide whatever it is they want.'

'I've been looked at so intently and for so long I've forgotten what it's like not to be. And now I can't imagine how I would even live without it.'

'That sounds, forgive me, like an unliveable life.'

'Not for me,' she said.

'The version of you that is in the gaze of others is the one that is focused. The version of you – it's not a version, I would argue, but the original – that is not available in that way is out of focus, blurred.'

'Goodness, how . . . Hitchcockian.'

Miss March shivered in the cool night air. Going from hot to cold, from drawing room to back garden, was like having the flu. And then she recalled coming round from her faint to Gillian Smith looking down at her from between her opened legs. The thought was so awful she said out loud, 'Jesu mercy, Mary pray!' like a spell to neutralise the shame that spread across her face and made her suddenly hot again.

'What was that, Miss March?' said Theo.

'Nothing. But what a scene I just made!'

'Would you like to sit?' There was a bench by the

back door where he liked to have a cigarette. 'Do you mind if I . . .?' He produced a packet of Silk Cut. Miss March did mind, but she shook her head. 'Would you like one?' She shook her head again. 'It was just a faint. And you've had one hell of a day. And you haven't eaten. Do you want a banana?'

'To lose control like that. And in front of Miss Smith! I feel I've let the side down. Causing a scene at your mother's when she's cooked a fish pie for a film star . . .'

'Don't worry about Mum, she won't mind the drama. She likes drama. And her triumph was assured the moment Miss Smith consented to grace us with her presence.'

They were interrupted by a series of angry barks.

'That sounds like Cosmo,' said Theo. 'Did we let him out?'

'I don't know, I didn't see. I wonder what he's barking at.'

'A leaf. A shadow. A twig. It doesn't take much.'

The barks came again.

'It doesn't sound like he's in the garden. It sounds like he's in the park,' said Miss March.

Then a figure appeared out of the darkness. To Miss March he looked like an unusually large child, dressed for the playground rather than an autumn night.

Theo thought, what the hell is he doing in the back garden?

Brandon stepped into the pool of light cast from the kitchen window.

Miss March fainted again.

15

Neil's torch flickered along the path that led from the rectory into the park. He couldn't see anyone, but then he heard a dog barking, a bark he thought he recognised. It came from the little stand of trees that stood in the corner made by the wall to the park and the rectory garden wall. And then he heard a voice he recognised come out of it.

'You little brute, where are you?'

There was a sound of something heavy crashing through undergrowth.

Neil peered in with the torch. 'Lord de Floures? Is that you?'

'Must you shine that damn thing in my eyes? Who are you? What are you doing in my park?'

'It's Detective Sergeant Vanloo, sir. Are you in some difficulty?'

There was a pause and then Bernard said, 'Are you any good with dogs?'

Neil headed through the thickets and the under-growth and the low-hanging branches to where the voice had come from. It was only September, but there was already that faint, gamey smell of decay as autumn approached. He shone his torch in front of him and it soon found Lord de Floures, who had got into a bit of a state, looking dishevelled and with muddy shoes.

He shaded his eyes and said, 'Sergeant, I've lost the damn dog. He heard something and ran into the trees. I can hear the little bugger, but I can't see him and he won't come when I call.'

'What was it he went after, sir?' said Neil.

'No idea – a rabbit? A fox? Whatever it is, I think he may have it cornered. He's still barking.'

At that moment Cosmo started off again.

'Who would have thought that small a dog could make such a fucking racket?'

'They don't know they're small,' said Neil.

'Spirited too. Did you know they were bred to hunt badgers?'

'I did, sir, yes.'

'Imagine him taking on a big bruiser brock? Do you think we might be dealing with one here?'

'I don't think so. Bit early for badgers. And they're more down Holly Walk, aren't they?'

'They are. He went after one there a while ago and had to be dug out.'

'I remember,' said Neil.

'Were you there?'

'I heard about it.'

Bernard was not interested in the goings-on of his children – he preferred not to know – but he was not blind and deaf to a frisson, and he knew something had happened between this policeman and his daughter. By his calculation, Neil owed him, at least, a favour. 'Perhaps he will heed your call?' he said.

'Cosmo! Cosmo!' shouted Neil, and then he listened for the scrabbling sound of a miniature dachshund running through scrub. No sound came.

'Doesn't come for you either,' said Bernard. 'Perhaps you might fetch him? I can't see anything, and I am no longer lithe.'

Neil pushed through towards the sound of the barking. He found Cosmo in the torch's beam, but he had not cornered a badger, or a rabbit, or anything. He was standing as tall as he could on his little legs and barking at the wall directly in front of him. Neil called him, but he was completely absorbed in his hunt. So Neil went to get him, picking him up in one sweeping movement and tucking him under his arm. This caught Cosmo by surprise and he was immediately compliant, from fierce hunter to tiny pet in one move.

Neil was about to return the dog to Lord de Floures but stopped and cast the torchlight over the wall. It looked like something had scrambled up it recently. Could badgers climb? Maybe a rat? He went to have a closer look, and noticed a tear in the mossy surface of the coping. Had something, someone, been over?

'Have you got him?'

'Yes, got him,' Neil said. He brought the dog to Lord de Floures, who tucked him under his arm. 'Maybe put him on the lead if he's in the habit of running off.'

'I'm not going to put my dog on a lead just to take a walk in the park,' said Bernard.

'He's not a Labrador, sir. If they see something, they run.'

'He'll come back when he wants to,' said Bernard. 'Why are you still here? I thought you were done for the day?'

'We are. But I'm having supper with you at the rectory tonight. Mrs Clement asked me to see if you'd got lost.'

'Christ, what time is it?'

'Suppertime. And we're joined by Miss Smith.'

'So we're keeping the ladies waiting. That will never do.'

They walked down the path towards the rectory. Cosmo turned his head once to look towards the copse where his quarry had fled and disappeared.

The dog was still there. Every time Brandon had shifted it started barking again, like an Alsatian guarding the perimeter of a military base in a film. He had stayed still and then heard a second voice shouting for Cosmo. He saw the flicker of torchlight in the trees on the other side of the wall. A search party. He moved again and the dog barked again, but he would have to risk it because he did not want to get caught. He moved across what was once the floor of the greenhouse, still dangerous with broken glass and half-bricks, but was lucky this time and got to the other side without making things worse. He crouched down for a while behind a bed of nettles, in case the person with the torch decided to take a look over the wall, but the dog had stopped barking and whoever it was seemed to be insufficiently curious. He saw the flicker start to move away. Maybe he could find a way of making himself more comfortable. It was cold now, his hoodie and T-shirt were not warm, and he had been lying low. Maybe he could find a way of getting Theo to come to the door. Could he ring on the doorbell and ask for him? He didn't think that would be a good idea. Theo would have to explain who he was and what he wanted.

Then he had heard the sound of a door opening. It was the back door of the rectory. A rectangle of yellow light appeared and a figure passed across, and then the rectangle disappeared as the door shut. It was too dark to make much out, but who else could it be but Theo? If it was, he could do what he needed to do, and go home.

A spurt of light illuminated a face and then the red laser dot of a lit cigarette end brightening as Theo took a drag.

Brandon stood up and walked towards it. It was only when he got within the field of light made by the kitchen window that he saw that Theo was not alone.

He stopped, and the figure sitting next to Theo fell sideways.

'Christ, Brandon!' said Theo. 'You gave me a fright. And Miss March – she's fainted again!'

'I've got your gear,' he said. 'I was passing.'

'I can't do anything about that now. Hang around, out of sight. I'll sort her and slip back when I can.'

Audrey was in the kitchen wondering if the fish pie could take another ten minutes in the Aga. It had been out for long enough now to congeal and another blast of heat would loosen it and, she hoped, make it more or less palatable, but it was well past its best. Curse these guests, turning up late. The peas had been on and were now off and wrinkled and hard, so she was going to make a new panful. The pastry rim of her mincemeat tart had become browned to the point of combustion. It was only a midweek supper, and a scratch supper at that, but this was like school food. Her most glittering table ever and she was about to serve congealed fish pie and burnt mincemeat tart.

Theo stuck his head around the door. 'Mum, it's Miss March. She's fainted again.'

'Again? This is like the Beatles at Shea Stadium!'

'I wonder if she needs to see the doctor.'

'Nonsense, it's just a long day and an empty stomach.'

Audrey patted down her pinny and came through the back door to find Miss March sitting a bit groggily on the bench.

'No need to elevate my legs, Mrs Clement, if you don't mind . . .'

'Are you all right?'

'I'm absolutely fine, thank you, but perhaps it would be better if I just slipped away?' said Miss March.

'But you must eat something!'

'I can have a sandwich at home, really. Please don't make a fuss.'

'Oh, *really* . . .'

Audrey's inability to disguise her disappointment at another mishap befalling her supper party may have been construed as disconcerting by someone as finely balanced as Miss March, but she knew Audrey, and her inability to disguise what she felt about anything.

'Yes, really, I don't want to end up face down in a plate of fish pie, so better if I go.'

Audrey recovered herself. 'Theo, could you see Miss March home?'

'There's absolutely no need,' said Miss March. 'I would much prefer not to put people to any trouble.'

Theo, seeing a double opportunity to be gallant and to effect his transaction, said, 'Yes, of course. Did you have a coat, Miss March?'

'It's hanging up in the cloakroom,' said Audrey. 'Wool, Jaeger, grey herringbone, four double buttons.'

'I'll get it for you.'

'And your bag?' said Audrey.

'With me,' said Miss March, patting it, partly to make sure she really did have it.

Theo left Miss March to Audrey.

'Let me at least make you a plate to take home. I don't like to think of you on your own and too feeble to slice bread.'

'I would rather be on my own, Mrs Clement. And I don't feel up to a full meal.'

Audrey found it difficult to imagine why someone would want to be on their own, especially when a peer of the realm and a film star were on offer thanks to her. 'As you wish, Miss March. Anyway, by the time we actually sit down to eat it will be inedible.'

'I am very sorry to bow out like this, really, but I think it's for the best.'

Audrey said, 'Well, yes . . .' There was something about the form of words in which English stoicism is expressed – make do and mend, we soldier on, it's for the best – that pleased her, although she was not especially conscious of it. Miss March had noticed this in her and wondered if it came from experience, surviving a war, or perhaps was more deeply rooted than that, in a form of English Protestantism that thought suffering was not so bad if it encouraged one in the virtue of endurance. It was an unfashionable virtue, but one Miss March rather admired, and she thought of St Paul's helpful exhortation in the Epistle to the Romans, to 'glory in tribulations also, knowing that tribulation worketh patience; patience, experience; and experience, hope'. It was a text that had spoken to her in her own times of tribulation.

'No fuss, Mrs Clement,' she said. 'You understand?'

'Naturally,' said Audrey in the bell-like tone she used to smother irritation she would rather not confess.

Theo returned with Miss March's coat and helped her into it with the same courtliness he had shown to Gillian Smith.

'Thank you, Mr Clement. It's really not necessary for you to walk me home.'

'Of course I'm going to walk you home, Miss March.'

'And make sure she gets up those stairs safely, Theo,' said Audrey. 'I couldn't live with myself if you were to be found at the bottom of them in a heap.'

'Mrs Clement,' said Miss March, 'I do hope I haven't spoilt your evening. Goodnight.'

'Goodnight, Miss March. Please don't give it another thought.'

Theo gave Miss March his arm, which she declined, and off they went into the darkness.

Audrey was annoyed, not only at the added disruption to the evening, but because she thought it uninspiring for people to retire from the field of battle. She had expected more of Miss March, and while she had indeed endured a very difficult day, it would do her no good, let alone anyone else, to sit gibbering alone at home with a pot of hazelnut yoghurt when she could be part of Audrey's triumph. Her laurels were now in danger of wilting before they had even encircled her brow – worse than wilting, crisping, as desiccated as the fish pie that was at the very edge of viability in the Aga's warming oven. Audrey may have had the body of a weak and feeble woman, but she had the liver and lights of a High Church parson's mother, and the evening was not lost yet.

The rapport between Miss Smith and Daniel might have surprised some – what did a film star and parson have to do with each other? – but it did not surprise Daniel and Miss Smith. Daniel's character and vocation had given him a capacity for rapport with all kinds of people in all states of life. It did not matter to him very much whether someone was a princess or a beggar; both were equally important to God and so it behoved him to treat them also as equally important. And, curious by nature, he quietly and intently studied what people did, when they did it and why, and what they did not do. This was not especially to understand them better – he had discovered that people are not there to be understood, as he had once thought – but to broaden his sympathies, to become more imaginative about what it would be like to fight in a war, to have twins, to like calypso, to rob a security van. So he was in one sense particularly interested in outliers, those whose lives were unusually unusual, and a film star was certainly in that category.

Miss Smith had also made people her study, for while she liked to think of her vocation as a sort of magic, her work was created out of the base ingredients of gait and tic, of deftness and clumsiness, of how we tie our shoelaces and how we brush our hair, and above all of the tiny tensing and relaxing of the muscles around the eyes and in the throat. Motive, character, the larger themes of a life, came after that; in the first instance, it was the way they filled the space around them. She was fascinated by Daniel's calmness. It was not, she thought, his natural temperament, but acquired. There was a suggestion about him of consolidation, someone who had put together something that was in discrete parts, and she wanted to know more about that. It made him curiously attractive, and he had absolutely no idea that he was, which made him even more attractive. She was also difficult to intimidate, not, like him, because she thought all people equal, but because she had rarely met anyone she did not think she could defeat.

'How did you start in all this, Daniel?' she said.

'It's the only thing I've ever wanted to do,' he said, 'apart from be a monk, and that did not work out.'

'What happened?'

'I tried it and discovered there was something else intended for me.'

'Didn't you solve a murder in a monastery or something like that? Carrie told me.'

'That's what the newspaper called it.'

'I suppose monasteries are full of murderous impulses.'

'They are.'

'Like drama schools. But there are other physical exertions that also occupy the student body, and I don't mean tap dancing.'

'I suppose not. I have seen that in a very pronounced way in Theo's life. He seems to share his bed more readily than his postcode.'

'Lots of actors are like that. It gets you where you want to go quicker.'

'Where's that?'

'Intimacy.'

Daniel very faintly recoiled from that, but not faintly enough for Miss Smith to miss it.

'Not your thing, Dan?'

Daniel opened his mouth to speak but shut it again to think. Then he said, 'To do what I do, to be available for those who I am responsible for, I have to keep roughly the same distance from everyone. A significant other − isn't that what you say? − would not fit into that.'

'Your mother? Your brother?'

'I mean, to have a first choice, and to be someone's first choice.'

The moment he said this he felt an embarrassing liquefaction at the corner of his eyes and looked away.

'Oh dear,' said Miss Smith, 'where did *that* come from?'

'It is difficult sometimes,' said Daniel. 'Lonely. It never used to bother me but now it does. Middle age.'

'How old are you?'

'Almost fifty.'

'A real fifty or a Hollywood fifty?'

'Real.'

'That's nothing.'

'I look in the mirror and see my grandfather looking back at me.'

'But think of everything you've done. Everything you are.'

'I do. And I see what I haven't done and am not and the horizon in front getting closer every day. You know?'

'I know. But beyond the horizon is your payday, if I can put it like that. I don't get that.'

'You're not a believer,' Daniel said.

'No.'

'It all feels a little abstract sometimes.'

'I don't think you really believe that,' she said. 'Sounds to me like a mid-life crisis. Get a . . . whatever vicars have for fun. A Morris Minor?'

'I already have an ancient Land Rover.'

'And you know what you crave is not what you would get?'

'Yes, I know.'

'Oh,' said Miss Smith, 'you got it.'

'No. But I wanted it.'

Miss Smith suddenly burst out laughing.

Daniel flinched. 'Why is this funny?'

'Oh, the comedy of life, Daniel. I don't mean to sound unfeeling, but can't you see that?'

'It doesn't feel very amusing to me.'

'No, dear, I don't suppose it does, but you will laugh about this one day. I hope it's soon.'

Audrey came in. 'I'm so sorry you're having to wait, Gilly, you must be famished, only we're still not all here. Bloody Bernard.'

'But you have the Detective Sergeant on the case, so I'm sure it won't be long,' said Miss Smith.

'And we're down a guest too. Miss March, I'm afraid – she decided to go home and didn't want to make a fuss.'

'Oh, what a shame. All the more for us, though.'

'If there's anything left that's edible.'

'I hardly eat anything, Audrey, so don't worry about it.'

'And for the other guests?'

Miss Smith ignored this. 'Daniel's been telling me all about being a parson. Fascinating!'

'I don't suppose you come across them very often,' said Audrey.

'Country parsons, not really. Not in LA. But I grew up in a religious family, a very religious family.'

'Oh, I see. And is that why you became an actress?'

'How do you mean?'

'You went to the other extreme?' said Audrey.

'I don't follow.'

'It's not unusual, is it, for someone from a very conventional background to run away and join the circus, seek a life of excitement and applause . . . the roar of the greasepaint, the smell of the crowd?'

'I didn't run away and join the circus, Audrey, I got into amateur dramatics. And that was quite a battle at home, I can tell you. My parents were strict enough, but my grandparents! You'd think I'd become a streetwalker!'

'That must have been very difficult,' said Audrey.

'It was, but a girl's gotta do what a girl's gotta do!'

'For them.'

Daniel interrupted. 'Did you know actors were declared excommunicate by the Council of Arles in 314? For John Chrysostom, the theatre was the Temple of Satan . . .'

'Oh dear,' said Miss Smith, 'are you going to excommunicate me?'

'What they understood by theatre is not what we understand by theatre,' said Daniel. 'This was closer to gladiatorial combat, not *French Without Tears*.'

'*French Without Tears*,' said Miss Smith. 'I must have done it a dozen times!'

'Did you play Diana?' said Audrey.

'I did,' said Miss Smith. 'I loved that part!'

'Could have been written for you,' said Audrey.

'And what about you, Audrey?' said Miss Smith. 'What was the lovely Theo running away from when he joined the circus?'

'Theo?' said Audrey. 'Oh, quite different. He's more Royal Shakespeare Company, the Old Vic – classical rather than, you know, Tinseltown.'

'Then how versatile of him to move so effortlessly into the soaps.'

'*Appletree End* is not really a soap, per se, it's a serial drama.'

'Daa-de-de-da-da-daa,' sang Miss Smith, the theme tune from *Coronation Street*. 'I suppose if Shakespeare were alive today, he'd be writing *Coronation Street*.'

'Who could possibly say?'

'The Merry Wives of Weatherfield.'

'How funny.'

'Antony and Ena Sharples.'

'I didn't know you could get ITV in America.'

'You can't. I have it couriered out, Audrey. On VHS.'

'In a diplomatic bag?'

Daniel interrupted again. 'The Council of Arles in 314 also aimed to settle the tricky matter of the celebration of Easter. It had been locally decided up until then, but they fixed a specific day, a Sunday, for all the churches to observe it. Much debated, of course, and remember Polycrates of Ephesus had been excommunicated for Quartodecimanism a hundred years earlier, or thereabouts . . .'

He knew he was gabbling, but he needed to come between Audrey and Miss Smith, and there was nothing like an early-Church controversy to smother a passionate surge of any kind.

'People often mistakenly believe the Synod of Whitby in 664 decided the matter, but it was not so; the Synod was to settle the question of the date of Easter, not the day on which the Resurrection was to be observed, and the churches that followed the practice of St Columba diverged from those that followed the reformed practice of Rome. Not just churches but individuals, and it is said that before the Synod there were three dates for Easter, and even in the royal court the king and queen, Oswig and Enfleda, differed and observed Easter on two different dates, so one was feasting while the other was fasting.'

'Fasting,' said Miss Smith, 'aren't we all?'

16

As Theo and Miss March made their way down the rectory drive, they met Neil and Bernard coming up it. Cosmo, still in a state of heightened alertness, scampered towards them and made Miss March flinch. Her nerves had been shredded all day, and she did not like dogs when she was at her best, so to have to endure a dachshund's guileless and incorrigible intrusiveness at this unusually testing time was too much. As he barked at her ankles she very much wanted to give him a kick, but she knew, even in her disrupted state, that if she did it would not be forgotten and only forgiven by Daniel, for that is what he would have to do. The elements necessary for Miss March's poise, so important to her, were, if not exact, defined, and the shock of the morning and the embarrassments of the evening had made her look longingly for the exit. She was out, but she was not yet alone, and she would prefer Theo not to walk her home, but he seemed determined to do so. She had an inkling this might not be simply for reasons of gallantry, but she did not wish to know what those other reasons were. And now another hurdle to leap before she could ascend her lonely stair.

'Have we missed supper?' said Bernard. 'My fault, I'm afraid. No, not my fault, it's that bloody dog's fault. He ran off after a rabbit or a fox or something. Audrey will be . . . well, you know Audrey.'

'I'm just walking Miss March home, Bernard,' said Theo, 'so you won't be the last to answer the summons of the dinner gong.'

'I hope you are not unwell, Miss March?' said Bernard.

'Fainted,' said Theo, 'twice. Or was it thrice?'

Miss March flinched again. 'A combination of fatigue and not having eaten, your lordship . . .' She immediately regretted the tone of deference she would normally employ in the shop for the more select of her clientele. It sounded overdone in the social world where the house and the rectory overlapped, but she had not yet worked out what the right tone should be.

'A most difficult day, Miss March.'

She could not think of anything to say, so nodded in a way she thought suitably solemn. How quickly, when we lose our savoir faire, she thought, we resort to little pantomimes.

Theo said, 'You'll feel better after a night's sleep.'

How could you know that? she thought, but just nodded solemnly again.

Neil said, 'Yes, I hope you will soon feel better, Miss

March, and I don't think we should stand in your way or keep Audrey waiting any longer.'

Bernard tried to call Cosmo to heel, but Cosmo was not that sort of dog and did what he wanted, not what Bernard wanted. He was torn between continuing his investigation of Theo and Miss March and wanting the rectory door to open so he would be home. He went backwards and forwards and backwards again before the draw of what lay ahead diverted him from the more proximate interest of the ankles on the drive. He finally decided on forwards and, with Bernard and Neil, approached home and hearth.

Miss March tried again to rid herself of Theo. 'I really am perfectly able to get home without your assistance,' she said.

'No way,' said Theo, 'Mum's orders. And what if you passed out and fell in the brook?'

She said nothing and the crunch of feet on gravel turned to the padding sound of feet on asphalt. It was colder now, the kind of early autumn cold that is much milder than what comes in November and December but has enough of a suggestion of it to make you think of jumpers and logs. Miss March did not think of jumpers or logs, because she would no sooner wear a jumper than a wet suit, and her little sitting room had an electric fire with unconvincing artificial coals and a sort of ruddy mini cyclorama to give the suggestion of flame. How she longed to be there and to be alone.

Theo was making conversation. 'Will you go back on

location, Miss March? Or, after today's . . . events . . . will you, entirely understandably, want to close that chapter?'

'I shall go back as soon as I am required to go back,' she said.

'The show must go on.'

'Must it? Won't there be at least a pause, an interval, before filming resumes? It seems so indecently casual to carry on as if nothing had happened, as if death was just a frustrating interruption to the schedule.'

'It's like a war,' said Theo. 'We must carry on, we must fight them on the beaches and all that, we must never surrender.'

'It's not a war, is it? It's an entertainment.' She suddenly felt a surge of anger. 'It's preposterous to go on about it as if it were D-Day. Nobody gets killed. Except today somebody was. Doesn't that mean something?'

'I'm not being serious, Miss March.'

'Perhaps you could try to be? For once?'

'I'm being satirical. Of course Margaret's death means something, of course it's a tragedy we should acknowledge properly, but there are still hundreds of people on payroll, there is limited time, and the West Coast are on the phone every hour. That doesn't just go away.'

'In the old days we respected the dead. We marked a passing, rang a bell, closed the shop, drew the blinds, put on black bombazine. What makes you so special?'

'I'd love to say the power of storytelling, or something

about dreams coming true, but it's really about money. There's so much of it at stake, so much that can be made.'

'It's not right.'

'I suppose not, but before we get too nostalgic for the old days, do you think the coal mines all stopped when there was an underground explosion? Miners who were killed before noon were docked half a day's pay. Thus, it ever was.'

'Miners dug out the coal that ran industries and power stations. Dressing up in doublet and hose – your ruff is all wrong, by the way – and dancing a minuet as a prelude to an orgy is hardly an essential service.'

'I don't know, I think it is in its way. It is not something for which the need is urgent, but we will need it. We need stories and flicks and televisions . . .'

'. . . and *Appletree End* . . .'

'And even *Appletree End*. I think what we do is not unlike what Daniel does.'

'You think you're the Church of England? I struggle to see the resemblance.'

'No, but we are both providers of stories that give people comfort, and challenge them, and offer a sense of who they are and how they fit in.'

'But you're pretending.'

'Yes, the stories are made up, but they tell the truth about what it is to be human. Some would say that's no different from what the Church does.'

'Do you think that?'

'I do,' he said.

'I don't.'

'What do you think?'

'That God was man in Palestine, and lives today in bread and wine.'

'Do you *really* believe it?'

'Yes,' said Miss March.

'Why?'

'It makes sense.'

'Really? How can it make sense that a man is killed and comes back to life and says that everyone else when they die will live again and it will all be all right?'

'I didn't say it sounded likely. I said it makes sense.'

'I don't see the sense.'

'It's not something I can easily describe. I used to think what you think. I assume you're an atheist?'

Theo nodded.

'So was I. The Christianity I had grown up with was a fairy tale, and no one could possibly want to live their life as if it were a fairy tale. So I put it behind me. I grew out of it. But as I got older, and lived my life, and fortune and misfortune came my way, I gradually started wanting to make a connection to it again. I didn't know what for. A memory, a feeling, hymns, an atmosphere – that got me through the door. It wasn't that my questions were all answered, my doubts overcome, not at all . . . I just wanted what it offered. So I started going to church, St Philip and James at Stow. I sat at the back and no one bothered me or asked how I was, thank goodness.'

'Sounds a bit cold.'

'No, not at all, it was very welcoming, but I think they didn't want to get in the way of what was happening.'

'Which was?'

'Discovering that it was not behind me, but in front of me.'

Theo said, 'But that *doesn't* make sense.'

'It made perfect sense. It was what I thought before that did not make sense. When I was a child I thought like a child, as St Paul said, but I was no longer a child, and I had to put that away and confront everything that was beginning to open up. Who am I? What's important? Do you see?'

'No, I don't think I do. I've never felt anything like that,' said Theo. 'And we're here. Elite Fashions.'

They stood outside the shop. Miss March had left a light on in the passageway that led down the side to the door to her flat.

'I have said too much, Mr Clement, forgive me.'

'Nothing to forgive, Miss March. Will you be all right? I would feel happier if I could see you in.'

'Really no need. Goodnight.'

'Goodnight.'

She turned and walked down the passageway, from the darkness of the street into its light, which seemed the wrong way round for an exit, he thought, until she let herself in and switched off the exterior light.

He started back to the rectory, took a cigarette and lit it. He walked at the pace he thought right for him to finish the cigarette at the moment he got to the rectory gate. He would then suck a Polo, a habit he had got into when he was a teenager trying to disguise his smoking. It had stuck with him in adulthood because he had to get close, and sometimes very close, to other actors and it did not help his performance if they recoiled from his ashtray smell. Then he saw someone waiting at the corner where Main Street turned into Church Lane. It was Brandon Redding.

'At last. I'm freezing,' Brandon said.

'You look like you've been at a rave.'

'I've been at Alex and Nathan's. And I've been hanging about waiting for you in the cold night air. That fucking little ferret came at me.'

'You mean Cosmo? I thought I heard his bark.'

'His lordship was walking him down from the house and he must have heard me in the cover by your wall. Came at me like a pit bull.'

Theo laughed. 'I'd have loved to see you chased by a little sausage dog.'

'It wasn't the dog I was worried about; it was the noise he made. And you should be grateful I got away – over your back wall; look what it's done to my jeans . . .' There was a dark stain across the thigh, and they were tatty, but they probably already were, thought Theo. 'All because the lady loves Milk Tray . . .'

'That's very thoughtful of you, Brandon, but you're insane to hang around a crime scene with police everywhere and your bumbag full of blow.'

'Not just blow. I've got Charlie and acid. And sinse-milla. What do you want?'

'I'll have a bag of sinsemilla and a couple of grams of Charlie.'

'No acid? I've got microdots.'

'No, thanks, it's mushroom season and I think we'll be going back to nature.'

'Where are you picking them?'

'I'm not telling you, Brandon, it would be like inviting a plague of locusts.'

Brandon shrugged. 'I have my own supplies. How about three grams of Charlie?'

'Can you do me a price?'

The deal was done.

Daniel's attempts to thaw the froideur that was forming between Miss Smith and his mother by smothering it with the credal controversies of the early Church was effectual in much the same way as throwing a kitchen towel over a fire retards flames. The two women, so different and so alike, had fallen silent from weariness rather than in a spirit of reconciliation. Then he heard the front door open.

'That will be Bernard and Neil,' said Audrey, obviously relieved. 'Dan, you look after them. I'll serve up.'

'Can I help at all?' said Gilly.

'I don't think so,' said Audrey, and headed to the kitchen but first intercepted the late arrival.

'Bernard, you're here at last! What on earth has happened?'

'A thousand apologies, Audrey. I lost Cosmo. He ran off. After a badger or something. I hope dinner is not ruined?'

'That rather depends on your expectations.'

'Oh dear. You should have started without me.'

'Would have done if we'd known you were going to be so late. But I can't stop, I've got to get the peas on. Dan will look after you.'

As she disappeared into the kitchen Daniel, looking emollient, appeared in the hall.

'Daniel, I am most dreadfully sorry,' said Bernard. 'It was Cosmo, he ran off.'

'Oh dear,' said Daniel, stooping to scratch Cosmo's head, 'who's been a naughty boy? Who's been such a naughty boy?'

Cosmo was the only creature on earth Daniel addressed in baby language. To others it sounded as unlikely coming from him as a rugby song from Nana Mouskouri, but Daniel could be fond and sentimental, only never towards another person, only to the dogs.

'It was the Detective Sergeant who found him,' said Bernard, 'in the stand of trees by your wall. Badger perhaps, or a fox. Doughty little beast, isn't he?'

'Utterly fearless,' said Neil, 'dangerously so.'

'He must be a hungry boy too,' said Daniel. 'I'll get him and Hilda their dinner.'

At that word Cosmo looked suddenly alert, scampered

to the kitchen door and looked round expectantly at Daniel.

'Miss Smith's in the drawing room. Supper won't be long now. Neil, could you sort Bernard out with a drink?'

In the drawing room Miss Smith had half curled up on the sofa. She was not used to being neglected, even for a moment, so her hackles, if not exactly risen, were on the up.

'Here he is,' she said. 'Lord de Floures, they seek him here, they seek him there.'

'My apologies,' said Bernard, only with less patience than he had mustered for his host, 'but . . . we were delayed unavoidably. Bernard de Floures,' he said, and advanced towards her with his hand outstretched.

'I won't get up, if you don't mind,' she said, extending her hand, 'only I've had a hell of a day.'

Bernard had to stoop to shake it, which made him feel like he was offering not only a hand for friendship but an act of obeisance, and he did not like that much. He knew perfectly well who Miss Smith was but thought her grandeur invited an enquiry.

'And you are?'

'We met already, don't you remember? Gillian Smith.'

'Can I pour you another, Miss Smith?' interrupted Neil. 'Same again?'

'How far off dinner are we?'

'Any minute.'

'Then I'll pass.'

'What about you?' said Neil to Bernard, not sure how to address him in a suddenly social environment with a film star making things more complicated.

'I'll have a whisky, if there is one.'

'There's Famous Grouse.'

'With a splash of soda.'

'Do you want to do it? I'm never sure how much to put in.'

'Oh, just a squirt, it's not difficult.'

Neil sensed the mood had stiffened since he had left to find Bernard, and suspected that relations between Audrey and Miss Smith had an element of difficulty – not a surprise, if so. Miss March's swoon had also added drama to the evening, and now Bernard, who was moody all the time, had arrived and introduced another difficult dynamic. How did the pecking order work if you had a peer of the realm and a film star at the dining-room table? Who would sit where? How could the appropriate honours be paid to two different but qualifying guests?

Neil handed Bernard his drink, and he took quite a large swallow – a swallow which reminded Neil of the dogs eating their dinners, not like gourmets savouring every nuance, but like whales hoovering up krill.

'Touch of autumn,' he said to no one in particular as a way of restarting things.

'I adore an English autumn,' said Miss Smith. 'It's one of the things I most miss in LA.'

'Don't you have the seasons in America?' said Bernard. 'My cousin in New York seems to think you do.'

'That's New York,' said Miss Smith. 'In LA there's summer and there's summer, we don't have fall.'

'Fall?'

'Autumn. I long for bonfires and conkers and . . . that fungal smell you get in woods.' She could not say the word fungal without wrinkling her nose, which rather gave the lie to her assertion of nostalgia for an English October.

'Not quite autumn yet, but you're here now,' said Neil. 'How long do you think you'll be in the UK?'

'That depends on you somewhat,' she said, 'and how our schedule can accommodate your investigation.'

'I think, Miss Smith, it's you who will have to work around us.'

'Yes, of course,' she said, 'but, practically speaking, we've got a movie to make and there has to be an element of give and take with these things. Don't get me wrong, I completely understand what the priorities are, but the world keeps on turning. Very sad to have to say so, but there you are. Does that sound very cold?'

'Margaret Porteous,' said Bernard, 'was very dear to us all at Champton.'

'Anyway,' said Miss Smith, 'let's not dwell on such sad things. Lord de Floures, how do you amuse yourselves at Champton? Do you all hunt and shoot and . . . other country things?'

'Not really, not any more. I can't remember the last time I took my gun out. Mostly I drink. I am a grave disappointment to the county.' He laughed in the heavy way he always did when he said something he supposed others might find amusing.

'What do you drink? I imagine people like you have cellars full of port and claret and champagne?'

'One standard I try my best to uphold is to keep a decent cellar. Are you fond of a drink, Miss Smith?' He said this with the air of a roué twirling his moustaches.

'Not that fond. I am particular, though; I bring my own gin wherever I go.'

'Why?'

'I like a certain kind, a Plymouth gin, and not everyone has it. It's so hard to find these days I have to have mine sent from the distillery.'

'I've forgotten what's different about Plymouth gin,' said Bernard.

'It's quite different from London gin,' said Miss Smith. 'It's earthy, it's citrus, it's smooth. It's the single malt of gins, or so they say.'

'I'm not sure I could tell a Plymouth gin from a London gin,' said Bernard.

'Oh, I could, but for me it's not exactly *nostalgic* . . . I just like it.'

'Are you sure I can't get you another?' said Neil.

'No, darling, we must surely be about to eat and I don't think G&T and . . . what are we having?'

'Fish pie.'

323

'. . . and fish pie go together. What would you have with fish pie, Lord de Floures?'

'A Muscadet, probably.'

'Do you like New World wines?'

'No.'

'We make gorgeous wine in California. I have a corner of a vineyard in Monterey. Our Chardonnay is spectacular.'

'I'm sure it's very good,' said Bernard, 'but I'm an Old World drinker, Miss Smith.'

Audrey appeared in the door. '*À table, à table,*' she said, 'and don't dilly-dally, this fish pie is one degree short of cinders.'

Bernard got up, stiffly. Neil offered Miss Smith his arm and with a soft rustle of natural fibres she hauled herself off the sofa.

'Would you like to come with me, Gilly?' said Audrey. She led her out of the drawing room towards the dining room; it was rather a daring innovation in Champton's orders of precedence to leave Bernard behind, who fell in beside Neil, unsure of where his place should be.

Then in the hall Daniel appeared from the kitchen. There was the sound of clattering and suddenly Cosmo burst from behind him, skidded across the black-and-white flags and hurled himself at Bernard.

'Cosmo,' said Daniel, 'get down, get down!'

But Bernard was not put out by the dog's barks and fussing. He stooped to scratch his ears and made a fuss back. No one at first noticed the reaction of Miss Smith. She had backed away into the corner beside the portrait of the Reverend Sir Gilbert Mackworth, Bt. Then she raised a finger and pointed silently at the dog.

'Don't be scared of him, Gilly, he's quite harmless,' said Audrey.

Miss Smith seemed to be trying to speak, but no words came, just a sort of gargling sound.

Daniel went to pick Cosmo up.

'Are you all right, Miss Smith?' said Neil. 'Are you frightened of dogs?'

But she said nothing, just went to the front door, pulled it open and disappeared out into the night.

At first, nobody did anything. Then Daniel said, 'Neil, take him,' and handed him the dog. He went to the top of the steps, but Miss Smith was already at the back door of the silver Mercedes waiting for her. The driver jumped out but she said, 'No, no, no, just get me home,' and he jumped back into his seat. She got in the back with considerably more litheness than she usually showed getting in and out of a car, then the red rear lights lit up and the engine turned, and before Daniel realised what was going on it was down the drive, through the gates and away.

17

Not long after Miss Smith's startling departure Daniel
and Neil departed too, summoned to the old stables by
Dick Alleyne. The dailies had arrived, transferred onto
a VHS video, with all the material they had shot that
day from the masque scene.

They had set up a television with a VCR in Dick's
office. Three chairs were positioned in front of it,
with the remote control and pads of paper and pens
on the coffee table. Neil raised an objection: the video
was only for him and Daniel; he thanked Dick for
arranging it, but they would take it from here. Dick
replied that much of what was on the tape would
need explaining – who people were, when it was shot,
by whom – and he was the person best placed to do
that. Daniel agreed, so they sat down as a trio, with
coffee, a basket of snacks and a bowl of fruit for sus-
tenance. Jasper had got up from his bed and looked
at each of them in turn with an expression that often
secured a titbit, but none of them were interested

in him, so eventually he went back to his bed and fell asleep.

'Are you ready?' said Dick. They nodded. He pressed play.

The television lit up with an image that seemed wrong to Daniel, not the right proportions for what he was expecting, and there were numbers in a little window at the bottom of the screen – a timer, he thought, only some of the numbers were running too quickly. It was timecode, Dick said, showing not only the time in hours and minutes and seconds but in frames per second too, so they could synch sound to images. It also served as an index so they could know exactly when whatever happened occurred.

The image was beautiful, the picture gallery lit like an Old Master painting itself – how brilliant, thought Daniel, that those great lamps on stands could make something look like it was lit by candles and lanterns. It reminded Daniel of the toy theatre Theo had as a child. He had been fascinated by the way the stage and the flats and the curtains and the scenery all conspired to make you think you were looking through a window at a real world until you looked round the back and saw it was an illusion concocted from light and paper and Theo's elementary stagecraft.

'This is the first sequence we shot from the morning,' said Dick, 'you can see the whole sequence from a distance, but it will show you where the key figures were and when.'

There were dancers on the floor in position for something formal and courtly. The queens rippled and shone in their costumes and headdresses, but the effect was cumulative rather than individual, and it was difficult to tell who was who. This became even more difficult when the figures around the edge of the floor, the spectators, began to press onto the floor, and what was intended as a dance became a throng and order broke down. The floor filled with more spectators, and then more, as figures from the very back, who looked like servants, followed them into what was becoming a scrum.

To Daniel this was unimaginable and required a poetic licence that he was unwilling to give. 'This would never have happened,' he said.

'We don't know what actually happened,' said Dick, 'but I need this to happen for dramatic purposes.'

'And those pictures,' said Daniel, 'I'm fairly sure those curtain-and-carpet portraits were later than the 1600s . . .'

'This is why advisers suggest but do not decree,' said Dick. 'I expect you're right, but we're trying to conjure a feel, a mood, not a forensic level of accuracy.'

'But . . .'

'Forensic accuracy is our concern,' said Neil, interrupting. 'Can we concentrate on what we're seeing, not what you think we should be seeing?'

The video spooled on.

Daniel said, 'Stop!'

'It's only just begun.'

'Is that you? Walking away, top left?'

Dick said, 'Yes, probably.' He peered – a bit too obviously? – at the screen. 'Yes, definitely.'

'So you were on set too?' said Neil.

'In and out from time to time, giving a note, summoned by Gilly, trying to figure out why something doesn't look quite right.'

'Why didn't you say?'

'Didn't I say?'

'No, you said you were watching off set on a little screen.'

'I think perhaps you don't understand what happens with filmmaking. Most of what goes on is not in shot. There wouldn't be a shot if there wasn't a crowd of people making it happen, like me, the director of photography, the crew, wardrobe and make-up, everyone just beyond the edge of what you see. I watch what happens from the camera mostly, but I step onto the set sometimes, in and out, and after the end or before the beginning of the action. That's not important. This is important.'

He pressed play and it spooled on. 'This is where it's happening,' said Dick, and he pressed pause again. The image froze. 'You see top right? That's where the queens are, you can see the headdresses. They form a sort of cordon around the real queen when they sense the spirit of misrule is getting out of hand. Margaret is in there, and Gilly, but as you can see it's a press.'

He hit play. More figures came onto the floor and started to dance.

'What are they dancing to?' asked Daniel.

'A consort, but we put that on properly later. It's really just an outline and a rhythm they hear on set.'

'A Tudor rave,' said Neil.

'Jacobean, just,' said Dick, 'but I suppose so. Isn't all dance a way of getting close to a line? A way of testing a boundary? And then sometimes you go over the boundary.'

'Who's meant to be on the set now, Mr Alleyne?' said Daniel.

'Everyone, more or less. We have the queen – the real queen – and the other queens and the courtiers and the dancers, and the I suppose you might say rude mechanicals. We're seeing the breakdown of societal values happening in real time, the release of inhibition, the unbridling of desire . . .'

'You make it sound like *Hair*,' said Neil.

'Nothing like it,' said Dick with a note of asperity, 'but we need to show how Anne's subversive presence released the suppressed impulses of the court and the society the court represented. Here, deference and politesse give way to instinct and desire.'

'Would she really have done that?' said Daniel.

'A woman of boundless intrigue would have been capable of just about anything, no? But that's not the point right now. The point is – if you're right – murderer and victim meet in the middle of this.'

'But it could be *anyone*,' said Neil, 'if *everyone's* on set. In that scrum there's Margaret, Miss Smith, Brandon Redding – your brother,' he said to Daniel, unnecessarily. 'We need to go through it frame by frame. Identify who each individual is and plot where they are and when.'

'There's more', said Dick, 'to look at.' He rewound the tape and as it whirred in the machine he took another from its sleeve. 'This is from camera two, from a different angle, and it's closer.'

He replaced the first tape with the second and pressed play. The screen filled with a clock face showing some numbers, some coloured bars, some geometric shapes.

'What's that?' asked Daniel.

'It's just a card that tells us what it is and when it is and how the picture is balanced.'

A single hand on the clock began to tick towards the twelve o'clock position, then the screen went dark. After a couple of seconds it brightened again and revealed what they had just watched only from the other end of the picture gallery and to the right of the cluster of queens.

'There's Margaret!' said Neil. 'Can you stop the tape?'

Dick stopped, rewound and froze the frame, and there was Margaret, caught for a moment in a gap, looking surprisingly convincing as a matronly woman of the early seventeenth century dressed as a queen from antiquity. Daniel felt a pang of sadness that Margaret, so splendidly costumed and having a ball on screen, half an hour later was dead.

'Shall I go on?' said Dick.

'Hang on, who else can you make out?' said Daniel.

'There's Gilly,' said Dick.

'How do you know it's her?'

'Headdress,' said Dick, 'bigger than the others.'

Daniel started to make a sketch in his notebook. 'Can you start it again?' he said.

Dick pressed play and Margaret, unfrozen, once again joined the dance.

'She doesn't look right,' said Neil, 'she looks stiff or something.'

'Extras tend to look like that,' said Dick. 'Not all of them, but the local recruits do. They're not used to it. But I like that, it makes it look how I want it to look, that's why I hire them.'

'What do you mean?' said Daniel.

'Hesitant, unsure, like people look when they're having to do something they've not done before. You'd never get that from professional dancers or actors.'

Then they saw Theo in doublet and hose looking exactly like someone who knew what he was doing.

'Freeze it, can you?' said Daniel.

Dick pressed pause.

'Can you make out if he's still got the dagger?'

'I can't tell.' Dick forwarded it frame by frame, but it was impossible to see whether he did or not. As Daniel started another sketch Dick said, 'We might have better luck with the section shot from the other side.'

'Hang on,' said Daniel, 'give me a moment.' He made a note in his sketchbook. 'OK.'

Dick pressed play, and more extras crowded in.

'Stop!' said Daniel. Dick pressed pause and Daniel peered at the screen. 'Brandon Redding,' he said.

'Oh, yes, Braunstonbury's King of Crime. Or Prince of Crime,' said Neil. 'What's he doing in this?'

'Same as everyone else,' said Dick. 'We threw everything at it.'

'Bloody hell,' said Neil, 'there's your mum.'

Audrey, too, span in and out of the shot. She reminded Daniel of Miss Brown who used to take Music and Movement classes in his first parish, though both ladies' exploration of the latter using the accompaniment of the former was at best stately. 'I didn't know she was in this scene.'

'Everyone's in this scene,' said Dick.

'Can we see it from the other angle?' said Neil. 'It might be easier, then, to see who's nearest to who and when.'

Dick took the next tape from the sleeve and put it on. The clock counted down and the scene was re-vealed from the opposite side, where a third camera covered what the first and second could not. They saw Candace and Bel-Anna, they saw Brandon, and Theo and Audrey, but they had to keep stopping and rewind-ing before Daniel was satisfied that he had charted the movements of as many of the participants as possible as accurately as possible. Then the movement stopped.

'What's happening?' asked Daniel.

'A pause,' said Dick, 'something to do with lights, or maybe wardrobe. Something must have needed fixing or changing.'

Then Daniel saw something at the edge of the frame. 'Can you pause it, please, Dick? Go backwards, and again, and pause. Look,' he said, and pointed to the edge of the frame. 'Unless I'm mistaken, that's Miss March.'

'Yes,' said Dick, 'she would have been on set. Wardrobe always is, to fix something.'

'Stop the tape,' said Neil. 'Look, she's fixing something for Theo.'

Even from a distance Daniel, with the discernment that came from years in the monastery, could see his brother's impatience. 'It's very stop–start, isn't it?'

'Yes, anything can happen,' said Dick, 'a hair out of place, a light that's not quite right, someone forgets something, and we all have to stop.'

'How do you keep the rhythm of the narrative going if you have to stop all the time? And you don't start at the beginning and finish at the end anyway?'

'It's all in the edit.'

'Oh. Like the New Testament.'

'I couldn't say,' said Dick. 'Shall I?' He pressed play. Daniel made notes.

Then Neil said, 'Stop the tape! Now she's sorting out Brandon Redding. Or something.'

Brandon and Miss March were facing each other and, even indistinctly, in freeze frame, Daniel sensed that this encounter was about more than a loose thread.

At the rectory, Audrey, unusually deflated, sat at the kitchen table surrounded by the debris of the disastrous meal. After Miss Smith had left so rudely, nobody quite knew what to do, but the food was on the table, so they sat and ate. Some effort was required, for the fish pie was chewy and the peas were hard, but they set to it and made painful small talk, for what they all wanted to talk about – the dramatic exit of the woman of boundless intrigue – was too tricky to discuss in polite conversation. Bernard had tried to be complimentary about the pie, but comparing it nostalgically with his favourite supper when he was a boy at school did not please Audrey. Theo had turned up just after Miss Smith had left – he had been caught in her headlights as he walked up the drive – but after complaining of being hungry, when supper was finally served he seemed to have lost his appetite and just had the odd forkful of peas, which he struggled to swallow. Audrey did not miss Neil exchanging a look with Daniel when he put down his knife and fork, having barely touched his food.

She kept up the sort of bright, empty conversation women of her age and type were able to turn on like water from a tap, and they spoke of Harvest Festival, the WI Winter Woollens Sale, Remembrance Sunday.

Theo, for all his listless appetite, was unusually ani-mated in his contributions to these topics but tried, once or twice, to talk about the film. Bernard was too dense to see that this was not a subject Audrey wished to discuss, but Daniel was quick and swerved in to change the subject before it could be developed into a theme.

They had got through the pie, and the mincemeat tart was to follow but then the phone rang, and Daniel and Neil were summoned to the old stables by Dick Van Dyke, as Audrey called him privately, though he was Mr Alleyne to his face.

She and Bernard and Theo had chipped away at the stony burnt pastry of the mincemeat tart and the dense, sickly filling, which she had smothered in Miss March's Elmlea intending to add a rich creaminess to soften the sticky sharpness, but it tasted like gruel poured on squashed fly biscuits, and nobody managed to finish it. No takers for coffee either, or a drink. Theo was tired, though he looked anything but tired, and wanted to go to bed, and Bernard said he had better get along. He paused at the door as if he wanted to say something, but then Audrey realised he was looking over her shoul-der for Cosmo. That would have to be dealt with, she thought again. Theo had half-heartedly offered to help with the washing up and she made him take the dishes through to the kitchen, but he had dropped a plate and broken it and then had said a very bad word, so she told him to go to bed.

And that was all but the end of the night for Audrey. It was to have been perhaps her greatest triumph, pot-luck supper in a simple country parsonage with a peer and a film star, but it had turned into a catastrophe. Not only was the food, when it came, all but inedible, but also one of her guests had fainted and had to go home, the peer had been delayed by a runaway dachshund, two had been summoned to assist in a murder inquiry, and the film star had experienced some kind of crisis and run away. Our triumphs, she thought, are come to dust and ashes – and then she wondered what that was from, Shakespeare or a hymn?

The doorbell rang. Most ladies like Audrey might wonder who on earth would come calling at this hour – it was past nine – but Audrey lived in a priest's house and the doorbell might ring at three in the morning with a summons to a deathbed or the hospital or the police station. The dogs stirred in their basket by the Aga; Cosmo raised a little yelp and poked his head over the top but with nominal rather than urgent interest.

It was Carrie. 'Mrs Clement? I'm Carrie Palethorpe. I'm Miss Smith's PA.'

'Yes?'

'I think Miss Smith left a bag.'

'And a trail of dust.'

'So I gather. May I take it?'

'You had better come in.'

'I can wait here, it's fine. I don't want to disturb you any more than I have to.'

'Oh, I would very much like you to come in.' She opened the door and stepped to one side in a magisterial way. 'It will take me a minute to find it. Let's sit in the kitchen.'

Audrey would not normally invite a caller at the door into the kitchen, but she wanted Carrie to see that the supper her employer had spoilt had been quite an operation.

'Sit, sit,' she said, and with an over-strenuous effort she cleared some dishes from the table. 'I don't want you dragging your sleeve through the butter dish, or a dirty plate . . .'

'Really, please don't go to any trouble, Mrs Clement.'

'Digestif? I'm having one, not that there was anything much to digest. A Cointreau?'

Carrie nodded. 'Thank you.'

'I won't be a minute,' said Audrey, and she left Carrie to survey the table of broken meats and congealing cream substitute.

There was a growl from a woven basket lying in front of the Aga and Cosmo poked his head over the side again to see who had invaded the kitchen. Carrie stared back at him.

Audrey reappeared with two tiny glasses of Cointreau. Carrie had been expecting it in a tumbler and poured over ice, like in the advertisement with the sexy Frenchman, but she took it gratefully enough.

'Cheers,' said Audrey.

'Mrs Clement, whose is the dog?'

'Dogs,' said Audrey. 'There are two, but the one who makes all the fuss is Cosmo. He's ours.'

'Little brown dachshund?' She pronounced it 'dashund'.

'Dachs-hund,' said Audrey, 'yes.'

'I thought he was Lord de Floures' dog.'

'No, Daniel's, but Lord de Floures has taken rather a shine to him, and vice versa. Daniel should never have let it happen, but we were staying up at the house after we had a fire here – Bernard was so kind – and he and Cosmo formed a bond. Now he fusses over him all day and borrows him whenever he wants. It was Cosmo who ran onto the set and caused all the hoo-hah yesterday.'

'Oh, of *course* . . .' said Carrie.

'Of course? Of course what?'

'Nothing. I heard about it – of course.'

Audrey's eyes narrowed. 'Tell me, why did . . . she told me to call her Gilly . . .'

Carrie raised an eyebrow.

'. . . I know, she insisted. But why did she take off like that? She looked like she'd seen a monster, and he's only a little sausage dog. Does she not like dogs?'

'No, she's scared of them,' she said, not adding 'when it suits her'.

'Why?'

'I don't know. Perhaps she was frightened by a dog when she was a girl.'

'I find it easier to imagine a dog being frightened

of her,' said Audrey, baring a bit of fang. 'Why didn't someone say? We could have kept them in the kitchen. I'm surprised it's not on your list of dos and don'ts.'

'I thought it was Lord de Floures' dog. And it was a very last-minute thing, I didn't have time to prep you, and she said she didn't want a fuss.'

Audrey said, 'Gilly's idea of not making a fuss reminds me of Queen Mary going to live with the Duchess of Beaufort at Badminton during the Blitz. She took so many servants the Beauforts were obliged to live in two rooms.'

Carrie nodded, then knocked back her Cointreau in one gulp. 'Do you have the bag, Mrs Clement? Only I can't keep her waiting.'

'What a fuss you all make of her. It won't do her any good at all. Like the dog.'

Carrie shrugged. 'I just do my job.'

Audrey said, 'It's in the cloakroom. Why don't you come with me?'

Miss Smith's bag was hanging on a hook. Carrie took it down and had a look inside.

'I don't think anything was stolen, dear.'

'Just checking, she's very particular.'

'What on earth does she keep in there?'

'Her gin, her lemons, her inhaler, her medication, a hairbrush, make-up and so on. I think it's all there. Thank you, Mrs Clement, I am sorry to trouble you. Miss Smith asked me to thank you and to apologise for her sudden departure.'

'Did she? How kind. Do send her my best wishes and I hope she feels better now.'

Audrey saw Carrie out. A large silver car was waiting for her, and she got into the back without saying anything to the driver. Audrey thought that rather grand.

It was after midnight when Neil finally switched off the VCR and Daniel closed his notebook, filled now with sketches and notes. Dick had fallen asleep in his chair, so Neil gave him a nudge. 'I think we're done for now, Mr Alleyne.'

'Oh,' he said, 'I sparked out. Long day. Was it helpful?'

'Yes, very,' said Daniel, clipping his Pentel R50, his new favourite pen, onto the front of his notebook. He liked it especially for the way it managed italic, almost like a proper nibbed pen, but without the faff of nibs and bottles of ink, and in its green designer livery he felt the faint but exciting throb of new technology. With it, he had written down the details of who was where and when, with the relevant timecode, and from comprehensive notes was already beginning to assemble a mental three-dimensional picture of the whole scene. He had refined it to what he thought were the essential elements, where Gilly was, where Theo was, where his mother was, where Brandon Redding was, and where the two until-now-unknown attendees were, Dick and Miss March. Their presence on set was harder to fit into that picture, for they only stepped into one or two shots after the action had finished.

Dick said, 'I am done in. Can I give anyone a lift?'

'No, you're all right,' said Neil. 'My car's here.'

'Daniel?'

'I think I'll walk. But thank you, Mr Alleyne.'

'Dick.'

'Thank you.'

'Come on, Jasper.' The black Labrador slowly levered himself up from the blanket and padded towards Dick. Daniel thought how oddly out of proportion most dogs look when you are used to dachshunds, their long, spindly legs insufficient for the weight of their bodies.

'Tomorrow we'll be shooting exteriors, so we don't get under your feet.'

'Thanks,' said Neil. 'I don't know how long we'll be needing to keep you out of the house.'

'Not long,' said Daniel.

'I hope not,' said Dick, 'we're burning through the budget. Anyway, I won't go on about it. Goodnight. Just let yourselves out when you're ready.'

'You're not going to lock up?' said Neil.

'No need, we've got security.'

'Goodnight,' said Daniel. Headlights shone through the window. 'Is that your car?'

'Yes, taking me back to wherever it is we're staying. I should have stayed here, really, but Gilly wanted me with her. Access all areas.'

He let the dog out in front of him and went.

'Can I walk you to your car, Neil?'

'You can.'

Outside it was cold, with a bright moon that made the cobbles look bluish.

'Not long?' said Neil.

'I don't think so. Do you?'

'I can see you don't. You get this look when you're about to work it all out. You stick your chin out. Like you're thinking of going in for the kill.'

'Oh, that doesn't sound like me.'

'It is you, you know it is.'

Daniel laughed. Then he said, 'I don't think there's anyone else in the world who would notice that. Perhaps Mum.'

Neil said nothing for a moment. 'It's good to be together again, Dan.'

'It is, isn't it?'

'Things happen.'

It was Daniel's turn to be silent. Then he said, 'Or don't happen.'

'Nothing, like something, happens anywhere.'

'Larkin. Where did you come across that?'

'I wasn't completely ignorant before I met you, you know. But tell me, what are you seeing here?'

'Two things. I'm not sure which is the right one. Or perhaps how they fit together.'

'Can I expect to be making an arrest soon?'

'I imagine so, but I need to untangle these threads.'

'Anything I can do?'

'What do you know about Brandon Redding?'

'I know his form, of which there is plenty. I can

343

ask around the station. There are people who've been detaining him since he was a nipper. Is he our man?'

'I don't know.'

'Are you going to tell me your thoughts?'

'Not yet, they're not in focus yet. I think I can see the beginning of an outline, but I need to talk to one or two people and see if it gets any sharper.'

'Can I tell you mine?'

'Of course.'

'I'm not clear about Miss March.'

'The Grey Lady. Neither am I,' said Daniel.

'She could have stabbed Margaret with one of those needles.'

'The thought had crossed my mind.'

'On set? Possible. In wardrobe? We've only got her word for it that Margaret came there because she had a stitch.'

'If she did stab her, where's the weapon?'

'Maybe in the pin cushion. Forensics is looking at them, but it wouldn't be difficult to clean them, and they've got all the stuff there – bleach, you know – to do it properly, and if she did it would just be in and out, not like a knife.'

'That's all imaginable, but I can't imagine why Miss March would want to kill Margaret.'

'Neither can I. But there's something that doesn't make sense about Miss March.'

'Success in these investigations often begins, I find, with imagining the unimaginable.'

They were at the car. Neil said, 'Imagining the un-imaginable. That's a mixed blessing. Goodnight, Dan.'

'Goodnight.'

'I'll catch up with you tomorrow?'

'Not tomorrow. I'm going to the seaside,' said Daniel.

'OK. Call me when you can.'

Daniel watched the rear lights of Neil's car until they disappeared at the turn in the drive. He had an early start in the morning, but he wanted to walk home to get his thoughts in the sort of order they should be in before he slept on them. He knew the answer to his questions lay partly in the meticulous notes he had taken of who was where and when in the scene they shot that morning, and partly, he suspected, where he was going tomorrow. He had thought about driving, but it was too far for his creaky Land Rover, and too daunting for his nerves, so he was resolved to suffer the enormous expense of going by train.

He walked along the path, lit by bright moonlight, and into the park. An owl hooted distantly and there was the occasional splash from the lake – a little night music, after the clamour of the day. Champton, he hoped, would soon return to its normal state, when the circus left town and . . . But there was no normal state, he thought, there was only what happened, and the appearance of unchanging tranquillity was only an appearance, and after the film was finished, its in-substantial pageant faded, and everyone's thoughts had turned to Harvest Festival and conkers, there would be no Margaret Porteous, ever again. She had not slipped away like her husband but was forced out of this world by someone who either wished her harm and did her to death, or wished someone else harm and she had just got in the way, receiving the wound intended for another. A wound inflicted by whom? Daniel thought he knew, for he had been imagining the unimaginable since he first stepped into the Old Dairy. But he did not know precisely whom. He had a shortlist of two, but now perhaps he needed to add another? Suddenly there flashed into his head an image of Margaret, un-wigged and half corseted, and dead in a chair, with the dark stain spreading from her waist to the floor. It was like being slapped. He knew that in the coming days and weeks and months, the loss that now seemed too big to conceive would gradually assume a discernible shape, and something like a flavour or a colour, and they would start to get used to it, rather than Margaret's presence, and there was nothing to be done about that.

But he could find out what had happened, and bring to light the deed of darkness by which she had lost her life. He could catch her killer.

He was still in this mood of resolve when he got home, letting himself in as quietly as he could by the back door. Someone had left the kitchen light on again, which made him tut, but then Cosmo came rattling out of his bed and started to bark in delight at the un-expected visit. Hilda also seemed unusually moved and padded towards him wagging her tail. 'Who's a good boy? Whooo's a good girl?' he said, and scratched their heads.

A voice said, 'Hello, Dan,' and made him jump.

It was Theo. He was sitting at the head of the kitchen table where Audrey usually sat.

'Hello. You're up late.'

'Not by my standards.'

'Don't you go to bed early when you're filming something?'

'I did, but I can't sleep.' He touched his nose when he said this, in the way people are supposed to do when they're lying. 'I've been thinking about my lines.'

'I thought you didn't have many.'

'It's a tiny part, a *tiny* part, but I think now I've made friends with Miss Smith, with Gilly, I might make more of them.'

'Do you think you are friends?'

'Not *real* friends, showbiz friends.'

'I mean after her melodramatic departure this evening.'

'Oh. Was it *that* bad?'

'I thought it was quite bad.'

Theo nodded. 'Would you like a drink? I'm having one.'

'No, I've got to be up early.'

'Just a tiny one?'

Daniel sat down. 'What's the matter?'

Theo reached for Miss Smith's bottle of Plymouth

347

gin, which she had left behind. He added a splash to his glass.

'Are you having that neat?' said Daniel.

'Gin and ice, Dan. It's a very fashionable drink. Very pure, very clean, very 1990s.'

'You haven't got any ice.'

'Fifty per cent is a start.'

'What did you want to talk about, Theo?'

Theo took a sip of his gin. It was surprisingly close to petrol, and it made him nearly gag. 'It's the dagger.'

'What about the dagger?'

'I have absolutely no idea what happened.'

'You said.'

'But . . . I only remembered this today, it's probably nothing . . .'

'What?'

'The last person I actually remember handling it was Miss March.'

Daniel said, 'What do you remember?'

'She came on set in between takes and was fussing over my costume, and she said it was hanging wrongly or something and she fixed it.'

'Do you remember anything else?'

'No, but I must have had it then or why would she have wanted to fix it?'

'Was this towards the end of the scene or the beginning, or in the middle?'

'I can't remember.'

'Do you think she might have taken it?'

'I have absolutely no idea. But why would she? To stab Mrs Porteous?'

'That's a difficult thought to entertain.'

Theo took another sip. 'Am I going to get in trouble for this, Dan?'

'I don't think so, no.'

'Only I have absolutely nothing to do with Margaret Porteous's murder, Dan, I want you to know that.'

'I didn't think for a second you did, but thanks.'

'Absolutely nothing. Nothing at all.'

'Go to bed, Theo.'

18

Audrey heard Daniel moving around at an unusually early hour, so she got up too and by the time he came downstairs she was in her dressing gown, with a second cup of *déca* and yesterday's *Telegraph* crossword.

'Morning, darling,' she said, 'you're up very early.'

'I'll let the dogs out,' he said, and two tails wagged as they recognised this offer.

'Already done. Are you off somewhere?'

'I am.' He added nothing to this.

'Buckingham Palace? The Matterhorn? The Little House on the Prairie?'

'To Devon. I have to see someone.'

'So mysterious. The kettle's only just boiled.' She picked up the crossword again.

Daniel went to make a mug of tea.

Audrey squinted at the crossword. 'The return of the Ulster Unionist maiden, eight letters.'

'What?'

'Five across, Dan, eight letters, the return of the

Ulster Unionist maiden. Something, R, something, something, something, something, A, something.'

Daniel was not really paying attention. 'Something to do with Paisley?'

'Paisley?' Audrey looked again. 'Doesn't fit. And it's not eight letters.'

'Oh dear.'

'Dan, you're not concentrating.'

'I'm going to be away all day and not back until after supper. Can you sort out the dogs?'

'I'm going to be up at the house all day, and after last night's performance, I don't think I'll be taking Cosmo and Hilda with me.'

'Then I wonder if Bernard would look in on them.'

'If you wish him to then perhaps you should ask him.'

'I haven't time. It's too early to call and I've got a train to catch.'

'I can't just slope off from filming because someone has to let the dogs out.'

'You did yesterday.'

'Very different circumstances, Daniel.'

'Please can I leave it with you? I've got to go.'

Audrey sighed and nodded. 'Where are you going?'

'The seaside.'

'Don't forget your bucket and spade, dear.'

Daniel gulped down the last of his tea, petted the dogs and kissed his mother goodbye. She did not look up from the paper.

'Back later,' he said, 'thanks for looking after the dogs.'

'The return of the Ulster Unionist maiden . . .' she said, oblivious.

In the south lodge, Nathan and Alex were getting up too. Rather, Alex had sent Nathan to the kitchen in the lodge on the other side of the drive to make him a mug of coffee. He had no recollection of having gone to bed. The nearest thing he had experienced to Brandon's sinsemilla was the general anaesthetic when he'd had his tonsils out, when he'd woken from a dream of boundless bliss with a sore throat. It was not just his throat that was sore, his head was aching too. That was some powerful stuff they had smoked. He had always wanted to be a drug-taker like Thomas De Quincey or Aldous Huxley, seekers after revelatory truth, rather than just getting 'off his face', as Brandon called it. Most of the intoxications he had sought in this way had been disappointing. When he took acid it was not the opening of a portal of perception, more like having a migraine; hash made him sleepy; speed made him feel like he was having his blood pressure taken; but this sinsemilla was breakfast, luncheon and dinner for the discerning opium-eater.

Nathan appeared in the door with Alex's coffee in the lovely cup and saucer he had subtracted from one of the Derby services up at the house. 'Brandon's here.'

'Early for him.'

'No, he crashed here last night.'

'Is he awake?'

'He is now. I gave him a mug of coffee. He's on the sofa. But he must have been in the bedroom because he took a blanket.'

'That's either rather a thrilling idea or rather an alarming idea. Possibly both.'

Nathan shrugged.

'You don't mean we . . .?'

'I dunno. It's not his scene.'

Alex took a slurp of his coffee and ran a mental body check to see if there was anything to suggest how full the night's entertainment had been. 'I don't like the idea of Brandon creeping around here while we're unconscious. I'd rather be awake for it.'

'I can check his stuff to see if he's nicked anything.'

'If he did, he'd have legged it by now.'

There was a tap at the door.

'Yes?'

It was Brandon. 'Thanks for letting me crash,' he said. 'Can I jump in the shower?'

'Go ahead,' said Alex.

'Have you got a towel?'

'Use the one that's there,' said Nathan. 'And you have to pull the cord to make the shower run.'

'OK,' he said and went into the tiny bathroom, locking the door behind him. After a while there was the sound of spraying water and then Brandon singing, surprisingly well.

'I wonder if he would be that shy if we'd gone the nine rounds.'

'What do you mean?'

'He locked the door behind him.'

In the bathroom, Brandon was hiding more of his stash behind the lightly rusty, unused tins of talc on top of the medicine cabinet.

Miss March had a troubled night's sleep. In the end she'd taken a Mogadon, and she did drop off but woke feeling more tired than she had when she had gone to bed. It took a second or two to recall the events of the previous day and she let out a sound, like an ooff. She resolved not to think about it, had a bath and got dressed, in black today as a mark of respect.

She breakfasted on a Müller Corner and decided to go to Matins with the rector, for that seemed only right too. It was colder out today than yesterday, she thought, cloudy and with a lick of wind. She wondered if she should have worn a winter coat. The village was still quiet, just the odd car going towards Braunstonbury, and Gilbert Drage sitting with his dog outside his cottage. 'Good morning, Mr Drage,' she said, but he ignored it.

The church was still locked. Unusual for the church not to be open five minutes before the start. And there was no bell. Then she saw Jane Thwaite, the deputy organist, coming up the path. She looked, Miss March noticed, like Audrey fforbes-Hamilton's friend in *To the Manor Born*.

'Miss March, sorry to keep you waiting. It's me today; Daniel's had to go away, and of course no Margaret.'

She took the big key and the little key from their not very safe hiding places under the stone next to the porch and opened up the wired door, meant to keep birds out, and then the main door, which was so old and so massive it would have kept elephants out of the church.

'I've never done this before, Miss March, but Daniel says there are cards in his stall, which have everything on, for use in an emergency.'

'Where's he gone?'

'Don't know – put a note through my door saying he'll be back late tonight. I hope it's not like the last time. I'd hate to think he's become a bolter.'

They went into the building, where it still felt as though it was more like night than day. 'Can you see all right, Miss March, in this light?' said Jane. 'I can switch on some more but I'm never sure where the right switches are.'

'I can manage quite well,' said Miss March.

'Shall we sit in the choir? I won't sit in Daniel's stall, it wouldn't feel right. Shall we sit next to each other here?'

Miss March would rather sit on the opposite side in the arrangement Daniel preferred, but seeing as they were both unsure of what they had to do, they chose safety in proximity.

Jane found the laminated cards with very simplified

versions of the morning prayer, suitable for all days and occasions. Simplified, that is, by Daniel, whose first version had options on another card for the feast of the saints, organised Apostles and Evangelists, martyrs, bishops and teachers, and a whole extra card just for Mary. There had been a revolt about this degree of complication, and in the end he did just a very basic order of service with nothing that needed to be looked up.

'Shall I say the bits in plain type, and we can do the bits in bold together?'

Miss March, who knew her way around Matins and had views about such things, suggested an alternative.

'Perhaps I should,' she said, 'if you are not familiar with the service?'

'Would you, Miss March? That's so kind.'

'Shall we just keep silence for a moment before we begin?'

'Oh, yes, that would be jolly nice.'

Matins, if a little juddery, like a car driven by a novice driver, went well enough until they got to the intercessions. It was the prayers for the dead that did for them.

'We remember our departed sister Margaret and give thanks for her life . . .' said Miss March, '. . . and ask for comfort for all who mourn her and grieve.'

Jane began to cry.

'And for justice to come to those responsible for taking her life, and for all who perpetrate acts of violence on the defenceless.'

Jane let out a sob. 'Oh, please stop!' she said.

Miss March looked up. 'Are you all right?'

'It's difficult to hear when you've lost someone the same way.'

'Your poor husband,' said Miss March. 'I didn't think.'

'I know it was some time ago now and everyone moves on, of course they do, but . . . Ned was murdered. I rather struggle to move on.'

Miss March wondered if she should offer some comfort and hoped Jane would not expect a hug, for she did not offer those. She found a tissue in her bag and gave her that instead, hoping it would be enough.

'Thank you. It's just very difficult.'

Before she realised what she was saying, Miss March said, 'I know. The same thing happened to me, as a matter of fact.'

'Oh, Miss March, you too?'

'My father was killed. By louts.'

'I'm so sorry! When did it happen?'

'Five years ago. He intervened in a disturbance in the street and one of the boys was rough with him and he . . . he suffered a heart attack. He died in my arms.'

'Did they catch the boy?'

'No, he got away. I watched him run off.'

Jane said nothing for a while. 'Isn't it an awful club to be part of? To have lost someone to violence.'

'Yes.'

'I sometimes feel I am a bottomless pool of sadness.'

'I'm a bottomless pool of anger,' said Miss March.

Budleigh Salterton – which sounded like the name of a Hollywood matinee idol of the 1930s, thought Daniel, like Burton Latimer or Clayton-le-Dale – was quiet, the summer rush departed. But it was a bright September afternoon and Daniel's bus was not for an hour, so he went to the beach. With unusual wantonness, he took off his shoes and socks, rolled up his trouser legs and stepped into the cold waves, which broke and rolled onto the sand.

It then struck him that paddling in turn-ups, even if he was wearing a dog collar and a sports jacket, was hardly the fall of Rome. He wondered what it would be like to take everything off and run naked across the beach like an archdeacon he had once known who took his holidays at a nudist beach in Norfolk, where he had once surprised his rural dean, also on holiday, by wishing him a happy Corpus Christi in his birthday suit. Buttoned-up people secretly long to undo their buttons. Daniel's restraint was more than a match for his impulse to divest, but he had learnt in the past year that he, too, had a body that sought other bodies, and desire that sought quietus, and a longing to be another's first choice and to have another to be his first choice. But it was like football at school. He was no more a candidate for intimate love than he was for the position of centre forward, and in the selection process for another's intimate embrace he would always be the last to be picked – 'Oh, no, not *you*, Clement?'

On the field of sport, he had never minded much not being picked; it meant that he could go and play the organ, or read, or score in cricket matches, which he rather enjoyed – and anything was better than having someone throw a ball at you. He shuddered at the thought of the helplessness that fell on him like cold weather whenever he saw a projectile coming towards him, kicked by a winger, or struck by a bat, or thrown by a boy who was as at home in his body as Daniel was in the score of Stanford in B flat. He had learnt to go where his gifts were valued, his composure unruffled, his hopes manageable.

And then he had met Neil Vanloo, and a totally unexpected passion had knocked him down and roughed him up and made his life so miserable he had forgotten himself. So, he had picked himself up and smoothed himself down and buttoned up his cassock and put himself beyond a debilitating pain he had never experienced before and never wanted to experience again.

And then circumstances had reunited them again, and Daniel had found he could enjoy Neil's company again, for the longing that had caused him so much pain had passed. The rest of his life was back in focus. He could see the nature of his own desire and the impossibility of its fulfilment, and see Neil restored to his place in an orbit that did not threaten his own. '*And let our ordered lives confess the beauty of thy peace,*' he sang out loud, and he thought of the disciples beside the Syrian Sea instead of Budleigh Salterton beach, sat down on a wall, and put his socks and shoes back on.

He turned away from the sea and its limitless depths and faced the town, with its streets and shops and church and chapel, and the little house with a sitting room that he recognised from every parish he had served, furnished to the taste of the occupant's parents, and grandparents, whose life she had lived rather than her own. From the unfashionable sofa, he took a biscuit from the plate of best, brought out only for visiting clergy.

'What did you want to see me about, rector?'

He knew before he asked what she would say, and she said it and confirmed it – why Margaret Porteous had died and who was responsible.

Or, rather, one version of why Margaret Porteous had died and who was responsible. There was another, and that he did not understand, and until he did, the mystery of *The Masque of Queens* would be unsolved.

19

Nathan and Alex were lying on the sofa in the north lodge watching *The Generation Game*, which had returned to BBC One with the original presenter, Bruce Forsyth, after an absence of what felt like a fortnight but was nearer a decade.

'Dear old Brucie,' said Nathan, 'hasn't he done *well* . . .'

They were both listless, wrung out after the past two days of excitement and indulgence: a murder, a film star for tea, Brandon's sinsemilla to befuddle them and cocaine to liven them up.

There was a flash of lights outside and the sound of an untuned engine. The gates swung open – someone had got past the security guards still on the door, posted not to keep people in but to keep them out; photographers and journalists had started gathering there like vultures after carrion – and then the engine stopped and the lights went out.

'Visitors?' said Nathan.

There was a knock on the door.

'Answer it,' said Alex irritably.

It was Daniel.

'Dan,' said Alex, 'nice to see you, to see you . . .'

'Oh, yes, how nice to see you too,' said Daniel, unaware of the reference. 'I'm sorry to bother you, but I was passing and I thought I'd call in.'

'You never just call in, Dan,' said Alex.

'It's been a very difficult two days. I wanted to see if you are all right.'

'I suppose it has,' said Alex languidly, 'but we're fine. A bit wasted, but fine.'

'I'm not sure what that means,' said Daniel. 'Do you mean you have wasted your talents, or opportunities, or your time?'

'No,' said Alex, 'just tired.'

'I see.'

'Would you like a drink, rector?' said Nathan. 'Or a cup of tea?'

'Cup of tea, if you have one.'

'Alex?'

'Not for me,' said Alex, 'but you could pour me another gin and tonic if you like.'

Alex and Daniel were alone in the drawing room. 'Where have you been?' said Alex.

'Budleigh Salterton.'

'I don't think I know where that is.'

'It's in Devonshire. A pretty little seaside town with a lovely beach.'

'May I ask why you were in Budleigh wherever-it-is?'

'A funeral visit,' said Daniel.

'A long way to go for a funeral visit.'

'Not in this case,' said Daniel, 'when it is where the deceased's next of kin lives – in fact, her only kin, and even then, kin spiritual rather than familial.'

'Margaret Porteous?' said Alex.

'I couldn't say,' said Daniel.

'Well, I assume it is Margaret Porteous. No other funerals on the books. Do you know, I thought about her today and I couldn't think of a single reason why anyone would want to do away with her.'

'She was a very private person.'

'So there was a reason?'

'Not what I said, Alex.'

'But you discovered something? I can't imagine you'd go all the way to Devon unless you thought it would be worth your while.'

Daniel said nothing. The clock on the chimneypiece struck a quarter with a lovely silvery sound. Daniel said, 'Is the clock from the house?'

'Everything's from the house, Dan.'

'Who is it by? Graham?'

'I have no idea.'

'May I?'

Alex nodded. Daniel got up and peered at the clock. 'Hmm, not Graham – George Graham, the pre-eminent clockmaker of his day – but Thomas Mudge, who was his pupil, I think. His father was Zachariah

Mudge, a most interesting man, a nonconformist from Exeter who became a Church of England parson. He was something to do with Sir Joshua Reynolds, but I can't remember what, and he sang the "Old Hundredth" from the top of Eddystone Lighthouse when Smeaton finished it in 1759. Mudge, of course, invented the lever escapement, which—'

Alex said quickly, 'I don't know what's keeping Nathan. I'll give him a hand,' and he left Daniel to explain the horological innovations of Mudge to an empty room.

Nathan was letting the tea – lapsang souchong with a spoonful of Assam – steep in the pot in the way Alex liked it.

'It's only the rector, Nathan, don't give it the full tea ceremony.'

'I thought I'd do it properly.'

'Have you done my gin and tonic properly?'

'It's by the sink.'

Alex took a sip. '*Very* good. You are indispensable!'

'Shouldn't you be entertaining the rector?'

'He's being boring about the clock. It's by some clockmaker he's interested in. Smudge or someone. It's like having *Antiques Roadshow* live from your drawing room.'

Nathan poured the tea through a silver strainer into a cup and added half a slice of lemon. The other half he had dropped into Nathan's gin and tonic. Such commendable thrift, thought Alex.

'I'll take it,' he said, and with a gin and tonic in one hand and lapsang souchong in the other, he went back into the drawing room.

But Daniel had gone.

Miss March sat in her sitting room on her uncomfortable sofa, PG Tips in her father's mug untouched on the coffee table on which she never had coffee. It was not late, but she was already in her winceyette pyjamas and her dressing gown and her fluffy slippers, which made her look, she once thought, like one of the Muppets. But this was the private Miss March, not the composed, impeccably dressed Miss March, in whom her customers placed their absolute trust to make them also look impeccable.

Also on the coffee table was a shoe box. She normally only took it down from the top of her wardrobe on her father's birthday and at Christmas, when she liked to look at their documented lives – birth certificates, death certificates, swimming certificates, school reports, an order of service for his Requiem Mass, a copy of her parents' decree absolute.

A bittersweet experience. She liked order, she liked to know that her life was registered, and his life too, entered into the record in black ink. She had noticed Daniel writing out a marriage certificate using a fountain pen reserved for that purpose. She knew him to be exceptionally punctilious about all matters to do with record-keeping, but why that pen? Because, he said, it was filled from a pot of registrar's ink, made with iron gall to resist the depredations of time. It wrote grey but faded paradoxically to black and remained black down the decades and the centuries, unerasable, as near to eternal as could be. It had been used for record-keeping, he said, for well over a thousand years. She liked to think that a thousand years from now, in a forgotten and unvisited archive, there would be a record of March and March, father and daughter, as crisp and clear as the day it was written. She thought of one of the tombs in the de Floures' chapel, erected a hundred and fifty years ago in pristine white marble for a virtuous and short-lived daughter, showing the recording angel entering her name in the Book of Life on her arrival at eternity.

There was one final document that she kept at the bottom of the pile, like a love letter from a superseded suitor that she could not quite bear to throw away. It, too, was written in unfading registrar's ink, but she held it to her heart in a gesture that would not have disgraced a pious Victorian maid. The tears, when they came, were neither dainty nor ennobling.

Brandon Redding finally got home to his hot little flat, infrequently visited, over the television repair shop in Braunstonbury. He had been especially busy, concealing his stash in various places around Champton: in Theo's trailer, at the lodges and in derelict outbuildings he had discovered while pursuing the art and craft of poaching. A murder investigation meant too many police around for him to conduct his business in the usual way — how typical of Mrs Porthole in death to mess him around as she had in life — but there was nothing he could do.

He had the extra worry now of placating his suppliers, who conducted their business in a notably unsentimental way, and if he could not shift the product, they would find someone who could, and he didn't want that. So his priority, after reducing the risk of being caught in possession, was to get back into business as soon as he could, and that meant exploiting opportunities in Braunstonbury rather than at Champton. He had done quite well there since the movies came to town, thanks to boredom and bad habits among both crew and cast, and he had ordered a ton of gear to provide for them, which now he would struggle to get rid of.

It had been two days of stress, and stress he did not need. He had a small stash of heroin, which he used to make his 'sinsemilla' and to cut with amphetamine, or whatever he had in, to sell as MDMA to ravers too stupid and too desperate to tell the difference between his junk and the real thing. He had a little sachet in his bumbag for emergencies and he decided to jack up. He was only ever an occasional user — he had seen the ruin it could bring — but he also understood why it was such a popular product with the more unfortunate of his customers. No matter how wretched your existence, a dose of this was instant bliss.

He lifted a corner of the carpet and then a floor-board and took out a toiletries bag he had long ago shoplifted from Boots. It originally contained Opium by Yves Saint Laurent – how appropriate, for now it was heroin, by the mujahideen probably, though his contact was in Luton, not Afghanistan. He smiled at his own joke.

He prepared his fix, cooking up the white powder with water in a tablespoon over a candle, and drawing it up into a syringe through a cigarette filter. He wound a belt round his upper arm and held it tight with his teeth, found a vein and injected. The effect was almost instantaneous, and his head fell back while the needle was still in his arm.

There was a wave of nausea, but he was used to that, and it soon gave way to a gentle rush of warmth and peace and bliss.

What Brandon did not know when he injected the solution of heroin into his vein was that the batch it came from was not his normal supply, and the dose was considerably more potent than any he had taken before. As he drifted off into bliss he may have felt for a moment an intimation of drowning, but drowning in the loveliest way imaginable.

Gilly Smith was sitting up in bed in a fresh pair of cashmere pyjamas. A sheaf of *Country Life* magazines, which Carrie had insisted the hotel provide, was spread across the counterpane. Gilly was taking them one by one and flicking through the property pages, imagining what it would be like to live in a mansion in Wiltshire, or a Tudor manor house in the Cotswolds, or an old rectory in Norfolk. Not for her, she thought, not enough luxury, insufficient bathrooms, no decent pool, and what would she want with a manège, whatever that was – something horsey? She much preferred the houses in places convenient for the airport, the millionaire mansions of Berkshire and Surrey, as fake as the streets of Venetian palazzi and Swiss chalets in LA, but with spas and home cinemas and garaging for twenty cars. She could buy any of them if she wanted, but it would mean living in England and she did not want to do that, for the distance she had put between Iris Butters of Clapham and Gillian Smith of Hollywood was not something that could or should be narrowed. 'Iris had her life, and I have mine,' she said out loud, as if she needed to hear it.

There was a knock at the door. 'Come!' she said, the 'in' being a particle of speech too far.

It was Carrie. She was in her dressing gown and slippers and looked like she had just woken up. 'Dick on the phone,' she said. 'You'll want to take it.'

'Précis! Précis!' said Gilly.

'He should explain.'

'Tell him I'll call him back.'

Carrie shuffled out and Gillian looked at the particulars for a house in Sunningdale so wreathed in wisteria it looked like a tart's boudoir. Handy for Pinewood, she supposed, and there would be change out of a million quid, but that would probably have to go on plumbing it to twentieth-century standards.

Carrie returned. 'You're not going to like this.'

'Fire away.'

'We are summoned to Champton House tomorrow morning, all cast and crew. Dick's going to make a speech, give an update, and then some sort of God for Harry and Saint George thing, I don't know – a rabble rouser.'

'What about me?'

'All cast and crew.'

'Is that supposed to mean me?'

Carrie paused, then said, 'He asked for you especially.'

'How thoughtful,' said Gilly, 'but I find I cannot oblige. Tell him I have other plans.'

'What plans?'

'Might have a spa if this flophouse can run to a box of Radox.'

'I really think—'

'What do you think?'

'I think you should go.'

'Why?'

'Morale.'

'But I don't want to go.'

Carrie sat down on the end of the bed. 'Makes you look queenly.'

'Queenly?'

'Yes, like Anne mucking in at the masque. Going

among the ladies as first among equals. Makes you look good for minimum effort, and no one really thinks they're your equal.'

'I don't want to go,' said Gilly, but her reluctance was not from her usual caprice; Carrie knew what that sounded like and this was different.

'Why not?'

'I don't like the sound of it.'

At the rectory, Daniel's arrival was heralded by the peremptory barking of Cosmo and Hilda, who heard the Land Rover hitting the gravel of the drive before Audrey did. They were sitting at her feet, nestled in the crumpled remains of two or three *Daily Telegraph*s, which she had discarded once no longer useful, for while Daniel was away, she had been filling in the crossword clues she hadn't got by checking the next day's edition in the vain hope that when he tidied them up he would think she had done it unaided. She had been stuck on one, for which the answer had not yet been published, and had fallen asleep until the dogs woke her, their barking rising to a frenzy as the back door opened.

Even in the warmth of the drawing room Audrey felt a whisper of cold air steal through the hall and nip at her ankles. 'Close the bloody door, Dan,' she shouted.

'Just letting the dogs out,' he shouted in reply.

Audrey tried to bury her feet in the nest of newsprint scattered around her chair, but when Daniel came into the drawing room he was still wreathed in cold air, and Audrey shivered.

'Typical you to go to the seaside when everyone else is leaving it. Wasn't it perishing?'

'No, it was quite mild,' said Daniel. 'I had a choc ice on the beach.'

'Prodigal!' she said.

'That may be so, but don't kill the fatted calf on my account.'

'No, you fathead, the crossword. Return of the Ulster Unionist maiden, do you remember? Proddy gal. Prodigal.'

'Oh. Very good.' He went to go but then stopped. 'Prodigal. Very good indeed. See you later.'

20

What a contrast, thought Daniel, between the early seventeenth century that filmgoers would see in *gloooorious* Technicolor – he could only hear the phrase pronounced this way by his Welsh housemaster at school announcing the feature for Film Club on Sunday afternoon – and the means of realising it. It looked like a cross between a favela and a junkyard, tents and containers heaped around a sort of improvised town square, all held together with nuts and bolts and marvellously efficient nylon bindings called cable ties – a new invention, at least to Daniel, which he thought at least as brilliant as Velcro.

The town square was full, with cast and crew assembled – even Gillian Smith, who was late, but not monstrously late, and apologised to all for keeping them waiting with uncharacteristic team spirit. This did not go far, for she was given a special place and a special chair, attended by Carrie and Martin, and fussed over by Dick. A queen at a masque, thought Daniel, so like

Anne of Denmark going among her people, but as *deus ex machina* rather than a peer.

The present dwellers of Champton House had turned out, Bernard and Alex, on a three-line whip for appearances' sake, and Mrs Shorely too. Miss March stood between them and Sandy and Angela, positioned between her two worlds as costume adviser and wardrobe assistant.

Audrey was there, standing not with the other kitchen menials, grouped in their lowliness, but with the principal actors, hovering around Theo, as mother of a son, but also trying to get subtly nearer to Miss Smith, whom she had hosted at dinner, even if not for long. Miss Smith seemed to be oblivious to her, even when Audrey deliberately stood in her line of vision and waved.

The prop people had found a dais, and sound had rigged a microphone, and after the first AD called everyone to order Dick took to the stage.

'It's been a tough couple of days,' said Dick to the crowd, 'as difficult as any I've known on any shoot, and I want to thank you all, every one of you, for being so flexible and cooperative. We have a new schedule, a new plan, and production will be back on track, and I hope back on schedule too, very soon. Thank you in advance for your continuing cooperation and flexibility. Before I take you through what that means, it's important to remember why we've had this disruption. One of our cast, Margaret . . .' – he glanced at a note

– 'Porteous, tragically lost her life, only a couple of days ago, so I think it's only fitting that I ask the Reverend Clement, who you will have seen around the place, vicar of Champton, to lead us in a moment of remembrance.' He nodded to Daniel and stepped aside.

Daniel said, 'Thank you. Perhaps you remember Margaret Porteous, perhaps you don't. Though familiar to all of us from Champton, if you weren't from here, she was someone you would probably not notice: a background artist. In film, in life, we all have our parts, some more exalted than others. But God does not give anyone special billing, and heaven is not Hollywood, so, if you are a person of faith, pray for Margaret as you would want to be prayed for yourself, and for those who mourn her. If not, call to mind your best, most generous thoughts. Before I offer a prayer, let us keep a minute's silence for Margaret . . .'

Everyone shuffled, some bowed their heads, some clasped their hands together in front of them – universal attitudes of prayer.

A minute went slowly by. After twenty seconds, those unused to this special use of time looked around at each other – surely that was enough? Some looked at their watches, some who knew timecode did not need to, some just listened to the wind in the trees and the distant cawing of rooks.

Daniel did not time the minute, for he knew what a minute was – eight repetitions of the Jesus Prayer: 'Lord Jesus Christ, son of God, have mercy on me a sinner' – but when it was done, instead of the prayer provided for such occasions, he prayed another.

'Almighty God, who hast created man in thine own image; Grant us grace fearlessly to contend against evil, and to make no peace with oppression; and, that we may reverently use our freedom, help us to employ it in the maintenance of justice among men and nations, to the glory of thy holy Name; through Jesus Christ our Lord. Amen.'

There was a murmured 'amen', like an uncertain echo, from the crowd. Dick looked a bit puzzled and turned his head to the dais, but Daniel was not done.

'What do we lose when we take away an element of the background?' he said. 'Nothing we notice at first, or not directly or consciously, but to lose something even if you do not notice it is still to suffer a loss, and it matters. Margaret's death matters. It matters not only because she is unique and irreplaceable and there will never be anyone like her ever again, but because her death is an affront to justice, and an affront to God, and in the silence we just kept, I wonder if that felt as urgent for you as it did for me.'

Dick advanced towards the dais, but Neil stepped in front of him.

'Indulge me, Mr Alleyne, for a moment,' said Daniel.

Dick looked at Neil and made a face. Neil ignored him.

'Surprising what you can hear in silence. You know the story of Cain and Abel? When Cain, in secret, murders Abel, God says, "The voice of your brother's blood is crying to me from the ground." Margaret's blood cries out too. And we must answer.'

'Christ, must we have a sermon?' said Bernard. 'Is this the time and the place?'

'It is time for Margaret's blood to be answered by the person who killed her. That person is here.'

'You don't need to be a detective to work that out,' said Gillian Smith. 'Of course it had to be one of us.'

'Yes, but we can narrow it down,' said Daniel. 'We've been looking at the footage shot at the time of the murder. If you hadn't heard this already, and I imagine you have, it looks like Margaret was stabbed during the masque scene. The wound was narrow but deep, and it was only when she went to wardrobe and her corset was unlaced that she bled, and that was how she died. Miss March was the one who unlaced it. What she did not tell us was that she was also on set when Margaret was stabbed.'

'I didn't tell you?' said Miss March. 'But of course I was, checking costumes between takes. I made no secret of it.'

'You gave a detailed statement, Miss March,' said Neil, 'impressively detailed, but you missed that out.'

Miss March looked flustered. 'Only because it was obvious, and not relevant to your questions. You wanted to know what happened in the Old Dairy, not on set. I didn't know – I don't know – what happened on set. I can't even be sure that I was there when you say this happened.'

'We can,' said Neil. 'We have videotapes of everything that was shot during the scene, three cameras, three angles, and there you are.'

Miss March suddenly was stung. 'What are you saying? That I had a hand in Mrs Porteous's death?'

'You did,' said Neil, 'you unlaced her corset. You may not have meant to cause her to bleed, but you did.'

'I would never have intentionally hurt Mrs Porteous!'

'It is difficult to see a reason why you would,' said Daniel, 'but we need to work through the possibilities. You might have had a reason, and you did have the means.'

'The dagger? But I did not have the dagger,' said Miss March.

'You had the farthingale needles. One thrust in the right place is all it would have taken,' said Neil.

Miss March went in an instant from pale grey to white. 'This is absurd! Why would I want to?'

'I don't know, Miss March,' said Neil, 'but I don't think you're telling us everything.'

Miss March was silent, but a blush spread across her cheeks.

'Guilty conscience, Miss March?' said Miss Smith.

'Not guilt, anger,' said Miss March. 'I did not kill Mrs Porteous, although God knows . . .'

'Knows what?' said Neil.

'The secrets of our hearts,' said Daniel.

Neil, getting impatient, said, 'I'd be obliged if you could share them.'

'It's from the funeral service,' said Daniel. 'In the midst of life we are in death – thou knowest, Lord, the secrets of our hearts.'

'Well?' said Neil.

'Miss March may have her secrets, but I don't think murdering Mrs Porteous is one of them.'

'Aren't you missing something?' said Alex. 'You're assuming Margaret was the intended victim. Why would anyone want to kill her? Isn't it more likely that the intended victim was . . . someone more significant?'

'Whom do you mean?' said Daniel.

'Forgive me,' Alex said, looking at Gillian, 'but what about Miss Smith?'

Gillian raised one eyebrow.

'I don't imagine anyone rises to her heights without ruffling some feathers along the way. She's well known for being difficult. We've all heard the stories about her. Professional jealousy? A broken heart? Long suppressed resentment? Motive meets opportunity. Imagine if you had hated her for years and years, or if you felt she had rejected you after years of faithful devotion, and then suddenly there she is in front of you, there's a weapon to hand, and in a surge of passion, of rage, you strike. Only you strike the wrong person, a queen, but not the queen.'

Miss Smith gasped. Carrie knelt beside her and took her hand.

Alex said, 'I'm only saying out loud what we are all thinking.'

'So, who?' said Neil.

'You tell me,' said Alex.

'Anyone on set, anyone in proximity, in between takes as well as during takes. Any of the supporting artists. Any of the main cast. Dick, Carrie?'

'They wouldn't have mistaken Margaret for her,' said Alex. 'They would know who she was.'

Carrie said, 'Made a mistake? I would never hurt Miss Smith. I've looked after her for years. And she's looked after me. What about actors? What about your brother? It was his dagger that killed her. His dagger that's still missing. Why don't you ask him?'

Theo said, 'Me? Why would I want to kill anyone?'

'I don't know,' said Carrie, 'but you had the opportunity and the murder weapon. And you wouldn't be the first actor to resent Miss Smith. Her talent, her brightness, her—'

'Fondness for sucking up the light and air,' said Alex.

Daniel interrupted, 'I think Theo lost the dagger before Mrs Porteous was stabbed.'

'How do you know?' said Carrie.

'I don't exactly know, but I'm fairly confident. From who was where and when. And from who had a motive.'

'To attack Miss Smith?' said Carrie.

'To attack Mrs Porteous.'

'Like who?' said Alex.

'Your friend Brandon Redding,' said Daniel. 'When he was a boy, it was Mrs Porteous who had him expelled from school.'

'Brandon would get expelled from the Medellin Cartel, Daniel. Getting chucked out of primary school would have meant nothing to him.'

'It was not just school he was expelled from. It was from Champton, the only place he knew, the only security he had in life. Motherless, fatherless, thrown out of his foster home and exiled. Abandonment on abandonment. Imagine what that does to a child.'

Miss March suddenly blurted out, 'It kills the soul.'

Everyone looked at her.

Neil said, 'Is there anything you want to tell us, Miss March? About Brandon Redding?'

Miss March looked flustered again. 'No. Why would I? Some lout from town . . . I'm not even sure who he was.'

'On the video,' said Daniel calmly, 'you approach him, between takes. In fact, you stand in front of him.'

'Checking his costume,' said Miss March. 'Why don't you ask him?'

'He's not here,' said Neil. 'Make of that what you will. We've sent uniform to his flat to see if we can find him.'

'Did you take the dagger, Miss March?' said Daniel.

'From your brother? I may have done. Checking his costume.'

'Could you have taken it and forgotten to replace it?'

'It's possible,' said Miss March.

'Is it?' said Daniel. 'Very unlike you to make a mistake like that.'

'I said it was possible, not that it was likely.'

'I've been trying to think of reasons why you might take the dagger,' said Neil. 'Here's one: you wanted a weapon.'

'To attack Mrs Porteous? Or perhaps Miss Smith? Or perhaps everyone?' said Miss March.

'To attack Brandon Redding,' said Neil.

Miss March blinked. 'Why on earth would I want to do that?'

'Because you blame him for your father's death.'

Miss March seemed to crumple for a second, as if she had been winded. 'No,' she said, 'no . . .'

'Five years ago your father was involved in an altercation with a group of youths in the street outside your shop in Stow,' said Neil. 'It was late at night. One of them urinated in the shop doorway. Your father went down to challenge them and there was a fight, and your father suffered a fatal heart attack. No one was ever called to account, though there were some names at the top of the police's list of suspects. Brandon Redding's was among them.'

Miss March said nothing.

'Did you recognise him? Did you work it out?' said Neil.

'You knew who he was, I think,' said Daniel. 'But I don't think you wanted to attack him.'

'What a peculiar thing to conjecture,' said Miss March. 'Not really becoming for you to . . . throw out . . . such things.'

'I just need to be clear, Miss March, that it was not you who stabbed Mrs Porteous,' said Daniel.

'I did not stab Mrs Porteous, no.' She paused. 'And neither did Brandon Redding.'

'How can you be sure?'

'Because he did not have the dagger. He's not your murderer.'

'Why are you only telling us this now?' said Neil.

Daniel interrupted, 'First things first. If you took the dagger from Theo, who took it from you?'

'I don't know.'

'Please explain what happened.'

'I put it in the pocket of my pinny, along with sewing things. When I got to the Old Dairy it had gone. I thought I must have dropped it. I was going to go and look for it and then Margaret came staggering in.'

'Did you ever find it?' said Neil.

'No. I don't know what happened to it. It seems to have disappeared.'

Daniel said, 'Until I found it.'

Everyone went: 'Oh!'

'Yesterday. When I realised who killed Margaret – a shortlist of two – I worked out where it must be. And there it was.'

'Where?' said Alex.

'At yours,' said Daniel, 'hidden in plain sight.'

'What do you mean?'

'It was in that cutlery fan over the fireplace, all those

old swords and bayonets from your military ancestors. Clever place to hide it.'

'The clock. Yesterday evening, you got boringly studious about the clock. But it wasn't the clock, you were looking at the fan,' said Alex.

'Yes, sorry about the subterfuge but I had to. I was not sure then who had hidden it there, and if it were Brandon . . . well, he's hidden quite a lot of things at your place, I think, so a certain discretion was necessary.'

'But it wasn't Brandon?' said Alex.

'No, which meant it could only really be one other person.'

Everyone looked at him.

'Who?' said Miss Smith.

'You,' said Daniel.

Some gasped. There was the sound of rustling as some turned to look at Miss Smith, and some looked at each other, unsure of what had just been said.

Dick was the first to speak. 'What exactly are you saying?'

'Miss Smith killed Mrs Porteous,' said Daniel. 'It had to be her. It couldn't be anyone else.'

Gillian Smith said, 'I'm sorry, are you talking about me?'

'I'm afraid I am,' said Daniel.

There was a pause, then Miss Smith said, 'But that is nonsense.'

'It is unexpected. But it isn't nonsense.'

'Dear rector,' said Miss Smith, 'I know you have a

reputation as a kind of sleuth, but this is not the last scene of a Poirot, and your little grey cells, I'm afraid, have conjured this dramatic scene for nothing. I am not in the habit of murdering my fellow actors.'

Not literally, thought Dick Alleyne.

'And why would I want to kill Mrs what's-her-name?' said Miss Smith. 'I didn't know her.'

'Not as Margaret Porteous.'

Miss Smith looked at Carrie. 'Is this some sort of set-up? Is Eamonn Andrews going to appear with a red book?'

Carrie looked at Daniel and Neil. 'I have no idea what's happening.'

'*This Is Your Life*,' said Neil, 'although not the telly programme, but a visitor from Miss Smith's past who made her what she is now.'

Miss Smith blinked. It was the first time she had ever given even a tiny sign that she was not in control, thought Daniel.

'Are you going to cart me off? In front of everyone? Should I get ready for my close-up? This is ridiculous!'

'You will need to come with us, Miss Smith,' said Neil.

'Carrie . . .' she said, making a fussing gesture at her PA, 'can you . . . sort it?'

Carrie stood up and opened her mouth to say something, but nothing came. She made to sit down again, but then stopped and said to Daniel, 'What do you mean, it couldn't be anyone else?'

'No one but Brandon Redding or Miss Smith could have hidden the dagger where it was hidden. If we've got the sequence of events right – and we have, thanks to the videos Mr Alleyne kindly arranged for us to see – then it could only be one of them.'

'Anyone could have taken the dagger,' said Miss Smith, 'anyone.'

'But only you or Brandon could have hidden it . . .'

'. . . when you went to pee,' said Carrie. 'We stopped at the lodges when they wouldn't let the car out.'

'Yes,' said Daniel.

'I thought that was odd,' said Carrie. 'You could have gone before we left the lodge for the car but you didn't. You went back because you saw an opportunity, didn't you, to take the dagger and hide it with all the other knives.'

'Carrie!' snapped Miss Smith.

'You took the dagger,' Carrie said slowly.

Miss Smith looked suddenly like Ceauşescu on the balcony at Timisoara, facing the suddenly hostile crowd.

'You took the dagger,' said Carrie. 'You took it from Miss March's pinny pocket. You took it and you killed Mrs Porteous . . . and you didn't tell me?'

And then she realised what she had said.

It had been a day of unusual drama. The police had arrested Gillian Smith and had got her into the back of the police car with quite a different degree of care and attention to what she was used to. Neil later said that she took the prospect of life imprisonment for murder with more equanimity than something touching her hair. Carrie had gone to the police station too, in a different car, not as Miss Smith's PA but as a future witness for the prosecution. Down the long drive they went, past the lodges, where Alex and Nathan were standing outside in a sort of guard of dishonour for Miss Smith, and then through the gates, and the crowd of press and photographers and cameramen who bubbled up in turbulent predation.

Dick Alleyne had spent hours on the phone to the West Coast telling them their bankable star was not only absent, but in custody and charged with the murder of one of the background artists. After the humiliation on humiliation of exposure and revelation, Miss March had been driven home by Neil the back way, past the rectory, with the firm request to come to the station to give another statement. Audrey had been on the telephone all afternoon, making outgoing calls to everyone she could think of to pass on the startling news 'to spare you finding out from the wireless or the telly or the papers . . . all of them . . . ALL of them . . .' and receiving incoming calls from journalists and editors, which she dealt with using the rude politeness that came so readily to her.

She also invited Bernard to tea, so as the afternoon came to its end, and Champton began to settle into its routine like a collapsing soufflé, Audrey shifted the dogs, asleep in their Aga-adjacent basket, to one side with her foot, fetched the kettle from the boiling plate and poured water into the Brown Betty teapot she thought suitable for a kitchen debrief on a day of surprises.

'When we are young,' said Daniel, 'we read and believe the most fantastic things. When we are older, we learn with regret that these things cannot be.'

'What's that from?' said Bernard.

'Margaret's last words?' said Neil.

'Yes, more or less. The epigraph from *Blithe Spirit*, by Noël Coward.'

'What's the significance?'

'It's how Margaret Porteous met Gillian Smith. Or rather how Peggy Greenslade, as Mrs Porteous was then, met Iris Butters, known today as Gillian Smith. At the Devonport Operatic Society. I found the programme for *Blithe Spirit* yesterday.'

'*That's* what your trip to the seaside was all about,' said Audrey. 'I didn't think it was for the donkey rides.'

'Yes. I went to see Margaret's god-daughter, Heather. She grew up in Devonport, Plymouth docks as was. Her parents were in the Operatic, so was Margaret and so was Miss Smith — it was the gin that put me onto it, by the way, a taste for Plymouth gin acquired in Plymouth — they were friends, young people spreading their wings. Amateur dramatics was their passion. Until the incident.'

'What happened?'

'The Operatic Society autumn show, 1963, Noël Coward's *Blithe Spirit*. It's all in the programme . . .' He picked up a shiny booklet from the table. 'Peggy Greenslade, stalwart of the society, was Madame Arcati. Iris Butters . . .'

'Sounds like a wartime food supplement. I can see why that would have to go,' said Audrey.

'. . . Iris was Elvira. She caused a sensation, apparently. Everyone could see she was unusually talented, even at that age. She took the Society by storm. I don't think Peggy Greenslade was entirely delighted to be eclipsed by the ingenue.'

'An old story,' said Audrey. 'They fell out. But why would that provoke Iris to murder Margaret a quarter of a century later?'

'Oh, it wasn't that,' said Daniel. 'It was a dachshund.'

There was the sound of stirring from the basket by the Aga.

'A dachshund?' said Audrey.

'Iris had a little dog. She doted on the little dog and the dog doted on her.'

'I thought she was scared of dogs,' said Audrey.

'She wasn't scared of Dick's dog, Jasper.'

'She was *terrified* of Cosmo,' said Audrey.

'Not terror exactly. Look.'

He turned to the back of the old programme and showed Audrey the page with the biographies of the actors and their portraits, black-and-white head-and-shoulder shots, the men in cravats with pipes clamped between their teeth, the women all eyes and teeth, looking like they were laughing at the comedy of life, and one of Iris Butters looking adoringly at her dog.

'Like Zsa Zsa Gabor with her Yorkie,' said Audrey. 'Only it's a dachsie, not a Yorkie.'

'Caspar,' said Daniel, 'whom she adored and who went everywhere with her. Until one day at Devonport, after the matinee, Peggy Greenslade reversed out of the car park in her shooting brake and ran him over. Killed him. Heather showed me a cutting from the local paper. "*Blithe Spirit* Actress's Dog Killed by Madame Arcati"'.'

'How awful,' said Audrey as she inspected the tea in the pot.

'It was more than awful for Iris. She loved the dog. It was the only thing in her life she loved, and possibly the only thing that loved her. She'd had a dreadful time growing up in a very strict religious family, the Taylorites, a rigorous offshoot of the Plymouth Brethren, who were already pretty rigorous. No wireless, no fraternising outside the Brethren, no pets . . . no life insurance.'

'Why no life insurance?'

'I think they thought it was trying to anticipate the will of God.'

'Makes the Moravian Brethren sound like the Young Generation,' said Neil.

'They were obsessed with the purity of the Church,' said Daniel. 'Any contact with the fallen — everyone but them – meant contamination and the need to be cleansed. So anyone who offended, and it could be a very minor offence, like going to the pictures, could be shut up, put under a form of house arrest, really. And if the offending continued, the sinner unrepentant, they would be ostracised. Parents refusing to speak to children, siblings turning against siblings, the whole community – which was everything – closing its doors to you.'

'Poor Miss Smith!' said Audrey. 'I can't imagine her lasting five minutes without lipstick, let alone life insurance . . .'

'Iris loved the theatre, she loved boys, she loved going out, she loved music . . . So her expulsion was inevitable and came at the first opportunity, when she was just eighteen; she was exiled from her community, and from salvation. She had chosen hell, and from that moment she went her solitary way. Imagine what that does to you? When she got a dog she poured all that repressed love and passion into a pet.'

'I've never understood why people do that,' said Audrey.

'It's very common. If you can't love people, love a dog.'

'Or God,' said Audrey. 'That's another way of loving when you can't manage a person. I've never really understood that either.'

Neil interrupted, 'So the dog was everything to her.'

'Until she found some better-matched objects for her

passion,' said Audrey, 'or at least members of the same species.'

'I don't think she ever loved her lovers,' said Daniel. 'I don't think she was capable of loving another person after what had happened to her. And then a creature came into her life – Caspar – who was always pleased to see her, always devoted to her, loved her come what may – and did not choose to be with her or not to be with her, so she was safe.'

'And then Margaret killed him. The only thing she loved,' said Neil.

'Yes. It ruined her life and nearly ruined Margaret's, according to Heather. Iris was unforgiving of the loss of her beloved Caspar. Everyone knew it was an accident, a very unfortunate one, but an accident. Margaret would never have done it intentionally. Iris saw it differently, though, as if Margaret had been not negligent, but deliberately cruel, inflicting an awful revenge on the ingenue who had outshone her. There was a showdown, Iris all tears and innocence. A faction of the Operatic, dazzled by that, turned on Margaret and something about it ended up in the local paper. Heather's mother suspected it had been put there by Iris herself. Margaret was the subject of the most awful gossip; somebody shouted at her in the street and the town clerk had to have words with Dennis. He confronted Iris and there was a scene, and it was decided that Iris should move on and shine her precious light elsewhere. But Margaret and Dennis were never the same; they left the Operatic and then faded into the background. Iris went back to London, but to stand on her own two feet now, and reinvented herself as Gillian Smith. Very soon she was in the West End, then a Rank starlet, then Hollywood. Perhaps she had put the tragic events at Devonport behind her. Until Cosmo.'

'Cosmo?'

The little dog stirred in his basket.

'Yes. Do you remember, Bernard, you let Cosmo out and he ran onto the set during a take the day before the murder? It was Margaret who rescued him. Suddenly Gillian saw a dachshund like Caspar in the arms of the woman she immediately recognised as the one who had killed him. Something snapped.'

'I remember,' said Bernard, 'she stormed off set. I thought she was just being hysterical.'

'Wasn't she frightened of dogs?' said Neil.

'So we were told,' said Daniel, 'but she showed no sign of fear of Mr Alleyne's Jasper. Didn't you notice that?'

'I didn't,' said Neil.

'But why didn't Margaret say something?' said Audrey. 'If she knew Gillian Smith, I don't think she would have kept it to herself.'

'Don't you? When their last encounter had been so awful? I suppose she thought it so long ago that Miss Smith would not recognise her. And she didn't, until Cosmo connected her with Caspar.'

'So, motive and opportunity,' said Neil.

'Imagine someone like Gillian Smith nursing a resentment like that all her life. Then decades later, in her prime, in her power, the person who had deprived her of the one thing she loved in all the world appeared in front of her. Worse than that, appeared in front of her taunting her with the very creature she had killed. She saw the dagger, she took it, and struck.'

'I still don't understand how the dagger ended up in her hand,' said Audrey. 'Isn't it far likelier that Brandon Redding took it from Miss March, not Miss Smith?'

'He had a motive,' said Neil. 'Mrs Porteous banished him from Champton. He had already been deserted by his birth family, and then he was chucked out of the one place he thought of as home. He was expelled from school and his foster family gave up on him . . . he blamed her for it. And he had the opportunity – we could see from the videotape that he could have taken it.'

'Give that lout a dagger and he'll stick it in someone,' said Audrey.

'Perhaps,' said Daniel, 'but that's not what happened.'

'What stopped him?'

'In a sense, Miss March.'

Audrey looked at him. 'Miss March, able in so many ways, is not the first person I would pick to disarm a murderer.'

'She did not disarm him. She did not need to.'

'What on earth do you mean?'

'He did not have the dagger. On the videotape you

see her stand between him and Theo. Costume adjustment. Only it wasn't a costume adjustment, I think. It
was a confrontation. You see Brandon recoil.'

'Why would Brandon be scared of Miss March?' said
Audrey.

'Because she knows who he is, what he did,' said
Neil. 'The boy responsible for her father's death.'

'Oh, yes,' said Audrey, 'if she thought the Redding
boy was responsible for her father's death, she would
have been implacable. She could face down a tiger.'

'The *peccata clamantia*,' said Daniel, 'the sins that cry
to heaven for vengeance.'

'And she's quite Old Testament about that sort of
thing,' said Audrey. 'Who would blame her for sticking
it in him?'

'She would never do that,' said Daniel.

'I think you underestimate Miss March,' said Audrey.

'I think you misunderstand Miss March,' said Daniel.

'And vengeance has come to Brandon Redding
anyway,' said Audrey, 'by his own hand, not anyone
else's. Rather fitting that he should be laid low by one
of his own pick-me-ups.'

'Heroin is not a tonic, Mum,' said Daniel.

'Any news on his condition, Detective Sergeant?'
said Bernard.

'Critical,' said Neil. 'If we hadn't gone to bring him
in, he would be dead. And even in ICU, he's still not
out of danger.'

★

Neil offered to walk with Daniel to church for Evensong. It was getting colder now as autumn set in, and Daniel was glad of his cassock. It would soon be time to put on the heating, an event at least as significant in the church calendar as Michaelmas, with which it more or less coincided.

Neil held open the little gate from the rectory garden wall to the churchyard.

'When did you actually know it was Miss Smith, Dan?'

'Oh, late. Late for me. At first, I thought she was the target. She seemed so likely a candidate for being murdered.'

'Me too. And Margaret so unlikely.'

'Yes, but I try not to hold on to assumptions; they never really help. And then I worked out who might have taken the dagger from Theo, or Miss March, or whomever, and why. In the end it came down to Miss Smith. Brandon, I thought, capable of violence and harbouring an understandable grudge, might have gone for it. Then Miss March. If she thought Brandon was responsible for her father's death then an opportunity for vengeance presented itself. But no, she faced him down, he never took the dagger, so he could not have stabbed Mrs Porteous, even if he were capable, which we don't know, and Miss March I was sure would never have hurt Margaret.'

'Her need to protect an innocent was greater than her need for revenge?'

'Well, yes, in a sense. . . but in the end the truth revealed itself when everything fitted together. Very satisfying when it happens. It's like . . . well, God is in His Heaven and all is well with the world.'

Neil would normally have noticed the ambiguity of that 'in a sense', but there was something else he wanted to say. 'Is all well with us, Dan?'

Daniel said nothing for a moment, then stopped and said, 'Yes, I think so. Don't you?'

'It's always been fine with me.'

Daniel said, 'I remember once, when I was in . . . my period of turmoil . . . standing here in the churchyard and suddenly realising I was standing on a millennium's deposit of dust. The countless dead, buried here, all of whom had their loves and their losses and their triumphs and their disappointments, predictable, unimaginable. And then I thought my own disappointment was not so much. My embarrassment. I remember at the time you said one day I would see the comedy in it. I didn't then, but I think I do now. More than that, though, I just feel very grateful that we met and became friends.'

Neil said, 'I hope we will always be friends.'

'Who else do I have,' said Daniel, 'to instruct me in the mysteries of the offside trap and the scrum?'

'Do you fancy the rugby next Saturday?'

'Yes, why not?'

'I'll ring you when I've got a plan.'

Daniel watched Neil walk down the path towards the lychgate and out into Church Lane. Then he went to the vestry door and let himself in. It was five minutes to Evensong and he needed to ring the bell to summon people to church, only no one ever came to Evensong except on Sundays, when there was a choir and sausage rolls afterwards.

He lit the two candles on the altar and went to sit in his stall.

'Oh Lord, open our lips,' he said but did not reply, for there were only his lips to open. The rest of the service he said silently and quickly, for he had somewhere to be, urgently, and alone.

He slipped out of the church still in his cassock, stopping only to pick up a purple stole from the vestry and the bits and pieces he needed from the aumbry. He locked up and went to the front of the rectory, hoping the dogs would not hear him on the gravel. He got into the old Land Rover as quietly as he could and started the engine. No barrage of barks came from within, no face appeared at a window, as he put it into reverse and manoeuvred with unusual smoothness into the drive and down the lane.

Braunstonbury General stood on the edge of town, accessible now from the new bypass; the red brick of Braunstonbury lay on one side, and a jumble of ugly new buildings on the other: a superstore, a bowling alley, and a fake pub that sold burgers and fries and something called key lime pie. Daniel wondered if it caused the hospital car park to fill up, not with doctors and nurses and outpatients and visitors, but with customers for these attractions, and he found it hard not to feel irritable as he searched for a space. He made three circuits of the car park – always a nerve-racking experience – before he found a space and bought a ticket with higher-than-normal resentment, for charges had only recently been applied to visiting clergy. He checked himself, remembering his training incumbent, Canon Whitehead, counselling impeccable patience when visiting the hospital, for the dithering or ungenerous person you encounter may be having the worst day of their life.

The Intensive Care Unit was in the main building rather than one of the shanty sections that sprawled across the site. It was divided from the rest of the hospital by a corridor with double doors at both ends. Daniel pressed the buzzer and the first set of double doors opened, admitting him to a sort of airlock between the departments people tended to get better in and the department where outcomes were more uncertain. ICU generated more prayer requests on the cork-board in the chaplaincy than any other, though maternity came close. There was another buzz and the second set of doors opened.

'Hello, Daniel,' said the charge nurse at the desk. 'You're here for Brandon, yes?'

'Yes. How's he doing?'

'Still here. Michelle's nursing him – she can tell you better than I can. I don't know if she's on the ward at the moment, but she won't be far away. He's in room six.'

'Thanks.'

'And his mum's with him.'

Daniel nodded.

He knocked at the door of room six and went in. Brandon was lying on a bed connected to machines to monitor what was happening to him, and to machines to help him stay alive. They blinked and whirred and beeped, and Daniel looked at them as if he knew what the information they displayed meant. It was a way, he supposed, of not confronting so bluntly the circumstances of the patient, suddenly small, vulnerable, more child than man, and out of reach, save from his mother's hand, which rested on his.

'Hello, rector. I wondered if you would come,' said Miss March.

'Of course I came,' said Daniel.

'I meant, he is not your parishioner.'

'No, not that it matters; but you are.'

Miss March said nothing for a moment. Then she said, 'Would you like to sit down?'

He took a chair from the wall and drew it up to the other side of the bed. It was not really a bed, which implied rest, but more workbench, or trolley; a gurney they called it in American English.

'How is he?'

'He was only just alive when they found him. Only just breathing. He had seizures, I think they said. His brain, his liver, his heart. Insufficient oxygen.' She looked at Daniel. 'Are you just enquiring after his health as a matter of politeness, or do you need to know in order to choose the appropriate sacrament? Are healing and dying separate or does one cover both?'

'What would you like me to do?'

'Why do you ask me?'

'You're his mother.'

She looked back at Brandon. 'It still sounds so . . . unwonted.' There was silence again. Then she said, 'How did you know?'

'It was a crossword puzzle,' said Daniel, 'in the *Telegraph*. The return of the Ulster Unionist maiden. Eight letters. Prodigal. My mother got it. And the moment I thought of the prodigal son everything fell into place.' That banal observation in Dennis Porteous's funeral address, he thought, the one clue that holds the whole puzzle together. 'Brandon was not your father's tormentor; he was your son.'

'He *is* my son.'

'He is your son. I was so wedded to the idea that you thought he was responsible for your father's death that I assumed your interest was vengeance. There it was on the videotape, you confronting him. But you did not strike. And neither did he. Miss Smith did. I knew it had to be one of them, and when I discovered Miss Smith and Margaret's awful history, I knew which. But the videotape . . . I could not think of an explanation that made sense of what passed between you and him. Until I did. Does he know you're his mother?'

'I don't know. I don't think so. But when I looked at

him and he looked at me . . . perhaps something. I suppose you will want to know our . . . familial history?'

'Not especially, but I would recommend full disclosure to the police. Clarity is so important in these matters.'

'So it will all come out?'

'I expect so.'

She grimaced. 'The thought of people talking about me.'

'Yes, but you will find people surprisingly merciful.'

'As well as judgemental?'

'Some. But there aren't many families without a story like yours. And it is not the first time I have ministered to someone in your circumstances. Not by a long way.'

'In the old days you would have made me come to church and be shamed in front of the whole community.'

'I hope I would not have done that. I hope I would have had the sense and grace to see that you had everything you needed and that your dignity was respected.'

'You would have been unusual.'

'I doubt it,' said Daniel, 'but what is not known is not remembered.'

'Known to God.'

'Yes. A characteristic feature of omniscience.'

Miss March sighed. 'I don't think I can talk about it at the moment. My son has never been more precious to me than now, and the story of his . . . begetting . . . is not savoury.'

'You really don't have to tell me anything you don't want to.'

Miss March nodded. 'Thank you. When this is done, one way or another, perhaps then?'

Daniel said, 'Yes, of course. May I?' Daniel produced the little black carrying case he had taken from the aumbry with the Blessed Sacrament and the holy oils.

'Do I have to do anything?' said Miss March.

Daniel shook his head. He took from the case a little silver pot with a screw top, about the size of a pot of eyeshadow, thought Miss March. He unscrewed it and pressed his thumb into a piece of wadding inside, soaked in a greenish oil.

He leant over Brandon and very gently with his thumb marked his forehead with a cross, saying, 'Brandon, I anoint you in the name of the Father, and of the Son, and of the Holy Spirit.'

From reflex, Miss March said, 'Amen.'

'The Lord bless thee, and keep thee,' said Daniel. 'The Lord make his face to shine upon thee, and be gracious unto thee. The Lord lift up his countenance upon thee, and give thee peace, both now and evermore. Amen.'

Miss March was unable to speak after that.

Acknowledgements

I would like to thank my editor, Juliet Annan, and everyone at Weidenfeld & Nicolson.

My agent, Tim Bates, and everyone at PFD.

Charles Spencer.

Richard Cant, David Moore, Radford Neville and Alison Owen.

And Martin Clancy for logistical assistance in the City of Chester.

The Reverend Richard Coles is a writer, broadcaster and an Anglican priest. He co-presented *Saturday Live* on BBC Radio 4 for a number of years and appears, from time to time, on *QI*, *Have I Got News for You* and *Would I Lie to You?* He has won Christmas *Celebrity MasterChef*, *Celebrity Mastermind* twice and captained Leeds to victory in Christmas *University Challenge* in 2019. A contestant on *Strictly Come Dancing* (2017) and a third-place finalist on *I'm a Celebrity . . . Get Me Out of Here!* (2024), he exhibits huge bravery.

He writes regularly for the *Sunday Times* and is the author of half a dozen books, including a bestselling autobiography, *Fathomless Riches*, and the bereavement bestseller *The Madness of Grief*, written after the death of his partner, David Coles. The first three books in the Canon Clement series have all been no.1 *Sunday Times* bestsellers. *Murder Before Evensong* is currently being adapted into a six-part series with Acorn TV and Channel 5.